Beth Kery .... thor of *Because You ....* ....ere she juggles the demands of her career, her love of the city and the arts and a busy family life. Her writing today reflects her passion for all of the above. She is a bestselling author of over ....irty books and novellas, and has also written under the pen ....me Bethany Kane. You can read more about Beth, her ....ooks and upcoming projects at www.bethkery.com or ....ollow her on Twitter @bethkery

Praise for Beth Kery:

'....eth Kery just became an auto-buy' Larissa Ione, *New York Times* bestselling author

'....ne of the best erotic romances I've ever read' *All About Romance*

'....he successful marriage of emotion and eroticism will make Beth Kery a big name in erotic romance' *Dear Author*

'....icked good storytelling' Jaci Burton, *New York Times* bestselling author

'....ome of the sexiest love scenes I have read' *Romance Junkies*

'....owerful characters ensnare you from the first page of this ....toxicating and exhilarating story' *Fresh Fiction*

'....ivid descriptions and sensual prose' *USA Today*

'..... fabulous, sizzling hot friends to lovers story. You'll be addicted from page one!' Julie James, *New York Times* bestselling author

By Beth Kery

Wicked Burn
Daring Time
Sweet Restraint
Paradise Rules
Release
Explosive
Because You Are Mine

One Night of Passion series
*Addicted To You
*Bound To You (e-novella)
Captured By You (e-novella)
Exposed To You

*previously published under the pseudonym Bethany Kane

Daring Time
BETH KERY

ETERNAL
ROMANCE

Copyright © 2009 Beth Kery

The right of Beth Kery to be identified as the Author of
the Work has been asserted by her in accordance with the
Copyright, Designs and Patents Act 1988.

Published by arrangement with Berkley,
a division of Penguin Group (USA) Inc.

First published in Great Britain in 2013
by ETERNAL ROMANCE
An imprint of HEADLINE PUBLISHING GROUP

1

Cataloguing in Publication Data is available from the British Library

ISBN 978 1 4722 0041 9

Offset in Sabon by Avon DataSet Ltd, Bidford-on-Avon, Warwickshire

Printed and bound by CPI Group (UK) Ltd, Croydon, CR0 4YY

Headline's policy is to use papers that are natural, renewable and
recyclable products and made from wood grown in sustainable forests.
The logging and manufacturing processes are expected to conform to the
environmental regulations of the country of origin.

HEADLINE PUBLISHING GROUP
An Hachette UK Company
338 Euston Road
London NW1 3BH

www.eternalromancebooks.co.uk
www.headline.co.uk
www.hachette.co.uk

Daring Time

∽ ONE ∽

His partner Ramiro Menendez turned and stared at him, his mouth gaping open comically. Ryan suspected his own face shared the same expression of stunned incredulity. He felt like a wide-eyed kid in a candy store.

"You got an effing *ballroom* in your house."

"Yeah. I noticed. Strange place for a cop to live, huh?" Ryan murmured as he studied the enormous room in the Prairie Avenue mansion. He'd just received the keys from his old professor and good friend Alistair Franklin this morning. When he'd told Ramiro as they left their west-side gym that he planned to stop by and take a look at his awesome, totally unexpected windfall that evening, Ramiro had said he wanted to join him.

Sunlight spilled from a row of four exquisite stained-glass windows, casting a landscape of rosy light and trellis-like shadows onto the mahogany floors. For a brief moment, Ryan Daire perfectly envisioned what it must have been like: the crystal chandeliers alight with newly installed electricity, a fire leaping in the marble-encased fireplace, the ladies in their gowns and jewels, the men in their evening attire, the rich, acrid smell of fine cigars, the tinkling sound of champagne glasses being removed from a tray.

A woman wearing a blue satin gown with a black fur border stood by the grand piano. She glanced over a creamy shoulder and met his stare, her velvety dark eyes amazed and a little alarmed. She spun around, gifting him with the vision of full, satin-encased breasts contrasting with a waist so narrow he could have almost encircled it with his hands. A silver locket glittered on the flawless skin of her chest.

Ryan blinked the sunlight out of his eyes and the ballroom returned to its former barren state.

Christ. This old house must have really fired his imagination.

"I thought that old guy who gave it to you said it was fine if you sold it," Ramiro said as he walked over to the fireplace, slightly bent his tall frame and stood completely erect in the enormous hearth. He looked out at Ryan and laughed.

"He did, and I will sell it eventually. The heating bills alone would probably break me," Ryan mused as he glanced around appreciatively. The property description he'd received from Alistair's lawyer said the paneling, floors, staircases and wainscoting in the late-nineteenth-century mansion were all imported African mahogany. The stained-glass windows had been designed by Tiffany's greatest rival, John La Farge. Even Ramiro had been stunned into an uncustomary silence earlier when they'd gotten their first glimpse of the sweeping, majestic grand staircase.

Ryan couldn't help but feel a stab of pride at actually *owning* the stately old jewel. The regal bearing and elegance of the house spoke to something deep within him.

"Hey, you know what we should do? We should turn it into a gym," Ramiro suggested, pausing as he walked toward Ryan and, crouching into sparring position, gave a tight jab with his fist.

"Right. Put up a boxing ring and fill the ballroom with a bunch of sweaty, smelly guys. Maybe we could turn on the Tiffany chandeliers and hire a string quartet for matches."

Ramiro gave a sharp bark of laughter. Their loud footsteps on the wood floor echoed hollowly off the barren walls. Ryan wondered idly what the elegant ghosts of the past would think seeing he and Ramiro stalking along the corridors—a spic and a mick storming the grand entry hall like a couple of bulls in a china shop.

The sun had sunk below the horizon, leaving the old house draped in shadows so thick they seemed to have weight.

"It'd be amazing. Tons of guys would pay you for boxing lessons. Guys with real money, that is," Ramiro added pointedly. "You'd have to give up coaching kids for free."

"Not gonna happen," Ryan replied casually, used to Ramiro's doubts about the wisdom of volunteering his time to coach boxing to inner-city youth. Ramiro and he had been partners on the vice squad of the Chicago Police Department for the past four years and he'd trust Ramiro with his life—*had* trusted him with his life on several occasions. They were as close as brothers, but they didn't have much in common besides their fanaticism for their work.

"Yeah, I figured you'd say that. Who'd you say the guy was who gave you this house? Marshall Field or something?" Ramiro joked, referring to the nineteenth-century magnate who owned the famous Chicago department store.

"No, I think Marshall Field lived down the street a little bit. So did George Pullman and Philip Armour, from what I hear." He noticed Ramiro's blank expression despite the dimness in the entry hall. Ryan searched for a light switch. "Pullman was the creator of the Pullman sleeper train car and Philip Armour was the meatpacking millionaire. You have him to thank, at least partially, for all those hot dogs you eat by the gross. Armour bragged about using everything on the pig 'but the squeal.'"

Ryan recalled how he'd temporarily gone cold turkey as a teenager on any kind of packaged meats after reading about Philip Armour's revolutionary meatpacking techniques and the infamous Chicago stockyards.

Suddenly the opulent crystal chandelier blazed to life, bathing the grand foyer in soft, gleaming light. Ramiro glanced at him in surprise. Ryan hadn't yet located the light switch.

"Must be a short circuit. Who knows when this house was wired for electricity," Ryan mumbled as they headed for the stairs.

"So you inherited a house on millionaire's row, in other words," Ramiro said as he followed.

"I don't know if I'd call it that anymore, but the property it sits on is a hot ticket. The Prairie Avenue District is becoming revitalized." Ryan switched on a light in the second-floor hallway, chasing encroaching shadows into the distance.

"This professor guy must have liked you a hell of a lot to leave you a mansion," Ramiro muttered, a hint of envy flavoring his tone.

"I was knocked flat on my ass when Alistair told me what he planned, but there was nothing I could say to change his mind. He insisted I was doing him a favor by taking it. The value of the house is appreciating hugely because of the real estate development in this area. Alistair's lawyers advised him to reduce his taxable estate with a gift."

"Some gift. Better he'd left you some cash, though."

Ryan stepped into a room and flipped on a light. He studied the large, spacious bedroom suite, the plaster ceilings and intricately carved mantel. Alistair knew Ryan loved Chicago history. He must have guessed how much Ryan would appreciate the mansion.

"Cash's got *nothing* on this place."

Ramiro snorted. "They broke the mold when it comes to you,

Daire. Six feet and four inches of pure pushover. At least to little kids and stray animals. Can't say the same about you when it comes to assholes like Jim Donahue."

"You wouldn't want me any other way."

"Who wants you? I'm shackled to you," Ramiro grumbled.

They stepped into the bedroom. Ryan ran his hand admiringly over the carved mahogany mantel. Unlike the majority of the house, this room retained some furniture—stuff that looked to be the same vintage as the house, Ryan realized with a sense of amazement. The green-and-white floral wallpaper beneath the wainscoting had faded but still retained a fresh, feminine charm. Obviously the bedroom had once belonged to a woman.

The foot- and headboard of a brass bedstead leaned against the wall between two antique mahogany tables. Ryan fingered the cool metal thoughtfully. The brass needed to be cleaned but the bed was perfectly intact. An image of himself polishing the brass and putting together the bed for his own mattress flashed vividly into his mind's eye.

He'd be *nuts* to even consider moving into this place.

"Look at this. Looks like something you'd have your nose buried in." Ramiro held up an old leather-bound book that he'd found in one of the table drawers. The color of the once-crimson leather had faded to a dull dark red.

"Shakespeare's sonnets," Ryan murmured. He owned a copy of his own, nearly as well read as this old tome. Ryan had cultivated a love of Shakespeare from his father that had been nourished by Alistair. The book parted to a well-worn gold-leafed page when he opened it. He immediately recognized the 116th sonnet.

He raised the book toward his face and inhaled. His brow furrowed at the scent of gardenias mixing with the odor of leather and mildew.

"I'll bet you can get a couple grand for this old chest, Daire. People pay out their asses for antiques. Holy shit, check it out."

Ramiro moved aside from the opened door of the massive mahogany wardrobe so that Ryan could see the full-length mirror attached on the inner side of the door. The frame had been carved into a meticulous iris design beneath the gilt. Time had taken its toll on the mirror itself. Six or so inches all along the exterior had gone foggy with age. Only the center portion reflected true. Still, the mirror was so huge that Ryan didn't have to stoop his tall frame to see his face in the reflection.

Only it wasn't his face that he saw. He started in surprise.

"Jesus."

He whipped around so fast that Ramiro jerked back in alarm.

"What?" Ramiro asked. The whites of his brown eyes showed as his gaze shifted warily around the room and then back to Ryan. "What's wrong, man?"

Ryan turned back to the mirror, this time seeing his own bloodless face and greenish-blue eyes staring back at him.

"You didn't see her?"

"See *who*?"

"That woman. She was just right here, standing in front of me. I saw her in the mirror." He quickly inspected the empty wardrobe, scanned the bedroom and rushed to the door.

The hallway stood empty and silent, the dozens of closed doors along both walls reminding him of watchful eyes.

"There's no one here but us, Daire," Ramiro said from just behind him.

Ryan shook his head. He *knew* what he'd seen with his own two eyes: a stunning, lithesome-limbed beauty with pale, flawless skin and a long mane of soft, curling dark hair hanging loose down her shoulders and back.

The same woman he'd imagined briefly in the ballroom, he realized. But this had been different. In the ballroom it had just been like a super-vivid flash of his imagination. This had been real.

Realer than real.

Laughter had curved her lush, dark pink lips. She'd worn a sheer negligee, the bottom of which barely covered the dark nest of hair between her slender thighs. She might as well have been standing there naked for as much good as the nightgown did. The only other thing that adorned her flawless skin was a locket hanging around her neck. Ryan could still see perfectly with his mind's eye the detail of the filigree carved into the silver and the throb of the woman's pulse at her throat.

"No. I definitely saw her," Ryan insisted firmly, but even as he said it, he began to question himself. He'd seen the front of her in the mirror . . . as though she'd stood directly before him with her back to him.

His breath froze on an inhale.

There hadn't been anyone standing in front of him. She'd *just* been in the mirror, staring out at him as if the space between the gilded frame had been a doorway, not a pane of glass. He crossed the room and touched the surface of the mirror. Despite the bizarreness of what had just happened, he didn't really believe he'd feel anything but the cool, smooth surface of the glass.

Shock jolted through him for the second time that evening when the molecules of his fingers seemed to meld with those of the mirror. He wondered if it hadn't been his imagination when a second later he pressed his fingertips against a solid pane of glass.

"You really didn't see anyone?" he asked Ramiro as he turned around.

Ramiro shook his head.

There was no way in *hell* Ryan wouldn't have noticed the back of that woman if she stood in front of him. That flimsy excuse for a nightgown wouldn't have completely covered her bare ass.

Uh-uh—not a possibility. As a healthy, red-blooded male, Ryan knew for a fact he would have noticed *that*.

"*Dios*, Daire. I think you saw a ghost."

Ryan shot Ramiro an annoyed look. "I didn't see a ghost. She was perfectly solid."

Perfectly gorgeous.

He recalled the startled expression in her velvety black eyes. "She looked as surprised to see me as I did her," Ryan said.

"What'd she look like?"

A pair of full, shapely breasts and succulent, fat nipples pressing against transparent cloth that did nothing to hide their rosy hue flashed into Ryan's mind's eye. The potent eroticism of the recalled image made his cock jerk in his boxer briefs.

What'd she look like? *Edible. Delicious. Like an angel on a mission of sin.*

"Dark hair. Dark eyes," he muttered. For some reason he felt hesitant about sharing even a basic description of the woman with Ramiro.

"You saw a ghost all right. This house is haunted," Ramiro declared as he glanced around, his feet shifting nervously.

Ryan couldn't help but grin. "I thought you were a big, bad vice detective. Since when are you scared of a little tiny female?"

Ramiro gave him an insulted look. "Ever since the 'little tiny female' is dead."

"She's *not* dead."

Ramiro looked a little taken aback by Ryan's hard tone. "Whatever, man." Ramiro shivered and started toward the door. The image of his brawny partner shuddering reflexively struck Ryan as markedly odd, not to mention alarming for some reason.

"The only time I saw you get so pale was when you got shot," Ramiro said. "Take my advice and sell this place quick as you can. I'll take the likes of a slimy rat like Anton Chirnovsky any day versus a haunted house. Come on. Crenshaw will be waiting for us at Bureau Headquarters. We're making sure Chirnovsky has his story straight and is in good voice before we strap the wires on him for Donahue's downfall this weekend."

Ryan closed the heavy wardrobe door with a brisk bang, perhaps hoping to shatter the fey spell wrought by the vision of the stunning woman. He didn't believe in ghosts and he was every bit as eager to nail Jim Donahue for human trafficking as Ramiro was.

Still, he lingered in the doorway, casting his gaze around the empty bedroom warily before he shut out the light.

∽

Anton Chirnovsky seemed to sense Ryan's stare when he exited the conference room. His pale blue eyes met Ryan's and then shifted away nervously. The FBI agent in charge of guarding him while he colluded with the police and FBI to have his boss Jim Donahue arrested tapped his elbow. Chirnovsky willingly headed down the hallway away from Ryan.

"Rat bastard. Guy's as much of a scum as Donahue," Ramiro muttered bitterly under his breath.

"Uh-uh. Donahue's worse," Ryan stated flatly, his tone not inviting one of Ramiro's typical glib responses.

They'd been working on the case against Jim Donahue for a year now, ever since Ramiro and he had followed a tip in regard to a supposed brothel operating in an upscale high-rise on the Gold Coast. They'd instead uncovered a white slavery operation; eight young women being held against their will and forced into performing acts of sex with strangers in exchange for food and freedom from heinous brutalization, never seeing a cent of the money that changed hands. They'd been primarily from Mexico, but several had come from eastern European countries after being promised jobs as waitresses and bartenders, but instead being taken captive and filtered to the United States across the porous Mexican-American border.

Jim Donahue was perfectly poised to mastermind a human trafficking operation that extended way beyond those eight girls. As the
owner of Donahue Landscaping, Donahue received approximately
forty million dollars a year in contracts from the city of Chicago for
street and park landscaping. Donahue cut costs by regularly im-
porting illegal immigrants for cheap labor. He was a slick operator,
though, and decided to put his network of illegal immigration contacts to more profitable use. It wasn't too far of a leap for him to
expand from illegal transportation of aliens to the sex-slave trade.

The bureau had become involved after their discovery on the
Gold Coast, but Ryan and Ramiro had been assigned to an FBI-
CPD combined task force created specifically to stamp out human
trafficking in Chicago and the northern Illinois area.

"Daire, wait up!"

He and Ramiro paused on Roosevelt Road on the way to Ryan's
car while Dale Crenshaw, the special agent in charge of the human
trafficking task force, caught up to them.

"What do you think?" Crenshaw asked.

"Chirnovsky will play. He's scared shitless Daire'll turn his pretty-
boy face to hamburger meat if he doesn't. It's amazing the cred you
get for being the Amateur International boxing champion for three
years running," Ramiro bragged as if he'd been talking about his
own titles instead of Ryan's. He had a habit of compensating for
Ryan's extended silences and terse explanations in a manner that
didn't even remotely resemble anything Ryan would say.

"I didn't hear that," Crenshaw said resolutely, his thin lips twitching with amusement. In the past year of working with him, Ryan
had found the older man to be fair-minded and relatively easy to
work for, especially considering the problems Ryan'd encountered
on multidisciplinary task forces in the past.

"Got your tuxes all brushed off and ready to go?" Crenshaw
asked, referring to the undercover sting operation to nail Donahue
over the weekend. Donahue was expecting to meet with Chirnovsky

at a black-tie charity event sponsored by the City League at the Field Museum to discuss future importation plans for women to Milwaukee, St. Louis and Kansas City.

"Yeah, but I'll still be staying background. Donahue and I have met. Took an instant disliking to each other," Ryan said as they walked down the sidewalk.

Crenshaw paused, an anxious look on his thin face. "*What?* You never mentioned that."

Ryan just shrugged and kept walking, but Ramiro spoke for him yet again.

"He met him years ago through his father. Daire's dad was a hotshot lawyer, did legal work for the city and county. You can imagine how disappointed he was when his precious only son joined the ranks of the common soldier."

Ryan shot Ramiro an annoyed look. Ramiro's eyebrows went up and Ryan knew that he'd gotten the message to shut up. For the most part, Ryan was as used to his partner's garrulousness as Ramiro was accustomed to Ryan's extended silences, but occasionally Ramiro went too far. Ramiro knew perfectly well that Ryan's father had eventually become proud of his son's work on the CPD despite his early misgivings about Ryan's choice to drop out of law school and become a cop.

For the past year or so Ryan had been having some doubts about the career decision he'd made ten years ago, though, and maybe that's what made him extra testy about Ramiro's off-the-cuff comment. Ryan wanted to make a tangible difference. That's why he volunteered his time to coach boxing to inner-city youth and chose to fight crime and human greed as a cop instead of a lawyer.

Sometimes he wondered if it was enough, though.

"Don't worry. I only met Donahue once years ago. I doubt he even remembers it, but I'll stay background, anyway. I wouldn't let anything get in the way of nailing Donahue's hide," Ryan told Crenshaw.

"Good. Make sure of it," Crenshaw said with a pointed glance before he said good night and headed toward his own car.

"You got a date with the society princess tonight?" Ramiro asked later when Ryan pulled up in front of Ramiro's Wicker Park condominium building.

Ryan shook his head, not bothering to elaborate. He'd only been out with Carrie Prince twice. They hadn't slept together yet and Ryan was suddenly convinced they never would. His heart just wasn't in it, which was damned strange for him.

The realization that he'd never get to know Carrie any better than he already had didn't warrant much interest on his part, let alone a pang of regret. He doubted the delicate, blonde-haired Carrie was the type to be overly thrilled to discover that Ryan's sexual preferences included not just fucking a woman in his bed but tying her down to said bed in the process—among other things.

"You driving tomorrow?" Ramiro nodded. "Do me a favor, will you?"

"Shit. Don't make me pick you up one of those nasty milkshakes from that health-food store on Damen before I get you. Drinking those things is like chewing a mouthful of vitamins and that nut-ball lady who owns it gives me these suspicious looks, like she can smell the bacon on my breath."

"She probably can. Pick me up on Prairie Avenue."

Ramiro gaped at him. "You're fucking with me."

"I'm serious."

"Then you're just *fucked*. You're not actually thinking about *living* in that place, are you?"

Ryan shrugged. "Maybe. Just until I sell it." He saw Ramiro open his mouth. "Can it, Ramiro. Just pick me up there in the morning, will ya?"

Ramiro shook his head as he unfastened his seat belt. "That ghost bitch must have been smoking."

"I told you—I didn't see a ghost."

"You saw something that fried your brain, *hermano*," Ramiro told him pointedly before he slammed the passenger door shut.

∽

Ryan was inclined to agree with Ramiro's parting shot when he turned on the light in the Prairie Avenue bedroom using his elbow. He set down the stuff he'd grabbed from his west-side loft before driving over to the mansion—a portable heater, two insulated sleeping bags that he'd zip together to accommodate his large frame, a pillow and a hastily packed duffle bag filled with camping equipment, clothing and toiletries.

He'd bring a carload of stuff over tomorrow, maybe ask Ramiro's cousin if he could borrow his truck to transport his mattress so he could set up the brass bed.

You've gone off the deep end at about 120 miles an hour, he told himself as he walked across the room, the wood floors creaking loudly beneath his boots. He felt like he'd penetrated the depths of a massive, sentient creature, as if the house itself was alive around him and regarding his intrusion with cold skepticism and a hint of amusement.

For the life of him he wouldn't have been able to say when he'd made the decision to move, at least temporarily, into the mansion.

He only knew for a fact that he wouldn't have been able to sleep in his familiar bed in his loft tonight. Thoughts of this house—of that woman in the peekaboo nightgown—would have hounded him . . . *haunted* him, until he'd finally risen from his mussed bed, dressed and driven over here at some ungodly hour of the morning.

Might as well do the inevitable right off the bat, Ryan thought grimly.

Once he'd turned the heater to a high setting, unrolled the sleeping bags, zipped them together and cleaned up in the antiquated but functional bathroom down the hall, Ryan stripped down to his boxer briefs. He retrieved the leather-bound book of sonnets from the drawer in the table where he'd left it earlier and started to head over to his sleeping bag.

Something caught his eye.

A portion of the mahogany mantel protruded forward an inch at chest level. It wasn't hugely obvious, but Ryan thought he would have noticed it when he and Ramiro were there earlier, considering how he'd touched and admired the workmanship of the carved wood. He pulled on the section of wood gently and then with more force, but it didn't budge. He stopped when he realized the only thing he was going to succeed in doing was ripping the beautiful mantel apart.

The piece of wood snapped forward another inch. The skin on the back of Ryan's neck prickled and roughened. It was as if someone had just pushed an invisible button and sprung the release.

He pulled, revealing a nine-by-nine-by-nine-inch compartment—like a drawer that had been installed into the woodwork. He reached inside and withdrew several aged black-and-white photographs. After a tense few seconds of staring at the first one, he went over to his sleeping bag and flipped on the battery-operated lamp he'd brought along for reading. He shuffled through the photos—seven in all—slowly. When he'd seen them all, he studied each one again.

And then again.

What he was looking at was a prime example of Victorian-era erotic photography—images of a bound, dark-haired beauty and a big, muscular man in various arousing stages of a session of mild BDSM sex.

Ryan lowered his head to better examine the woman's face in one photo. The man's hand was on the nape of her neck, appearing to hold her head down on the mattress of the bed while he knelt behind her. Her eyes were closed, but every nuance and angle of her face reflected a sense of profound, intense arousal.

He moaned harshly, his hand jerking up to his crotch to alleviate the painful stab of lust that shot through his cock like a sizzling bolt of lightning.

It wasn't just the nearly tangible ecstasy on the woman's face while the man thrust into her. No, it wasn't *only* that that made Ryan hard enough to pound nails with his erection. Nor was it *just* the arousing photo of her mouth open in a silent scream of pleasure while the man's face was buried between her slender thighs or the image of her restrained to the bed while her lover used a crop on her full, shapely breasts.

The thing that had him jerking his cock out of his boxer briefs and pumping himself like a madman was the fact that the woman being sexually dominated and pleasured in those pictures was the same woman he'd seen in the mirror.

The same woman who—if he allowed himself to examine the issue for even a split second—was the sole reason he'd come here tonight to sleep in this cold, hulking, rattling skeleton of a house. Seeing her in that mirror had made the blood simmer in his veins.

But seeing unmasked desire on her beautiful face made him burn at the center of a raging, white-hot fire.

⌒ TWO ⌒

His portable alarm clock went off at seven a.m. Ryan stuck his head up and looked blurrily around the sunlight-filled Prairie Avenue mansion bedroom before he hit the snooze button on the alarm clock and buried his face back in the pillow.

He groggily recalled how he'd jacked off not once last night, but three times in a shockingly short period of time thanks to the volatile fuel of those erotic photos. Now that morning was here, it struck him as amusing that he'd gotten as horny as a teenage boy over photographs of a woman who'd likely been dead for the greater part of a century.

He scowled at the thought, turning his head on the pillow, willing the warm, enticing embrace of sleep to enfold him once again. He heard the heater blowing out its hot air and the sound of a car backfiring on a far-distant city street. Ramiro was going to be as pissed and mouthy as a shortchanged whore if Ryan wasn't ready when he arrived.

He was weighing the consequences of sleeping in and leaning toward getting up rather than endure Ramiro's complaints when a floorboard not five feet behind his back creaked, as though someone had just placed a cautious foot on it and then paused at the subsequent sound. The hairs on his arms rose and prickled.

For some reason instead of springing up out his warm cocoon and lunging for his gun, like he logically should have, he remained still, his breath frozen in his lungs.

"You're such a hog with the covers. Let me in there with you. I'm freezing out here."

Ryan's eyelids popped open; surely he must have imagined the low, sultry voice laced with laughter.

Slowly, almost as though he believed he moved right at the precipice of a cliff, the ground beneath him fragile and crumbling, he turned around.

She sat next to him. The morning sunlight cast her pale, naked body into a luminous landscape of feminine curves and planes. The brilliant, breathtaking vision of her blinded him for a second. He blinked . . . but no, she didn't disappear in a sweet, gardenia-scented mist. Instead she continued to stare down at him, puzzlement mixing with the amusement in her large, midnight eyes.

Ryan whipped back the covers and spread his hands over her ribs, desperate to know if she was real. Her skin flowed like silk beneath his fingers. She hadn't been lying; she *was* chilled. But beneath the surface he felt her heat.

He groaned and pulled her down beside him, yanking the blanket over both of them before he came down over her, belly to belly.

"Who are you?" he grated out as he brushed aside a cloud of fragrant dark hair and kissed her neck with feverish intensity. But it was a stupid, superfluous question and he knew it. His cock had hardened into a lead pike and the only thing that mattered in that moment was burying himself in her heat. His brain might be clueless, but his body seemed to know *precisely* who she was. The degree of distilled lust he experienced at the sensation of her soft, firm body beneath him, her erect nipples pressing into his ribs was like a blade lancing into his flesh—in truth, like nothing he'd ever experienced or imagined in his life.

He moaned when he felt her hands in his hair and then running hungrily over his shoulders.

"You've accused me of being a witch often enough. Is that the answer you want?" she teased in that smoky voice that had the effect of a low-level current of electricity running just beneath his skin. His cock lurched against her smooth belly.

"It's the only answer I'm going to get for now. The only conversing I like doing while I'm fucking is dirty talk."

He saw her black velvet eyes surrounded by a lush thicket of lashes widen. She pressed two fingers to her smiling lips as though to seal them.

"*Witch*," Ryan muttered before he fell on the luscious pink bow of her mouth. When he registered her taste he growled deep in his throat, his body transforming into pure flame. He stroked the sweet cavern deeply, sweeping his tongue everywhere, eager to discover more of her flavor. She kissed him back with equal hunger, sliding her tongue against his teasingly and then engaging in a sinuous, hot duel with him. His fingers sought out the heat between her thighs, glorying at what he found as he glided over creamy, plump labia and a slick, erect clit.

He penetrated her snug slit with his forefinger.

Ah, God. Fantasy eyes, fantasy mouth, fantasy pussy. She'd be the dream fuck of a lifetime.

"You're so wet. I'm sorry, I can't wait." He rolled to the side, putting his upper body weight on one elbow and fisted his cock, positioning the tip at her juicy slit. He flexed his hips.

She gasped as he came down over her. He bent to take a tender bite from her fragrant neck and pushed his cock into her to mid-staff. It felt so good the sensation nearly ripped at the limits of his consciousness. Heat emanated from the muscular walls of her pussy, taunting him. She squirmed beneath him and moaned, trying to seat him further in her tight channel. Her writhing movements almost made him come then and there. He grasped her hip with one hand.

"Keep still," he grated out as he fought for control amid a cyclone of desire that pummeled him from all directions. He grabbed her wrists and pinned them down above her head with one hand while his other continued to immobilize her hip. "Quit twisting around or I swear I'll turn you over my knee when I'm done with you."

The little witch had the nerve to smile at his threat. His cock jerked in her clasping sheath. He bent down and nipped at her plump lower lip with his teeth. "After I fuck you I'm gonna—"

"Daire!" a man called somewhere far outside the confines of the battering, relentless storm that held him and this amazing woman as its hostages. She squirmed beneath him and he instinctively accepted her challenge, seating himself in her to the balls. His shout of triumph blended with her cry of excitement and Ramiro's call . . . louder this time.

"God damn it, Daire. I'm going to make you tie your left hand behind your back tonight so I can kick your ass in the ring for making me wander around this freaky fucking house alone!"

"Shhhh, don't move. I'll get rid of him," Ryan soothed when he looked into the woman's eyes and knew from her shocked expression that Ramiro's voice had penetrated her thick arousal. Their bellies expanded and contracted wildly against each other's as they panted.

What'd Ramiro done, picked the damn lock on the front door?

He held her stare, the uncertainty in her velvety eyes the only thing keeping him from fucking her like a crazed degenerate. She started beneath him when Ramiro banged loudly on the door. Ryan opened his mouth to shoo him off but the door swung inward before he got out a word.

"*Shut it*, Menendez," Ryan roared over his shoulder. "I'm not alone."

He caught a glimpse of Ramiro's startled face before his partner grabbed the handle and slammed the door shut. "Just meet me at the station," Ramiro yelled irritably.

Ryan bowed his head and sighed in relief as he listened to Ramiro's retreating footsteps. He cursed viciously when the annoying buzz of his alarm clock struck his consciousness.

"Sorry about that—" He paused, realizing he'd never allowed the amazing woman to tell him her name. The cruel, crashing waves of his arousal had abated somewhat, suddenly making it imperative that he find out who she was that instant. He lifted his head and opened his mouth but his query dissolved on his tongue.

He found himself leaning up on his elbows in a sleeping bag that looked like he'd staged a wrestling match in it. His cock was still rock-hard, despite the fact that instead of being sheathed in the stunning woman's pussy it merely throbbed against the pressure of a wood floor.

A half hour later Ryan reentered the bedroom, feeling miserable and grouchy after folding his large frame into a bathtub. Christ, he couldn't remember how old he'd been the last time he took a bath—three? At least there'd been plenty of hot water, although it ran through a separate tap from the cold, making it necessary for him to constantly check the water and attenuate the outflow of the two nozzles.

He got a strange, masochistic satisfaction from the fact that he didn't feel comfortable jerking off in the bathtub like he would in the shower. He deserved to suffer for getting more turned on than he'd ever been in his entire life over a dream woman.

But it *hadn't* been a dream, at least not like any dream Ryan had ever had.

Ramiro had called her a ghost.

"She's *not* dead," he said abruptly out loud.

Great. Now he wasn't only having hallucinatory sex that was so hot it'd probably put him off fucking forever for fear of the bitter disappointment of comparison, he also was talking to himself out loud.

And his cock still throbbed next to his thigh, indignant at being left unattended.

One brief recollection of what it'd been like to be buried fast in the woman's heat while she looked up at him with those big, velvety eyes stiffened him to full readiness once again.

It was going to be a day planned gleefully for Ryan by the devil himself.

He grabbed his jacket and shoved his hand in the pocket, poking around for his car keys. His gaze landed on the red book of poetry. It still lay on the floor where he'd left it after becoming bizarrely obsessed over those damned old photographs.

He bent slowly and picked up the book, hesitating for several seconds before he opened it. He impatiently flipped through the first few pages. The inscription was written in a long, spidery scrawl in ink that had faded to near invisibility.

September 14, 1904
Dearest Hope:

Happy twenty-third birthday. If the love you so generously show to your fellow man comes back to you even in partial measure, you will be a wealthy woman indeed. God loves and cherishes you.

As I do,
Father

Ryan remained immobile, reading the inscription repeatedly as if he thought he'd discover something new and crucial amongst the relatively innocuous words.

A strange feeling of helplessness overcame him. He raised the book to his nose and inhaled, searching for the elusive fragrance of gardenias amongst a host of other scents like a miner panning for a bright flash of gold in a pile of rocks.

Before he could question his sanity, he reached into his breast pocket for a pen. He allowed the book to fall open to the well-thumbed page and wrote rapidly in the margin. He tossed the book on his sleeping bag.

"Hope?"

His gaze swept over every corner of the room before he walked out, feeling every bit the fool that he undoubtedly was.

∾

Chicago, 1906

Hope Stillwater lay in her brass bed and sweated.

The gas radiator rattled loudly in an ineffective attempt to heat her chilly room, so she couldn't blame her overheated state on anything but herself and her scandalous thoughts. Much to her chagrin, her eyes kept returning to her wardrobe despite the fact that she tried her mightiest to keep them trained on the dull essay she attempted to read. Her father was a leading member of the Purity Foundation and had given her the tract earlier this evening to peruse.

Yes, *yes*, we know that white slavery is wrong, she thought impatiently as she set aside the essay and picked up her favorite book of Shakespearean sonnets instead. What creature in their right mind would condone such abhorrent practices? Hope herself engaged in an almost daily personal campaign to stop the kidnapping and rape of innocent young women with the eventual purpose of selling them to brothels in the infamous Levee District.

But why must organizations like the Purity Foundation continually couch the issue in the black-and-white terms of keeping "decent" women safe from the slavering, bestial nature of men? It seemed to Hope sometimes that the strict sexual prohibitions placed upon women made the ideal environment for white slavers like the notorious Diamond Jack Fletcher to flourish at his trade.

Once again, her eyes went to the wardrobe. The negligee was in there—the shockingly sheer, nearly nonexistent garment that the madam of the Marlborough Club, Addie Sampson, had given to Hope with a gamine grin just yesterday afternoon.

Despite their vastly different backgrounds and the fact that Hope's father championed the cause to shut down the brothels in the Levee District, Addie and Hope had formed an unlikely friendship. The bold, brassy madam and Hope shared one common goal—to put a stop to the rampant practice of white slavery. Their opinions differed on many topics, but unlike most Levee District madams or the vicious brothel owner Diamond Jack Fletcher, Addie seemed to truly care about the well-being of the young women who worked for her.

"Go on, take it, Hope. With your figure you'll do a Marlborough gown far more justice than even my most tempting girl. Oh, come on now," Addie had teased when she'd seen Hope's scandalized expression as she held out the negligee. "I'm not trying to tempt you to the devil. You yourself have admitted that if 'decent' wives weren't so uppity and tense in the bedroom, men might not find the Levee District so appealing."

"But I'm not a *wife*," Hope had whispered as she glanced around nervously for Dr. Walkerton. Hope had spearheaded a program under the auspices of the Women's Social Reform and Welfare League to provide medical services to women in need, including the Levee District brothels.

Although *in truth*, only the Marlborough Club and the Golden
Parrot had agreed to participate thus far. And *in fact*, Hope had
not yet successfully coaxed other women from the Welfare League
to join her cause. She had high hopes for further Levee District
reform, however, despite Addie's patient head-nodding and occa-
sional exasperated rolls of her eyes when Hope launched into the
topic with her typical militant zeal.

Addie had merely laughed at Hope's display of nervousness
about the nightgown and shoved the frothy confection into Hope's
hand.

"You'll be a wife someday, honey. Might as well get some practice. Wouldn't want your future husband lining up at the Marlborough Club's front doors, would you?"

Hope had opened her mouth to argue but heard Dr. Walkerton
descending the stairs. By the time the elderly doctor had put out his
arm for her in preparation to leave, Hope had secreted one of the
negligees that the Marlborough Club prostitutes were famous for
wearing into her reticule. She'd glowered at Addie's saucy grin before lowering the thick black veil she'd promised both her father
and Dr. Walkerton to wear in the Levee District to protect her identity.

She'd quickly discovered that the Marlborough gown she'd
shoved into the furthest, darkest corner of her wardrobe had some
kind of strange, powerful hold on her imagination. The idea of allowing a man to actually *see* her wearing the transparent garment
scandalized her.

Thrilled her.

It was the latter reaction that had her sweating as she lay on her
bed in the frigid bedroom.

She slowly set down her well-thumbed book of sonnets and approached the wardrobe, a tickle of excitement spreading from her
lower belly to her sex. After she'd withdrawn the negligee she cast

a guilty glance at her bedroom door before locking it. Her father would never bother her this late in the evening after she'd retired, but her maid Mary sometimes knocked to see if she'd like some logs added to the fire.

She shed her long-sleeved, high-necked linen nightgown and shoved the negligee over her head before she could second-guess her impulsive actions. The sheer fabric fluttered across her naked skin as softly as a butterfly's wings, thrilling her heated flesh. Her eyes went wide when she saw the gown barely covered the dark hair between her thighs.

Her breath burned in her lungs as she raced across the room and opened the wardrobe door wide. She stared into the full-length gilt mirror for several seconds before she finally exhaled harshly. Her cheeks turned a vibrant shade of pink.

Who was this lush, wanton creature?

Her breasts heaved shallowly in excitement, the slight abrasion of the fabric making her nipples prickle with pleasure. She watched as the crests stiffened and distended, the tea-rose pink hue darkening in color. Hope resisted an almost overwhelming urge to put her hand between her thighs. It was one thing to rub that secret, delicious place beneath all of her covers in the darkness, but touching herself while she wore a whore's nightgown and stared at herself in the mirror was quite another matter.

Hope turned, her chin craning over her shoulder as she inspected her appearance from the back. She gasped. The rear view was even more scandalous than the front. The filmy negligee left the bottom curves of her buttocks completely bare! How could the women at the Marlborough Club even *consider* walking around in the company of men wearing this thing? It somehow seemed more lewd than complete nudity. How did they keep a straight face?

Hope snorted with a burst of laughter before she spun completely around, her loose hair flying around her shoulders. Her mirth froze on her tongue when she found herself staring into the startling cerulean blue gaze of a tall, dark man who looked every bit as shocked to see her as she was him.

Hope barely stifled a scream. She tripped on the edge of a rug in her anxiety to get away from the mirror and the man. By the time she'd grabbed her robe, flung it around her and scurried toward the door, a modicum of reason penetrated her panic. A quick survey of the room assured her she was completely alone.

She panted shallowly in fear a second later as she peered into her large wardrobe. Of course it was empty. And the only image that stared back at her from the gilded mirror was her own pale, shocked face.

Hope shook her head in amazement and guiltily removed the negligee, shoving her modest nightgown over her head. Unlike the gossamer-thin gown, the linen felt scratchy and uncomfortable next to her skin. She seriously considered burning the Marlborough gown for a few seconds before she tossed it back into the dark corner of the wardrobe and crawled into her bed, throwing the covers over her head. Her heartbeat thundered alarmingly loud in her ears.

She'd heard of drugs causing phantasms but had never before known that sexually sinful behavior could promote hallucinations. Because if her wickedest desires had been given free reign to conjure up a man, surely it would have been the man she'd just seen in the mirror.

She peeked over the covers cautiously and stared at the wardrobe.

Why had he been dressed so strangely? His trousers reminded her a little of the thick hickory cloth the men who worked for the railroad wore, but the man's in the mirror had been uniformly dyed indigo blue. She would have assumed those pants marked him as some sort of laborer if it weren't for the short coat he wore made completely of sleek, supple leather.

He'd been so large—not fat, if anything his hips had been trim and narrow—just *big*. Taller than any man she'd ever seen, with wide shoulders and long thighs the size of a sturdy, young tree trunk. She blushed as she recalled how well those blue hickory cloth pants fit those strong thighs. He'd worn an unusual sort of beard that reminded her of the kind she'd glimpsed on Chinese men. It'd been as dark as his hair, short and well trimmed.

Who—or *what*—in God's name had he been?

If everything about him seemed strange and exotic, his eyes had struck her as wholly familiar. They'd been a singular greenish-blue hue that brought to mind the color of the Mediterranean Sea on a crystalline day. He'd clearly been shocked to see her, just as she was him, but when he'd glanced down over her ever so briefly something else had flashed into those compelling eyes; something even more exciting than the illicit thrill of seeing herself in a Marlborough gown.

After several minutes Hope's heart finally began to slow. She sat up in bed and sighed shakily. Had her bizarre, hysterical episode entirely passed? She felt jittery, her nerves still jangled by the incident. Knowing she wouldn't be able to sleep for hours, if at all tonight, she reached for her book of sonnets on the beside table and flipped it open.

For a long moment, she stared in rising confusion.

Someone had written in a bold hand in the margin of her favorite sonnet *Ryan Vincent Daire, 1807 S. Prairie Avenue, Chicago, Illinois, 2008.*

The book trembled in her hand. The page had been clean just before she'd stood and put on the Marlborough gown. She'd have bet her life on it.

She flipped through the pages anxiously but found no other anomalous messages. After staring at the name, her own street address on Prairie Avenue and the number—surely that wasn't supposed to signify a year, was it?—for several more minutes, Hope realized that the mysterious writing had been placed directly next to a line from the sonnet.

Love is not time's fool.

⌒ THREE ⌒

Ryan studied a translated statement from a twenty-year-old illegal immigrant who was being extradited. The kid claimed his sister and cousin had disappeared at approximately the same time two men had come to their village in Mexico recruiting men for work in the United States. One of the men fit Anton Chirnovsky's description, the other matched that of a former Colombian drug importer named Manuel Gutierrez. Gutierrez had apparently joined the recruiting division of Donahue's white slavery operation.

A file suddenly plopped down on his desk.

"You going to explain to me what that's all about or not?" Gail Edgerton asked archly when he looked up. Gail worked in the Computer Crime Research Lab. She'd kindly agreed to do a little digging for Ryan earlier this morning even though her blonde eyebrows had shot up on her forehead in disbelief when she'd seen his written request.

"Thanks, Gail. I owe you one," Ryan muttered as he opened the folder. The words *Hope Virginia Stillwater, born: 1881, died: 1906* immediately leapt out at him.

She'd been twenty-five years old when she died? What the hell had happened to her? Ryan wondered as something that felt akin to panic unfurled in his gut.

"How about if we take you to lunch to return the favor, lovely lady?"

Ryan kept his head ducked when he heard Ramiro. Damn. He hadn't particularly wanted his partner to know about this bit of research he'd requested from Gail. He hadn't expected Gail to bring him the information in person. It was a given that Ramiro would be all over Gail once she came into the vice squad room. Ramiro'd had a letch for the attractive blonde for years, not that Gail ever gave him the time of day.

"You trying to tell me you wanted that information as well, Menendez?" Gail asked doubtfully. "This has gotta be one for the record books. There isn't enough crime in the year 2008, so you two top cops gotta go solving hundred-year-old murders?"

Ryan's head reared up.

"Murder?"

Gail grinned, obviously pleased she was telling him something he didn't know. She tilted her chin at the file. "It's all in there, and you *do* owe me for it, Daire. Extra. I had to call the Chicago Police Department Regional Archives Depository to get information on a homicide from 1906. The guy up there was a real pain in my ass. I think I deserve a lunch with tablecloths and waiters, don't you?"

"Definitely," Ryan murmured evenly, despite the fact that it felt like ice water had just been shot down his spinal cord.

"Nineteen hundred and six? What the hell are you talking about? That doesn't have anything to do with the Donahue case," Ramiro said with a scowl. Ryan deftly moved the file away from Ramiro's fingers when he made a grab for it.

"I think I'm coming down with the flu or something. Not hungry. But I've got a great idea, Gail. Why don't you let Ramiro take you to lunch? You can pick the spot and I'll spring for the check. I really do appreciate this."

Ramiro's attention was instantly diverted. His eyes zoomed over to Gail's face. Gail's expression of slight disappointment deepened to stark suspicion when Ramiro pumped his eyebrows and flashed a white smile, shamelessly using the single, deep dimple in his right cheek to seduce his wary prey.

Gail sighed.

"All right. It's got to be better than the cafeteria food."

"You won't be disappointed, beautiful lady."

"Especially if Daire's going to reimburse you for the check, right?" Gail asked, her amusement tinged heavily with skepticism as she gave Ramiro the once-over. Still, Ryan heard her laughing at one of Ramiro's dumb jokes as they exited the squad room together.

Ryan's stomach growled for its lunch but he turned his complete focus onto the meager file about Hope Stillwater's life.

About Hope Stillwater's murder, he added to himself grimly.

Ryan lay in the old-fashioned claw-foot porcelain tub and stared into space while the water cooled around him. He should get up and move or his well-used muscles would stiffen and ache. He'd both worked out at his gym and moved a pickup truck full of items from his loft to the Prairie Avenue mansion. It was past midnight. He should go to bed.

Still, he remained unmoving, his mind churning.

The sound of water splashing made his head swing around. Funny. He knew he'd been preoccupied but he hadn't moved. The sound of lapping water followed by what had sounded like a soft sigh hadn't matched with any of his actions. The dim overhead light cast shadows in the corners but Ryan could still see that the large bathroom was silent and empty except for him and his thoughts.

Ruminations about a woman long dead.

His jaw tightened at the thought. He used his toe to turn on the hot water tap and forced himself to relax once again.

She's not dead.

Despite his stubborn, illogical assertion he'd discovered today that Hope Stillwater, of 1807 S. Prairie Avenue, Chicago, Illinois, had been reported as missing by her father on November thirteenth of the year 1906.

"Three days from now—give or take a hundred and two years," Ryan mumbled out loud.

The woman from his dreams had been declared dead four days after her father reported her missing when her severely beaten and disfigured body had been found floating in the Chicago River. For a few seconds the image of her luminescent pale skin, lithesome limbs, lush breasts and curving lips flashed into his mind's eye like a perfectly clear film clip. His muscles tensed.

He couldn't make it work—*couldn't* rectify that breathtaking, vibrant image of stunning beauty with the report of a beaten, bloated, lifeless body.

Ryan hadn't been able to reconcile those erotic photographs with what he'd learned of Hope's background, either. What he'd read about her life seemed to suggest that the bizarre things he'd been experiencing since stepping into the Prairie Avenue mansion must be wrought by an overworked, stressed-out brain.

Hope's father had been rather famous in his day. Gail had made a few photocopies of old *Chicago Daily Herald* articles about Jacob Stillwater, a wealthy minister, social reformer and alderman of the first ward who had campaigned vociferously against the white slave trade and the shutting down of Chicago's notorious red-light district. A few of those articles speculated that his open warfare against graft, prostitution and white slavery had been the motive for the murder of his daughter.

Hope's murderer had never been found, although one man, who had been colorfully dubbed Diamond Jack Fletcher, had been a prime suspect. The police had investigated Diamond Jack, a man one article had called the "King of Vice" of the Levee District, the area where most of the houses of prostitution could be found.

Although Gail had complained about the person at the Chicago Police Department Regional Archives Depository being a pain in her ass, whoever had compiled the data had done an admirable job finding public and police records in regard to Hope's life and death. In fact, the file had included photocopies of old, handwritten notes from a detective on the Chicago police force, a man by the name of Connor J. O'Rourke.

In his notes, Detective O'Rourke described Jack Fletcher as the most powerful crime boss in the city, owner of multiple brothels and gambling dens, extortionist, blackmailer and white slaver. He ruled the first ward and the Levee District with an iron fist. Jack and his cronies conducted the majority of their business dealings at one of his seedier brothels on the 2400 block of South Dearborn Street. Detective O'Rourke had no difficulty painting a black picture of Jack Fletcher in his notes, although he admitted with a hint of frustration that "certain foul circumstances" prevented him from pinning Diamond Jack with the murder of "that angel of mercy," Hope Stillwater.

Ryan had long taken an interest in the history of Chicago and especially the Chicago Police Department. He had a suspicion that the "certain foul circumstances" O'Rourke referred to was the rampant corruption and graft that plagued the CPD's commissioners and captains in the early 1900s. Detective O'Rourke's boss was likely indebted to Diamond Jack for his heralded position and received some healthy payoffs in order to ignore the vast landscape of illegal activities that occurred in the Levee District.

At any rate, if Diamond Jack Fletcher had thought to silence Jacob Stillwater with his daughter's abduction and murder, he'd made a critical mistake. Jacob Stillwater became even more vocal and active after his daughter's death, spearheading a political campaign that eventually closed down the Levee District. Stillwater launched some of the first federal anti–white slavery legislation. Apparently he was one of the pioneers for drafting laws that Ryan upheld even today by investigating scum like Jim Donahue.

Meanwhile, Detective O'Rourke's shackled attempts at investigating Diamond Jack were stymied even further by Jack becoming sicker and sicker from a reported "blood disorder" that drained him of all his vitality, including his proclivity for violence. He died after a lingering, painful illness a year after Hope's death. That fact didn't provide Ryan with the measure of satisfaction he would have thought it would.

He would have wished something a hell of a lot more decisive if Diamond Jack truly had been Hope Stillwater's murderer.

She's not dead.

Ryan rolled his eyes when he recognized his own stubborn thought. Before he had time to mentally admonish himself for clinging on to delusions, the sound of splashing water once again entered his awareness.

Goose bumps rose on his damp, exposed shoulders, neck and chest. Another wary inspection of the bathroom assured him it was empty, however. Experimentally, Ryan raised his hand from the tub. The sloshing water made a much louder sound than the one he'd just heard. That other noise had possessed a soft, trickling quality, but there was something odd about the sound . . . almost as if he'd heard it through a tin can. There'd been a muffled, slightly metallic quality to it.

When he realized he was holding on to both sides of the deep tub and listening with an intense focus, he sat up with a jerking motion. The sound of water splashing around him as he sat up forcefully was anything but subtle, instantly shattering his tense, expectant mood.

Maybe Ramiro really was right. Not about the Prairie Avenue mansion being haunted. About his brain being fried.

He grunted in irritation when he saw that he'd left his towel on an antique wooden bench that looked as if it'd been made for a child's playhouse. It had been there when he arrived in the house and he hadn't seen any reason to move it yet. It stood a good six feet from the tub. Water streamed off his body when he stood quickly. He lifted one foot to step out, looked up and almost fell out of the deep tub when he lost his balance. His breath burned in his lungs as he stared in openmouthed disbelief.

He gaped at a very alive-looking, half-naked Hope Stillwater.

⌒ FOUR ⌒

Her eyes looked enormous in her delicate face as she peered at him over a damp, creamy shoulder. She stood at the bowl of the sink, masses of curling dark hair pinned up on her head. She held a sponge in her frozen hand. It dripped into the filled basin, the resulting sound perfectly real, soft and somehow soothing to Ryan's stunned brain.

He had caught her in the private ritual of a sponge bath.

After a moment the weird vibrations of shock resonating through him lessened. He'd been mistaken. His imagination had gotten the best of him. This was a very real woman. She must have been living in the mansion illegally. Perhaps she was the former owner and had never vacated the premises?

Despite his logical thoughts, when he finally spoke what he said was completely irrational.

"Hope?" he asked, his volume level barely above a whisper. It was as if she existed inside a fragile bubble and he was afraid his robust male essence would pop her into oblivion.

The sponge she clutched dropped into the basin of water as though she'd lost muscular control. He watched, mesmerized, as she slowly turned to face him. She met his gaze and nodded her head once.

"Hope Stillwater?" he clarified.

Again she nodded, her huge eyes never leaving his face.

Ryan blinked in amazement. Her beauty was so immense, however, that it drew his attention away even from the fact that he was impossibly standing in a bathroom with a woman who'd lived a century before him.

The light that fell upon her naked shoulders and chest wasn't the same dim electric fixture that shone in Ryan's world. Her source of radiance caressed her like a lover, making her flawless, damp skin seem to glow with a dark gold light. He saw her elegant neck convulse as his gaze lowered over her body.

She wore a pair of frilly white pantaloons—at least that's what Ryan *thought* they called the woman's undergarment—but her upper body was bare excerpt for the silver locket. Her arms were beautifully shaped and graceful, her carriage slender and proud. Her breasts were full, but thrust high and firm off the plane of her chest and ribs. His penis tugged in arousal as he stared at the large pink nipples. The fantasy of suckling the tender crests and feeling them tauten under his tongue played across his mind in graphic detail.

"Ryan?"

Her breathy whisper did the impossible and removed his hot stare from the most beautiful breasts he'd ever seen. Like her, he merely nodded when he met her gaze. She'd temporarily stolen his wits along with his voice. He noticed the silent query in her velvety eyes, the amazement mixing with anxiety shaping her features. He raised his hand in an instinctive quieting gesture.

"Shhhh," he soothed, as though he were afraid her nervousness was like a loud noise—something that would rob him of the exquisite, otherworldly moment. "There's nothing to be afraid of. I'm just a man who lives in your house. I'm not sure why we're able to see each other like this."

Her breasts trembled slightly at his words.

"Why wouldn't we be able to see each other?" she whispered cautiously. She took a step toward him, her eyes searching his face. "Are you a spirit?"

"Not that I'm aware of. I was about to ask you the same question . . . even though I don't believe in ghosts."

She started slightly, as though she hadn't expected the amusement in his voice at such a moment.

"I'm just a man, Hope."

Her eyes lowered down over him.

"I see that," she murmured, her tone slightly dazed.

Her stare felt like the equivalent of a touch on the prickling skin of his chest and abdomen. When it lowered even further his cock jerked in arousal.

He couldn't stop himself. He laughed softly when he saw her startled expression of amazement as she stared at his cock with a mixture of 20 percent trepidation and 80 percent fascination. When she realized where she was staring her eyes darted to his face. She blushed.

"I'm sorry," she murmured, clearly bemused even further by his laughter. "I've never seen a man without his clothes on before. You're the largest man I've ever seen."

"That would go without saying, since as you said, you've never seen a man naked before," Ryan said through a smile.

"I meant your overall size . . . not . . . not the size of . . ." Her voice quavered and trailed off. This time a bloom of color rose all the way from her chest to her cheeks, but that didn't stop her curious gaze from flickering back to his groin.

"I know what you meant," Ryan said quietly.

The bizarreness of the situation soaked into his awareness fully for the first time at that moment. She existed but she *didn't* exist. The information Gail had given him today proclaimed that without a doubt, Hope Stillwater had been dead for over a century.

And yet she stood before him vibrant with life. What's more, he was naked and she was nearly so, and they were both obviously highly aware of each other sexually if his lengthening erection and her stiffening nipples were any indication.

Or perhaps she'd just grown chilly, damp as she was?

Her dark eyes lowered over him once again, lingering on his cock, and Ryan knew that her tightening nipples and flushed cheeks weren't caused by a chill in the air and embarrassment—at least not entirely. With her eyes still fastened on his growing erection, she spoke.

"If . . . if you are not a spirit, then what are you?"

"A flesh-and-blood man," Ryan replied even as said flesh and blood pulsated with a primitive need to mate with the luscious female who stood before him. His muscles clenched when her gaze traveled up his torso, pausing to linger on his chest before she met his stare. He inhaled slowly to stave off a powerful wave of lust.

"Maybe I should get my towel—"

"You're even more beautiful than the Michelangelo sculptures I saw in Rome and Florence."

Ryan's mouth fell open at her spontaneous, sweet words. He'd never experienced such uncontrived honesty. He was accustomed to guarded, defensive women . . . to people in general playing it cool in order to protect their vulnerable inner selves. To have such a beautiful woman compliment him so openly given the bizarreness—no, the *impossibility*—of the situation acted as an aphrodisiac just as potent as her naked, flame-gilded flesh.

"Hope," he began gruffly. He started to step out of the tub but hesitated, not sure if he could stop himself from touching her without the small barrier between them. "Do you understand what's happening here?"

She shook her head slowly. "Not really. I know that you're Ryan Vincent Daire and that you live in my house . . . somehow."

"How do you know my name?"

"I saw it. You wrote it, didn't you? In my book of sonnets?" She harried her shapely lower lip with her teeth anxiously when she paused for a moment. "You put the number 2008. That referred to a year, didn't it? To the year in which you live?" she asked in a rush, as if the question had required a burst of courage.

Ryan nodded cautiously, not sure what sort of an effect the news would have on an early-twentieth-century woman—if that was indeed what she was. In that moment, it seemed equally both ludicrous and self-evident at once that he held a conversation with a woman born in 1881. Didn't women at that time period swoon as regularly as sitting down to a meal?

Instead of fainting dead away, however, this incredible woman stepped closer to him, her magical eyes widening in excitement.

"Did you build a time machine, perhaps? Something similar to what Mr. Wells wrote about?"

Ryan blinked. And he'd been thinking she might faint . . .

"No, I haven't done anything intentional to make this happen. Well, except to unexpectedly gain ownership of 1807 Prairie Avenue. You read *The Time Machine*?"

His brow crinkled in confusion when she looked vaguely embarrassed by his question. It surprised him, considering this singular woman hadn't shown a trace of embarrassment over the fact that she stood before him wearing only some sheer pantaloons. The thinness of the garment had become uncomfortably more obvious to Ryan the closer she came to him. He'd never had reason to think about an early-twentieth-century woman's underwear before and was surprised at how sexy the garment was. He could easily see the dark pubic hair between her legs and map the shape of her curving hips and slender thighs through the wispy material.

"I assure you that I temper my reading of novels with that of serious, thoughtful texts, Mr. Daire."

His eyebrows shot up on his forehead at her sudden formal tone. She must have noticed his reaction because she bit her lower lip before the excited gleam entered her eyes once again. Apparently Hope Stillwater's enthusiasm was not a thing so easily repressed by convention.

"But Mr. Wells—and Mr. Jules Verne as well—write such *amazing* adventures. And now we are in one of our own!"

When she saw his wry smile, her eyes dropped to his naked body and then to her own. Clearly Hope Stillwater hadn't meant *adventures* of the sexual kind. That was just Ryan's dirty, twenty-first-century male mind working. He wondered, though, when she jolted visibly. Ryan guessed the full impact of the strangeness—not to mention the potent eroticism—of their situation had just slammed into her consciousness.

"Don't. Don't move," he said.

"Why?" she asked breathlessly.

"I don't know what will make it stop. I don't want you to go."

She swallowed convulsively. "I . . . I don't want you to go, either."

A charged silence ensued.

"Do you . . . do you suppose we should try and touch? To see if it's . . . real?" she asked cautiously.

Ryan hesitated. Hope Stillwater certainly matched none of his ideas about what an early-twentieth-century woman might be like, not that he'd ever given it much thought before. The power of her singular personality smashed all stereotypes to dust. Her lively curiosity and freshness left him stunned and aroused. He also sensed her impulsive, headstrong nature, however . . .

"I want to. Very much," he admitted slowly.

"But you're afraid it will break the connection. Aren't you?"

Ryan's pulse escalated both in his neck and his cock at her reference to a connection. Did she feel it, too, then?

"Yes. But I want to touch you so badly right now, I'm afraid I'm going to have to take the risk."

She took another step toward him. He drowned in deep pools of ebony fringed with the thickest, longest eyelashes he'd ever seen. Her eyebrows arched gracefully on her pale forehead, their shape somehow highlighting her animated expression, the sheer vibrancy that seemed to exude from her being.

Her gaze lowered. She held up one elegant hand just inches from his chest. Her pulse throbbed madly at her throat.

"*Wait.*"

"What?" she asked a trifle impatiently, her hand still outstretched.

"Do you understand what's going to happen if you put your hand on me?" he rasped.

Her gaze flickered over his naked body and back to his face.

"Yes."

"Touch me, then. And be prepared to be touched. But first, tell me this. What is the date there . . . where you are?"

The hand that was suspended in the air trembled slightly.

"November the tenth of the year 1906."

Ryan's jaw tightened. In three days in her time period—perhaps sooner—Hope would be abducted. Her murder would soon follow. The untenable thought was the only thing that kept him from stepping out of that tub and pulling her into his arms. If he didn't feel her dewy, silky-looking skin slide next to his body sometime soon, he worried he might die from thwarted lust.

"Listen to me," he said, his voice sounding harsher than he'd intended. "I want you to be careful. Someone intends to harm you."

"What do you mean?" she asked, clearly confused.

Ryan studied her uncertainly. If he could touch her, hold on to her, perhaps he could keep her here with him in the twenty-first century. Keep her safe?

"Come closer," he demanded quietly.

His hands rose to just an inch above her creamy shoulders. The need to touch her felt imperative. He realized his gaze was glued on her breasts and that he was imagining his hands cradling the weight of them while his forefinger whisked over the tightening, rosy nipples. The heavy head of his cock strained for her almost as though it was made of metal and Hope was a powerful magnet.

He forced his eyes up to her face.

"If something should happen . . . if this"—he glanced down to the narrow space between them—"connection should be broken when we touch, I want you to try and contact me through the mirror."

Her eyes widened. "The one in my bedroom? You were there. You saw me as well?"

"Oh, I saw you all right," he muttered grimly. He thought of the way the mirror had felt yesterday for a second when he touched it: not solid, not liquid, but not like empty space, either. More like . . . a fullness, an indescribable web of possibilities. "Use the mirror, Hope. Do you understand?"

"Yes."

He frowned slightly when he heard her solemn whisper. God, she was sweet. Not to mention sexy as hell without ever intending to be. He really didn't want anything to happen to her—

"And under *no* circumstances should you venture out alone over the next few days. Agreed?"

She nodded.

"Don't go *anywhere* with a stranger. Am I making myself clear?"

"Even you?" She looked dazed as her hand sunk toward his chest.

"I don't understand what's happening here, Hope, but I'm no stranger to you," he growled before he reached to claim her . . .

. . . And hissed in monumental frustration when his hands closed on empty air.

∽

Ryan charged into his bedroom down the hall still naked and damp, but impervious to the chill in the hulking old house. He swung open the wardrobe door and stared at the image of himself in the antique mirror. His wet hair spiked up from his head at haphazard angles. His cock and balls hung heavy between his thighs, still semi-aroused . . . still expectant.

"Hope?" he demanded. After he'd repeated her name several times, each time the volume of his voice escalating, he closed his eyes in profound frustration. Christ, what did he think he was going to do? *Scold* her into the year 2008?

He shouldn't have tried to touch her. Since when did he let his cock rule his actions? How was he going to reach her now? How the hell was he going to keep her from being murdered?

And did he really believe such a thing was a possibility?

Ryan thought of the dazed arousal in Hope's dark eyes when her hand had hovered above his chest.

It didn't matter what he believed. He *knew* he'd just spoken with a woman named Hope Stillwater. He *knew* danger and death hovered over her.

He *knew* he'd do anything in his power to stop her from being harmed.

When it came down to it, belief and bone-deep knowledge were two very different things, Ryan realized for the first time in his life as he stared blankly into the looking glass.

His gaze sharpened on the outer edge of the mirror. Was it his imagination or had an inch or so of the fogginess cleared? He touched the cool, hard surface and cursed. No give to the solid object. No bend to time.

No Hope.

∽

Ramiro looked pissed off enough to bite through metal the next day as he and Ryan left the Immigration and Naturalization Service Detention Center in Chicago's Loop. Although he doubted his expression gave away much, Ryan was every bit as furious as Ramiro after interviewing the twenty-year-old kid who would be extradited back to Mexico within the week.

"My grandparents live in a village about the size of that kid's! So do my aunts and uncles and cousins. It could have been *their* village Donahue sent Chirnovsky and that other asshole Gutierrez to rape. One of my cousins could have been lured with all their lies into doing slave labor for Donahue, just like that kid was. A woman from my family could have been kidnapped for their white slavery ring. Saturday night can't come quick enough for me," Ramiro exclaimed heatedly, referring to their sting operation to finally collar Jim Donahue.

"Donahue's done," Ryan stated flatly.

Ramiro took a deep breath and nodded as they walked out onto Monroe Street, seeming partially mollified by Ryan's steadfast assurance.

When Ryan parallel parked on Eighteenth Street at eight p.m. later that night, he just sat for a moment and stared out the car window at the imposing French Châteauesque–style limestone mansion he now owned, the multiple towers and cupolas, the ornate ironwork, the sloping mansard roof. Ryan couldn't imagine a more unlikely place for him to live or a house more perfectly suited to Hope Stillwater's elegant, lush American beauty.

He'd been preoccupied all day with the final details of Jim

Donahue's downfall but thoughts of Hope had never really left him. It felt a little bizarre to be entertaining concerns and worries about such an ephemeral woman when the very real details of his job demanded his attention. But just behind the scenes of his awareness he'd been forming a plan to try to contact her tonight.

Just like he had last night, he took another hot bath in the deep claw-footed tub. He had to admit he was getting used to bathing, the hot water loosening his muscles after his daily workout in the gym beyond what a shower could do. He was hyperalert the entire time for sounds of Hope, but she remained distressingly absent.

Afterward he opened the wardrobe door wide and stared into the antique mirror. He willed Hope to appear, but only his tense face looked back at him.

He left the wardrobe door open so that he could keep an eye on the mirror and sprawled on the newly assembled brass bed, watching the ten o'clock news on the portable television that used to sit on the kitchen counter in his loft.

Once he looked back at the television after glancing at the mirror for the hundredth time only to see Jim Donahue's beefy face filling the screen. He spoke at a local charity event for Children's Memorial Hospital. Ryan sat up slightly in bed, his attention narrowing to a sharp focus like a predator's when it sights prey.

Donahue still carried the vestiges of handsomeness, but his body and face were going to fat. He was already a big man—maybe an inch or two shorter than Ryan—but the rich foods and alcohol that his lifestyle afforded him and which he partook of liberally were finally taking their toll. At forty-eight years old, Donahue was a heart attack waiting to happen.

Maybe a prison diet would tack on a few extra years to his worthless life, Ryan thought with a sense of grim satisfaction as Donahue flashed a sharklike smile at the end of the sound bite. It really steamed him to see scum like Donahue being kowtowed to by the press as a community leader and respectable businessman.

For Ramiro's sake, Ryan hoped his partner wasn't watching the sickening display.

He irritably clicked off the television and stood to look into the mirror again.

"Hope. I need to speak with you. You're in danger," he said, feeling like an idiot for talking to himself but just desperate enough not to care.

Two more nights. All he had was *two more nights*.

He stalked across the room and picked up the leather-bound book of sonnets. He'd already checked the pages once this evening for some kind of message—hadn't Hope said she'd seen what he'd written? But there was nothing. Although he hadn't completely ruled out writing her a message of warning, he'd rather give her such an alarming message in person.

He needed more than just to leave her a message. He needed to reach her.

Protect her.

When he approached the mirror again there was still no sign of her, but Ryan noticed that the band of fogginess at the edge of the glass was definitely narrower. He ran his hand along the filmy band. He'd wondered if it wasn't decreasing last night, but tonight it was evident that it was.

Did the clarifying mirror somehow relate to his connection to Hope?

"Hope, *please*," he entreated, feeling foolish.

Feeling *helpless*.

How the hell could he reach her?

As he stood there and talked to himself, wearing nothing but a pair of dark blue sweats, his skin roughening as he caught a chill in the drafty old house, Ryan started to wonder if he wasn't losing it.

Should he schedule an appointment with one of the police counselors? He and Ramiro had put in a lot of long hours on the Jim Donahue investigation. Maybe the stress was finally getting to him.

Maybe his visions of the delectable Hope Stillwater were all part and parcel of a stress-induced psychosis?

If that were the case, his libido must be playing a major part in his hallucinations. He recalled the way Hope had looked last night bared to the waist, her flawless skin dewed with moisture, her high, full breasts quivering slightly as she trembled. Or when he'd seen her in the mirror wearing that sinfully sheer gown, her large, pink nipples pressing against a fabric so translucent it did nothing to cover the triangle of dark hair between her shapely thighs.

Ryan groaned as his cock stiffened against his thigh. He shoved his hand down his sweatpants and fisted it, trying to alleviate the pain of lust that had sliced through him at the graphic memories of Hope. How was it that the daughter of a wealthy social reformist minister wore such a revealing garment?

And more important, why had Hope Stillwater been in those erotic photographs?

It had been a mistake to think of those photos, Ryan realized as he withdrew his cock and shoved the waistband of his sweats below his balls. He stroked the length of his penis as he stared into the mirror, but he wasn't really seeing himself masturbate. Instead he was imagining those erotic images of Hope: her thighs spread wide and her lips opened in a silent keen of pleasure as her pussy was being eaten; the crop frozen in the action of smacking against the voluptuous curve of a white, shapely breast crowned with a stiffened, distended nipple.

God, what he wouldn't give to tie down that gorgeous creature and make her scream with need and desire.

He groaned as his pistoning motions on his cock became more rapid. He briefly considered getting the photographs out of the bedside drawer where he'd placed them and bringing himself off several times just like he had the night he'd found them. But he found that his imagination was all too sufficient when it came to fantasizing about Hope.

So he remained in place, his right hand jacking his cock with more and more force. If only it were her small, elegant hand caressing the straining column of flesh. He squeezed just beneath the head and a stream of clear pre-cum oozed out of the slit. He imagined the liquid melting on Hope's pink tongue as she looked up at him with huge, velvety eyes that always seemed to convey a sense of her innocence and a profoundly carnal nature all at once.

The image was so real he groaned roughly. A light seemed to flash. He opened his eyelids, startled, only to find that it was no longer his own image staring back at him from the mirror.

Hope stood there, her cheeks flushed a bright, vivid pink. She once again wore the tiny, sheer gown.

And her hand was every bit as busy between her thighs as Ryan's was.

∾ FIVE ∾

Hope turned the last page in her book of sonnets and set it down dispiritedly on her bedside table. What had she really expected, after all? Ryan hadn't told her to try to communicate with him using the book. Instead he'd specifically mentioned the mirror. Her gaze traveled to the opened wardrobe door. Despite the fact that she'd been quite busy today—taking up her post at Central Station and planning her father's birthday celebration with the housekeeper—she'd still managed to stare into the depths of the gilded mirror at least a hundred times today.

Never once, however, had she caught a glimpse of Ryan's handsome face.

The memory of how he'd looked standing in that tub, like a naked statue of some warrior god come to life, left her breathless yet again.

It surprised her a little that she believed wholeheartedly that he was a man from the future. Hope supposed the reason for the relative ease for her faith in the impossible was Ryan himself. There was something about him that she couldn't see with her eyes or put precisely into words, but she sensed it nonetheless.

Ryan Vincent Daire was different. He wasn't *of* her world.

There was something else she knew about him instinctively. She desired him. Hope supposed desire is what one called this overpowering need and hunger that overcame her in his presence, anyway.

And even in his absence.

She had said she would use the mirror to try to contact him again, but what, exactly was she supposed to do to penetrate the barrier of time? All she possessed were her too brief memories of him . . . and her desire.

She stood slowly from the brass bed. A moment later she extricated the balled-up Marlborough gown from the deep recesses of her wardrobe.

The last time she'd seen Ryan in the mirror she'd been wearing the Marlborough gown and he'd been looking at her with a mixture of surprise and stark arousal. Hope had become all too familiar with that addicting hot look in his eyes when he'd studied her half-naked body last night in the bathroom. She moved quickly before she could change her mind, locking her bedroom door and lifting her cotton nightgown over her head.

The Marlborough gown slipped over the sensitive skin of her breasts and belly, finally tickling the tops of her thighs as it settled on her naked body as lightly as a lover's whisper.

Her throat spasmed convulsively when she once again stood before the gilded mirror. Did Ryan enjoy seeing her in the Marlborough gown? What sort of women did a man who lived in the twenty-first century find attractive?

At five feet six inches, Hope considered herself relatively tall for a woman. But Ryan towered over her. Were people perhaps larger in the future? He was so big. Everywhere. Her cheeks and chest flushed with color when she pictured his long, shapely penis. Hope knew she had nothing to compare Ryan to except the statues she'd studied in France, Italy and Greece during her grand tour with an avid curiosity that could not be termed wholly artistic in nature. From what little knowledge she possessed, however, she suspected very strongly that most men were not as fortunate in their proportions as Ryan.

Or sheer beauty.

Not just of his genitals, Hope thought as her color deepened. All of him. There'd been a scar on his left shoulder, the whiteness of it contrasting with the darker surrounding skin. She'd ached to touch that old injury, to feel his smooth, thick skin and the beat of his heart beneath her fingertips. He was male power personified—all those firm, rounded, delineated muscles on his chest, shoulders and arms, those strong thighs dusted with dark, crinkly hair. His testicles had hung like ripe, round fruit between his thighs.

And his penis . . .

Surely it wasn't possible to put such a large member inside of a woman, was it? But it must be so, Hope thought with wonder and increasing arousal as she lifted the hem of the Marlborough gown and stared at the thatch of hair between her thighs. The thought of Ryan's penis coming into such close, intimate contact with her body made her groan in stark arousal.

That forbidden piece of flesh that nestled so secretly between her thighs ached with longing. She slid a finger between the tender folds and found herself to be creamy. Her finger glided easily over her aroused genitals. She understood why she'd grown wet—that her body instinctively readied itself to accept a man when she became excited.

Her body prepared itself to receive *Ryan*.

Even though she couldn't see or touch him, she trusted the knowledge of her body. She rubbed herself with increasing desire, thinking of those electrifying, steamy moments as she looked her fill at not just any naked male, but the most glorious specimen of manhood she'd ever conjured up in her admittedly overactive imagination.

Would it hurt to have intercourse with Ryan? Hope wouldn't care if it did. She had learned from various sources—the most honest and matter-of-fact of which was Addie Sampson, the madam of the Marlborough Club—that if the man was patient and skilled at arousing a woman, the discomfort for her the first time was minimal and short-lived.

Hope had little doubt that Ryan would be a skilled lover. He made her so aroused and hungry and he'd never so much as touched her.

She burned to join with him . . . to discover the raptures of sex. Surely it must be awe-inspiring if everyone thought about it so much—whether they be preaching the sinfulness of it or lining up to spend a last hard-earned dollar on it at one of the Levee District whorehouses. Even her idol William Shakespeare seemed quite preoccupied by the topic.

She closed her eyes and imagined touching Ryan's hard muscles with her fingertips. She pictured the hot look that would gleam in his eyes if she placed her lips on his chest, ribs and belly and discovered his textures with that sensitive flesh as well.

A soft moan vibrated her throat when she imagined him pushing that engorged pillar of flesh into her body.

She wanted to touch him, to merge with him so much that her desire focused her will to a powerful white-hot flame. Something flashed in her room and her eyelids flew open in surprise. She looked around in slight disorientation only to find that everything was as it should be—

She gasped. Everything was *not* as it should be, or at least, not as it *had* been. Her room looked as it always did, with the fire crackling in the fireplace and her bedclothes tossed back on her bed. But it was no longer her own reflection that looked back at her through the looking glass.

"Ryan," she called out in shock when she saw him standing in the mirror, their distance from each other only two or three feet. She was so stunned at the apparition that it took her a moment to realize what he was doing and to recall what *she'd* been doing the moment before she saw him. She gaped when she took in the swollen organ in his hand. Her own flesh sharply twanged with arousal beneath her fingertips.

She took a step forward and reached in blind need for him, her face collapsing in anguish when it encountered hard glass.

"*No,*" she whispered in profound frustration. But at least his image hadn't disappeared. Her hand tightened into a claw on the mirror. When she saw his tensed expression she noticed that her fingertips had smeared a thin coat of liquid on the glass.

The juices from her sex smeared on the mirror, put on display for Ryan to see.

His stare on her fingers felt palpable. His lips shaped the word *Hope*, but she heard nothing. He released his penis. Hope watched in fascination as the heavy head of his member pulled the stalk down, although it still remained suspended in the air at a downward angle.

She licked her lower lip in nervous excitement, starting when Ryan pressed his hand to the other side of the mirror.

She glanced up, held prisoner by his gaze.

"Hope," he repeated, although she only saw his lips move, never hearing the sound. The degree of longing and frustration she saw in his singular eyes made her want to weep.

"Ryan, why can't I touch you?" she whispered shakily. She was hardly aware of what she was doing as she pressed closer to the mirror . . . closer to him. She whimpered in desperate need when she saw his erection spring up at her movement. He came closer, too, and lowered his dark head. He stood so near his eyes looked like millions of sea green, cerulean blue and aquamarine points of light when she looked up at him. She saw that the continuous beard and mustache had been clipped very short and neat. The nearly black hair looked sleek as it encircled and highlighted his hard yet sensual mouth. It would be such a pleasure to trace her fingertip over it.

She raised a hand and pressed her finger to the glass just over his angular chin. He inched even closer. Hope glanced down and saw that the smooth head of his penis pressed directly against the glass. She looked up quickly, her cheeks heating with embarrassment and arousal. He said something. She strained to read his lips, but out of everything he uttered she only comprehended one word.

Danger.

Her lack of comprehension and confusion must have shown on her face because Ryan cursed silently.

Damn.

She'd understood that word perfectly well, especially since she shared in the stark frustration behind his exclamation.

For a moment he seemed indecisive, but then he glanced pointedly at his hand where it pressed against hers on the glass, as though he tried to tell her something. The barrier of the mirror and 102 years separated them, however, and she felt uncertainty swell in her breast as she followed his gaze.

His hand was so much larger than hers. Her own fit in his palm, her fingertips reaching only his second knuckle. She shivered with excitement when she realized this was the same hand that had been holding his dense erection when she first spied him. Was it her imagination, or could she feel heat emanating from the cool surface?

She started in surprise.

It'd seemed for a split second that her hand had sunk into the surface of the mirror.

She glanced up into Ryan's face and could tell by his rigid expression that he had felt that give in the solid object as well. His lips shaped her name once again. He held her gaze and began to lower his hand. Hope followed his movement even as her gaze remained fixed on his fiery eyes. She definitely sensed heat now coming from the smooth surface of the mirror and followed it unerringly.

They both glanced down when their hands reached the area over their bellies and continued to slide down the mirror. Hope stopped breathing when Ryan fisted the stalk of his ruddy penis and pressed the head directly into the space over her opened palm.

She cried out sharply, raw need scraping at her throat. Heat scorched the center of her palm, but she pressed closer . . . desperate with wanting. His arm moved and she realized he stroked himself as he shared in her arousal. Her fingers rose to her own sex. She strummed slick, burning flesh.

He lowered his other hand and made a protective cupping motion over the juncture of her thighs. Hope whimpered shakily.

They pleasured themselves, separate but connected. Their eyes held. Ryan's hot, almost furious gaze left her in little doubt that he longed to be touching her as much as Hope wished she could touch him.

When his hand moved more rapidly between his thighs, her actions matched his pace. Desire swelled both in her sex and her chest, feeling like it would burst out of her.

She cried out in alarmed excitement when she felt a new, divine friction between her thighs. Her hips pressed instinctively against the pressure even as the fingers over Ryan's cock reached more insistently.

The solid pane of the mirror gave way to her desire.

Her fingertips pressed against steely flesh encased in warm, surprisingly soft skin. Her gaze sharpened on Ryan. Did he feel it, too? His mouth had fallen partially open. His nostrils flared. Hope felt his penis surge beneath her moving, curious fingertips.

He felt it, to be sure.

Which means he must feel her as well. She glanced down in wonder, and sure enough four long fingers protruded from the mirror. The first two were buried in her labia and making small, firm circular motions over her tingling flesh. She moaned shakily. It felt delicious . . . like he knew precisely what he was doing, exactly how to stroke her to make her burn.

She jumped when he suddenly raised the hand that wasn't playing in her heated flesh and slammed it against the mirror. The strike made a distant, hollow thumping sound. Hope tried to penetrate the glass over his splayed, pressing hand but felt only the smooth surface of the mirror.

He wore an almost frightening look of intensity as he looked down at her and his fingers rubbed and fired her sensitive flesh. Hope understood that he'd tried to reach through the mirror to her to feel her more fully, but whatever force was restraining their contact continued, only the area above their aroused sexes thinning enough to allow this minimal contact.

Her thoughts made her sharpen more on the miracle of actually touching Ryan. The head of his penis felt incredibly smooth. She looked down and used her thumb to outline the circumference of the thick ridge beneath it. When she pressed gently against the slit at the tip, a stream of clear liquid leaked onto her forefinger.

Ryan's fingers slowed on her sex. Hope glanced up in dazed arousal. He held her gaze while he reached down and touched her fingers. They rubbed their fingertips together in a slippery, sensual quest, his seed spreading on their skin.

While they gently discovered one another's touch, Ryan began stimulating her sex again. He burrowed his long forefinger between her folds and moved the hard ridge of it up and down and in tiny, firm circular motions. Hope bit her lip to stifle a sharp cry of pleasure. He stroked her so masterfully, as though he knew her flesh even better than she.

He once again fisted his erection and began to stroke himself with long, sure movements, twisting his fist slightly when he reached the area just below the fat, plum-sized head. Hope watched him, wide-eyed with excitement, still clutching the damp tip of his penis. She started out of her trance when she realized he was showing her how he wanted to be pleasured. She closed her hand into a fist, frustrated she couldn't completely encircle his girth like his own large hand did.

She began to stroke him. His movements on her sex grew more rapid. She found herself spreading her legs, wanting more of the sensation . . . more of Ryan.

He watched her hand pumping his penis and Hope realized he did it for more than mere pleasure at the visual stimulation. Ryan wanted to see how far she could penetrate through their window into each other's reality. She gripped his penis tightly and slid along the dense shaft. She spied his testicles nestled just above the cotton pants that he wore and longed to stroke them. Just like the classical sculptures of the male nudes she'd studied so intently, his testicles were free of hair, hanging like round, succulent fruit between his thighs.

A more arousing, awe-inspiring sight Hope couldn't have imagined if her life depended on it.

She slid her hand along his penis but a few inches from his testicles she encountered a strange barrier. It gave to pressure, but no more than a half an inch or so.

Hope groaned. She wondered if Ryan did the same thing in his world when she glanced up at his face and he wore a pinched expression of frustration . . . and something else. Her hand gripped him tight and stroked him long and hard when she recognized what she saw was arousal near the breaking point.

She may not be able to stroke his entire length or his testicles but her touch clearly gave him pleasure. It was an intoxicating experience, to realize she had the power to put that hot, almost wild look in his eyes.

He pressed as close to the mirror as he could while still giving her room to pump her hand up and down his shaft. She twisted her hand just below the head like he'd showed her. She pounded her hand over his straining penis again and again even as his fingers made her burn unbearably. She would explode any second she was so excited to touch him and to be touched by Ryan in return.

Her hand paused in its rapid pumping motion when he suddenly pressed his middle finger to her slit and pushed into her. A shaky cry leaked past her lips. Her forehead fell against the mirror with a dull thump. He continued to stimulate that burning piece of flesh between her swollen outer lips but at the same time he insisted upon entrance to her body.

She saw him spread his long legs, bringing him down closer to her height without altering her hold on his penis overly much. His face lowered to hers. He watched her, their eyes less than an inch apart even though they were separated by the barrier of the glass and 102 years. He gently worked his finger into her. Her lips fell open and she gasped softly, her breath causing a patch of circular mist to grow on the mirror when he twisted his finger and impaled her to his knuckle.

She beat his erection with her hand, wild with cresting desire. She clenched her eyelids shut as the tension broke and pleasure ripped through her flesh. Her body tightened around Ryan's stroking finger but he continued to plunge into her, faster and faster.

Still in the midst of a thunderous orgasm, Hope felt his penis swell and then spasm in her hand. The sensation was so amazing that she looked down despite the shudders of pleasure that tore through her. Thick, white fluid began to spurt from the slit on his penis. Hope stared in aroused fascination as his seed streamed onto the floor in his world.

She cried out in surprised excitement when his still climaxing member suddenly plunged through the mirror and she found herself stroking a long, climaxing penis in her very own bedroom.

Hope looked up at Ryan in shock. Her mouth fell open in awe when she saw his large body directly next to the mirror, his muscular arms draped over the top of it, his lips curled in a small snarl of thwarted desire . . . his gaze on her feral in its intensity. For a second she couldn't draw breath under the impact of the powerfully erotic image of him. She thought sure he'd lunge directly into her bedroom, for what could possibly restrain such a powerful force of nature as Ryan at that moment?

His muscles spasmed visibly.

And then he was gone. Just like that. One moment he was there, looking like he would storm straight through the barriers of time in order to claim her. The next she stood alone as aftershocks of pleasure still vibrated through her flesh.

Hope glanced down at her outstretched hand and gave a soft cry of loss when she saw Ryan's warm seed still clinging to her skin and pooling on the wood floor.

∽ SIX ∽

Ryan bared his teeth when he realized he could no longer see Hope. He still tried to catch his breath following a blistering orgasm as he lowered his arms from the top of the wardrobe door. He felt like he'd been humping the damn thing.

The thought made him glance down quickly, relieved to see his cock had come back to the year 2008 with him. Wouldn't it have been a new definition of nightmare for both Hope and him if it hadn't?

"Thank God for small favors," he mumbled.

He searched the mirror and saw only his sad self panting like a madman, his cock still dripping for a 127-year-old woman.

Jesus, if this didn't beat all.

He jerked up his sweats and stalked back and forth in front of the mirror like a caged beast. After a few turns he paused and drew close to the mirror once again.

The fog around the edge was definitely clearing. The band that remained was perhaps only two or three inches thick. Still panting, he went to the bedside table and grabbed one of his credit cards out of his wallet. He held it up to the mirror a few seconds later, using it as an ad hoc measuring device.

Ryan stepped back and tried his best to review the unlikely events of the past fifteen or so minutes. He'd touched Hope and she'd touched him. His cock had done the impossible and punched right through the barrier of time.

Either he was going completely, utterly insane or it'd happened just like that.

Don't be a coward, Daire. Pick your sides—believe or don't, but don't be a waffler, Ryan thought. If there was one thing he couldn't stand, it was a fence clinger.

He either needed to believe that for some bizarre reason he was having contact with an amazing, beautiful woman who lived in the year 1906 or he needed to decide what he was going to do about his encroaching madness.

Time was of the essence, either way. If what he'd been experiencing was true, Hope was in a crisis; if he was hallucinating, *he* was the one in dire trouble.

That pretty much decided him. Hope took precedence, although Ryan knew deep down there'd never been a chance of him abandoning her to such a horrible fate.

He began his pacing again back and forth in front of the mirror. Every time he had contact with Hope the fog around the mirror narrowed. Every time he encountered her their ability to commune with one another deepened.

If he had it his way, he was going to touch and pleasure Hope repeatedly until the mirror opened wide enough for him to walk straight through into her world. Once he was there, he could try to coax her into coming back with him to the year 2008 where she'd be safe. There was plenty of time for him to do that and still be back with time to spare for Jim Donahue's sting operation this coming Saturday.

He wouldn't allow himself to dwell on what the hell he was supposed to do with Hope after that.

All he needed to worry about for the moment was seeing her face looking back at him once again. With any luck, he could handle things from there. He paused in his agitated pacing and lifted his fingers to his nose. He inhaled deeply before he plunged his first two fingers into his mouth, sucking strongly so as to capture every last remnant of Hope's exquisite essence. His cock swelled and stiffened into complete readiness once again.

I've got your scent in my nose, Hope. I've memorized your taste. Nothing's going to keep me from you now.

∽

Ryan found a rare spot in front of his mother's Lincoln Park boutique and parallel parked. Ramiro answered his call just as Ryan shifted the car into park.

"Shit."

"Didn't your mother ever teach you how to answer a phone?" Ryan asked mildly.

"Ah, fuck. My alarm clock never went off."

"That's because you never set it," Ryan heard a woman say groggily in the distance. He couldn't help but grin.

"Is that Gail? You owe me seventy bucks."

"For what?"

"I reimbursed you for taking her out to lunch."

"So? You were supposed to," Ramiro replied scornfully.

"You owe *me* for setting you up with her. You've been after her for almost two years now, but all she ever gave you was a view of her ass as she ran away from you."

"She's not likely to run now that she's had a taste of my hard, delicious Latino flesh."

"I wouldn't bet on it," Ryan heard Gail say acerbically.

"Drive yourself into work today. I'm taking a few days off," Ryan said, thinking it would be best for Ramiro if he changed the subject posthaste.

"Is everything okay?"

"Yeah. I just need to take care of a family matter. I'll be back on Friday for the final briefing about Donahue."

"It'll finally be over Saturday night. I can't wait to see that asshole's face when he realizes he's just dug himself a grave clear to China. Hey, Gail, you're seeing stars after that last round, but you're not gonna know what hit you when you see me in a tux—"

"See you Friday," Ryan muttered before he hung up, not particularly wanting to hear Ramiro as he dug himself his own hole with Gail.

His mother's shop wasn't open yet, but she knew he was coming and was at the door before he ever knocked.

"Is something wrong?" she asked as he leaned down and kissed her cheek.

"Has the traditional greeting gone the way of handwritten letters and eight-track tapes?" he asked in amusement, thinking of Ramiro on the phone a moment ago. His smile faded slightly when he recognized the truth of what he'd said for Hope and him last night. Forget "How are you feeling on this chilly fall evening in the year 1906, Miss Stillwater?" and move straight to hand jobs and blistering orgasms.

As a detective Ryan knew the world was a strange place. But thanks to Hope, he was learning it was *much* more bizarre than he'd previously thought. And if it turned out he wasn't in fact delusional, and what he planned actually occurred, he was about to discover the world was even more strange than he'd ever imagined.

Ryan became aware that his mother regarded him worriedly.

"Everything is fine. I'm just going to be hard to reach for the next day or two so I wanted to warn you."

Eve Daire's tawny eyebrows rose on her forehead. "Are you going undercover again?"

Ryan didn't answer for a moment as he glanced around his mom's boutique. He could tell her business was thriving by the amount of stock on the racks. His mother was a talented dress designer although she carried more than her own products in the store. It had taken her ten years to get the balance just right between creating her own designs, marketing and selling them in a bustling Internet business and also running her own boutique where she showcased not only her dresses but those of a few other designers she intimately knew and respected. She had a loyal and growing customer base.

"I guess you could say that," he murmured evasively. "I'll be back by Thursday evening at the latest. I'll give you a call when I return to the land of the living."

Eve frowned and crossed her arms over her tailored suit jacket. "That's not very funny, Ryan."

"Sorry, Mom," he muttered sheepishly when he realized what he'd said. His mother had never grown as comfortable as his father had about him becoming a cop. She worried about him incessantly. "It's not going to be dangerous. It's not what you're thinking."

Nobody would be thinking what you're planning to do, Ryan thought wryly. And if it wasn't precisely dangerous to try to travel backward 102 years, it sure as hell wasn't a ride on the kiddy merry-go-round, either.

When he noticed that his mother's forehead continued to crinkle with concern, he gave her a hug. She laughed at his impulsive act of endearment and gave him a healthy squeeze in return.

"I always forget how big you really are until I wrap my arms around you," she said a second later as she gazed up at him fondly. "Your father was the same way. Ryan, are you still worried about accepting the house Alistair left you?"

Ryan sighed. He really needed to work on his poker face. Then again, he could never hide his worries very well from his mother.

"There's just . . . something so *strange* about him giving it to me."

"What do you mean?" his mother asked, obviously sensing Ryan meant something beyond the obvious.

Ryan hesitated, not sure how to put into words the haunting, watchful atmosphere of the Prairie Street mansion, the bizarre yet strangely *right* circumstances of having gained ownership of it.

"You have to admit, Mom, it's over-the-top generous on Alistair's part. That property is worth millions."

Eve ruffled his hair before she stepped back. "He wanted to do it, Ryan."

He glanced at his mother in mild surprise. He'd become friends with Alistair Franklin while he was a student at the University of Chicago. Alistair had been a professor of history who was well known among the students for his charismatic personality and entertaining lectures. Alistair had taken an instant liking to Ryan and the feeling had been mutual. Ryan had ended up doing a senior thesis with Alistair as his counselor. Their friendship had only grown after Ryan graduated, went to law school and eventually joined the ranks of the Chicago Police Department. Ryan's father had passed away two years ago, but while he'd been alive Alistair had also grown close with both of his parents.

Still, he was surprised to hear his mother had been talking to Alistair about the mansion.

"When have you seen Alistair?"

"We speak on the phone every few weeks, ever since he had his stroke," Eve explained. "He can't get around like he used to, but we both know what a social person Alistair is. He loves to talk. He *wanted* to give you that property, Ryan."

"He said it's helping him out tax-wise," Ryan mumbled doubtfully.

Eve's eyebrows arched. "Well, that may be. But he also thinks of you like a son, Ryan. You know he lost a child. I think it helps him to be able to do something like this . . . helps fill in the empty spaces that the death of a child leaves."

"Alistair had a kid?" Ryan asked, genuinely shocked. Never once in all the time he'd spent with the older man had Alistair ever hinted at that fact.

"He doesn't speak of it often, but he has told me that he lost a child years ago. Maybe he felt more comfortable telling me since I'm also a parent," Eve explained when she noticed what must have been a look of shock on his face. "At any rate, you're doing a good thing by accepting the house from him. When are you going to show it to me?"

"How about next Tuesday?" Ryan asked.

"Perfect," Eve replied cheerfully. "I'm looking forward to seeing it after hearing Alistair's and your descriptions. Imagine—you owning a house on Prairie Avenue."

"Come on," Ryan said with a tilt of his chin toward the back room of her store. "You can show me where those shelves are that you wanted me to put together."

Eve clapped once, her blue eyes going wide with delight. "Oh, today *is* my lucky day. I've been trying to get you over here to put those shelves together forever."

Ryan shrugged nonchalantly as he followed her. "If forever is the same as a week and a half."

Eve snorted with laughter. "Okay, you caught me exaggerating. Seriously, though," she continued as her gaze sharpened on him. "What'd I do to deserve the favor on today of all days?"

Ryan gave her a smile. "Just figured it was time, Mom."

∞

Now that he had everything in place to take his jaunt through time, Ryan wasn't exactly sure how to proceed. He only knew that his sexual desire for Hope had always been involved in their contact.

He wasn't sure if there was a genuine link or if it was just inevitable that Hope and sex went together like two sides of a coin, but it was the only place he could figure was a good starting point for the journey.

So he stripped off his clothes, lay in the brass bed and engaged in some good, old-fashioned masturbatory fantasizing. Maybe imagination was the key to time travel. If that were the case, what more powerful, vivid type of fantasy was there than that used to instigate sexual arousal?

He stroked his cock slowly, recalling what it had felt like having Hope's soft, elegantly shaped hand doing the same thing. He recalled the scent that he'd caught on her in the bathroom when they'd both been bathing—the fresh, floral fragrance he'd also caught in her book of sonnets and inhaled at her neck during that hyper-vivid dream.

He'd never forget the way she tasted on his fingers. God, he'd give anything to bury his nose in her skin . . . to plunge his tongue into her pussy and surround himself in her essence. She'd been so wet when he'd explored her last night. His fingers had glided over her erect clit like he was moving through warm oil. Her pussy had almost been too snug for him to gain entrance at the limited angle the mirror afforded them.

The thought of pushing his cock into that tight sheath made his fist piston over his cock more stridently.

He cursed and forced his hand to drop to the mattress. He didn't want to come. Well, he did, just not right here and right now. Instead he needed to build his desire as he envisioned Hope with as much clarity and focus as he could manage. Something told him this would provide a path to her; that their combined desire melted the barrier of time that stood between them.

He would keep her safe. He *would* have her. There really wasn't any other possible option as far as Ryan was concerned.

Fifteen minutes later he stood and approached the mirror. *She'll be there*, he thought, shaping reality with a burst of stubborn will.

He didn't bat an eye when he saw Hope standing in the gilt mirror clutching together the lapels of a robe, the silver filigreed locket gleaming between the V of the dark green fabric, her long, dark hair spilling around her shoulders.

This time he'd known she'd be there.

∽

Hope chastised herself for her modesty when she saw Ryan standing in the mirror, naked, aroused and proud. Her intuition had told her she'd find him there. She'd already locked her bedroom door and stripped out of her clothing, draping her velvet dressing gown over her naked body before she opened the wardrobe door.

She read his lips unerringly this time.

Hope? Can you hear me?

She shook her head sadly. His mouth pressed into a grim line. He pressed one large hand to the glass.

Hope inhaled slowly, drawing on her reserves of courage. She pulled back her robe and let it drop to the floor.

Upon reflection she'd come to understand why Ryan had purposefully stoked the fires of their desire last night. Their mounting need for one another somehow penetrated the very limit of time.

She met Ryan's eyes, her chin tilting up with a mixture of pride and stubbornness. She would not cower because of her sex or her nakedness.

Besides, the way Ryan's eyes scorched her as they trailed over her body hardly called for a show of embarrassment. If anything, that hot look made her feel like a queen. She took a step toward him, pausing in mixed excitement and wonderment when the hand on the mirror reached further for her.

Ryan's entire forearm extended into her bedroom.

A small burst of laughter escaped her lips when he turned his hand palm up and made an unmistakable gesture.

Come here.

She saw amusement curving his handsome mouth as well. That small smile erased all of her uncertainties. She took another step toward him and reached for him. For a long moment they grasped hands and locked gazes. He tried to reach for her with his other hand, but Hope knew he'd been stopped short when his palm pressed to the glass. His fingertips skimmed lightly up her arm before he cupped her shoulder, the caress gentle and cherishing and yet fiercely possessive as well.

Hope watched his face fixedly as he began to move his hand over her body. He slid it slowly over her neck and back down the slope of her shoulder before he palmed her upper arm and flexed his fingers into the flesh, his actions causing her nipples to grow achy and tight. Before she could stop herself she reached up and pressed her fingers to one of the sensitive tips, desperate to alleviate the prickling pain that plagued it.

He stared at her fingers on her nipple before his gaze leapt to her face. Hope moaned softly at what she saw in his fiery eyes. His penis flicked forward, drawing her gaze. Then his big hand was cupping her left breast from below. He held her up for a few taut seconds while he examined her.

Her head fell back, her long hair tickling the tops of her buttocks, when he began to mold and shape her breast to his palm. He pressed her stiffened nipple to the center of his hand and lightly rotated, causing her to cry out in pleasure. His actions seemed to strum a magical cord between her breast and sex, making her throb with excitement. As if he knew about this invisible connection, his hand dropped and he traced it down her belly. He paused over her navel, his splayed hand over her center seeming to encompass her entire being, before he swept over her hips languorously. His fingertips and the upper ridge of his palm were slightly calloused, causing a slight abrasion on her smooth skin that excited her immensely.

"Ryan," she moaned, lifting her head. She reached for him but stopped abruptly when she saw him shake his head.

Let me, first, she thought she understood him to say.

He tried to push his other hand through the mirror again. Hope's eyes widened slightly in amazement when he at first seemed to be succeeding and the glass bulged toward her like thickened water. Then it sprung back into place. She read Ryan's frustration from his tensed muscles, but then he met her eyes and gave her a reassuring nod.

Don't worry. I'm going to reach you soon enough, his determined gaze seemed to say.

Hope shivered in anticipatory excitement.

Ryan moved his hand, perhaps sensing the trembling in her flesh. He ran his fingertips over her thighs, then sandwiched his hand between them. In her nervous excitement Hope found herself clamping her legs tighter together, not because she wanted to avoid Ryan's touch. Her muscles clenched to alleviate the stark pain of longing that stabbed through her at that moment. She noticed Ryan's eyebrows go up wryly and smiled shakily as she parted her thighs several inches. She almost bit her lower lip clean through in anticipation when he raised his hand toward her sex, but he merely cupped it ever so briefly before he rose back up, stroking her belly and waist.

She gasped in rising desire when he lightly ran his fingers against the side of her breast, making the crests bead into pointed little darts of sensation. Her reward was to have him lightly pinch a nipple between his thumb and forefinger.

Hope whimpered. Before she'd met Ryan she would have thought having her nipple pinched would be unpleasant and painful. But at that moment of sharp, intense desire it seemed the only way to alleviate the ache that plagued her. Ryan's fingers on her breast caused a sympathetic tug in her womb, making her feel an aching emptiness.

Ryan glanced up into her face before his head dipped. For a breathless moment she thought he was going to penetrate the mirror and kiss her upturned lips. His hand opened and he cupped her breast in his palm. His massaging movement was neither soft nor forceful, only sure.

"No," she murmured in protest when he dropped his hand from her breast.

Yes, she saw him mouth.

His fingers dug lightly into her hip. Hope's eyes widened when she realized he wanted her to turn around. She stared over her shoulder in trepidation as she turned. It'd been monumentally thrilling and embarrassing to stand before Ryan naked while he stared boldly at the front of her, but she was surprised at how excited she became at the thought of him inspecting the back of her.

Liquid warmth bubbled from her sex.

When she continued to try to crane around to watch his outstretched hand, Ryan shook his head slowly. She felt his fingers on her neck, gently urging her to face forward.

Hope panted as she stared unseeingly at the fire leaping in the hearth while Ryan parted her hair at the nape, gently moving the heavy weight of it over each of her shoulders, baring her body to his gaze.

For a moment nothing happened. The air burned in her lungs as she held her breath. When she tried to look over her shoulder to quiet her curiosity over what Ryan was doing, she felt his hand on the back of her skull, keeping her in place. She gasped. For some unknown reason that firm, restraining gesture made her sex twinge with painful arousal. She resisted a powerful urge to bend over, to offer herself to him more fully like a female animal in heat.

Her cheeks burned when she registered her thoughts. Was *this* what sex was? Is that why so many preached against the evils of it? Because it turned civilized people into primitive savages?

Hope couldn't help it. Now that she'd encountered Ryan, she was even more greatly inclined to trust in not only the wisdom of the bard but the wisdom of another one of her secret idols, Mr. Walt Whitman. She kept a copy of his amazingly carnal book, *Leaves of Grass*, secreted in the compartment she'd discovered in the mantel. Perhaps God *wanted* them to celebrate their fierce, savage human nature.

God was the one who made them so able to appreciate their bodies so immensely, after all, Hope thought as she slowly bent at the waist while Ryan trailed his finger down her spine.

⟋ SEVEN ⟍

Hope's skin was unlike anything he'd ever touched. Did they perhaps use some emollient a hundred years ago that had been lost to the ages? Or maybe the relative lack of pollution and differing bathing techniques kept the skin more healthy, Ryan mused as he traced the elegant line of her back and spread his hand over the enticing curve of her hip.

It drove him crazy not to be able to touch her more fully. But he only seemed to be granted the ability to penetrate at one point in the mirror. For now, anyway, he added to himself.

When Hope bent forward, her pale, plump bottom coming within an inch of the mirror, Ryan's cock leapt up and thumped against the glass.

"Little witch," Ryan muttered between clenched teeth. She'd literally presented herself to him when he was doing his best to control himself while touching her gorgeous body.

He ran his hand over a buttock and gently swatted her.

Her head whipped around. When he met her startled dark eyes he arched his eyebrows in a wry expression. Her cheeks colored becomingly so he smacked the other cheek, more firmly this time, wishing like hell he could hear the popping noise his palm made on her supple flesh.

Best she learned early on what happened when she teased him, Ryan thought with a small grin. His smile widened in deep gratification when he palmed a shapely ass cheek and sunk his forefinger into her pussy.

She was soaking.

Her lips parted as she looked back at him and he almost heard her cry of excitement. He withdrew and plunged back into her, marveling at how her sleek, muscular channel pulled subtly at his finger. She was tight. Snugger than any woman he'd ever been with. Was she a virgin? Weren't young ladies of Hope's class usually virgins when they married?

So why the hell had she been in those photos? *That* woman was no virgin.

With the evidence right at his fingertip, so to speak, Ryan had to concede that at this point in time, it was highly unlikely that Hope Stillwater had ever had intercourse with a man. But did she ever seem eager to, Ryan thought as she began to buck her hips back and forth against his fucking finger. He watched her face carefully while he stimulated her, studying her reactions. From the looks of things he'd found her G-spot. He concentrated on rubbing there every time he plunged deep into her sweetness. She looked magnificent, bent over with her bottom in the air and her hands on her thighs. Her head was turned in profile, her face gleaming with a coat of light perspiration, her dark pink lips parted as she panted and sighed in mounting excitement.

The head of his cock pressed against the mirror, spreading a thin coat of pre-cum on the glass. He fisted himself with his left hand and held Hope's gaze as he stimulated both of them. Hope twisted her chin and met his stare.

"I will have you," Ryan said quietly. He didn't know if he was telling Hope or assuring himself, he only knew he spoke the truth.

Her dark eyes widened, making him wonder if she'd understood him. Ryan regretfully withdrew his finger from her pussy and pushed back one round ass cheek. He felt her muscles stiffen as he looked his fill at her treasures: the delicate, glossy pink folds of her sex and the tiny rosette of her asshole. He groaned when the muscular ring clenched tight as he examined her. She was uncomfortable having him stare at her, but it was best she understood early on that he wouldn't be denied any part of her.

He held her wide-eyed stare as he plunged his forefinger back into her pussy. When he withdrew he brought her abundant juices to lubricate her clit, but he needn't have. Her clit nestled in warm cream. Much to his satisfaction, Hope's cheeks turned vividly pink almost immediately at his touch. The color of her lips deepened to a lush shade of red. God he wanted to pillage that mouth with his tongue and teeth. Kissing Hope seemed like the height of eroticism at that moment. When she was finally his, he was going to spend an entire day discovering the pleasures of that sweet, carnal-looking mouth.

Her lips formed an O of awe not five seconds later as she cried out and came against his hand. He'd barely been stimulating her clit for five seconds.

"Amazing woman," Ryan mumbled as she shuddered in ecstasy. He plunged his middle finger into her, wanting to feel her pleasure trembling through her most intimate flesh. She contracted and convulsed around him in a powerful orgasm. When he saw that her eyes were shut as her entire focus rolled on the waves of ecstasy, he pushed another finger into her clinging sheath.

A pussy straight from a man's personal rendering of heaven,

Ryan thought as he penetrated her again and again. His cock was so stiff he felt like it was going to burst straight through the skin.

By the time Hope opened her eyes and her convulsions had lessened, his two fingers thrust into her forcefully. He used his forefinger to stimulate her clit and soon enough her red lips parted in a cry of release and she was shaking again in climax.

"Jesus," Ryan mumbled as he worked her through her second orgasm, stunned by her responsiveness as well as the short refractory time between her climaxes. He gripped his cock tightly, his desire becoming unbearable. When Hope's spasms had waned he withdrew his fingers and grabbed her hip. He pushed her soft, firm flesh directly against the mirror.

He would have her. Hope was *his*. He knew it just like he knew she'd be standing in that mirror a short while ago.

He used his fingers to spread her slit as best he could. He felt her shaking beneath his hand. Should he wait for this? Restrain himself until a time where he could hold her, soothe her?

He pressed his cock against her waiting glory. He couldn't wait. If it truly was his objective to hold her in his arms . . . to protect her, then he needed to fuel the fires of their desire.

Now.

He gasped raggedly when the tip of his cock penetrated her tight slit. Her heat resonated into him. Hope started in shock, but Ryan was glad to see when she met his gaze in the mirror that excitement twined with her amazement. Realizing he should test the limits of his luck, Ryan tried to reach with his other hand. Although the glass gave beneath his fingers as though it were made of pliable elastic, the barrier held firm.

He could only be grateful for Hope's obvious fearlessness, because it was going to take some effort and patience to work his cock into her snug vagina. He took a deep breath, trying to muster his restraint.

But then Hope pressed back against the mirror. Ryan groaned, his eyes rolling back into his head when the head of his cock slid into her sublime heat. He popped her bottom once with his palm in warning, not to be cruel. He needed her to realize how hard this was for him. His control had never been so sorely tested.

She stared at him, biting her lower lip when it trembled.

"You want it so much?" Ryan mouthed slowly.

She nodded.

"Witch," he muttered before he held her hip steady and sunk his cock into her humid heat another few inches. She tightened around him; he suspected the instinctive clenching of her muscles was in protest to his presence but he'd never felt anything so welcoming. He groaned gutturally. Fuck, it felt good. She squeezed him in a silken, muscular fist.

God, he needed to get *in there*. He tensed his leg and ass muscles, ready to claim more of her. But then he focused on Hope's face. It was pinched with a mixture of desire and discomfort.

"Shhhh," he soothed, forgetting she couldn't hear him. "Try to relax. It's going to be so good, honey. Please believe me."

He pulled his cock out a fraction of an inch and slid back into her, stroking her with tiny, electrical pulsations. Her muscular walls writhed and tightened around him with each stroke, making him grind his teeth as his restraint diminished with alarming speed. He held Hope's wide-eyed stare and reached around to find her clit with his fingers. He saw her lower lip drop.

Jesus he wanted to hear her scream.

He found he needed to be firm in his strokes to make any progress into her wet, clinging walls, but he tried his best to be gentle. He was less delicate with his fingers on her clit, rubbing and circling, plucking and gliding. She pushed back against the barrier of the mirror, her buttocks pressing tightly against the glass. Ryan glanced down at the bizarre, highly arousing site of his cock as it sunk into the mirror to mid-staff . . . into Hope's pussy to mid-staff.

He checked her face again, seeing that her cheeks were once again the livid pink he'd come to associate with incipient climax. He pressed his cock further into her, piercing her gripping, tight tunnel, moaning harshly at the immensity of the pleasure that tore through his body. His mouth twisted into a snarl. Hope started and stiffened, her body momentarily resisting him, but Ryan raised his hand and gripped her hip tightly, holding her into place while he withdrew his cock and sunk back into her pussy using the same insistent but controlled strokes.

When he felt her begin to move against him, pushing his shaft further into her heat with each small thrust, he released her hip and dipped his finger between her drenched labia once again, stimulating her. Her pussy clamped around his cock. Ryan looked up. Her head was still turned but her chin rested on her shoulder. He studied her rigid features turned in profile and knew she was about to explode.

He thrust hard at the same moment that the first wave of orgasm hit her, shouting out uncontrollably at the sensation of being buried in her sweet, tight flesh to the hilt while she quivered around him in release. Her clinging sheath milked him as she came, the resulting shivers that crept up his spine making him think he'd reached the limit of his control and was about to come deep inside her.

The realization dismayed him. He'd promised himself not to come inside her. Dammit, why hadn't he thought to use a condom? Women in the year 1906 didn't have birth control pills at their disposal. Regular condom use was such an ingrained habit for Ryan, he could only figure that the quality of miraculous otherworldliness to his encounters with Hope had been the reason he hadn't automatically reached for a condom before he'd single-mindedly looked into the mirror tonight.

He clenched his eyes shut and endured the most intense version of blissful agony he'd ever experienced in his life as Hope's heat gushed around him and her pussy squeezed his cock ruthlessly.

Sweat poured off his abdomen. He panted like he'd just sprinted the last leg of a marathon. When the exquisite torture of being buried in the midst of Hope's fires waned, Ryan pried open his eyelids. He stroked her hip softly before he took her in a firm grip.

He flexed his muscles and began to thrust in and out of her with short strokes. He grunted in satisfaction when he realized that the barrier between them had thinned sufficiently for him to hear his hips smacking against her thighs and ass with each downstroke of his cock. He wanted to caress her bottom more than anything, but she was so tight he required a firm hold on her body. He tried once again to penetrate the mirror with his other hand, growling in frustration when he was once again rebuffed.

His eyebrows drew together in confusion when Hope turned as fully as she could and he saw surprise in the dark pools of her eyes. If he'd needed any further evidence that she'd been a virgin until tonight, he'd just got it in spades. Her lower lips dropped open in aroused incredulity while he pumped into her more forcefully. She might have thought she understood the mechanics of intercourse, but this gorgeous, amazing woman clearly just now comprehended what it meant to be fucked.

But just as in all things, it was best she learned the lesson right off the bat, Ryan thought as he held her gaze and jackhammered his cock into her.

He saw her cheeks flush even redder. It may have been a new experience for her but she was a quick learner. She bucked her hips in perfect synchrony to his driving thrusts, creating a burning friction along his cock that made his eyes roll back in his head.

"*Fuck*," he sputtered in desperation when he felt Hope start to convulse around his pummeling cock yet again. His eyes sprang open in disbelief but the evidence of her immense cache of sensuality was writ large on her strained, beautiful face.

Ryan wondered briefly what would be most painful: plunging a knife into his own flesh or jerking his cock out of Hope's clamping vagina at that moment. He roared as he erupted in a scalding climax. His consciousness was temporarily engulfed by the fiery blasts of pleasure that wracked his mind and body.

But when he gained a measure of awareness he realized that he held Hope's smooth, firm hips with both hands, his fingers digging demandingly into the soft flesh as he continued to shoot his seed on her lower back and in the crevice of her ass.

When she suddenly started and tried to stand, he held her tightly, consumed by the most powerful orgasm he'd ever experienced.

"Don't . . . don't move, honey," he grated out as he shuddered violently. He pressed his spasming cock more tightly to her satiny, warm flesh. He gasped for air as a measure of sanity sluggishly wormed its way into overwhelming pleasure. He was touching Hope with both hands.

Step through. Now, he told himself.

Ryan lifted a foot in preparation to do just that—to step into Hope Stillwater's world in the year 1906—when her struggling against his hold penetrated his awareness more fully.

"What the hell?" he muttered in rising confusion when she twisted in his hands. Had he harmed her in the mindless midst of his orgasm? He automatically released her, stunned and alarmed by the wildness of Hope's actions . . . by the wretchedness of her expression when she spun to face him.

∽ EIGHT ∾

Hope had never imagined anything like it in her life.

As much as she'd wanted to join with Ryan, doubts had swamped her in all directions when he'd pushed his thick, throbbing member into her body. He stretched her delicate tissues, overfilled her until Hope had become desperate.

It hurt.

But then it didn't hurt. It just burned. Soon she'd been shuddering in climax yet again and Ryan pressed to the very core of her. She'd been shocked when he began thrusting his penis in and out of her, having no idea this was how things were done.

It was as if he kindled a fire inside of her with the friction of their rubbing flesh. The burning, tingling sensation had escalated until she felt it in the strangest places: her flaming cheeks, her throbbing nipples and the soles of her feet.

She knew what it was to climax, but this was different. This sensation was even more imperative. The fat, delineated head of Ryan's penis rubbed somewhere she could never hope to reach, a place that made fire shoot up into her belly, created a sizzling sensation in that piece of flesh Ryan had stimulated with his finger and even tingled at the tail of her spine. It was unbearable, wonderful . . . so mandatory to her very existence she'd thought she'd die from the sheer physical necessity of reaching that divine pinnacle so she could fall gloriously.

He held her in a steadfast grip and plunged into her ruthlessly. She loved it. *Needed* it. She closed her eyes and cried out sharply as she reached the peak of her desire . . . and tipped over into sheer bliss. Her entire body vibrated in an electrical storm of pure pleasure that completely stole her very identity for a blinding moment.

She gasped wildly for air, her eyes opening wide at the sensation of Ryan jerking his penis out of the tight embrace of her body. Her heartbeat hammered so loud in her ears she couldn't at first differentiate the separate sound of someone pounding on her bedroom door.

Her panting ceased, her breath burning in her lungs. Ryan's heavy, swollen member thumped onto her lower back. He held her with both hands as pleasure shuddered through him, his penis spasming next to her skin. Mrs. Abernathy called out worriedly as Ryan's hot seed spurted along her spine.

"Miss Stillwater. Miss Stillwater! Are you all right?"

Hope choked back an instinctive cry of wonder at the sensation of Ryan climaxing—all that awesome fierceness exploding in a single moment of concentrated power.

"I—I, yes, I'm fine, Mrs. Abernathy," she called breathlessly. Ryan shifted his hips, causing his still spasming penis to press deeper between the cheeks of her bottom. Mrs. Abernathy knocked again. Dear God, she *had* locked the door, hadn't she? Her heart resumed beating when she saw the knob turn but the door remained stationary.

"Come quickly, dear. It's your father. He fell in his den. He's quite ill."

Hope tried to stand in rising alarm, whimpering softly when Ryan held her tightly, still in the midst of his release. Her father's health had not been good recently. He was having increasing periods of fatigue and exhaustion.

"Oh, I'm sorry, Ryan," she whispered desperately as she once again tried to stand. Her mother had died of a particularly savage form of influenza when Hope was a child of twelve, and she was quite anxious about her father's health as a result.

Nothing else could have made her move away from Ryan at that moment.

"I'm coming, Mrs. Abernathy," she called loudly. "Please send someone to get Dr. Walkerton!"

"I already have, dear. Hurry now. He's asking for you," Mrs. Abernathy called through the door, the slight trace of condemnation spicing her tone causing Hope to struggle more forcefully in Ryan's hold.

Ryan must have finally sensed her rising panic because he released her abruptly.

He'd held her with *both* hands, she thought miserably as she spun around. Even though they lived in different centuries, they'd breached the barrier. They'd been *so close* to being able to touch and speak to one another at will.

She stared into the empty mirror. Even though her flesh still tingled in the aftermath of ecstasy and Ryan's seed was still warm on her back and where it pooled in the crack of her bottom, Hope was utterly, completely alone.

She stifled a sob of anguish as she knelt to retrieve her forgotten robe.

Hope fastened her lined forest green plush coat while Mary stood waiting with her muffler and hat. It would be chilly as she made her usual rounds at the Central Station, but the cold Chicago weather had never put off Hope in the past. This afternoon she was more worried about her father, although Dr. Walkerton had proclaimed after his examination last night that Jacob Stillwater would be fine.

"He's just been working too hard, that's all," Dr. Walkerton had explained to Hope last night as she anxiously hovered by her father's bedside.

"But, Dr. Walkerton—"

"He has an upper respiratory infection, Miss Stillwater. Nothing more. Jacob needs several days of quiet and rest and he'll be as good as new," Dr. Walkerton had interrupted with his calm, authoritative manner. He'd given Hope a sidelong glance, letting her know that he realized she thought of her mother's death thirteen years before.

"How is he?" Hope asked presently when Michael approached. She had asked her father's manservant to go and check on her father and report to her before she left on her almost daily missions to Central Station and later to Hull House. Her father had laughed and rolled his eyes earlier when she told him of her intention to stay home because of his bout of dizziness last night. Nevertheless, Hope had put off her errands in order to see how he fared after his midday meal.

"He is doing very well, miss, and was up reading by the fire when I left him just now."

"Are you sure he should be out of bed?" Hope fretted. "I'm still not convinced it isn't the right thing to do to cancel his birthday celebration next week."

"Come, miss, Dr. Walkerton says there was nothing more to Mr. Stillwater's weakness than a bad head cold and overwork. Surely a party would do him some good if he's mended by then," Mary assured her.

Hope chewed on her lower lip doubtfully. "My mother died of *nothing more* than a case of the influenza, you know."

Mary's kind face collapsed. "Oh, miss, I didn't mean—"

"I know you didn't, Mary. I'm sorry for being so melodramatic. Forgive me," Hope said gently before she took her hat from the maid, giving the young woman an apologetic smile. She tied the velvet ribbons beneath her chin. "My father is undoubtedly right to recommend my usual activities. It will hopefully alleviate my boorishness. A brisk walk is precisely what I require."

"But, miss . . . you're not taking the carriage?" Mary asked as she opened the front door for her.

"I've asked Evan to follow. It's the exercise I need, Mary, to clear the worries in my head."

She marched down the limestone front steps, determined to see to her daily duties instead of hover over her father—who was clearly doing well following his spell of near fainting last night in his study— or to alternatively stare like an idiot into the mirror searching for Ryan.

What did Ryan think of her struggling to be free of him? Would he never try to reach her again? The thought was so unbearable that it made her pace quicken and her shoes tap more forcefully on the pavement. She gave a polite nod to a waving Mr. John Glessner as he proceeded sedately in his carriage down Prairie Avenue. Although she picked up her step, her anxieties and questions would not be so easily chased away.

She'd slept restlessly last night, haunted by dreams, tossing and turning until her bedclothes grew damp with perspiration and tangled around her legs like a snare. For some strange reason Ryan's warning that she was in danger had melded with the dread associated with her father's illness, creating a profound sense of foreboding that she could not shake.

Once she'd heard Ryan call out to her, clear as a trumpet's call. She'd gasped at the sound and sat bolt upright in the mussed bed.

"Ryan?" she'd answered shakily.

The fading light from the fire in the hearth had told her she was alone in the large bedroom, however. Although she'd left the wardrobe door open, the mirror remained impervious, reflecting everything it should and nothing she most desired to see.

The coachman Evan tipped his hat to her from where he waited on Eighteenth Street. He allowed her a head start down Prairie Avenue before he followed slowly in the shiny black brougham. Hope's breath created a cloud of vapor around her mouth as she progressed down the quiet, tree-lined avenue.

The silence was short-lived, however. She paused and considered crossing the avenue when she saw a young man trying to get into his carriage, staggering and laughing uproariously as he tripped and fell forward. His driver hopped down and drew the man up off the carriage steps. She knew she was too late, however, when she saw Colin Mason, the sole inheritor of the Mason Haberdasher fortune and known Prairie Street reprobate, had noticed Hope as she walked down the sidewalk.

"Well, if it isn't that rose o' purity, that angel o' the mount . . . or is it that angel every man in Chicago would like to mount? He'p me out, Agnew . . ." Colin queried his driver as poor Agnew tried desperately to keep his wavering employer standing. Agnew winced involuntarily when Colin Mason exhaled an alcohol-saturated breath into his face. Colin pointed his walking cane at Hope, his action causing both men to lose balance again. Agnew barely prevented his employer from causing them to spill headfirst into the carriage. ". . . Should a woman who looks like her be polishing the neighborhood's virtue or polishing her appreciative neighbor's cock with her tongue?"

"*Sir*," Agnew exclaimed, turning bright red as he glanced around at Hope.

Hope's chest swelled with angry indignation. It wasn't the first time she'd been insulted by Colin Mason after he'd taken his daily gin bath. She felt nothing but pity for the frail, seventeen-year-old heiress from Schenectady who had married him earlier this year.

Hope was vaguely aware of Evan's concerned eye as he approached in the carriage but she wasn't worried about her safety from a drunkard louse like Colin Mason. She gritted her teeth as she neared him and his gaze rolled over her body, the effect similar to the crawl of a gin-soaked slug on her naked skin. She waited to speak until he finally looked up into her face again, his mouth slanted into a lascivious sneer.

"In your drunken state, Mr. Mason, it might be pointed out that the polishing of either your soul or the other item you mentioned would be an utter, dismal failure and therefore should be considered a waste of time, not only for me but for every individual alive on this planet. I will no longer detain you, sir, from an undoubtedly wasted trip to the Levee District."

Agnew made a loud choking sound and turned his wide grin into his shoulder. Hope spun around and continued her journey down the street.

"Frigid li'l viper," Colin yelled after her, ignoring Agnew's attempts to quiet him. "Take me to the Sweet Lash this instant, Agnew. I'll show every damn whore in that place the only good use for a female's mouth!"

Hope stewed in anger as she progressed down Prairie Avenue and then turned left on Seventeenth Street. Before Colin Mason's marriage had been arranged, Colin and his puffed-up, arrogant father had both approached Jacob Stillwater in an attempt to arrange a marriage between Hope and Colin. Hope's father had proclaimed in no uncertain terms, however, that the choice was his daughter's to make.

Hope had been shocked and highly discomfited when she'd turned down Colin's proposal to learn he'd actually believed she would agree to marry him. She'd known Colin since they were children. He'd always been a sullen, selfish boy. He'd begun being sexually aggressive with her when they both turned fourteen. Hope had never made it a secret how much she despised being in Colin's presence, so the realization that he genuinely seemed to think she'd agree to be his wife had left her stunned.

Colin Mason was the sort of specimen of manhood who might put a thinking woman off the concept of marriage forever.

Her temper had mostly calmed by the time she reached Indiana Avenue. It was foolish to waste one's energies on the likes of Colin Mason, after all.

Reaching Michigan Avenue was like making an abrupt turn from sleepy suburbia into the crashing liveliness of the proud, industrious city of Chicago. A parade of carriages progressed down the street, their ironclad wheels hitting the macadam pavement causing a ceaseless clatter. The chill of the November afternoon had set the city's coal furnaces to full-out action, inevitably deepening the gloom of an already cloudy day.

Visibility was so poor that Hope couldn't even see the thirteen-story clock tower of Central Station until she was a block away. Near Central Station the passage of trolley cars, trains and the calls of newsboys joined the cacophony of continual sound and movement.

Hope walked along briskly, as at home amidst the young, brash city as she was in the elegant silences of Prairie Avenue. Several of the mainstay families of Prairie Avenue had begun to migrate to the north shore to places like the suburban town of Lake Forest, disgusted by the industry and crass urbanization encroaching on their somber, august neighborhood.

Hope and her father were determined to stay in the midst of the city they both loved, however, even if some of their more elegant neighbors found their preference to be odd. Many Prairie Avenue denizens already considered Jacob Stillwater to be an idiosyncratic gentleman, anyway, especially for the way he allowed his headstrong daughter to run free about the city, engaging in so many questionable, unladylike social reform activities.

And the Prairie Avenue matriarchs didn't know half of what she did, Hope thought wryly.

Hope's father was a new alderman of the ward, the first to be elected outside of the patronage of the crime boss Diamond Jack Fletcher. As a minister of the Second Presbyterian Church on Michigan and Cullerton, this was also Jacob Stillwater's parish. Hope knew the Loop and the first ward as well as any young woman might know the sleepy avenues and Main Street of her small town.

Chicago was a city of industry, a town that knew where it was headed. As a young woman of determination and purpose, Hope innately understood and appreciated her place in the sprawling miasma of bustling humanity.

A shrill scream of terror suddenly pierced the loud clatter of the city. Horses neighed in panic. Hope turned in anxious dread. It was a horrible fact of urban life that on any single day, an average of two people were killed at rail crossings in Chicago's Loop or by merely stepping off the curb and being plowed down by a charging horse. She was extremely relieved to see that the screaming woman was very much still alive, grasping her elderly companion and looking shocked and whey-faced.

"Did you see him? Did you *see* him?" she shouted repeatedly. Every time her companion shook her head in rising confusion the woman asked the question more loudly.

"Poor unfortunate creature," Hope murmured under her breath. Progress marched triumphantly in the streets of Chicago, but so did its inevitable companions illness and mental stress. The rates of alcoholism and drug abuse were also rising alarmingly.

She paused in mid-stride when she realized that most people

would think *she* was a "poor unfortunate creature" if they learned she had visions of a god in man form who made love to her through her bedroom mirror.

Not that Ryan Vincent Daire was a hallucination. Hope would never believe that in a million years. When she returned home later this evening she planned to prove it, too, by contacting Ryan again in whatever fashion she could contrive.

One did not become deflowered by hallucinations, after all. Even now she felt the slight soreness of her genitals, the pleasant tingling just beneath her skin that signaled her sensual awakening. Her cheeks heated as she recalled in a flash of detail her unlikely joining with Ryan. Strange such a thing should be termed "deflowering." Hope felt, in fact, that in some immeasurable, intangible fashion, she'd burst into full bloom beneath Ryan's touch.

She looked back one more time at the woman, feeling a tad guilty for assuming she was mad or drunk. Her companion appeared to have calmed her but she was talking nonstop and kept pointing to the middle of Michigan Avenue. She sighed as she crossed Lake Park Place, looking around to locate Evan and waving before she opened the wood-and-glass doors to Central Station. She would enter here and meet Evan at the drop-off, pickup port designated for carriages with her new charge in tow.

She lingered cautiously by the marble archway to the waiting room of the busy intercity train station. Sure enough she spied Marvin Evercrumb reading a newspaper as he sat on one of the polished wooden benches.

In her private thoughts, Hope referred to him as Marvin *Everscum*.

Like Hope, Marvin had come to Central Station on this gray, dingy Chicago afternoon in order to meet the arrival of the Milwaukee Road, the southbound train that brought hundreds of people to Chicago daily, including the inevitable few young women interested in finding work as stenographers, typists or secretaries.

Unchaperoned, friendless women flowed into the urban center of Chicago in the year 1906 at unprecedented levels in history.

The Milwaukee Road was just one of many trains that Hope might meet on a given day. Marvin was just one of many sleazy operators employed by Diamond Jack Fletcher who came to greet these vulnerable, wide-eyed women at Central Station.

They came from countless towns on several different trains. They immigrated from Missouri, Indiana, Wisconsin, Ohio or Kansas. Hope came to welcome them in her small way to a city she loved and to do her damndest to keep them out of the hands of men like Marvin. She took them to one of several respectable boardinghouses that she knew of and put them in contact with someone who could assist them in finding a job.

Marvin and his ilk lured their prey with enticements of high-paying jobs and luxurious, cheap housing. Sometimes the white slavers pitched their lines for the first time at the train stations and other times they utilized a network of females who befriended these women in other cities and towns; female operatives who told their companions of the glamour of Chicago and the high-paying jobs to be had for the asking. Guileless young women then boarded trains in St. Louis, Bloomington or Milwaukee, clutching their life possessions and a note with Marvin Evercrumb's or one of his oily peers' names on it. Once they reached Chicago, Marvin proceeded to deliver these women directly to hell, taking them to one of several white slavery way stations in the city.

The victims were drugged and brutalized by men who were the equivalent of professional rapists. Afterward they were sold to the seedier Clark Street and Levee District brothels, forced into a life of degradation and imprisonment. Even the madam Addie Sampson, who was far more experienced in these matters than Hope, visibly shivered when she considered the fate of these young women once they were taken behind the closed doors of Levee brothels like the Sweet Lash.

Hope had been infuriated to the point of losing her appetite for a week when she discovered that Diamond Jack's reach extended to most of the police officers in the first ward and that very little if anything was done to stop this outrageous kidnapping and brutalization of young women. Once she'd gotten past her initial fury, however, Hope's practical nature had taken over. She left the speeches and lawmaking up to her father, deciding to counteract the white slavers in her own small way.

Perhaps she couldn't save everyone, but she could save a few. For now, that had to be enough.

Unfortunately, Marvin knew her by appearance and often did his best to circumvent Hope's circumventions. Hope had taken to coming to meet the trains earlier and earlier each time, but apparently Marvin was one step ahead of her today and had arrived even earlier than she. She frowned as she studied the criminal appareled in his expensive, sleek clothing. A portly gentleman entering the station caught her attention.

"Your pardon, sir," she called out, giving the startled man her best smile. "I am new to this station and also abominably late. I wonder if you could be bothered to show me to the train shed?"

"It would be my honor, my dear," the man said, gallantly putting out his elbow for her to take.

Hope peaked over the man's shoulder as she rattled off some ridiculous story about visiting a sick aunt in St. Louis, glad to see that although Marvin had set down his paper he had not noticed her behind the man's bulk.

Her luck held strong. After she'd given her heartfelt thanks to the portly gentleman, she saw through the smoky train shed that the Milwaukee Road pulled into Chicago early. With any luck, by the time its arrival was announced in the waiting room, Hope would have plucked a potential victim right out from beneath Marvin Evercrumb's nose.

Minutes later Hope studied the faces of the stream of new arrivals with an expert eye. When she saw a slender, full-breasted young woman with the dark curls and expression of mixed excitement and panic on her pretty face, Hope stepped forward as decisively as if she were greeting a distant cousin on her first trip to the city.

"Good afternoon. I hope you had a smooth journey."

The woman glanced down over Hope warily but whatever she saw seemed to chase away her caution.

"That's the prettiest coat I've ever laid eyes on! My sister Eloise told me women in Chicago knew how to dress real smart."

"Thank you. I like your hat very much."

"It's nothing compared to yours."

"My name is Hope Stillwater. I belong to the Welcoming League, a group of Christian women whose mission it is to greet new visitors and familiarize them with our beautiful city," Hope lied effortlessly. In truth, she was a one-woman army. Her attempts at getting other female social reformers to join in her efforts had thus far been unsuccessful, as the train depot was considered to be nearly as unsavory of a locale as a tavern. She was still confident in her efforts to form a future Welcoming League, however.

Hope held out her hand. "The city can be a bit overwhelming on your first visit."

"I'm Sadie Holcrum, miss, and you're right about that," Sadie said as she shook Hope's hand and looked around slack-jawed at the bustling activity of the train shed. "I used to think Kenosha was a big city but it's nothing to what I saw as we pulled into Chicago."

Out of the corner of her eye Hope saw Marvin standing on the platform of the train shed. She gave Sadie her most winning smile.

"May I help you with your luggage, Miss Holcrum?" She grabbed a suitcase from a dubious-looking Sadie, cradled her elbow and maneuvered her to the doors furthest away from a glowering Marvin. "My goodness, you pack light," Hope exclaimed when she lifted the suitcase with ease.

Sadie's cheeks flushed. Her gaze flickered over to Hope a tad nervously. "I'm afraid I haven't got much to pack, miss. None of my family does. I come to Chicago to get a job as a typist, see. I've been practicing on my mother's Remington. I hope to be able to send 'em back a portion of my wages."

Hope nodded in understanding, having heard a similar story countless times before. Once families in monetary need had sent off their sons to bread-win in the cities, but now out of necessity they sent their daughters as well. Hope saw nothing wrong with the practice in theory, but unfortunately the city had not yet compensated for the hoards of single, friendless women or provided them with appropriate avenues for security and guidance.

And white slavers like Diamond Jack Fletcher took blatant advantage of the situation.

"Have you a place to stay while you look for a job, Miss Holcrum?" Hope asked once they'd entered the waiting area. Sadie didn't respond immediately as she was busy gaping at the three-story-high bay window that overlooked Lake Michigan.

"Oh . . . well, as to that, my sister Eloise says there's a boardinghouse on near every corner in Chicago," Sadie replied stoutly.

"There are a good number, such a plethora in fact that it's far too easy to make an error and choose one of the more . . . dodgy variety," Hope explained with a significant look. "It is part of the Welcoming League's mission to take young women to respectable boardinghouses and provide directions and contacts for employers in the Loop who are looking for workers."

Sadie's blue eyes widened in amazement. "Well, ain't it lucky I ran into you, then?"

"Indeed," Hope replied as she gently nudged Sadie toward the exit where Evan would be waiting with the carriage.

"There's just one thing, miss." Hope blinked in surprise when the young woman's cheeky grin revealed a gleaming gold tooth. "I'll be needing to use the facilities after that long trip, if you don't mind."

"Of course, I should have asked. Right this way, Miss Holcrum," Hope said as she nodded in the direction of the ladies' lounge.

She got a measure of satisfaction when she saw Marvin slink back into the main waiting room notably with no young woman on his arm. A shiver of apprehension went through her when he gave first Sadie and then Hope a narrow, assessing look before Hope lost sight of him in the crowd.

∽ NINE ∽

Ryan's heart still hammered like a locomotive going full steam inside his chest as he stared at his laptop computer. He tried to take a slow, steadying breath and forced his attention on the black-and-white photo of men in the stands at Marshall Field watching a University of Chicago football game in the year 1905. None of his jackets would pass as suitable, but his long, black overcoat would work along with a white shirt and black tie.

Apparently it was time for him to fully enter Hope's world. He knew that because he just had.

The jarring experience had taught him that he needed to be a bit more cautious and prepared on his next attempt, although he didn't know how he could have prepared himself for *that*.

Five minutes ago he'd noticed that the fog on the mirror had completely cleared. Although he couldn't see Hope or the interior of her bedroom, he found that the surface of the mirror had enough give for him to penetrate it completely.

Like a fool he'd stepped through and ended up in the middle of a clamoring city street with a team of horses bounding straight toward him. The animals' shrieks of terror and the image of them rearing in panic—the lethal, kicking hooves and the whites of their rolling eyes—would likely be emblazoned on Ryan's memory until the day he died. He'd experienced some pretty significant shocks in his life, but that had to be one of the biggest ever.

He didn't have the opportunity to be dismayed over the fact that the window of the mirror had disappeared by the time he turned in panic. He'd dived through the space where it *had* been and smacked into the wooden floor of the Prairie Avenue bedroom so hard that'd it'd knocked the breath clean out of him for ten seconds.

Obviously this mirror didn't work precisely in the way he'd imagined, he acknowledged when he was finally able to draw air again.

He grinned distractedly when he pulled the ivory felt, short-brimmed hat from a still unpacked box of memorabilia from his college days. It was a replica of the hat Coach Amos Alonzo Stagg used to wear. The University of Chicago Hall of Famer had long been one of Ryan's sports idols. He'd bought the hat for fifty cents at a Hyde Park garage sale while he was still in college because of its similarity to the one Coach Stagg wore in the very picture Ryan had pulled up on his computer.

He put the hat on his head and studied himself in the gilt mirror. There was no way around it. He was going to have to shave his goatee.

Fifteen minutes later, clean shaven and wearing his best facsimile of early-1900s apparel, Ryan reached into the mahogany wardrobe and extricated his SIG Sauer semiautomatic from the holster. He slid the weapon into the chest pocket of his overcoat. After showing up in the middle of the street with those horses charging straight

at him, Ryan didn't know what to expect. The last thing he needed
was to find himself in a situation in 1906 where he was required to
remove his coat, thus revealing his holster and gun. He checked
that the clip on his Spyderco Captain knife was secure before he
tucked it out of sight in his boot.

He stood before the mirror and concentrated on the poignant
memory of Hope last night, the mixture of anxiety and trust on her
face when she'd pushed her robe off her shoulders and gifted him
with the sight of her naked beauty.

Gifted him with all her. Period.

Ryan didn't understand what had happened there at the end of
their lovemaking, couldn't comprehend why she'd tried to escape his
hold. He only knew it was the image of her giving herself so trust-
ingly to him that he needed to cling to if he ever hoped to reach her.

If he ever hoped to save her.

He took a deep breath and stepped into the gilt mirror.

And found himself staring at a long bar in a dark, dingy room.
Each empty wooden bar stool had a none-too-clean-looking brass
spittoon directly beside it. A man with flaming red hair behind the
bar's polished glasses. He glanced up and met Ryan's reflection in
the dirty mirror behind the bar.

"Mother o'—" The bartender spun around. "How'd ya get
there all of a sudden?"

Ryan took in the man's thick mustache and hair that had been
slicked back with so much oil that it dripped onto his dirty white
collar. His accent seemed strange and yet familiar at once; some exotic mixture of Irish and south-side Chicago.

Ryan's tongue had seemingly become glued to the roof of his
mouth. Reality slammed into his brain with the effect of a baseball
bat whacking his skull.

Holy shit. He really was in the early twentieth century. If Alistair
could only see *this*.

At first the man seemed angry at Ryan's muteness.

"The Sweet Lash ain't open yet fer business, mister, so scram."
An idea seemed to occur to the bartender whose forearms reminded
Ryan of Popeye. "Hang on! I know who ya are. Shoulda known,
from the size of ya. At least Shapiro sent someone decent this time.
Well, sit yerself down there, fella. How 'bout a nice glass of cold
beer? Something to take the sting outa Big Marlo's fist?"

Ryan didn't care for the bartender's knowing look. He scowled
at him while he struggled for how he should reply. Would something about his speech give him away? Did he really need to say
anything at all? He needed to get out of this place. He needed to
find Hope.

The Sweet Lash? Ryan thought in rising amazement. Wasn't that
the name of the south-side restaurant and nightclub that his nem-
esis Jim Donahue owned in the twenty-first century? And hadn't
he read in the *Tribune* at the time of the nightclub's opening a few
years back that the establishment had once been the home of a
late-nineteenth-century brothel?

Despite his eagerness to find Hope, Ryan couldn't help but look
around him in wonder. He quickly saw, however, that the Sweet
Lash hardly warranted awe. Neither did the rancid, mildew odor that
filled his nose. The room was large—perhaps a hundred by seventy
feet—and contained a multitude of round tables and chairs. Four gas
chandeliers with red lampshades cast as many shadows in the dim
room as it did lurid light. Ryan realized that one of the dark corners contained a piano because someone started plunking out a
raucous tune on the keys.

There were several raised platforms. The ones at the side of the
room were cordoned off with frayed and dirty, gold velvet ropes. The
floor consisted of some sort of black substance of unknown origin
but had a slight give to it beneath Ryan's shoes. He suspected it
might be solid earth and grime pressed down into solidity by thou-
sands of hard leather soles.

Either that, or the wooden floor had long ago been covered by years of dirt, spittle, sweat and God only knew what other types of human and animal excretions.

The bartender obviously took note of Ryan's preoccupation.

"Yeah, maybe ya got a right to look down yer nose at me, fella. Beer won't do the trick, will it? No, sir, whiskey's yer only hope if yer climbing in the ring with Big Marlo, friend. Ah, here we go. Doors have opened. Yer audience arrives."

Ryan glanced over to see dozens upon dozens of boisterous, black-suited men swarm into the room, their faces alight with excitement. A few of them had women draped on their arms. It struck Ryan as comical to see the manner in which the males ogled the prostitutes and then joked with their companions, almost as though they followed a socially prescribed script for brothel behavior. Despite their relatively low-cut gowns, their heavily painted faces and the brassy color of their hair, the women didn't look all that racy to Ryan's twenty-first-century eyes.

"I'd hoped you were going to take part in the Slip and Whip. That's why I came tonight, you know, Molly," one mustachioed man told the woman on his arm suggestively as they passed Ryan.

"I never do the Slip and Whip on the night of a Big Marlo match. I know that fight and the gambling is the real reason you boys showed up here tonight," Molly sulked.

"Molly, m'dear, you malign me. I'd forsake all to see you again with the reins in your hand and your"—Molly shrieked dramatically and giggled when her suitor swatted her bottom—"gleaming promises at me from the stage."

"And there's the man who'll pay ya," the bartender spoke in an undertone to Ryan as the couple passed out of hearing. "Here's yer man, Jack!" the bartender called out more loudly to a large man standing at the end of the bar whose girth strained at the fabric of a pristine white suit. "Big Marlo's latest meal."

Jack paused and wiped what very much looked like blood off his hands onto a white cloth resting at the end of the bar. When he was finished he flashed a sharklike grin. Ryan should have been bedazzled by the hundreds of diamonds flashing on rings that encircled every single one of the man's sausage-like fingers.

Instead he was preoccupied by another unexpected reality.

"*Jim Donahue*," he muttered incredulously.

"What's that ya said?" the bartender asked quietly, obviously to shield Ryan's ignorance from the immense presence of the man at the other end of the bar. "That's the owner of the Sweet Lash, the owner of the whole Levee District, if the truth be told. Don't ya know, fool? That man's none other than Diamond Jack Fletcher."

Ryan nodded numbly. The bartender could say whatever he wanted. Some things a guy knew just like he'd *known* he'd do whatever it took to come after Hope Stillwater. No matter what the bartender said, the man who currently stood at the end of the bar giving Ryan a cold, appraising once-over while he gnawed on the end of a soggy cigar was most definitely *other* than just Diamond Jack Fletcher.

In Ryan's time, the rotten spirit that currently inhabited Diamond Jack animated the flesh of the man Ramiro and he had been working to put behind bars for the past year.

Diamond Jack and Jim Donahue were one and the same soul.

∽

Tacky.

That was the first fuzzy thought Hope had when she pried open her eyelids and found herself staring at scarlet velvet curtains surrounding a large alcove. She lay on a four-poster bed that had been tucked inside the alcove. Little gold pom-poms dangled off the mullioned fabric of the curtains. The gold-and-scarlet material clashed awfully with the worn green-and-blue wallpaper featuring sea creatures and bare-breasted mermaids.

Hope shifted her gaze around the room, wary to move her head for some reason. For a long moment she stared uncomprehendingly at a photograph hanging on the wall framed in gold leaf. It featured a nude young woman looking over her shoulder coyly. A single red rose sprouted from the crack of her bottom.

The framed photograph brought the strangeness of her situation home at last.

"*What* in the—"

She gasped as pain lanced through her head. She'd tried to rise from her supine position only to be stopped abruptly by the stabbing pain. For a full minute she remained very still, eyes clamped shut, perspiring profusely, deathly afraid to move lest she experience that unbearable sensation yet again.

"I wouldn't bother trying to get up if I was you," a woman said from somewhere to the left of the bed, her tone smug and contemptuous. "I've got you tied down good, see? 'Sides, for what Diamond Jack's got planned for ya, lying on the bed with your legs spread wide is the only position you'll be needin' to take anyhow," the woman finished with a self-satisfied laugh.

At the mention of Diamond Jack Fletcher's name Hope's heartbeat escalated until it beat frantically in her chest like a bird trying to escape a cage. She subtly flexed her arms and legs, not wanting the woman to notice her struggling. Sure enough, her wrists and ankles were bound with what felt like snugly knotted velvet cord. The woman's voice struck a familiar resonance in Hope's memory but pain and vertigo prevented her from focusing too hard on anything.

Very cautiously and slowly, Hope opened her eyes. Thankfully the sharp pain seemed to have abated for the moment. Sadie Holcrum looked down at her with a satisfied smirk on her pretty face.

"Ain't so high and mighty now, are ya?" she taunted. "*Welcoming League*, my dimpled arse. Pretty soon you'll be no better'n the likes of me, missy. Good sight worse, I'd say."

"Miss Holcrum? I don't understand . . ."

"Don't ya, *Miss* Stillwater?" Sadie grinned, her gold eyetooth gleaming. She seemed to be enjoying herself immensely. Her sharp-featured, sneering face didn't look so pretty now, Hope realized. She recalled Sadie's wide-eyed wonder at the size of the train shed and gaping mouth as she looked at Central Station's enormous bay windows on Lake Michigan.

Sadie Holcrum would have made a fine actress.

"What's the last thing ya remember?" Sadie asked.

Hope tried her best to focus her thoughts. "I . . . at the train station. We . . . went to the ladies' lounge and . . . and . . ."

"*Crack*," Sadie finished happily as she mimed someone striking downward forcefully. "I did my part and got ya somewhere secluded and ol' Marvin did his as well. Used his pistol to do it. Knocked ya out cold."

"May I have some water, please?" Hope whispered, biological imperatives taking the forefront in her consciousness before she could even begin to consider her bizarre predicament. Besides, focusing on the basics helped keep panic at bay. Sadie curled her lip in disdain and Hope thought sure she'd refuse her request. Suddenly the willowy brunette turned away, however. When she once again came into Hope's sight she carried a green glass. Sadie lifted it to her lips.

Hope sighed shakily and rested her head back in the pillow after she'd taken several huge swallows of the deliciously cool water.

"Where am I?" she managed hoarsely.

"Why, your new home, o' course, the Sweet Lash. An' when you ain't servin' Diamond Jack and the men, you're gonna fetch and clean fer me, I think. I always fancied having a lady fer a slave."

"Shut your mouth, you good-for-nothing whore."

Although Hope was already stunned into silence by Sadie's proclamations, she blinked in even more profound shock at the sound of a man's cutting words being delivered with the smooth, beguiling accent of the south.

Diamond Jack Fletcher himself entered her range of vision.

"I let you leave this house for two hours to go on a special mission for me and even in that little bit of time you managed to get juiced up. What was it? Did you and that fool Evercrumb actually stop in the alley and do business with those damn cokies while you had Jacob Stillwater's unconscious daughter in the carriage? Or have you two just been hitting the bottle?"

He grabbed Sadie's hand and pushed back her sleeve, checking her forearms. Hope knew very well from her social reform activities that the term *cokies* referred to the panderers and lowlifes that both supported and sustained an underground traffic in cocaine and morphine in the Levee District.

She jumped when Jack slapped the woman's face with a big, meaty hand. He must not have liked what he'd seen on the woman's arm. Sadie's chin flung around hard at the impact, causing several ringlets to dislodge from her upswept hair. She sobbed.

"What're ya mad at me for, Jack? Me and Marvin . . . we did whatcha asked, didn't we?" Sadie whined. "We brought ya Miss High and Mighty Stillwater. If me and Marvin did make a quick stop on the way home, no harm come of it. Ain't I right, Jack?"

Hope's heart seemed to stop in her chest when Diamond Jack Fletcher's small, dark brown eyes shifted and settled on her. She'd seen Jack on several occasions around the first ward. He was rather a hard man to miss, large, charismatic and infamous as he was. Everyone—including Hope and every shop boy, minister, prostitute, Prairie Avenue matriarch and panderer in the neighborhood—knew Diamond Jack.

She'd been unfortunate enough to be the object of his notice on a few occasions, but he'd never stood as close to her as he did presently. Near as he was now Hope saw that fat had swelled the angular features of his large face, making them seem to pop out from the flesh, the result being almost caricature-like.

Jack still possessed the cold, calculating gaze of a predator, however, even though he regarded her through puffy eyelids. It was most unpleasant to have him pin her in his sights while she lay spread-eagle and naked on a bed, a thin sheet her only covering. She shivered uncontrollably when his beady eyes ran slowly over the outline of her body.

"What *lies* have you been telling this young lady, Sadie?" Jack shook his head as though saddened. His voice had once again slowed and softened, reminding Hope of sweet, flowing syrup. "My apologies, Miss Stillwater, for my employees' mistreatment of you."

"Then untie me from this bed and give me my clothes so that I can leave."

Jack sighed. "I'm afraid that's an impossibility at this point, miss. I do need you for a very specific purpose, you see, and I won't be able to let you go until I have what I need."

"And what purpose would that be?" Hope asked, although she wasn't at all sure she wanted to know.

"Well, let's just say I needed to do something to stop your father, Miss Stillwater. From what I've come to understand, he holds nothing in this world dearer than his daughter, which is just as it should be. I respect a man like Jacob Stillwater. Respect him more than ninety-nine percent of the fools I'm forced to do business with daily." He threw a dark glance at the sniffling Sadie. "Your father's a man of commitment and values."

"I'm surprised you're able to respect something of which you have no personal knowledge, Mr. Fletcher."

Surprise flickered across his large features at her jibe before they settled into a cold mask. Gone in an instant was the façade of a sweet-tongued southern gentleman. He raised his hand and something slipped and dangled between his fingers.

Hope clenched her teeth when she saw what it was—the silver locket her father had given her before she went on her European tour. Inside of it were two photographs—one of her mother, Virginia Stillwater, when she was a young woman of nineteen and one of Hope at the very same age. Their likenesses were striking enough to make them look like twins. Hope prized it above all her possessions and rarely removed the locket from her neck. Seeing it dangling beneath fat fingers decorated with dozens of tacky diamonds made her so angry she lurched up on the bed, her restraints bringing her up short.

"Give that back, you foul creature! You have no right to touch it."

Jack grinned and made a tut-tutting noise as though she were a two-year-old behaving poorly. "I'm going to keep this necklace. I think it'll bring me luck. You may not know it, young lady, but I was an avid, yet distant admirer of your mother. Beautiful, passionate woman. How your dried-up excuse for a father ever managed to win her is beyond my understanding."

He ignored Hope's hissing sound of fury as he examined the swaying locket.

"The thing you don't understand is that I have a way of life here, little lady. It may not be to your father's liking. It may not be to yours. But that's just something you'll both have to live with, the way I see it. Last I checked, God never elected you and your holier-than-thou father to be the judges of everyone else on this planet."

"You're right. Something much higher than you or I will stand in judgment, Mr. Fletcher. But until that day, I'm going to keep right on trying to stop individuals such as yourself who prey on the weak and innocent to feed your insatiable greed. My father feels the same way and will continue to do so no matter what you have planned for me," Hope bluffed. In truth she knew her father would be decimated if Jack continued to hold her captive or killed her, but she'd never let Jack know that.

Jack's dark brows rose in wry amusement, but Hope sensed his anger beneath the surface—a cold, dangerous kind of fury.

"I can see you've learned the skill of speechmaking from your daddy, Miss Stillwater." He chuckled as he idly reached into his white suit jacket. Hope's ire rose because she believed he was pocketing her locket. Instead he withdrew something larger from his jacket, something that Hope couldn't quite see. "The thing of it is," Jack continued, "speechmaking will do you about as much good in the Sweet Lash as being a drunkard, drug-using, loudmouthed whore."

Hope never had the opportunity to be frightened before it happened. Neither did Sadie, which she had reason to be thankful for later.

Jack almost casually grabbed Sadie's hair, pulling her head back and exposing her throat. He reached around her neck. Hope leaned up as far as she could go, ignoring the pain that throbbed at the back of her head. She watched in puzzlement as a scarlet band grew around Sadie's throat.

Jack let go and Sadie dropped to her knees heavily.

When Hope recognized that the gurgling sounds she heard were Sadie choking on her life's blood as it spilled out of her, horror flashed through her like a blinding white light.

"*No*," Hope cried as she pulled so wildly at the restraints that the bed creaked in protest. Sadie's body made a muffled thumping noise on the floor as she fell. Hope's terror magnified when she realized she no longer heard the woman trying fruitlessly to draw air from a severed windpipe. She looked up at Jack, who watched the dying woman with the detachment one might afford a swatted fly. "Help her. *Damn you*, help her!"

Diamond Jack Fletcher's image wavered before her gaze, but she was still able to make him out as he stepped back and used a handkerchief to carefully wipe off the blade of his knife.

"My deepest sympathies for distressing you, Miss Stillwater, but Sadie had to go. She couldn't keep quiet once she caught a whiff of whiskey, and never mind what she turned into when someone put some morphine in her veins. You heard how mean she could get. Her mouth turned her into a real liability for a man like me . . . a man with secrets of the Stillwater caliber."

Hope's eyelids began to close as the room spun dizzily. She knew she was about to lose consciousness—whether from the blow to her head or sheer horror, she didn't know—but she managed to stay awake long enough to see Diamond Jack bow slightly to her in a parody of gallantry before he exited the room.

∾ TEN ∾

Diamond Jack picked up the glass of whiskey the bartender set in front of him, checked the gold watch he kept on a chain and walked toward Ryan with a broad grin on his fat face.

Ryan was reminded of an overfed shark dressed up in the clothing of a southern gentleman. He'd had similar thoughts about Jim Donahue innumerable times in the past—or the future, however you wanted to word it. In truth, Jim and Jack weren't a matched pair in physical appearance. They might have been brothers instead of twins. But their physical inexactness did nothing to sway Ryan's firm conviction that they possessed one and the same soul.

"I didn't catch your name," Jack said as he came toward Ryan.

"I didn't give it."

The bartender made a hissing sound and flexed his Popeye forearms as he formed fists. Ryan suppressed rolling his eyes in barely contained frustration. God damn it, he'd come here for Hope. What'd it mean that he'd run into Jim Donahue's former incarnation in the meanwhile?

And what the hell? He didn't even believe in reincarnation, did he?

"Now, now, Alfie. Keep your fists busy pouring drinks. We have a thirsty crowd here tonight, and this boy looks like he'd hold his own, anyway," Jack said as he shrewdly studied Ryan's stature and then swept his gaze across the quickly filling room. A line of patrons still streamed in, making the fifteen or so women that circulated in the crowd highly outnumbered. Another bartender had joined Alfie behind the bar and was pouring whiskey and beer for two women who, given their listless expressions, relative lack of face paint and drab dresses were there to serve drinks instead of entertain the men.

Jack waved a diamond-laden hand in Ryan's direction. "Looks like this young man could use one of those drinks. He's likely just a mite nervous about meeting Marlo. Wouldn't we all be? A glass of my finest will put him at his ease."

Alfie looked vaguely surprised at his boss's request but he followed his order quickly enough. Ryan sat down, placing the short-brimmed ivory felt hat on the bar. When Alfie set a glass in front of him he automatically took a swallow, pausing before he took a second, more appreciative sip. Diamond Jack chuckled.

"That's from my private stores. I have it shipped to me from the finest distillery in Tennessee not far from where I grew up."

"Not bad," Ryan conceded.

"I can see you're a man of good taste. Now . . . are we ever to know your name, son?"

"Daire," Ryan muttered. He gave Jack a sidelong glance, curious despite his wariness. Hadn't the frustrated detective whose notes he'd read—Connor J. O'Rourke—written that Diamond Jack Fletcher was the prime suspect in Hope's murder?

And now he'd discovered Diamond Jack and Jim Donahue

were the same man. Perhaps he wasn't in the wrong place, after all. Now he just needed to figure out without blowing his cover who the hell Alfie and Jack had mistaken him for.

"Where's Marlo?" Ryan asked, hoping it was a safe question.

"He's taking care of some business for me. He'll be along. I've told the girls to carry on with the Slip and Whip for the first show tonight." Jack paused, beady eyes fixing on a tall, thin, disheveled-looking man who staggered into the main room, a woman supporting him on each side.

"Excuse me for a moment," Jack murmured, obviously irritated. Ryan tried to pretend he wasn't listening as Jack approached the half-soused dandy.

"Are you sure you should be down here, Mason?" Jack asked silkily.

"Course I am. I've slept it off and am now good as new, isn't that right, ladies?"

The bold-featured, blonde female on the right of him winked slyly at Mason. "Everything seems to be in perfect working order, wouldn't you say, Betsey?"

The redheaded Betsey giggled and petted the drunk guy along his thin chest and belly sycophantically. "Oh, he's a perfect specimen of manhood, Mel."

Jack leaned against the bar. Although Ryan wasn't fully looking into his face he got the distinct impression he rolled his eyes in disgust. "All right, you two, cut the act. Get up there and put on just as good of a show onstage or I'll set Big Marlo on the both of you afterward for not keeping him upstairs to sleep it off like I told you to."

The sly, seductive expressions on both women's faces vanished in an instant. The threat of Big Marlo was obviously not taken lightly.

"I thought Nancy and Sadie were doing the Slip and Whip tonight," the blonde woman said a tad bit suspiciously.

Jack pulled back his hand as though he were about to strike her for her insolence. "Who makes the rules here, Mel? Get up on that stage."

"Big Marlo keeps the girls here in line?" Ryan mumbled when Alfie paused in front of him after pouring a glass of bourbon.

"Sure. Big Marlo keeps *everyone* in line if Diamond Jack tells him to. He does more than just discipline the girls, though." Alfie leaned across the bar and spoke more intimately. "He breaks in the new ones, if ya get my meanin'. Everyone knows how much Big Marlo likes doing that. Ain't exactly gentle with 'em, but maybe that's best considering their new profession an' all." Alfie nodded knowingly toward the stairs Ryan could just make out in the distance through the doorway. "Word is, the girl Diamond Jack's got upstairs for him tonight is special . . . beautiful as a real princess."

Ryan took a sip of whiskey. "I guess that's what Diamond Jack meant when he said Marlo was 'doing something for him.' "

Alfie looked confused by his statement. "No, Marlo won't be breaking the new girl in until he wins her later tonight."

"*Wins* her?" Ryan asked slowly.

"Sure. Diamond Jack awards the winner of the match not only prize money but a virgin. Shapiro didn't tell you that before they sent ya over?"

Ryan kept his face impassive to hide his repulsion.

"No. Must've slipped Shapiro's mind. *I'm* the man who's taking on Big Marlo tonight," Ryan said, covertly measuring Alfie's expression to see if he'd gotten that guess correct. When Alfie just shrugged like what he'd said was obvious, Ryan continued. "So how come you don't think I have a chance of winning the prize money and the lady?"

Alfie's blue eyes popped open wide. He guffawed like Ryan had told him a hilarious joke. "That's priceless," he muttered as he shook his head, laughing. The other bartender scowled at Alfie for leaving all the work to him. Alfie scurried away momentarily, setting several drinks on a tray. When he returned he took one look at Ryan and started laughing again as if his mirth had never been interrupted. He glanced at Ryan's face and stopped suddenly.

"Wait . . . ya weren't serious, were ya? Uh . . . sorry to have to be the one to break it to ya, fella—you'll still get yer pay, fair and square—but nobody . . . I mean *nobody* beats Big Marlo in any fight, least of all one-on-one in the Sweet Lash's boxing ring." He pointed into the room and Ryan turned. Two men had been busy since he'd last looked and had roped off the center platform with sturdy, utilitarian rope versus the gold braid used on the sideshow areas. It hadn't struck Ryan when he'd originally noticed the center staging area that it was the approximate size of a boxing ring.

He stared incredulously. He was supposed to box some unbeatable foe named Big Marlo for a virgin? This situation became more bizarre by the second. In the back of his mind it kept niggling at him, however, that if he walked out of there in search of Hope, he left the girl upstairs that Alfie had mentioned with a chance of being brutalized by Big Marlo. The detective O'Rourke had obviously been correct about one thing: Diamond Jack Fletcher was most definitely a white slaver just as the twenty-first-century version of him was.

Ryan realized that the room was now entirely filled. Several gaslights suddenly flamed to life along the rim of one of the smaller stages to the right of the boxing ring. The rowdy crowd began clapping and whooping uproariously when they saw Betsey and Mel strut onto the stage. Several of the men pulled women into their laps and began to caress and grope them familiarly while their eyes were trained on the stage. Betsey and Mel flashed their most seductive smiles, occasionally parting the robes they wore to the tops of their large, powdered breasts.

Suddenly Mel, who was the taller and older of the two women, went behind Betsey, reached around her and began lowering Betsey's robe. The men whooped when Betsey pretended to look scandalized and afraid, shaking her head and trying to clutch the robe around her shoulders, conveniently plumping her breasts in the process. Mel swatted her bottom, however, and Betsey, now chastised with head lowered, stood still while Mel removed the robe. She was naked beneath it with the exception of a too tight, black corset that failed to cover either her voluptuous belly and hips or the majority of her generous breasts. The crowd's cheers swelled as Mel possessively ran her hand over Betsey's breasts, belly and thighs. She turned the younger woman's back to the audience and massaged Betsey's curving buttocks to the men's obvious delight.

Mel now made a show of removing her own robe, glancing seductively over her shoulder and lowering it inch by inch. She also wore only a scanty corset, but her costume was supplemented by a pair of supple brown riding boots.

Both women possessed abundant amounts of round flesh, their looks strikingly different from the twenty-first century's concept of svelte beauty. Ryan liked a woman with curves; he found Hope's elegant carriage, narrow waist, full breasts and generously curving hips and ass to be his idea of female perfection, for instance. Betsey's and Mel's dimpled flesh, on the other hand, struck him as blowsy and unhealthy-looking. Not that the Sweet Lash was likely to offer its residents the healthiest of living and working environments, Ryan thought wryly.

He watched with mild interest as Mel picked up a bottle from the stage and gave the men a suggestive look. The men roared their approval, especially when Mel pointed sternly to the floor and Betsey obediently went down on her hands and knees. Mel proceeded to rub oil into Betsey's skin, making her hips, thighs and ass gleam in the gaslights. Their performance was almost as over-the-top contrived as the men's frantic, chest-beating excitement.

The crowd cheered rock-star loud when the blonde parodied a look of stern dissatisfaction and picked up a small, black whip and the redhead reacted with a similarly dramatic expression of anxious desire to please. Betsey squealed when the blonde woman flicked the whip threateningly on the stage to loud applause and appreciative catcalls. Much to Ryan's amazement, at this point of the performance several of the men grabbed a female and hastily headed for the exit and the rooms upstairs. Jack glanced up from his conversation with Mason, smiling and nodding his approval as the couples passed. But Ryan sensed from his narrow-eyed gaze that Jack was checking which men had taken their satisfaction early so that if they should want another round later, Jack got his extra pay.

"There's no chance I'll beat Big Marlo, is that what you're saying?" Ryan asked when he faced Alfie again. Like him, Alfie seemed relatively impervious to the enactment on the stage, matter-of-factly filling a beer from the tap and pouring a glass of gin at once. "Why is that, exactly?"

"Ye've never seen him, eh?" The bartender seemed a tad pitying.

"No, but I'm guessing he didn't earn his name from the size of his heart," Ryan muttered wryly.

Alfie gave him a blank look. "He's a monster. Jack bought him off the Algerian contingent from the Chicago World's Fair years back. They claimed he was the strongest man on earth, and nothing any of the other participating countries or America had to offer could ever prove the Algerians wrong. He dead-weighted more than any man ever before recorded in history. Marlo's so strong he can pull a tree up by its roots and stop a carriage in its tracks."

"What about his boxing skills?"

"What about 'em? Who needs to worry about skills when ya can hammer a guy's head into the floor with yer fist anytime you—"

The last part of Alfie's sentence was cut off when the crowd roared in approval.

Mel's subtle gestures and Betsey's growing excitement made Ryan suspect the two women were familiar lovers. For the first time since they began their theatrics he felt an inkling of arousal. It wasn't so much that he found either of them attractive or that he particularly got off on watching lesbians. It was the glimpse of Mel's dominance and Betsey's submission, the exchange of their energies that had caught his attention more than anything.

During the height of the crowd's excitement over the tawdry spectacle unfolding on the stage, three men had entered the room and immediately approached Diamond Jack and Mason. The five of them retired to a solitary table on a platform directly by the entrance. A big man with a square jaw stood several feet away, staring in a hawk-like manner out at the crowd. Ryan assumed he was one of Jack's henchmen. One of the waitresses brought the men drinks and also handed Jack several sheets of paper and a pencil.

All of the men except for Mason began conversing soberly. Ryan realized Diamond Jack was conducting high-level business. What better place to carry on in secret than in this boisterous crowd where they were sure to go unheard? Both the table and Jack's chair were perfectly positioned for Jack to see everything going on in the large room. Every time a man left with a woman on his arm he made a note on the paper in front of him and another note when they returned. Ryan observed that when the women returned from their forays upstairs they wore significantly less clothing, often nothing more than a petticoat and revealing corset. A few came down wearing frothy negligees, their breasts almost fully exposed beneath the sashes of their robes.

For the most part Mason ignored the men's talk and sat slumped in his chair, watching the Slip and Whip with a fixed, heavy-lidded stare. Despite the fact that he appeared to be no older than twenty-four or -five, he looked distinctly ill, like his body had been hard used. At one point Mason sat up to attention at something Jack had said. He questioned the owner of the Sweet Lash. Jack's terse response made Mason tilt his chin in the general direction of the upstairs of the establishment. When Jack nodded, Mason grinned widely.

Mason's leer made Ryan uneasy. He needed to find Hope. What

if his showing up at the brothel had been related to Hope, after all? There was a woman upstairs, "beautiful as a princess," who'd been forced into coming here. Detective Connor O'Rourke had suspected Diamond Jack of abducting Hope around this time period.

What if the woman upstairs was Hope?

Ryan jerkily stood from the bar stool. What if Jack or one of his henchmen had already killed her?

He was trying to think of a way that he could get past Jack's all-seeing eyes and poke around upstairs in search of the captive young woman Alfie had mentioned. Knowing what Alfie had told him about Marlo's role with the abducted females made Marlo's protracted absence alarming.

He paused when he saw Jack stand and put his hand on the henchman who'd been about to descend the stairs. Jack went down the stairs himself. He stalked over to a table where a balding man had pulled a pretty young woman into his lap and jerked down her dress and corset. He happily fondled a small breast while his other hand was busy beneath her skirts, his eyes glued to the Slip and Whip. When Betsey had begun her lewd humping motions up on the stage, the man had started hopping the prostitute's bottom in his lap at the same rate. Jack must've been wise enough to realize the man was looking for two pops for the price of one, having his pleasure here in public and also upstairs later on.

At first Ryan was thankful for the distraction. He unobtrusively started to move toward the exit and the wooden staircase in the far distance but Alfie almost immediately spoke to him.

"You're not gonna want to miss this, fella," Alfie murmured. Ryan turned to see both Alfie and the other bartender stopped dead in their tracks, eyes trained on Jack's intimidating figure as it progressed across the crowded room. Both men were directly behind Ryan, preventing a surreptitious getaway.

Like the bartenders, he watched as Jack approached the table, yanked the young woman up and shoved her out of the way roughly before he pounded the man's face with a beefy fist. The guy didn't know what hit him. He'd still been grinning lasciviously when he spilled over his chair backward.

"Get outa here. If you try and come back, they'll find you face-down in the alley," Jack snarled when the balding man sat up with a stunned look on his face.

"Big Marlo usually keeps house down here," Alfie told Ryan by way of explanation. "Jack's gotta watch over things while he's gone."

Ryan cleared his throat. "Look, I need to get some fresh air, you know?"

Alfie shook his head quickly. "Ye ain't going nowhere, friend. Marlo'll be here any minute." He nodded his head to the stage, where the whipping had now ceased. Mel knelt behind her lover, her face buried between a moaning Betsey's thighs. "The Slip and Whip's near finished. Ye're up next, fella."

Ryan sat back down on the stool while he narrowly studied the room. It was so dim he couldn't tell if there were any back entrances or not.

Betsey's moans became louder as she neared what appeared to be a genuine climax.

"Whip the bitch!" a muscular, stocky man who was clearly drunk yelled from a center table. Mel and Betsey had given their pound of flesh to the demanding men, however, and now appeared to be completely involved in each other. There were men in the audience who clearly appreciated the sensual display of Mel pleasuring Betsey with her mouth and tongue, but a few others echoed the man's desire for more brutality.

Ryan glanced over at Jack, curious as to how he would handle the belligerent man as he grew louder, eventually stood and moved toward the stage. Jack had returned to his seat, and although he glanced over when the man bawled again for more whipping, his attention clearly remained on business. Jack had his priorities, it would seem, and establishing that men couldn't come into the Sweet Lash and hope to cheat him of a dollar was one of them.

The safety of the women apparently was not.

Something about the jerk's fixed, ugly expression sent off a warning bell in his head. At first Ryan didn't understand what the guy was doing as he fumbled at his waist, but then Ryan saw him pull off his belt with a snap.

The man leapt onto the stage, the leather belt doubled in his hand, and began to viciously strike both Betsey and Mel. Betsey cried out in stark pain, her flesh having already been abused by the whip. Several people called out in anger, but a few others cheered on the stocky man.

Mel bared her teeth in fury and gripped the belt, stilling the attacker's actions. She kicked at the man's shins with her riding boots. He cursed and grabbed her shoulders, shoving her down forcefully. Mel's head smacked into the floor of the platform. The man with the belt raised his hand over his head, poised to beat the stunned woman.

Ryan caught the attacker's wrist and jerked his other hand behind his back at the same time. He pressed the man's body into him, taking his weight with relative ease and tilting the struggling man off balance, diminishing the power of his short, muscular legs. Ryan pushed the man's wrist up his spine until his fist pressed against his skull.

The man screamed in pain as bone threatened to pop out of a socket or break at any second given the amount of pressure applied to it.

Ryan let up slightly and spoke into the trembling man's ear. "If you don't get off this stage and walk out of the Sweet Lash right now, I'm gonna break your shoulder. Do you understand?"

The man grunted in profound pain.

"I need an answer. Yes or no?"

This time the guy grated out a "yeah." Ryan turned him around and prodded him off the stage. No sooner had he released him, however, when the man whipped around, fist clenched, and aimed at Ryan's gut. Ryan palmed his fist, stopping it instantly, and served him a brisk left hook to the jaw. The man whipped around like a ballerina doing a pirouette. He caught the velvet rope on his face-first fall from the stage, landing heavily on the dingy floor.

Ryan hopped down next to him but apparently the man'd had enough. He scuttled up onto his knees, gripping his jaw as he staggered away, the golden rope catching on his legs and making him trip and fall facedown on the grimy floor. The crowd laughed uproariously and applauded Ryan.

Ryan saw his chance to escape the room and forced the guy to his feet, prodding him toward the exit. The jerk went willingly enough this time, but suddenly the henchman with the square jaw was there to take over, shoving the stocky man ahead of him and charging threateningly behind, herding him out of the brothel.

Ryan cursed softly under his breath when he saw Diamond Jack heading toward him. He glanced back and noticed that Mel was gently settling Betsey's robe on her shoulders, careful of the abrasions on the young woman's back. She regarded Ryan with a mixed expression of gratitude and open curiosity. A strange sense of familiarity went through him when he met her brown-eyed stare. She nodded once in wary thanks. She looked much older up close and Ryan realized she was probably twice Betsey's age.

Ryan gave an answering nod and turned around to await Diamond Jack. He honestly didn't know how the crime boss would react to him jumping up on the stage to protect the prostitutes, and Jack's set, cold visage gave nothing away. Some of the members of the seedy crowd had enjoyed the violent spectacle of the man beating the women, after all. Ryan had seen some nasty business as a vice detective, but this was one hell of a depraved crowd. He supposed that made sense, because Diamond Jack was one hell of a scumbag.

He tensed when Jack reached for his breast pocket.

"Well, it looks like Shapiro finally sent us someone who knows what he's doing," Jack said as he withdrew a cigar from his pocket and handed it to Ryan. When Ryan refused to take the cigar, he merely shrugged negligently and shoved it in his own mouth. He spoke loud enough for Ryan to hear him but was careful to keep his voice from carrying to the crowd.

"I want to thank you." He nodded his head toward the stage. "I had the odds for the fight set at twenty to one. The last eight guys Shapiro sent over didn't last thirty seconds in the ring with Marlo. Betting has been sluggish. Guys come for the blood," Jack explained as he tilted his head toward a man sitting at a raised podium at the far side of the room. Indeed, dozens of men queued up and money was quickly changing hands. "Because of your little demonstration there, I've changed the odds to ten to one. Those guys think you might cause an upset."

"You think you know better, though, right?"

Jack gave him a viper-like grin before he plunged his own soggy cigar back in his mouth. "I'll take a couple hundred bets on ten to one versus twenty on twenty to one any day."

"Course if Marlo loses, you're not going to be so pleased," Ryan said quietly as he scanned the packed room.

"*Sure*, fella," Jack chortled around his cigar.

"Shapiro was a little hazy on the details, so I just wanted to clarify my pay before the match."

"Fifteen bucks cash at the end of the match," Jack replied briskly.

"And if I win?"

Jack removed his cigar although some of the tobacco remained clinging to his stained front teeth. His eyelids narrowed speculatively. "Alfie was telling me you've never seen Big Marlo. I can tell from your accent you aren't just off the boat," Jack mused. "Where do you live?"

"Bridgeport," Ryan said. Surely the distinctively Irish-American, south-side neighborhood existed in 1906, didn't it?

"I've got some Irish in my background as well," Jack finally murmured after a moment of studying Ryan with his beady, dark eyes. "The prize purse for the boxing match is fifty dollars. That's a lot of money for a mick like you."

"What else?"

Jack's eyebrows went up at Ryan's hard tone. "I see Alfie's been talking again. Well, can't see there's any harm in it. Most of these men know I fire Marlo's interest in fighting with the promise of sampling a young lady's charms upstairs. He enjoys the unplucked ones," Jack explained with a taut leer.

"So if I win the match, I'll be granted the same pleasure," Jack stated bluntly. He wanted Jack to put the deal into words.

"Like I said, you've got balls," Jack murmured. Ryan returned his stare unwaveringly.

Jack eventually shrugged. "Sure, that's the prize to the winner, even if the winner isn't Big Marlo." He once again gave Ryan a cool once-over. "You'd do just as well as anyone for what I have in mind."

"What's the girl look like?"

The laughter faded from around Jack's thin lips. "All of my girls are beauties. Haven't you been satisfied by what you've seen here so far tonight?" he asked, his cadence and tone reverting back to the easy drawl of a southern gentleman.

Ryan gave a small shrug and watched the money rapidly changing hands at the betting station. "They're all right. But if what you've got upstairs is nicer, you should speak up. You said you like to motivate Big Marlo before a match. Don't I deserve the same treatment?" He acutely felt Jack's assessing gaze on him and wondered if he'd gone too far.

"And what'd motivate you?"

"I don't like blondes or redheads. Only brunettes do it for me. Dark hair, dark eyes."

"Is that right?" Jack murmured. "Well, you're in luck, son, because I have the most stunning brunette in five states waiting most patiently upstairs for the victor to join her in bed. Eyes like liquid midnight and skin so white, soft and smooth it'd make a grown man want to weep. I've got some fine fun planned for the man who breaks this beauty in. I want to see some real action in that bed upstairs. Get the picture?" Jack asked, tapping his hand on Ryan's chest and giving him a shrewd, knowing look.

Ryan gave a closedmouth grin to hide his clenched teeth and raised his eyebrows in what he hoped was a passable expression of lechery.

"Don't get your hopes up, though, kid," Jack said.

"Why's that?"

"It'll never happen. Because *that's* your opponent." Jack pointed with his cigar to the entrance of the room. Diamond Jack laughed when he saw Ryan's eyes widen in shock.

"Still, you promise to make it interesting, kid, even if it is just an *interesting* slaughter."

∽ ELEVEN ∽

Ten minutes later Ryan could hardly hear himself think the din in the Sweet Lash had grown so loud. He carefully folded his coat and placed it on the floor of the platform just outside the ring. His tie and shirt soon followed. He glanced at the pile of clothing and frowned, knowing his gun was in there. He really didn't have anywhere else to leave the items, though, and there were more pressing matters to consider at the moment.

Ryan crawled through the ropes, testing their tautness and strength with a casual strum of his fingers. The men had drawn them sufficiently tight and tied them off on the four steel posts at the corners.

A tinny bell rang. Ryan batted his knuckles together twice in a habitual gesture. Strange to feel his own skin and bone. Big Marlo and he were expected to fight bare-fisted. Considering how much this crowd loved blood, he shouldn't have been surprised.

Ryan swallowed through a dry throat as he moved to face his opponent. A liquid-like, knee-weakening sensation sunk through him and it took Ryan a moment to recognize it as pure, unmitigated fear—fear for Hope if he didn't succeed in beating Marlo.

No sooner was he aware of the emotion than he pushed it back to the periphery. Ryan knew what unbridled fear and anger could do to you in the ring.

Jesus Christ, was it his imagination or had he seen Chicago World's Fair posters of Big Marlo posing as one of the many oddities on the circus-like atmosphere of the Midway Plaisance? Marlo was a behemoth. A freak of nature, as far as Ryan could tell. The bald Algerian towered perhaps six inches over Ryan's six feet four. He wore a thick black mustache beneath a curved hook of a nose. The abundant hair at his upper lip almost covered a vicious-looking slash of a mouth. Muscle bulged on his shoulders, chest and arms, but he'd started to go to fat on his belly and back. The guy was thick everywhere, the sheer bulk of him being what had stunned Ryan when Jack pointed out Big Marlo's entrance several minutes ago.

No wonder they claimed Marlo could stop a carriage in its tracks. He looked about the weight of one of the steel-clad vehicles. The guy probably had in excess of 150 pounds on Ryan.

He was slow, though, Ryan reminded himself, trying his best to still his racing heart. Ryan'd have to take advantage of his sloth-like movement.

Marlo lumbered forward to meet him at the center of the ring. He planted his big feet and came to a complete standstill, making it easy for Ryan to maintain the perfect distance. The giant looked confused by Ryan's limber footwork. He swiped at him with the biggest paw Ryan'd ever seen in his life. Ryan avoided the punch with an almost negligible fade of his torso.

Difficult not to miss a huge, slow-moving target like that.

Marlo took several more wide shots, which Ryan avoided with

ease. The crowd jeered the big man's ineffective efforts. Since Marlo was so cordial about leaving his big body as exposed as the desert to the wind, Ryan got in a few punches into the midriff.

Marlo snarled in annoyance and came at him throwing a barrage of punches, most of which Ryan managed to either avoid, duck or minimize. The giant's technique was sloppy, so Ryan had no difficulty landing three tight jabs to Marlo's midsection while his opponent continued to throw wide. The guy may have accumulated some flab on the gut, but he was solid as a rock beneath it. Still, he could tell by Marlo's grunts and widening eyes that he'd aimed well.

Some of his typical confidence in the boxing ring began to return until Marlo penetrated, landing a meaty, thwacking punch to Ryan's solar plexus. A guttural groan exploded out of Ryan's lungs and throat as pain slammed into him with the force of a charging locomotive.

For a few breathless seconds every nerve in Ryan's torso shrieked in protest. Even his heart throbbed in pain, utterly forgetting its purpose. Ryan barely had the presence of mind to clumsily duck beneath Marlo's swinging arm and stagger to the center of the ring, his eyes streaming tears down his face.

Damn, that fucker had a hammering punch when he managed to land it right. Ryan took his first full breath shakily and vowed then and there to make sure he minimized at all costs Marlo's chance of a dead-on swing again.

Now that he had the sure knowledge that Marlo could fell him with one well-placed blow, Ryan's focus narrowed and sharpened even further. This was do or die. He couldn't let that asshole win. The mere thought of Marlo even looking at Hope hardened Ryan's already stiff resolve.

The crowd booed when Ryan used his quickness and agility to avoid Marlo's punches for the rest of the first round and for a majority of the second, but Ryan could have cared less. His goal was to exhaust the slow-moving giant while at the same time to make every one of his own infrequent punches penetrate and pay richly.

By the time the bell signaled the beginning of the fourth round, Ryan conceded that his strategy of dancing just outside of Marlo's reach and taunting the behemoth like an annoying fly was having its effect. Marlo had swung thirty punches for every one of Ryan's, but the majority of them had been either entirely ineffective or glancing blows. Ryan's, on the other hand, had been far more accurate, including a nailing left that had not only put Marlo's right eye out of commission for the remainder of the match, but also caused the giant to sway on his feet for a few seconds while the crowd roared in excitement.

Ryan also showed the signs of battle, not having been able to successfully evade every one of Marlo's flurry of combinations. His ribs were bruised fairly badly and it burned like hell just to breathe. He tried not to dwell on the effect of using his bare fists to hammer flesh and bone. All in all, however, he had good reason to be hopeful, Ryan thought as he watched Big Marlo tip a tankard to his mouth in his corner, slopping what looked like beer all over his already perspiration-soaked body. Ryan's breathing was hardly escalated while Marlo still panted from his last bout of wild punches and ineffective pursuance of Ryan around the ring.

Now that he'd gotten Marlo used to his tactics of buzz and sting, however, Ryan was going to have to change things up and take a risk.

The bell went off and Ryan tapped his knuckles twice, this time much more tenderly due to the cuts and bruises on his fists.

Marlo's eyes went wide when Ryan stormed the center of the ring. His brief shock at Ryan's aggressive attack gave Ryan the advantage. He pounded the behemoth with a combination to the liver, ribs and head before he danced back to his typical out-fighter distance. His last jab at the giant's head had been particularly precise, causing Marlo to stumble back and blood droplets to spray through the air in an arc.

Ryan was only vaguely aware of the boom of approving cheers and applause from the crowd of men, every one of whom was on their feet at this point. Ryan narrowed his gaze on his stunned foe, knowing the fury and pain Marlo experienced at his offensive attack would be mixed with a good dose of adrenaline. That adrenaline would eventually exhaust Marlo even further.

But right at this very second, it would make the giant exponentially more dangerous. Ryan was going to have to take his punishment.

He'd tried to prepare himself but when Marlo's counterattack came, blind panic flashed through him for a second. Marlo may have been unsteady on his feet after that last right hook to his head, but he was mad enough to move three times as quickly as he normally did. It was like having a slavering, rabid bear charge him. Marlo gave a savage yell as he ran toward him, spittle shooting in front of his gray teeth, the whites of his eyes showing ominously. Ryan managed to minimize his first two wild punches by moving away from their momentum, but Marlo caught him with a tight jab to his right brow.

For a nauseating few seconds the lights from the gas chandeliers multiplied before his eyes. As if from a distance Ryan saw a sea of blurred, manic, frenzied faces and punching hands. The loud roar of the crowd slammed into his awareness after a prolonged peaceful moment of total silence.

A white-hot blade of pain pierced his head simultaneously.

He realized that Marlo's blow had spun him face-first into the ropes. He barely had time to turn around and put up his fists and forearms to protect his head and chest before Marlo flew into him.

Ryan relied on the ropes to absorb the impact of Marlo's swings while he tried to regain his equilibrium. He could tell by the Algerian's flurry of wide, blunt punches that he was not only frustrated, but increasingly exhausted. Ryan protected his head, chest and liver as best as he could and allowed Marlo the opportunity to tire himself out even further.

He wasn't above taunting him to add mental exhaustion to the physical.

"That all you got, big boy? *Huh?* What . . . do ya save all the good stuff for the women?" Ryan shouted behind the relative protection of his fists and forearms. "No wonder all these assholes think you're so tough. Anybody can look like the strongest man on earth when they hit a woman that's a third their weight."

Marlo growled between pants, his snarl showing off teeth stained even blacker with tobacco juice than Jack's had been. He let loose with another volley of blunt blows. Ryan grunted as one out of the dozens of glancing punches made direct contact on his ribs. His eyes popped wide. He ground his jaw together and shouted hoarsely through clenched teeth at the vicious explosion of pain that resonated through his flesh.

Ryan didn't think he could survive another direct hit like that. Still, he forced himself to wait, knowing there were crueler and more inevitable foes in a boxing match than a pounding fist. Marlo fought against an out-of-shape heart and lungs, fading adrenaline and sheer frustration at that moment, more than anything.

When he saw the Algerian stagger on his feet, temporarily losing his balance, Ryan put all the fuel he had into a rocketing uppercut to the jaw.

Marlo's huge bald head lurched back, his body following suit as he staggered to the center of the ring. He followed him with a barrage of punches, terminating with a chopping shot to the head powered by nearly everything Ryan had left in him.

When Marlo went down he went down harder than anything Ryan'd ever felled in the ring. Even so, the eruption of the crowd nearly drowned out the resounding crash of 340 pounds of deadweight against protesting wood board.

Ryan felt someone put his hand on his wrist and raise it. The audience roared its approval. It took him a second to realize Diamond Jack himself stood at center ring declaring him the winner.

"You did it, son. I'm still flat on my ass. And it was such a spectacular match I'm even going to forgive you for losing what I would have had if you hadn't changed the odds to ten to one. Besides, I'll make out like a sultan on the rematch," Jack informed him gleefully over the din of the crowd. "So what d'ya say to that?"

"I say I'm ready for my prize," Jack muttered through tight lips as he lowered his arm forcefully.

"I've got your money right over here."

"That's not the prize I was referring to," Ryan said, meeting Jack's dark, beady eyes. "Take me to her."

For a moment Jack looked slightly taken aback by his intensity but then he laughed uproariously. "You're eager for it, aren't you, son? Well, you won't be disappointed. Come on. A deal's a deal."

Jack signaled with his head toward the exit.

"Just a minute. I need to get my clothes."

"What's the matter?" Jack asked warmly when he heard Ryan mutter a vicious curse a second later.

"My clothes are gone," Ryan hissed.

And so is my gun.

"Damn," Jack said angrily as he glanced around the packed room. "Someone must have nicked them during the frenzy of the knockout. Slimy little sneak thief. Ah well, what can I do? I try to run a nice place but . . . Hey! Where you going, son?"

Ryan jumped down to the main floor and approached the closest table where four men sat, one of them with a half-nude woman sprawled in his lap. They all looked up at Ryan in surprise.

"Did you see someone steal my stuff during the match?" Ryan demanded. He studied each of their faces in turn. Three of them gave him blank stares but the woman and one of the men glanced nervously behind Ryan's shoulder before they shook their heads. Ryan turned to where they'd been looking.

"It's rough luck, son, but your prize money will get you plenty of new clothes," Jack shouted down to him with a winning grin. "Come on, I thought you were all fired up to go upstairs."

Several of the men at the table wolf whistled behind him. "Hope you're nicer to your gal than you were to Marlo, mister."

The full impact of Ryan's frustration must have carried in his glare at the men because they shut their mouths quickly enough. He followed Jack toward the exit of the room. When they reached the hallway, which was garishly decorated with gilt mirrors and crimson wallpaper, Ryan suddenly realized that all four of the men who had sat at the table with Jack followed them.

Ryan paused. Jack and the four men stopped with him.

"That was one hell of a match," a well-groomed man with thick gray whiskers told him.

"Spectacular," another said.

"I'll never forget it as long as I live, seeing you bring down the mighty Marlo," a third added jovially.

Ryan studied each of them in turn. With the exception of Mason, all three men were middle-aged and affluent-looking. He imagined he might find them in any number of "respectable" places during the day, church, family gatherings and even Prairie Avenue. Diamond Jack must afford them any number of opportunities for extra "business," not to mention an outlet for their more seedy desires.

"Thanks. But I don't need company to appreciate my prize," Ryan said quietly.

Mason rolled his eyes in disgust. "You can't let this lout have her," he whined to Jack. "Look at him. A big, sweaty paddy and you're turning him loose on Ho—"

"Keep your drunken mouth shut," Jack ordered. He gave Mason a wilting once-over. "I suppose you'd like her father to figure out it was *you* in the photos? Or maybe you'd prefer your *own* daddy saw them."

Ryan tensed, his eyes traveling up the stairs anxiously. "What the hell are you talking about?"

Jack pulled his withering glare off Mason. "I was about to explain about that, son."

"I'm listening, unless your explanation has anything to do with me not getting my prize."

Jack looked insulted. "I'm a man of my word. The girl is yours." He paused when Mason made a sound of disgust. Jack waved Ryan over to the periphery of the large hallway for a private word. He put his hand on Ryan's shoulder as he spoke. "Here's the thing. This girl's no ordinary whore. You're a lucky man to win her. As you might be able to guess from Mason's reaction, half the men in Chicago would give their left nut to be in your shoes at this moment."

"So?" Ryan prompted tersely. He grew more and more impatient with Jack's machinations. After Mason's near slip, Ryan was now 99 percent sure the woman upstairs was Hope. His desperation to see her pushed at him like a shove from the inside, making him want to forego the role he'd played unwillingly here tonight and rush up the stairs. A quick survey of the large foyer and the front door, however, had already told him that Jack's henchmen abounded.

A man wearing a black hat guarded the front door, taking the admittance fees of latecomers. A blond man stood like a sentinel at the foot of the stairs, a pistol shoved into his pants in clear sight for all potential troublemakers to see. Ryan would wager there'd be *at least* one more guard upstairs in order to control any situations that occurred while the prostitutes entertained the Sweet Lash's guests.

Escaping Jack's brutal, efficiently run brothel wasn't going to be easy. It'd be one thing if he was alone, but getting Hope out safely might require some finesse. Charging up the stairs and raising a ruckus as he searched room after room was likely only going to result in getting them both killed.

If only his gun hadn't been stolen.

"So I just want you to realize how fortunate you are," Jack answered with a hard look. "You'll have that girl, just like I promised. But there are some extenuating circumstances."

"Such as?"

"Well, first of all, these men here"—he nodded at Mason and the three sleek gentlemen—"will want to witness the event. Along with myself, of course. It's not every day one gets the opportunity to see something of this caliber."

"No."

Jack's eyebrows went up in genuine amazement at Ryan's simple, firm statement.

"There was nothing like that in the agreement. I want her to myself," Ryan added.

Jack removed his hand from Ryan's shoulder, forgoing the façade of a friendly chat. "You really don't have any choice in the matter, son. I need a man for the part. If you don't want the girl, I'll just turn her over to Marlo. He'll recover from his beating soon enough."

Ryan's nostrils flared in anger but he said nothing.

"You get the point now, I see. Best to just go along with the program, son. The young lady must be kept restrained during her initiation. If you release her before the deed is done, I'll be severely displeased. You will also be required to use some . . . implements: a whip, a crop, a flogger. In addition to sodomy, these are the things that make the Sweet Lash so popular, you see. The more scandalous the goings-on in that bed, the better. I have my friends to consider. For the price they've paid to watch, I won't be the only one who's highly displeased if you don't perform up to standards."

"I thought you said she was a virgin," Ryan muttered through teeth clenched in fury.

"She is, she is. You can see why my gentlemen friends are so eager to witness the event. The truth be told, she's a minister's daughter!" Jack laughed as if he'd just told the punch line to a joke. His humor faded quickly when he noticed Ryan's expression. "Haven't got much of a sense of humor, have you, boy?"

"Just take me to her," Ryan muttered, sick to the point of nausea from conversing with Jack. Nothing mattered more at that moment than seeing Hope. He'd have to figure out the rest when he fully understood the landscape.

"There's one other thing, son. One of my men will be photographing the . . . event. For posterity's sake," Jack added with a slashing grin.

Ryan went entirely still. Jack must have misunderstood his rigid, shocked expression.

"Don't worry. My photographer knows his instructions. He never photographs the details of the man's face; just the back of him and the . . . crucial body parts."

Jack took a wary step back when Ryan closed in on him. "You want the photographs to blackmail someone, *am I right?*"

Jack's clamping jaws loosened around his cigar. "I don't suppose it hurts if you know it. You're correct."

"A fiancé? A father?" Ryan prodded. Much to his rising dismay, he already knew the answer, however.

Jack merely shrugged.

Ryan's mind spun like an out-of-control carnival ride for a second. But then it was as if someone hit a switch and the flurry of activity slowed and settled into place.

He knew what he had to do.

"Any asshole with a cock and a sick mind can rape a helpless woman," Ryan told Jack stonily. "Has it ever occurred to you that the photographs would carry a bit more . . . punch, let's say, to her lover or her minister father if the lady in question was shown to be enjoying herself instead of merely being forced?"

Jack's glance down over Ryan was disparaging while his trip back up was more assessing . . . more cunning.

"You think that's a possibility, eh? Well, I've said you've got balls from the start. The girl's a frigid one, though, from the information I've been given."

"From assholes like Mason? Does it surprise you she'd be cold to the likes of him?"

Jack chuckled. "No, I suppose it doesn't."

"I can do it. I can entice her to respond. I'll give you what you want. You'll be happy with the photographs you get. There's just one thing. I won't be able to get her to participate to any degree if she knows she's being photographed. I can't do miracles. I doubt she'll be too interested in romance if she knows your . . . *business partners* are watching, either," Ryan muttered as he gave a disparaging glance to the four scumbags dressed in gentlemen's clothing. He was just playing for time and a little privacy with Hope. If he could just have that, he'd finagle a means of escape. He *had* to.

"Not a problem."

Ryan started at Jack's almost nonchalant acceptance. He hadn't expected that.

He glanced over in rising wariness when a tall, thin man carrying a black box that Ryan recognized as an old-fashioned brownie snapshot camera approached the other men. He nodded his readiness at Jack.

"What'd you mean it's not a problem?" Ryan asked cautiously.

"The bedroom where the young lady awaits you is equipped with a viewing room. Some of my patrons enjoy watching the goings-on in the boudoirs at the Sweet Lash as much as participating. Miss Stillwater won't know she's being viewed through the peepholes and there's a large enough knothole for my man to take photographs."

Jack stated things so confidently that Ryan was left in little doubt he'd had plenty of experience with this sort of sordid business in the past.

"Just take me to her and make sure you and your men stay well out of the way," Ryan muttered. He was already contriving a plan for snatching Hope once the men were secreted in the "viewing room," having her wait while he took on the guy at the base of the stairs and commandeered his gun, then escaping this hellhole with her in tow.

He started to step away but Jack stopped him with a hand on his elbow. Ryan froze when his eyes lowered and he saw Jack pointing his SIG Sauer directly at his chest.

"This is an extremely unusual weapon that you possess, Mr. Daire," he said softly. "It's making me mighty curious about you." Jack's eyebrows went up on his doughy forehead when Ryan remained silent. "Nothing to say, son? I'd sure like to hear where you got a contraption like this."

"It's manufactured in Switzerland. Very rare."

"Is that right?" Jack murmured silkily. "Strange, that a mick from Bridgeport would own such a weapon. It looks accurate and as deadly a gun as I've ever seen in my life. I just want you to know it will be trained on you the entire time from one of the peepholes in the viewing room. If you don't do everything as agreed, I'll gladly test out this strange-looking weapon directly on your head. Big Marlo will be all too glad to step in to take your place with the girl, I assure you. I've always found his methods to be most effective in the past."

Ice water streamed through Ryan's veins in a torrential rush when he glanced over to where Jack motioned with his head. Big Marlo had regained consciousness. He walked into the foyer. His fierce, furious, one-eyed gaze on Ryan belied the giant's blood-smeared face and unsteady gait.

"Just take me to her," Ryan muttered stiffly. "And keep that damn photographer from flashing any photographs when she has her eyes open."

Ryan felt a grim sense of inevitability several moments later as he walked with the rest of the men down a long, gaslit hallway. Jack nodded to a closed door. Ryan opened it, lingering for a second in the entrance. He watched Jack's cronies file into the next door down the hall into the room Ryan assumed was the "viewing room." Jack closed the door behind Ryan and turned a key in the lock.

He entered warily, taking in the garish decorations, the alcove where the bed was situated . . . the stunning, dark-haired woman that lay restrained to it.

The last time he'd seen the room it'd been in a black-and-white image, but he recognized it nevertheless. A quick glance at the wall to the left of the alcove confirmed there were plenty of peepholes cleverly concealed in the design of the wallpaper. Although he couldn't make it out without staring, one of them was obviously large enough for the lens of a camera.

He knew this for many reasons, the most important of which being that he'd seen the result of that camera's endeavors in the twenty-first century. As fate would have it, he—Ryan—had been the one in those photos along with Hope.

A sense of desperation pressed down on his chest when he noticed the items that had been placed strategically on the bedside table for the purposes of Hope Stillwater's ravishment and degradation: a leather flogger, a whippy-looking crop, a bottle of oil, a wooden paddle.

He approached the bed slowly. The dull ache of his injuries from the boxing match was nothing compared to the deep pain he experienced for Hope—for the ugliness of this situation. He took heart at seeing the flush of color in her cheeks. She was either unconscious or sleeping.

She would likely never forgive him when she learned about his part in the plan.

And even more intimidating to consider: what if his presence in the past made no difference whatsoever in Hope's death? That was *him* in those photographs with Hope, after all. Maybe his trip to save her had somehow already become an integral factor in the events that led up to her murder.

He heard a muffled knock coming from the wall to the left of the alcove and knew he couldn't deliberate on time paradoxes at the moment. He needed to focus on keeping them both alive—second to second. If he endangered himself, he endangered Hope. If Jack killed him, Big Marlo would be sent in and Hope would be photographed with her rapist instead of her lover.

Her rapist and quite possibly her murderer.

Ryan's mouth twisted slightly when he realized he'd referred to himself in his mind as Hope's lover. But that's what he was, wasn't he? What else would you call a guy foolish enough to come back in time in order to claim her from death's grip?

Love is not time's fool, Ryan recalled as he checked the pulse at Hope's neck, relieved to feel its strength and regularity.

He eased onto the bed, reclining next to her. The feeling of her curving, soft body felt good. The intoxicating scent of gardenias and sweet, succulent woman entered his nostrils. He inhaled slowly, letting the fragrance beguile him for a few precious seconds into forgetfulness of their foul circumstances.

God, he wished this could be different. But what else could he do? He was going to have to make love to this exquisite woman here, in front of these depraved assholes. He thought of waking her and whispering the truth to her, begging her to go along with Jack's plan until a more likely moment came for their escape. But something wouldn't allow him to do that to her. He didn't want to expose her to the details of the sordid situation.

He knew she'd never be able to let go . . . to find fulfillment instead of become humiliated if he told her about the greedy men who observed them. And if she balked, they'd send in Marlo . . .

Ryan swallowed convulsively as he pressed his mouth to her throbbing pulse, awestruck by the silkiness of her fragrant skin beneath his worshipping lips. The miracle of her presence, of being able to touch her at will penetrated his awareness fully for the first time.

He had to make this as palatable as possible for her. For Hope's sake, he needed to find a way to transcend this ugly situation . . . to take her to a place where only the two of them existed. When he'd viewed those photographs in the twenty-first century, it'd never occurred once to him that the woman was being forced. The expression that had radiated from her lovely face in those photos couldn't possibly be mistaken for anything but pure ecstasy. Hope would submit to him . . . submit to her own desire, no matter how unlikely the circumstances.

In that moment, Ryan *knew* he could do it, because thanks to the evidence of the photos . . . he already had.

⌒ TWELVE ⌒

Hope luxuriated in a delicious drowsy world where Ryan nuzzled and kissed her neck. His low, rough voice whispering in her ear caused shivers to race down her spine and her nipples to pinch tight against the cool sheet in anticipation of pleasure.

"Wake up, honey."

Her eyelids fluttered open. "Oh. I'm dreaming," she whispered through leaden lips when she saw Ryan lying beside her. He leaned his head on one braced hand and stared down at her. His scent filled her nostrils, making her dizzy with desire. He smelled rich, male and musky, but she caught the underlying odor of clean soap.

"I'm sorry. I had a . . . workout of sorts earlier and no chance to shower."

Her gaze sharpened on him. Her brow crinkled in puzzlement. "Workout? *Shower*?" Hope whispered, confused as much by his apologetic tone as his odd word usage. She blinked in rising disorientation as reality slammed into her. Her head jerked up off the pillow.

"Ryan!"

"Shhhh," he commanded tautly. He nuzzled her ear once again and whispered. "We're in a dangerous place, beauty. Speak very softly."

"But there's a cut on your brow. And you *shaved*!" she exclaimed in a muted voice as she turned her head toward him.

She watched as his sculpted, firm lips twitched with humor. Her heart seemed to surge against her breastbone. But *Lord*, Ryan Vincent Daire was a handsome man.

"Is that all you have to say?" he teased in a low rumble. "I came back from the year 2008 to find you, and the thing you're most concerned about is the fact that I shaved?"

Hope gaped at him for a long moment. Almost as if Ryan knew precisely that she was about to try to rise into a sitting position, examine her surroundings and demand he tell her precisely what was going on, he spoke tautly.

"Stay still, Hope. Trust me," he murmured. She felt his hand moving ever so gently along the back of her neck. She winced when his fingertips ran over the back of her skull.

"You've got a nice goose egg back here. Are you dizzy?"

"No, I—" She gasped as memory came crashing back. Panic rose in her gut like a swelling wave and stifled her lungs. "Oh God. Diamond Jack Fletcher murdered that poor woman!"

"Quietly," Ryan murmured. She saw a muscle leap with tension in his lean cheek. His nostrils flared slightly as he stared down at her. "The walls and doors in the Sweet Lash are thin. You saw Jack murder someone?"

"Sadie Holcrum. She worked for him here in the Sweet Lash. I think this is her room. Diamond Jack sent her to Central Station to lure me. Marvin Evercrumb, one of the men Jack employs for his white slavery operation, hit me over the head once Sadie got me to the ladies' lounge and they brought me here. Did you come through the mirror?" she whispered, abruptly changing the topic. She couldn't get over the fact that Ryan was here, lying next to her, incredibly real and solid. She was wild with curiosity and excitement over his presence, no matter how bizarre and dangerous the circumstances.

He nodded.

"Did you come to save me?"

His small, wry smile caused a delicious heat to spread in her lower belly.

"And doing a hell of a job of it, it would seem. I ended up at the Sweet Lash unexpectedly, but I suppose it makes sense considering you're here. I won't bore you with all the details at present; I'll just say Jack figured I was up to something. We're being held prisoner in this room for the night."

Her eyes sprang wide.

"Don't worry. I'll get us out."

"You know . . . I believe you will," she replied softly.

The heat spread to become an ache between her thighs when Ryan's singular greenish-blue gaze sunk to her mouth.

"Hope . . ."

His dark head dipped and she was inundated with the pleasure of his firm mouth moving over her own, shaping her flesh to his, nibbling and plucking at her lips as though he considered them to be the most succulent of sensual delicacies. He lightly caressed his tongue along the seam of her lips. A shiver rippled down her spine and her womb tightened in a spasm of desire. He continued to mold her flesh to his, sandwiching first her lower lip between his own, and then the upper until she reciprocated the caress hungrily.

"Open," he whispered, his breath creating a warm mist on her seeking lips. She parted her mouth although she was confused by his request. His sleek tongue penetrated, just the tip moving inside her mouth and making a gentle sweep to capture her taste. When

Hope touched her tongue to his, however, he groaned and leaned down over her.

Her eyes sprang wide at first when his tongue demanded full entrance, probing her depths possessively. He continued to seal his lips to hers, creating a slight suction that created a simultaneous tug at her sex. She gasped at the sensation. For some reason Ryan's penetration of her mouth called to mind how his penis had pushed into her body, how his flesh had rubbed and probed and agitated her own until she'd wanted to scream in mindless need and pleasure.

He came down over her further, his kiss becoming more demanding. He lightly pressed his chest to the tips of her breasts. Her back arched up into him, craving the sensation of his hard planes against her soft curves.

Ryan growled deep in his throat, the sound thrilling her.

When he gently sealed their kiss and lifted his head, Hope pulled against her restraints, her lips instinctively seeking out more of his taste and the intoxicating pressure of his molding mouth. He raised his hand, looking as though he was preparing to touch her face . . . her lips. He grimaced suddenly and lowered it.

"What?" she whispered.

"There's a bowl and pitcher of water over there. I need to wash. My hands are bloody."

Hope stared at his knuckles, seeing how they were bruised and cut for the first time. "Oh no, you're hurt. Did you fight someone?" she asked quietly as he moved off the bed and stood.

He nodded. She watched him as he went over to the bureau where Sadie had collected the water she'd requested earlier. Fear rose up in her stomach and tightened her throat in a powerful wave at the horrible memory of seeing Diamond Jack Fletcher murder Sadie in such a callous, cold-blooded manner.

"Ryan, how are we going to get out of here?"

He turned abruptly from his actions of pouring water into a bowl at her question.

"We're going to be safe. I'm not going to let anything happen to you. We're going to walk out of this hellhole by morning. I have a plan. The only thing is . . ."

"What?" Hope asked when he seemed to hesitate. He turned away, finding the soap and dipping his hands in the water.

"We have to sit tight for a while. They're not going to bother us until dawn at least. Diamond Jack locked us in here," he murmured as he washed his hands.

"But how will—" Hope began more loudly.

"Shhhh," Ryan interrupted her. He'd kept his face turned away from her while he'd hushed her, the resulting sound so soft it'd barely interrupted her question. Hope watched silently as he washed his face, her gaze moving hungrily over his flexing back muscles, trim hips and tight buttocks. His legs looked impossibly long in the black pants he wore.

He picked up a towel from the bureau and dried his face and hands, being extra tender around his cut brow. Hope opened her mouth to question him about his actions when he finished, but a warning seemed to flash in his cerulean eyes when he turned toward her. His handsome face looked rigid and shadowed, but his eyes seemed to glow in the dim light.

Hope bit her lower lip anxiously.

"I know this is frightening. But you have to trust me when I say that you're safe right now. And I *will* get you out of here."

"I do trust you," she whispered.

He gave a small smile and tossed aside the towel. Hope stared in rising awe and sexual awareness as his delineated abdominal muscles rippled subtly at the small movement. Perhaps he was aware of the way she examined him because she sensed a sudden stillness, a rising tension in him. His gaze toured her face and lowered down over her body, causing Hope's nipples to stiffen and prickle against the cool sheet.

He slowly approached the foot of the bed, reminding her of a stalking wildcat.

"So . . ." Hope asked. "We have several hours before we can act?"

"That's right," he rumbled softly. His lips twitched as he regarded her steadily. She watched his hand, mesmerized, as he dropped it to the sheet next to her bound ankle. His fingers flexed, pulling the sheet an inch lower over her chest. "You've suffered a head injury. Perhaps you'd like to rest until I awaken you before dawn?"

Hope's eyes widened when he pulled slightly again and the sheet slipped lower, this time revealing the top curves of her breasts. "I . . . I am not tired. And my head does not at all pain me as it did."

His smiled warmly. "That's a good thing. Have you any idea, then, how you might like to spend the next few hours?"

He tugged. The edge of the sheet lowered until it perched directly above the stiff peaks of her breasts.

"I . . . we could spend it . . . getting acquainted with one another?" she squeaked.

Her nipples popped out of the sheet, the crests looking rigid and pointed in comparison to the curving mounds of her breasts.

"You know, that was my thinking precisely."

Hope's startled gaze flicked up to Ryan's face. When she saw his expression she snorted softly with laughter. He twisted his mouth as though he was trying to prevent joining in her mirth.

"Untie me," she said.

Without speaking he unfastened her ankles from their restraints. Hope sighed in relief as she bent up her knees and then straightened into a taut stretch.

"Better?"

"Yes," Hope whispered, her voice nearly stolen by Ryan's fixed gaze on her exposed breasts as she arched her back into a stretch.

She sunk back again onto the bed although every muscle in her body was tense with anticipation. He leaned down over the bed and pulled the edge of the sheet down to her knees. For a taut, full moment he looked his fill at her naked body. A tingling sensation of heat flamed beneath her skin wherever his hot stare trailed. Her sex flooded with liquid warmth.

"Ryan," she whispered, desire making her whisper hoarse. He met her gaze. "Untie my wrists. I want to touch you so much."

She saw his throat convulse as he swallowed.

"I want that, too, Hope," he said so quietly she almost didn't catch the words. He came down next to her on the bed, the front of his big body pressing to the side of her. She gasped at the sensation of his bare torso sliding against her naked skin. She could tell by the rigid expression of his face as he encircled her waist with his arm and gently caressed her that he wasn't unaffected by their closeness, either. "But would it be all right if I left your wrists restrained for now?"

"Why?" Hope asked.

He paused, as if considering his answer before he looked into her eyes and answered her. "It would turn me on." He must have noticed her puzzlement at his peculiar turn of phrase. "It would arouse me. Well . . . honestly, you would arouse me anywhere, anyway I could get you," he added as a wry aside as his gaze briefly traveled over her face and down over her breasts. As if he couldn't stop himself his hand rose and slipped beneath one of the heaving mounds. He shaped her to his palm and massaged her while Hope moaned softly.

"It arouses you to restrain a woman while you make love to her?" Hope finally managed to get out as both of them watched Ryan fondle her breast. She pressed her hips down on the bed, desperate for pressure on her sex when he gently plucked her turgid nipple between thumb and forefinger.

"Not always. But yes. I'd like to have you at my mercy right now . . . to see trust on your beautiful face while I give you pleasure.

Have you ever wondered about the things men like to do with women in a bordello, Hope?"

Her lower lip trembled uncontrollably. She'd found the question uttered in Ryan's deep, raspy voice almost unbearably exciting. Her trembling only increased when Ryan leaned down and gently kissed her parted lips while he continued to play with her breast languorously.

"Yes," she whispered honestly against his firm lips a moment later when he lifted his head. "That doesn't mean that I believe in the necessity of prostitution. I believe . . ."

"What do you believe?" Ryan prompted gruffly when her voice trailed off. She'd become distracted because he'd buried his face in her neck and proceeded to make her shiver with pleasure as he kissed, nibbled and scraped his teeth gently against her sensitive skin.

"I—I believe that wives and ladies should feel free to please their husbands . . . and lovers in whatever ways they feel comfortable." Hope gasped when Ryan trailed hot kisses down her chest. "And . . . and I believe respectable ladies should take joy in the bedroom as well, for their bodies are their birthright, just as they are men's. Perhaps then men would not feel so compelled to come to houses of prostitution."

"That is a very modern, wise opinion." She saw a grin curve Ryan's mouth. She'd grown to love that small smile in such a short period of time.

"Ryan?"

"Yes?"

"You seem to have an understanding of what occurs in houses of prostitution. Does . . . does that mean you disagree with my opinion?"

He met her gaze, his chin still hovering over her heaving breasts. "I don't. In fact, prostitution is one of the main types of crime I fight at my job."

Hope opened her mouth to pursue the topic, but Ryan made her forget what they discussed by slipping one of her nipples between his lips.

Her back arched up uncontrollably as his warm mouth enfolded the hypersensitive flesh. She whimpered in stunned arousal at the delicious sensation. He suckled her gently, his tongue like a wet, sleek lash gently whipping her helpless nipple.

"Oh!" she cried out loudly. Distantly she wondered if Ryan would remind her to stay quiet, but her concerns were soon forgotten as he continued to suckle her nipple in his warm mouth while he tweaked the other aching crest with his fingertips. Fire prickled in her flesh and tore down to her sex. She writhed on the bed, but the restraints held her securely in place for Ryan's sensual torture.

Was this why he said he'd enjoy having her at his mercy? The fact that it was impossible to turn away from him or to deny her own hot, needy desire certainly added a sharp edge of excitement to their lovemaking. Her sex ached for him unbearably.

"Ryan . . . *quickly*," she groaned.

He looked up at her even as he continued to draw on her nipple. Her womb flexed painfully when she saw how his cheeks were hollowed out as he suckled. Hope didn't know precisely what she'd been begging him to do, but Ryan's heavy-lidded stare and unceasing, rhythmic suck informed Hope they were going at his pace, not hers.

She suppressed a moan when he finally lifted his head and inspected her glistening nipple. His constant, gentle suction had drawn blood just beneath the surface, making the crest red and defining and distending the center nubbin nearly twice its normal length. Hope knew that the sight pleased Ryan when he shifted his hips. She felt the hard column of his penis press against her thigh, his heat emanating into her skin.

He placed his hands under both of her breasts, holding them up and massaging them lightly. "You have the most beautiful breasts I've ever seen."

Hope gasped at his focused attention and gruff compliment. Warm fluid gushed at the gate of her sex. "Thank you," she murmured dazedly.

He stared longingly at the breast he hadn't yet suckled, but as if he regretted leaving the other, he lowered his dark head and kissed the damp nipple softly before slipping it between his lips. Hope cried out sharply in excitement—she couldn't seem to help herself—when he gently scraped the tingling flesh between his front teeth before he released her.

Then he proceeded to torment her other breast with his lips, mouth and teeth, all the while plucking and strumming her other nipple with his fingertips. Hope writhed beneath him in sweet agony. But she had to endure, for the ropes prevented her from moving.

Her sex grew so wet she felt moisture slicking her inner thighs. She knew Ryan was aroused, too, from the sound of his satisfied grunts and the feeling of his stiff penis pressing to her thigh. She pushed up on him, wanting more of the exciting sensation. He groaned, the sound vibrating into her breast. As if he couldn't help himself he flexed his hips, stroking her rhythmically with his erection.

Finally he raised his head. Hope panted in the break of sensual torture. He scraped his front teeth gently along her ribs just beneath her heaving breasts, making her cry out.

"You're so sensitive. I think you'll be able to come from nipple stimulation alone. We're going to find out in a moment. But first . . . I have to taste you."

Hope's mouth sagged open as he began to move his mouth over her ribs and belly. When he ran his teeth gently along the sides of her torso she moaned uncontrollably, her back curving into him for closer contact. Shivers prickled her flesh. Her skin roughened. His hands moved beneath her, lifting her even further until her back bowed up off the bed as he served himself her eager flesh. How had he known she would be almost painfully sensitive along the sides of her ribs or that she would cry out in sharp pleasure when he took a small bite at her waist and soothed her with his warm, sleek tongue?

By the time he transferred his attentions to her thighs, Hope was nearly out of her mind with stark arousal. He kissed her flexing muscles while his hands moved beneath her, tautly squeezing her buttocks in his large palms. She couldn't take it anymore. She just knew she couldn't. Ryan had her stretched on a sensual rack of pleasure and she would break apart any moment.

He released her bottom with one hand and pushed a thigh wide. Instinctively Hope closed it. No matter how aroused she was, she wasn't used to exposing such private flesh to the open air, let alone a man's hot gaze. He used both hands this time, pushing her legs apart and holding her in place while he stared at her sex. Hope moaned in mixed mortification and intense arousal.

The muscles of her vagina flexed inward painfully.

"Ryan . . . *please*," she grated out between a clenched jaw. She had no idea for what she asked, but something told her that Ryan knew.

His dark head dipped. Her entire body trembled in anguish when he licked her inner thigh, just a few scant inches from her sex. She sensed him stiffen. He looked up at her, his lips still parted. Something in the wild intensity of his eyes told her he'd found her essence on her thighs.

And that he liked what he'd tasted.

His hands slid beneath her again. He palmed her bottom and pushed her up at the same time his face lowered to her sex.

Hope jerked in the restraints. She cried out in mixed shock and pleasure as Ryan covered her outer sex with his mouth, applying suction like he had on her nipples. But the most scandalous and wonderful thing was his tongue. He worked it between her labia and rubbed and flicked and probed until her flesh sizzled unbearably.

"No . . . you shouldn't . . . ah, God . . . dear Lord, *don't* . . . don't stop," she beseeched. Her buttocks flexed hard in his hands as she writhed in the restraints. The pleasure was so forbidden, so sharp it was nearly untenable. She closed her eyes and wailed as climax crashed into her, battering her relentlessly in its fierce tide.

Hope's eyes blinked open a moment later. She whimpered and trembled when she realized Ryan's face was still buried between her thighs, now even more intimately than before. He'd pushed her legs even wider and tilted back her hips. He held her with her feet dangling up in the air while he drank from her sex like she was a fleshy bowl.

Hope clenched her teeth and forced herself to look away; the vision of Ryan's mouth on her was so powerful. He plunged his tongue into her slit again and again, pausing to suckle her juices every few seconds, opening his lips to strongly mouth her sensitive sex lips and the throbbing flesh they covered. Any lingering embarrassment on her part was melted away by the evidence of his hunger.

His intensity left her spellbound.

She moaned and twisted in the restraints as he built the pressure inside her once again, but he shifted his hands to her hips and held her firmly against his marauding mouth. Hope felt a drop of sweat roll between her breasts and down her heaving belly. Her face and teeth clenched tight at the rising tension.

"Ryan," she whispered, his prisoner at that moment . . . a hostage to her own desire.

He opened his eyes and looked into her face even as his mouth continued to work her ruthlessly. One hand held her in place while the other rose and parted her swollen, damp labia. Hope's desperation swelled when he waggled his tongue between the juicy lips as he continued to pin her with his fierce stare.

She cried out mindlessly as she came, her body shaking uncontrollably. He refused to grant her mercy, stabbing, licking, rubbing and sucking until every last shiver of pleasure had been squeezed, suckled and coaxed out of her.

"You have the sweetest pussy in existence."

Hope heard the deep, rough voice as if a thick pillow had been placed over both of her ears. Her eyes opened sluggishly when she felt Ryan's lips on hers, molding and plucking at them insistently with his own. He spread her juices on her lips. The tip of her tongue touched his and then swept along his lower lip, tasting her desire for the first time in her life.

He groaned deep in his throat. He held himself off her with his arms. Hope saw that he'd shoved his pants and underwear down to his thighs. She felt the hard, warm knob of his cock nudge at her wet slit.

"Just for a moment . . . I need to feel you. I can't stop myself."

She gasped as he flexed his hips. He looked into her eyes as he slid further inside her.

"*Happy dagger*," he whispered. That small, special smile tilted his lips, as though he was both amused at himself for his show of sentimentality and dead earnest at once.

Tears filled her eyes as her burning, clamping flesh stretched at his welcome invasion.

"*This is thy sheath*," Hope quoted back to him from *Romeo and Juliet*, her heart in her eyes as she stared up at him. How strange that the bard, who lived and loved in a world so different from both her own and Ryan's, should be a common bond between them. Even stranger that such a big, masculine man apparently treasured Shakespeare as she did.

He pushed, watching her face for a reaction, working his penis into her tight channel with gentle determination. They both gasped when he pressed into her to the hilt. She sensed the slight tremor in his flesh, the evidence of his intense, raw need making her eyes burn even more.

"*There let me die*," he finally replied.

They both seemed to hold their breath as he thrust in and out of her for several strokes, making Hope's eyes roll back in her head as he rubbed and agitated deep, secret flesh.

"I could forget the world existed buried inside you." Hope's eyelids sprang open when he withdrew from her. She felt a shudder go through him at the action.

"Ahhh . . . no, *please* don't," she begged. It felt like her soul had been cleaved a little when he separated his flesh from her own.

She watched in rising confusion as he moved away from her, his movements restrained and tense, as though he were in pain. He stood at the side of the bed. When he turned toward her in profile she saw that his cock hung heavy and fully erect between his strong, naked thighs, her own juices making it glisten magnificently. His color had grown ruddy and the surface veins swelled turgidly. He puzzled her further by pulling up his pants. He had to stretch his underwear forward considerably to capture the length of his swollen penis. She saw him glance almost surreptitiously out the window seeing, as Hope had, the discouraging sight of black iron bars blocking the view.

Why had he deprived himself of his own pleasure? The fact that he hadn't shared in her bliss made her ache in a way she'd never before experienced.

"Ryan? Are you in pain from the fight?"

His strained smile and uplifted eyebrows informed her he'd somehow found her question darkly amusing. "Not from the fight, no. I'm all right. I thought you wanted to learn about some of the things men and women do in a place like this."

Her eyes popped open in amazement. "What we were just doing were not some of those things?"

Hope loved the sound of the deep rumble of his laughter. "No, those apply. I just thought you might like to discover more."

He picked up a riding crop from the bedside table. She lifted her head and saw the other items lying there.

"It'll be all right, Hope," he soothed when he saw her eyes go wide in anxiety. "I would never harm you. Never. Some people like to use these things to cause pain, but that's not what we're going to do. I'm going to use them to heighten your pleasure . . . to set your nerves on fire. Do you trust me to do that?"

Hope looked up into his earnest gaze.

"Will it arouse you to do this? Will it . . . bring you pleasure as well?" she asked hesitantly. He couldn't know it, but what she was really asking was whether or not it would bring that blazing hot intensity into his singular eyes that putting his mouth on her most private flesh had.

She saw his expression tighten. The flash of fire in his eyes supplied her answer even before he spoke.

"Oh yeah."

"All right then," she whispered. "I want to bring you pleasure more than anything, Ryan."

She saw his throat flex convulsively before he stepped toward her naked, bound body.

∽ THIRTEEN ∾

Ryan's cock lurched in stark arousal when Hope told him she wanted to pleasure him more than anything. There really couldn't be a sweeter, sexier woman on the planet anywhere . . . at any time. It'd nearly killed him to withdraw from her a moment ago. If given a choice, Ryan thought he might have endured another one of Marlo's dead-on punches rather than suffer leaving Hope's clinging, warm little pussy before he filled her with his seed.

He studied her face as he lifted the riding crop toward her body. The crop was the genuine article, of course, not something manufactured exclusively for bedroom sport. Her eyes looked enormous with anxiety and rising excitement as he lowered the two-by-two-inch leather slapper and ran the surface over her abdomen. The image of the weathered, supple leather running over the pale harbor of her silky smooth belly was potently erotic. He slid the popper along the sides of her ribs and heaving breasts, all the while watching her reaction.

He could tell by her shallow, rapid breathing and the deepening color of her cheeks, lips and nipples she was excited.

"I'm going to slap your skin now, beauty. Not to hurt you. It'll make you tingle and burn."

She'd been tightly focused on the progress of the popper as it trailed across her body, but she met his eyes when he spoke. She merely nodded.

He smiled at her obvious courage and lifted the crop. She gasped softly when he slapped her belly and ribs several times, pinkening the white skin. His cock throbbed every time the leather made a popping sound against her taut flesh. When he heard her moan in mounting excitement he paused and quieted her fiery nerve endings by sliding the leather across her rosy skin.

"That's a girl," he soothed. Her lips parted as she panted in rising excitement, the vision making Ryan want nothing more than to sink his tongue between the lush red ring . . . followed by his cock. The thought aroused him so much his body shuddered slightly with restrained lust.

His thick arousal was suddenly pierced by the sound of a muted knock against the wall. Damn. He'd managed to forget about Jack for a few precious moments. Hope's beauty and responsiveness held him captive . . . made him forget everything but her.

His gaze flew to her face but she didn't appear to have noticed the thumping sound. Ryan gritted his teeth, guessing Jack's subtle message. He'd already noticed the flash of the camera going off while her eyes had been closed in ecstasy and her juices ran so sweetly down his throat, and then again when she'd briefly closed her eyes as he sank his cock into her pussy.

Now Jack wanted another shot, Ryan realized bitterly.

He slid the leather slapper along the sides of Hope's torso, already

knowing how sensitive she was there. He lightly caressed the sides
of her breasts. She whimpered softly.

"I want you to do two things, honey," he explained. "I want
you to spread your thighs. No . . . keep them wide," he demanded
when she initially followed his instructions and then closed her legs
several inches, as though she'd been programmed for modesty—
which she had been, of course. She followed his order, nonetheless,
spreading her thighs wider, allowing him to see her pink, glistening, fleshy flower. He looked into her strained face and knew how
difficult it was for her.

"That's right. You're so beautiful. That pleases me so much, to
be able to see you. Now . . . close your eyes . . . and just feel," he
ordered as he slid the popper over the curving flesh of her breast.

Hope immediately shut her eyes. She moaned and pulled against
her restraints, as though trying to get more of the sensation of the
leather stroking her breast. The evidence of her intensely carnal nature left Ryan stunned and immensely gratified. When she became
so insistent that she closed her legs partially as she strained up,
Ryan lifted the whippy crop and gently slapped her breast, garnering her attention.

"Keep your thighs spread wide, beauty," he chastened.

He landed several well-aimed swats on her breasts, thoroughly
enjoying the slight jiggle in her firm flesh and the visible tightening
of her nipples. He was so caught up in the eroticism of the moment
he almost didn't notice the flash of the camera.

Almost.

He forced his anger to the periphery, knowing he couldn't allow that volatile emotion to control him here any more than he
could in the boxing ring. There was a gun pointed at this head, after all.

And he'd much rather focus on pleasuring Hope, anyway.

She whimpered and writhed as he popped her firm breasts with
the crop again and again, turning them a lovely shade of pink. She

managed to keep her thighs spread the entire time. He watched her face, fascinated at how arousal tightened and transformed her lovely features until she literally emanated desire.

"*Ryan*," she murmured through trembling lips when he popped her left breast very near the center, carefully avoiding her stiff, pointed nipple. "I—I don't think I can do this anymore. You must . . . you must . . ."

"Make you come?" he suggested softly as he slapped the tender side of her breast.

"Yes . . . please." She scrunched her eyes shut and groaned through gritting teeth. Her hips shifted wildly on the bed. Ryan could see how rigid her thigh muscles were as she forced them to remain spread while desire tightened her body. The pubic hairs around her swollen lips were drenched with her juices as were her inner thighs.

He'd never seen a more arousing sight in his life. Such a strong stab of lust went through him that his balls tightened uncomfortably.

"I'll see what I can do about that," Ryan promised at the same time he gently popped first one pouting nipple and then the other, back and forth rapidly. Hope cried out, her back curving off the bed. The second he saw her flesh ripple in orgasm, he added a third taut slap to his rhythm, this one on her wet, spread pussy.

His pops continued, rapid and taut—nipple, nipple, cunt, nipple, nipple, cunt.

Hope screamed, her body shuddering in orgasm. He continued slapping her, his pace quickening as she convulsed in mindless pleasure. Ryan was hardly aware that he'd torn open the fly of his pants and shoved his hand into his boxer briefs. He stroked his cock madly as he played Hope's sweet, sensitive body with the crop like a maestro striking the finale on the keys of his instrument. When her screams segued to whimpers and cries as her climax slowed, he focused solely on her pussy, slapping her juicy tissues with firm, fast little vibrating strokes until she screamed full throttle all over again.

Moments later he tossed the crop on the table, careless as to where it landed, and put one knee on the bed. He leaned down, palmed her jaw and ravaged her mouth with barely restrained lust. Potent, sweet, addicting woman, he thought dizzily as he pillaged her depths and she whimpered into his mouth. By the time he lifted his head they both gasped for air—she, straining to recover after her orgasm and he, desperately trying to rein in his splintering control.

It took him a moment to realize she still clamped her eyes shut. He chuckled and gently kissed her eyelids. Not only was she intelligent, spirited and the essence of pure sexuality, Hope Stillwater was a natural submissive given the right man.

Thank God she'd decided he was such a man.

"Did you like that, beauty?" he whispered gruffly when she opened her midnight eyes and focused on his face.

"If it wasn't a sin for me to allow it, surely it won't be one for me to say I liked it very much."

Ryan chuckled. "You're a little witch, Hope Stillwater."

"What do you mean by that?" she asked, seeming more concerned about his statement than interested in the fact that he leaned over to unfasten her left wrist from the headboard.

"Turn over on your belly, beauty," he whispered. He waited while she flipped over and rapidly reaffixed the velvet rope. He recalled what Jack had said about keeping her restrained until he'd gotten all the photos he wanted and was extremely mindful of the gun pointed at him during those tense seconds.

"I called you a witch because everything you say and every glance you give me casts a spell," Ryan murmured. Part of him was surprised by his blatant honesty, although another part wasn't. A woman like Hope deserved nothing less, especially when she gifted him with her sincerity so generously time and again.

"Oh. It was a compliment."

"You seem relieved," he teased.

"Ryan . . . may I give you pleasure now?"

Ryan opened his mouth and closed it again, wondering all the while if he really would ever become accustomed to her sweetness.

"It would please me very much to turn your beautiful bottom the same fetching shade as your gorgeous breasts."

"Would it?"

"Yes."

"Is that why you spanked me last night when—"

"Shhhh," he hushed softly when eagerness made her voice volume escalate. The last thing he needed at this point was Jack realizing that he and Hope weren't strangers to one another. "Bring your knees up under you, Hope. That's right." For a second he just stared in mute amazement at the beauty of her naked back, narrow waist, curving hips and plump bottom.

He carefully removed her long, curly hair from her face, running his hands over the length before he settled it out of her way. He reveled in the softness of it, the erotic sensation of the curls coiling around his fingers. One day soon, if he had his way about it, he would thrust his cock into the silky mass of curls.

His cock throbbed dully at the mere thought.

Ryan picked up the leather flogger from the table.

"Lift up some more, beauty. Come up on your haunches," he said. "Put your bottom up in the air. Make it a nice target for me."

Hope moaned softly as Ryan slid his hand across her exquisitely soft skin, showing her how he wanted her positioned. When she'd settled she was up on her knees, thighs spread, her chest and cheek pressed to the mattress, her arms restrained over her head. Under his guidance she'd parted her legs sufficiently enough for him to glimpse the wet, swollen folds of her sex between her white thighs.

"That's right," Ryan mumbled. When he realized his hand was down his pants again, stroking his furious erection, he took a deep breath and released himself.

He remained standing by the bed and ran the leather straps of the flogger over Hope's ass with his left hand. He decided to tease her lithesome thighs and partially exposed sex with the flogger, but her luscious ass was meant to be paddled.

She squealed in surprise when he flicked the straps against her thighs.

"Too much?" he asked, his hand immediately there to soothe the silken flesh.

"No . . . not really. It stung at first. Now it just tingles," Hope muttered thoughtfully.

"Hold still, then."

Ryan wasn't sure what to make of the fact that she didn't moan and struggle against her restraints when he flogged the back of her thighs and the plump, tender curve of her lower ass like she had when he'd used the crop. It excited him to sensitize her pale flesh with the leather flogger, but he was concerned about her subdued reaction.

He paused in his flogging and slid the straps over her exposed pussy and up the crack of her ass. A visible convulsion rippled through her flesh. She gasped loudly, and Ryan realized for the first time she'd been holding her breath before.

"Okay?" he murmured as he lowered the flogger, once again lightly brushing the straps over her wet pussy.

"Yes . . . ahhh . . . yes. It feels so . . ."

"What?" Ryan prompted when her voice trailed off.

"Forbidden," she whispered so softly he barely heard her.

He smiled, despite the fierceness of emotion that swept through him at that moment. "Would you like to try something even more forbidden, little witch?"

She looked up at him with one eye in anxious excitement. He saw her force down a swallow.

"Yes."

"Good," he said, realizing the single word had come out of his throat like a growl. He was doing his best to be patient, but her beauty and responsiveness had nearly unraveled his tightly coiled control on several occasions. Hope's seduction under these foul circumstances was the most awful and yet exquisite sexual torture Ryan had ever experienced.

He felt her gaze on him as he returned the flogger to the table and picked up the stoppered bottle. He said nothing as he parted one of her ass cheeks and poured some of the oil on the tiny, pink ring of her rectum. She shivered when he used his fingertip to rub the oil into the sensitive skin of her perineum and then penetrated her asshole.

She twisted her hips away from him.

"Ohhhh . . . Ryan, I don't think that's . . . I don't believe you know what you're doing!"

He chuckled as he stilled her waving fanny and pushed his forefinger into her asshole further. He closed his eyes briefly at the sensation of being clasped in smooth, tight heat.

"I know what I'm doing, beauty." *Do I ever*, Ryan thought bemusedly as he began plunging his finger in and out of her tight hole. She moaned in mixed panic and arousal, still twisting her hips. He put his knee on the bed and used his elbow and forearm to still her squirming bottom against his chest.

"Ohhhh," she wailed as he held her immobile and finger-fucked her ass with gentle determination, lubricating and loosening the clenching hole. After a moment her wailing stopped, however. Silence prevailed. Both of them seemed to be holding their breath in tense excitement. When he gently inserted another finger into her ass, Hope groaned shakily.

"Shhhh," Ryan soothed as he began to move in and out of her tight channel, this time with two fingers. "You see? You've gifted me with more than one sheath, beauty."

He felt her muscles tighten around his fingers, the sensation making him grit his teeth in agonized arousal.

"You do not plan to . . . *no*, Ryan. That would never work in a million years," Hope hissed.

He glanced back at her and saw that the cheek that was turned up was floridly pink.

"Oh, it will work," Ryan assured, even as he slipped his fingers out of her ass and stood. "But not right this second. At the moment, I think I might have to give you a punishment."

"Why?" she asked in surprise.

Ryan set down the bottle of lubricant and picked up the foot-long wooden paddle from the table.

"Do you remember when we were in the bathroom together, how I specifically asked you not to go anywhere with strangers?"

"Well, yes—"

"And did you do what I asked?"

"Well, it was just Sadie," Hope mumbled, giving him a petulant look. She opened her mouth to defend herself further, but stopped when he opened his hand over her bare bottom. He couldn't stop himself from groaning in agony when he felt her soft, taut flesh curving into his palm.

"I'm going to cut you some slack since you're new to this. I won't ever demand much of you, Hope, but if I ask you to do something for your safety, you'd best know from this point on that I'll take your agreement of it very seriously."

She looked up at him, the whites of her eyes largely in evidence.

"Don't be afraid. I told you I'd never harm you," he reminded her quietly.

He placed one hand on her shoulder and swung the paddle back with his left hand.

Crack.

"Ooh!" Hope exclaimed in surprise, lurching forward slightly. His hand on her shoulder kept her steady, though. He'd been so enthralled by the way the blow had shimmered through her firm flesh that he landed two more in quick succession.

Hope moaned loudly. Ryan used the end of the polished wood paddle to soothe her burning bottom, moving the tip of it in tight circular motions over her plump flesh.

"I think you'll listen to me next time, won't you, witch?"

"I—I, I will do my best—"

Whap, whap. Whap.

"Ooh, I will! I certainly will."

Ryan couldn't help but smile. He released her shoulder and tenderly ran his hand over her bottom, soothing her hot, prickly flesh. He parted her buttocks to get a better look at her swollen outer sex, glistening slit and oiled rectum.

His guttural groan tore at his throat.

Her asshole clenched and she shifted her hips restlessly, as though she could feel his blazing hot stare.

"What are you thinking, beauty?" he rasped as he raised the paddle.

"I burn," she whispered shakily.

"So do I. You undo me, witch."

He briskly paddled her over her exposed asshole . . . not hard, just enough to make her whimper and her fanny twitch. He did it several more times in succession and each time her bottom gave a little hop and she yelped.

When he lowered the paddle and gently tapped it against her swollen labia and erect clit, she let out a howl of excitement.

"Shhhh," he quieted, but he couldn't help but laugh at how cute and sexy she was.

He really couldn't take much more of this. He supposed most would say he was teasing and tormenting Hope, but Ryan felt like he personally endured the most excruciating form of torture imaginable.

He set down the paddle and paused to lean down and brush the hair out of her face. His fingers came away damp with her perspiration.

"Are you excited, little witch?"

"Yes." Her breathy whisper charmed him as much as everything else about her.

"I can see I'm going to have to be more firm with your punishments in the future since you seem to enjoy it so much," he murmured as he leaned down and kissed her ear and then her dewy cheek, inhaling her singular scent. His cock lurched against his underwear, reminding him of a furious, ravenous, caged creature. He ignored it as best he could while he continued to nuzzle Hope's cheek and neck.

"Ryan?"

"Yes," he murmured as he nibbled along her fragrant hairline.

"Are you really going to put your . . . member inside of me . . . there?"

"You mean here?" he asked as he ran his down hand down her satiny, flushed flesh. He penetrated her snug asshole again. For a second he froze when light flashed. He ground his back teeth together even as he slowly stroked Hope and she moaned softly.

He'd managed to forget about Jack and his sleazy friends for long, glorious minutes, but they'd forced the knowledge of their presence back into his awareness. All of it slammed into him at once— the sordidness, the greed . . . the threat to himself and Hope.

"I am, honey," he whispered before he gently plucked at her parted lips. She turned her chin, trying to participate more fully in his kiss. *Sweet, sweet*, Ryan thought as he became more and more enraptured by her taste and lush, warm lips, and Diamond Jack Fletcher faded to a distant lurking shadow in his mind. Hope was so innocent and eager, so purely and profoundly carnal in nature that Ryan suddenly knew for a fact that Jack and his ilk could never begin to besmirch her.

"And it's going to feel so good for me. I'm going to make sure it feels just as good for you. Believe me?"

She gave him a long, searching look before she nodded solemnly.

"Witch," he whispered.

The smile that curved her red lips nearly made him explode in his pants. He grabbed the bottle of oil before he moved behind her on the bed. He unfastened his pants and jerked both them and his underwear down to his thighs. Having most of his clothes stolen had taught him to place uncommon value on what remained. He needed to be as prepared as possible in case he needed to move quickly.

They had a gun trained on them, after all. Knowing they were in imminent danger and yet feeling such intense sexual excitement created a bizarre, sharp mix of tension and emotion unlike anything Ryan had ever experienced.

He told himself not to stare at Hope's pink, paddled bottom, flushed thighs and swollen sex as he lubricated his cock with his hand but he couldn't stop himself from gaping at the extraordinarily erotic vision.

"Stay very still," he ordered before he moved into position behind her and pressed the tip of his cock to her lubricated asshole. He held his aching penis by the root and applied a firm pressure, already feeling her body's natural resistance.

"Now push yourself back onto my cock."

Hope squealed and then gasped when the fat head of his cock sunk into her.

"Shhhh, stay still now. That was the worst of it," Ryan soothed, praying it was true. She hugged him tighter than anything he'd ever experienced. It felt like an elastic band tugged beneath the head of his cock. The muscles of her anus writhed around him, subtly trying to push him out of her body. He needed to apply a firm pressure not to be ejected. Her heat resonated into him like a furnace, making him wild with longing to submerse his cock completely in that tight channel.

"Are you ready?" he asked gruffly.

He saw her nod.

"Then press back again."

This time while she pressed he reached around and massaged her clit. She howled in mounting excitement and pushed his cock into her several more inches.

"That's a girl," he murmured as he continued to stimulate her even while he held her hip and began pumping in and out of her ass gently.

It was really too much to take. Later on, Ryan couldn't think where he'd possibly found the reserves to endure it.

But endure it he did.

ᐧ FOURTEEN ᐧ

The viewing room grew uncomfortably hot.

Jack had long ago let Daire's unusual weapon drop to his side as he stood with his eye glued to the peephole. Subdued grunts, gasps and slurping sounds filled the still, stifling, windowless room. He watched, just as enthralled as the other five men in the room (for the photographer kept lowering his camera and staring slack-jawed through the largest hole in the wall) as the man who'd brought down the mighty Marlo in the ring breached an even more unconquerable foe.

"I don't believe it," Mason muttered every minute or so, despite the fact that Jack and Ambrose had hissed at him to be quiet at least a half a dozen times each.

All of the men except for Jack and the photographer had whores kneeling before them. Even Divorak, the photographer, couldn't keep his hand out of his pants, although Jack had threatened to throw him into a room with Big Marlo if he missed Hope Stillwater's most photogenic moments because he was playing with himself. Every time one of the men shuddered in orgasm while his whore slurped away at his cock, Jack grated his teeth in a strange brew of lust, irritation and envy.

It'd been several years since he participated in any type of communal sex. After a few instances of furious humiliation because his cock refused to respond as usual, he'd sworn off public and private displays altogether. Jack had traveled all the way to Indianapolis the year before last in order to have a specialist tell him how to get his cock to full working order again. It wasn't that Chicago didn't have plenty of good doctors, but Jack couldn't take the risk of his secret weakness being broadcast onto his home turf. Jack ruled in the first ward. Fools believed a man who couldn't nail a tail good and hard couldn't get things accomplished, couldn't send fear into men's hearts.

But Jack had shown them. If anything, he'd become more fearsome and ruthless ever since his body had betrayed him.

The damn doctor in Indianapolis had explained to him that there was something amiss with his blood, something that would eventually make his organs and eyes fail in addition to just his cock. He told Jack to stop smoking cigars and drinking whiskey.

But Jack could tell the physician didn't *really* know what the hell was wrong with him or how to fix it. He wasn't going to allow some tottering, gray-haired fool to tell him how to run his life.

Even though he couldn't take his pleasure as he used to, Jack had become almost obsessive about watching, always looking, searching for a display that would quicken his cock as he recalled. Usually he searched in vain.

Until tonight that is.

Watching that big, muscular paddy with the thick, long dick make Hope Stillwater scream with pleasure had definitely gotten the blood flowing into his cock in a way he hadn't experienced in years. He waited and watched, but his excitement didn't diminish as it often did. It only grew exponentially as he stared—afraid to even blink—while Daire coaxed the elegant beauty to submit to the crop, the flogger and the paddle.

Now it looked as if he was preparing to sodomize her.

When both Sinclair Ambrose and Lewis Lander shuddered in orgasm as they watched the mick hold the little minx's squirming bottom still and penetrate her asshole with his fingers, Jack finally dared to speak.

"You two—Mel and Betsey. Get over here," he ordered quietly, nodding to the floor before him. Betsey tried to move back off Lander's cock but he held her in place while his body continued to convulse, his penis pressed into her deep, his eye never wavering from the peephole. He finally went limp and released her. Betsey leaned back gasping, an obvious look of distaste on her face as she still struggled to swallow Lander's cream.

"Get over here, I said," Jack hissed, furious that the whores had hesitated even for an instant given who he was and how infrequently he made such a request.

Mel reached him first and knelt before him, unfastening his pants quickly and efficiently.

"This is a treat, isn't it, Betsey? Such a big, beautiful cock," Mel cooed as she licked the head of his penis.

"Shut up and suck," Jack muttered, sick to death of whores' dramatics. They'd tell a half-rotten leper he had the cock of a god if there was a buck in it for them. These two regularly did precisely that for that drunken lush Mason, whose cock was nearly as limp and unresponsive as his brain. The young fool paid Jack enormous amounts of money every week for unlimited use of his whores. Not that it took much away from the prostitutes' time or Jack's profits because the rotter was usually too soused to do anything but pass out in one of the beds upstairs, his mouth slobbering around a bare breast.

Tonight young Mason appeared to be as inspired by the show as Jack, however. The young woman kneeling before him was having a hard time keeping up with his rapid thrusts and jabs into her mouth and throat. Jack noticed, however, that Mason looked far from pleased. In fact, he appeared angrier than Jack'd ever seen him as he watched his innocent, lovely Prairie Avenue neighbor scream in pleasure under Daire's knowing hands.

He watched Daire move behind Hope Stillwater's plump bottom and press a huge, swollen dick to her ass.

"His cock is every bit as big as Marlo's," Ambrose said quietly, still panting from his most recent orgasm.

"Yeah, but this fellow knows what to do with his, and that makes all the difference in the world," Brett Newcomb muttered as he pulsed his cock between the clamping lips of a brown-haired whore named Martha. "You're going to have to keep him around for our pleasure, Jack."

Jack just grunted as Betsey ran her tongue around his lower shaft and Mel focused on the head of his cock. Mel might be getting on in years but she still could suck the tarnish off a doorknob. He watched intently as Daire flexed his taut, powerful muscles and slid his cock in and out of Miss Hope Stillwater's ass. He could tell by the tension in the big man's body that she resisted him, but he was firm and insistent.

"Tell that asshole Divorak to take a fucking picture," Jack whispered furiously to Ambrose, who stood closest to him.

"Are we going to be able to sample her when he's through? Can't tell you how many times I've watched that tail twitching down Prairie Avenue. Wouldn't mind having a go at it myself. You could always blindfold her, Jack," Newcomb reasoned, his eyeball screwed to the peephole so snugly Jack wondered if he'd ever be able to pop it out of the wall. Newcomb sweated profusely and made Martha groan whenever he plunged his cock into her too forcefully.

"Maybe. We'll just have to see," Jack mumbled noncommittally, too caught up in his own excitement over the fact that his cock was responding so wholeheartedly. He'd never seen anything this juicy. Something about that stoic Irishman with the unusual, large gun, big dick and a confidence to match also infuriated him, though.

But hell, *yes*, he'd keep Hope Stillwater around for a little private sport, even if it was just for a short while. She'd need to be returned to her father very soon. It had never been his desire to kill her, just to humiliate her and her father into silence. The last thing he needed was involvement in a murder investigation of the Stillwater caliber.

"If anyone is going to have her, it'll be me," Mason seethed. "I knew she was nothing but a begging whore every time she looked down her nose at me. I knew it all along."

Jack didn't bother to answer. He'd never give Hope Stillwater to the drunken idiot, but he happened to agree with the rest of his comment. All women were whores. His mother had been a whore who had given him to the owner of a tavern in Lynchburg, Tennessee, when he was two years old. There Jack had lived a barren slave's existence until he was twelve, never complaining about the callous, cruel treatment he received because it was all he'd ever known. He'd occasionally see his mother at the local brothel when he made deliveries. To his dying day he'd be able to perfectly envision her hard, contemptuous, vaguely amused face whenever she looked at him.

Sure, women were something *before* they were whores. He'd known Mel, for instance, the old whore who currently sucked his cock, since she was sixteen years old and her skin was as soft and dewy as a firm, ripe peach. He'd personally broken her in and even had indulged in a foolish little romance with the beauty. Jack had been young, after all, and although he'd been ruthless about clawing his way to the top and grasping for power any way he could get it, he was entitled to a few foolish moments.

He'd wised up quickly enough. Mel was nothing more than a piece of property, one of the many means by which he profited. It'd hurt him a little the first night he'd given her up for public consumption in a brothel he owned a few blocks south of the Sweet Lash called the Crimson Fortune, but the pain had been as short-lived as Mel's tears of betrayal.

Soon things had evolved into their natural order and Mel became quite comfortable in her true identity as a whore.

"Do you think he's going to get that thing all the way into her?" Ambrose speculated idly as he peered through the peephole.

"He damn well better if he doesn't want me to play target practice with his head from this hole," Jack replied.

He lifted the hand that gripped Daire's big gun and pushed Mel's head down on his cock while he thrust forward. The clunk of the hard metal against her skull made Mel grunt in pain, but Jack was too busy watching Jacob Stillwater's pretty daughter take it in the ass to notice.

He couldn't wait to see how that holier-than-thou son of a bitch responded when he saw the photographic commemoration of *this* special moment in his daughter's life.

The thought made him grin widely around his cigar.

∽

Hope twisted her head and pressed her other hot cheek into the mattress. She burned unbearably. Everywhere. What Ryan was doing to her was absolutely outrageous, but it excited her so greatly she felt as though she'd literally combust into a white-hot, roaring conflagration.

"Steady," she heard Ryan say when she moaned and twisted her hips in pleasure as he rubbed her sex with his knowing finger and thrust his penis in and out of her with gentle, firm strokes. Pathways of sensation that she'd never before known existed throbbed to life as he stimulated her sex and penetrated such a private, intimate place.

She was far more sensitive where Ryan plunged his penis than she ever would have imagined. She could perfectly feel the rim beneath the crown of his sex pushing and probing, claiming more and more of her with each pass.

Ryan paused and rubbed her hip, the action so tender and cherishing it made Hope want to weep, especially since the caress was combined with his outlandishly bold possession of her body and mind. He continued to rub her sex, making her burn. She pressed down subtly on his hand and clamped tighter around his straining erection, unable to stop herself in her excitement.

Ryan groaned gutturally.

"You feel so damn good," Ryan gasped, the rough edge to his voice pleasing Hope immeasurably. "I'm not going to be able to take much more of this."

Hope gritted her teeth together and made tiny, desperate movements with her hips against his finger. She felt so full of Ryan, so incendiary, like the end of a matchstick about to burst into flame. She pushed her hips against his penis, seating him several inches further in her body.

Orgasm slammed into her, lighting up every nerve in her entire body.

She heard Ryan curse harshly as if from a distance. Then he pressed her head down firmly into the soft mattress and sunk into her ass completely. He gave an uneven howl of pleasure before he began to plunge his penis in and out of her, his strokes no longer gentle, but demanding . . . conquering.

Orgasm still shuddered through her as she gripped onto the velvet ropes that restrained her and Ryan fucked her with just as much raw passion as he'd taken her with the night he took her virginity. His grunts and growls of pleasure fell like blessings on her ears.

She loved when he finally lost control, when she possessed sure, inarguable knowledge that she pleased him as much as he'd pleased her again and again and again. The sharp, staccato sounds of their crashing bodies and the rocking of the headboard against the wall blended with the rapid hammer of her heartbeat in her ears.

She felt Ryan's member swell inside of her, the sensation making her cry out sharply in agonized bliss. A rough growl tore at his throat, the sound thrilling every raw, firing nerve in her body. He held her hips and plunged into her one last time.

Hope's eyes opened wide. She'd been stunned at the power of Ryan's climaxes before—all that pent-up, concentrated energy being released in a single, enormous explosion of pleasure. But this—this feeling of him coming while they were joined, hearing his anguished groans, clearly sensing the rush of his warm seed inside of her while his penis jerked in her tight channel—this was an experience that scorched her very soul.

He slumped forward, his breathing ragged and heavy. For a long moment he struggled to regain equilibrium. It made her strangely proud that loving her could make this big, fierce man so vulnerable. As if he'd read her mind he leaned down and nuzzled her cheek.

"You slay me, little witch."

"I do not mean to," she whispered.

She caught a flash of his curving lips before he gently withdrew from her, making her gasp. She stuck her head up and watched him while he released her wrists from the velvet rope. Then he came down on his back next to her and enclosed her in his arms, pulling her upper body over him so they were face-to-face, chest-to-chest. He brushed her hair back from her face and lightly kissed her parted lips.

And Hope was left wondering if this was not the best part of all of their lovemaking—quiet, sated, different than the blazing hot tempest, but no less sweet for it.

"I'm kind of having a hard time believing that you're regretful about causing me to lose control," Ryan murmured next to her lips.

Hope's eyelids flickered open and she caught his expression of amusement. Her gaze lingered on his bold, rugged features, eating him up with her gaze. What a miracle it was that he was here with her.

"I—I wanted to bring you pleasure."

"If you had brought me any more, I'd probably be dead from a heart attack. I'd have died a blissfully happy man, though," he murmured as he ran his hands along the sensitive sides of her body. She shivered at his touch.

"That was a very"—Hope's cheeks flushed with heat—"*unusual* way of making love."

She wondered what he was thinking as he studied her for several seconds. His hand rose and he brushed back her hair from her face. "It *was* making love, though, Hope. Never forget it. You're very brave for giving yourself in that way when you hardly know me . . ."

He hesitated, as though he wanted to say something else but wasn't quite sure how to put it. She felt her lower lip quiver as she stared into cerulean eyes that reminded her of the color of the Mediterranean Sea around the Greek islands on a clear, balmy day.

"You're welcome, Ryan," she whispered.

His dark brows went up in slight surprise before he smiled. "Are you all right? Are you in pain?"

Hope shook her head. In truth, her bottom felt a little sore, but pleasure still tingled in her sex all the way up to her tailbone as well, making the slight discomfort seem more than worth the price.

Ryan leaned up and seized her lips in a kiss that struck Hope as both possessive and cherishing at once. He leaned back and spoke softly against her lips while her fallen hair created a curtain around their faces.

"Then it's time for us to escape, honey."

"Now?" she asked in surprise.

He nodded as he held her gaze.

"Very well. Tell me what to do."

"When I give the word, I want you to dive off this bed—quickly, you understand? One second you're here, the next not." Hope nodded. "Crouch down as low as you can to the floor, and move to that corner of the alcove," Ryan said, his eyes moving to the right side of the bed.

"But they took my clothing."

"Crawl across the hallway to that closet on the far wall and pull down one of Sadie's robes or dresses—something easily slipped on. Whatever you do . . . stay down low and keep hidden."

"Should I stay hidden because you want me to make a surprise attack on someone if they come in the room?" Hope asked, all too eager to vent her anger on Diamond Jack Fletcher or one of his minions after what she'd seen him do to Sadie Holcrum.

"What?" Ryan asked, looking stunned. "No. Of course not. I want you to stay down and keep hidden to keep you safe."

Hope scowled and opened her mouth to argue.

"Quiet, Hope. We're not going to do anything at all unless you agree to this. The chances of me getting you out of here safely are small enough . . ."

"What?" Hope whispered when she saw Ryan's expression stiffen. For a moment he didn't speak, seeming undecided.

"No. We must act. Staying put might be playing into the hands of fate just as much as choosing to act," he mumbled, as if to himself. His faraway expression sharpened on her once again. "The only thing you need to worry about is staying down close to the floor and keeping out of the way until I tell you to move. Okay?"

"But, Ryan, I want to help you—"

"You'll help me by promising to do what I ask. There are things you don't understand about this situation that I don't have time to explain right now. Do I have your word that you'll cooperate?"

When she hesitated his dark brows went up again, this time in an intimidating fashion. "This is not the time for an H. G. Wells brand of adventure, Hope. One or both of us may be killed if you don't follow my instructions."

"All right, I agree to—"

But Hope had no opportunity to tell Ryan to what she agreed or to hear any more details of Ryan's plan for escape, because suddenly a loud, furious voice that bizarrely seemed to be coming from the wall itself bellowed.

"Daire!"

∽ FIFTEEN ∽

Jack gritted his teeth in rising frustration when he heard New-comb stifle his groans of climax as he watched Daire fuck Hope Stillwater's ass with unrestrained lust. It infuriated him to know that even though he put on such a top-notch sex display for his most powerful business associates, he himself could not enjoy it.

Mel tried her damndest to suck his dick back to its former glory, but despite the fact that Jack was mentally as aroused as he'd ever been, his damn cock wouldn't respond. Hearing Newcomb find his pleasure was bad enough, but watching the starkly vir-ile Daire plunder the beauty was like having a knife twist in a wound.

"Get off it, Mel! You're losing your touch. You—Betsey—you take over," he demanded bitterly as he watched Daire slamming his big cock into Hope Stillwater's bobbing little ass.

The fucking mick hadn't been lying when he said he could make her respond. How had he been so confident? That self-righteous little minx seemed to love every moment of being sodomized, Jack thought grudgingly.

It became obvious that Betsey had nothing on Mel's skills at fellatio. He pushed down on her head roughly in rising frustration, heedless of her gags and cries of discomfort. He strained for his own pleasure so greatly that he was hardly aware that the photographer took another picture or that Mason finally gasped in a hard-won orgasm.

Daire bucked into Hope one last time before his body went rigid in climax. He let out a full-throated roar. His pleasure seemed so concentrated, so immense that Jack could almost feel it resonating through the walls. A profound sense of fury and jealousy made his gut burn like he'd just swallowed acid.

He pushed Betsey off his now-limp dick, scraping her cheek with one of his diamond rings in the process. She whimpered in pain. When Mel pulled back the young woman's head and checked the bleeding scratch with a concerned look on her face, Jack's fury escalated.

He pulled up his underwear and pants, fastening his suspenders. "The men who come here are idiots. I can't believe they pay me good money to sample such a worthless whore."

Mel looked up at him with glittering eyes.

"There are some things money can't buy, Jack. A sense of decency and a working cock are two of them," Mel said quietly.

For a few seconds a tense silence prevailed in the stuffy little room.

Jack's eyes widened slowly in stark disbelief. It was all because of his limp dick that he was losing respect, even among his whores. He raised his hand to backhand Mel's smart mouth when someone burst into the room, distracting his attention. He'd assigned

Big Marlo to stand guard in the hallway and not to allow anyone into the viewing room, so he couldn't imagine who dared to enter.

"What'd'ya want?" he barked in a surly fashion when he saw it was Big Marlo himself, still looking disgruntled and worse for wear after waltzing with Daire in the ring. Another man followed Marlo into the room. He only came up to Marlo's shoulder but the guy was barrel-chested and thick with muscle. Jack noticed his pale hair looked disheveled and that like Marlo, he also sported a swollen, black eye.

"This man's name is Kendall, Boss. He works for Shapiro in the stockyards. He says *he's* the one who Shapiro sent over to fight me tonight," Marlo said, fury spicing his deep baritone.

Kendall was busy staring at the women on their knees and the men standing before them, a puzzled look on his broad face. He finally cleared his throat and addressed Jack. "Some damn cokie jumped me on the way here. I just woke up twenty minutes ago in the alley. Damn thief stole all my money. So . . . is it true the fight's already over?"

For a second or two Jack just stared as the acid anger in his gut seemed to bubble up in his throat. It exploded out of his mouth along with one word.

"*Daire!*"

He shoved the barrel of Daire's bizarre pistol into an unused peephole at waist level. When he peered into the room he could no longer see Hope Stillwater at all and Daire perched at the edge of the bed, poised to spring. Jack's forefinger pulled on the trigger but nothing happened.

"No!" a woman cried out below him. His thumb fumbled and found a lever. Jack flipped it back. He had to squeeze with all his might on the trigger but he fired at Daire's moving chest even as he lunged off the bed. Someone jerked down forcefully on his wrist just as the gun went off. A light fixture on the far wall of Sadie's room exploded.

"You *bitch*," Jack snarled in disbelieving rage when he saw Mel still hanging on his wrist. He tried to pull back the hand that held the gun, but Mel held on to his wrist with all her might and pushed his hand toward the wall. The barrel of the gun shoved further into the hole.

Mel looked over at Betsey and said one word.

"*Marlo.*"

Then she sunk her teeth into Jack's wrist. He howled in stunned disbelief and pain.

Betsey scurried quicker than a crab threatened with a steaming pot across the small room and launched into Marlo's knees, giving an eerie, bloodcurdling scream as she did so. Maybe it was just surprise on Marlo's part, or maybe it was that he was still unsteady from Daire's pummeling earlier, but the giant wavered on his feet. When Martha followed Betsey's example and threw her body weight against Marlo's thighs, the giant toppled to the floor for the second time that night.

A piercing scream rent the air and the other prostitute in the viewing room flew into the fray. All three women fought like rabid dogs, swarming the still stunned Marlo and attacking with fists, knees, fingernails and teeth.

A door opened across the hall and someone gave a loud, piercing whistle. The next thing Jack knew Molly Sayles fell to her knees behind Marlo's head.

"You worthless piece of *shit*," she screamed as she jabbed a long fingernail into Marlo's only functional eye and gouged. Marlo roared and threw two of the women off him violently as he reared up in pain. They were back almost immediately, however, throwing their weight on Marlo and pushing him back to the floor, biting, beating and clawing like madwomen. Meanwhile a bare-breasted

Molly grabbed Marlo's ears, twisted them until he shrieked in pain and proceeded to whack his skull into the wood floor again and again.

"You'll never . . . ever . . . *ever* beat me again, you monster," she yelled, punctuating each word with a crack of Marlo's head.

"Stop them!" Jack bawled at Ambrose and Newcomb as he tried to pull his hand away from the wall, but Mel clamped down with her teeth on this wrist and pushed his hand tightly into the wall. Jack tried to use his left fist to beat her off him, but their positioning was awkward and Jack's right arm inadvertently protected Mel's head as he tried to take a swing at her. He refused to let go of Daire's gun for some reason, gripping it tightly as though he held on to it for dear life. The barrel fixed faster in the peephole the more Mel pushed on his hand.

"*Hey*," Jack bellowed at a stunned-looking Ambrose. "Get this bitch off me!"

Ambrose unglued his eyes from the spectacle unfolding before them as several more prostitutes rushed to the scene, a couple of them screaming balefully as though they were warriors running into battle. Ambrose wasn't the only one who had frozen in disbelieving shock. All the men in the room stared, pale-faced, at the horrible but mesmerizing sight of the mighty behemoth disappearing beneath a mound of writhing, furious women whose painted faces were alive with malice.

"What did Marlo *do* to them?" Lander muttered under his breath.

"I think we should get out of here. They'll be after us next," Ambrose said. His words seemed to galvanize Mason, Lander and Newcomb. Divorak was the first to bolt, however, clutching his black box camera and doing his best not to step on any body parts in the pile of twisting limbs before he finally leapt out the door to freedom. The rest of the men followed quicker than Jack could blink and shout, "Get your yellow asses back here!"

But the useless cowards were already gone. Jack struggled against Mel's clamped jaws, hissing curses at her, but his attempts only seemed to sink her teeth further. He hit her about her ear but she remained doggedly latched. It hurt so badly that tears flowed ceaselessly down his face. The thing that Jack was most aware of, however, wasn't pain. Pure, undiluted rage throbbed in every cell of his body at the fact that his authority was being challenged.

Pretty soon every whore in the Levee District would be looking at him with cold contempt, just like his mother had.

The man who was supposed to be Marlo's contender in the boxing ring looked frightened when Jack caught his gaze.

"*You*, Kendall," Jack said quietly. "If you don't get over here and get this bitch off me, I'm going to hunt you and every last member of your family down and treat them to a slow, terrible death."

Kendall swallowed and glanced longingly at the doorway before he came toward Jack and Mel.

∽

The sound of a shot and shattering glass made Hope yelp in surprise at the same moment that Ryan's body thudded against the floorboard.

"*Hurry*," he prompted a stunned-looking Hope before he army-crawled over to the fireplace and retrieved a metal poker. Out of the corner of his eye he saw that Hope had pulled down a frayed satin robe and struggled to pull it around her shoulders while she remained crouched. Ryan blocked her with his body and reached inside of his boot.

"Lie down flat on the floor," he ordered before he handed her his knife. Her eyes widened when he released the clip and removed the blade. "Use it if you have to. Don't hesitate."

He waited for her to look up at him and nod her head before he crawled along the hallway and rose to a crouching position. He'd half expected Jack to be firing like mad into the room—and

Lord knew Ryan's weapon was powerful enough to penetrate the wall at close range—but no shots occurred beyond the first.

The noises he heard emanating from the wall and hallway confused him: women screaming in a bloodthirsty manner and male grunts of pain and fury. Seconds later he heard footsteps running past, but no one tried to enter their room.

There was nothing for it. No matter what was going on out there, staying holed up in here wasn't going to help Hope escape.

He raised the poker and brought it down heavily on the door, breaking through the lock after two swings. He glanced back and saw Hope peering around the corner at him as she lay on her belly, her hair spilling wildly around her shoulders, the knife clutched in her hand, her expression livid with excitement.

There was no doubt about it. If Hope Stillwater lived in his time period, she'd undoubtedly spend her time bungee jumping or climbing harrowing mountain peaks.

Christ, what had he gotten himself into, anyway?

"Somebody has been kind enough to provide us with a distraction," he whispered, "but I want you to stay *down* for now, Hope."

She nodded in agreement and he eased open the door a few inches. The sounds of women shrieking in rage amplified along with increasingly fading grunts of pain. Ryan froze when he saw two men running down the hallway. A quick glance told him it was the tall, blond man who'd stood guard at the bottom of the stairs along with the doorman who wore a black hat. Both of them had pistols drawn as they passed him. Apparently the debacle that was going on next door was more of a concern for the henchmen than Ryan or Hope.

Ryan waved for Hope to come near him. Whatever was going on was a heaven-sent distraction. Just as he felt a tendril of Hope's soft hair brushing his bare waist, however, one of the men bawled over the din.

"I'll shoot your brains out, Molly, and you, too, Nancy! Get *off* him."

"Go back," Ryan mouthed fiercely to Hope. "*Go*," he whispered when she hesitated and grabbed his knife with both hands as though she were steeling herself for battle.

"Shoot 'em! Go ahead," Ryan heard Diamond Jack Fletcher roar.

"*Back*," Ryan ordered.

A scowl of mixed irritation and uncertainty creased Hope's forehead at Ryan's warning, but something she saw in his eyes must have made her fade back toward a place of safety—in regard to flying bullets, anyway.

No place was safe in this madhouse, at the moment.

Ryan gave a regretful glance to his cut and bruised knuckles before he entered the hallway. He had a quick impression of several women looking up from a pile on the floor just inside the viewing room doorway, their hair wild and tangled, their faces wary and showing clear signs of battle. He saw what appeared to be the bald head of Big Marlo beneath the heap. As Ryan silently approached, he saw the behemoth's head move sluggishly and then go still.

He tapped on the blond man's shoulder.

When the man turned in surprise Ryan served him an uppercut to the jaw, immediately following with a left directly to his face. Although the man already was falling, Ryan gave him a forceful shove into the other henchman. The guy with the hat stumbled, losing his balance.

Ryan kicked the blond in the groin and took his gun from him as he doubled over, falling heavily on top of the other man, both of them grunting loudly. By the time the man beneath shoved the deadweight of his coworker off him, Ryan had the pistol trained on him.

"Throw it down or I'll shoot you."

"Ryan, get down!" Hope shrieked from directly behind him.

He glanced around in alarm and saw Diamond Jack standing on the other side of the pile of humanity in the doorway, a snarl of hatred on his face, a bloody hand raised and ready to fire Ryan's gun. Ryan flung his weight backward in the direction of Hope, covering her with his body. They both hit the floor with a crash, Hope unfortunately taking the brunt of his weight. The knife she'd been carrying skittered across the wood floor, but Ryan figured it was better off there than accidentally in his back.

He quickly aimed and fired at Jack. Without bothering to wait and see the result, he transferred his attention to the henchman on the floor, who was in the process of raising his pistol and aiming. Ryan winged him like he had Diamond Jack. The man grunted; the pistol clattered to the floor.

Ryan sprung up and surveyed the area for threat. Both of Jack's guards lay unmoving and there was no sign of Jack. The prostitutes stared at him slack-jawed, their faces pale with shock.

"Let's go," Ryan told Hope tensely once he'd helped her up off the floor. He pulled her with him toward the staircase, pausing to retrieve his knife. His eyes widened in disbelief when he felt her jerking back on his hand, resisting him.

"Hope, get back here," Ryan ordered furiously when she yanked her hand out of his and ran over to the prostitutes.

"Quickly! Diamond Jack will kill you when he recovers," Hope hissed at the stunned women.

"Hope, get your butt over—"

She turned around to face him, her expression anxious and desperate.

"Do you want to just leave them all here to die? What do you think Diamond Jack will do to them? They attacked that man. They helped us escape!"

"We haven't escaped yet," Ryan muttered as he scanned the

hallway warily. Was it possible that only these two—the guard at the front of the stairs and the doorman—had been warned of what was occurring upstairs at the Sweet Lash? It seemed too good to be true, but Ryan had to admit the large, interior room that housed the bar and staging areas was quite a distance from the front stairs.

Several of the prostitutes started out of trances of shock and looked into the interior of the viewing room. Ryan glanced around in time to see Mel, the elder of the pair who'd performed the Slip and Whip. Her blonde hair hung askew and her cheeks and mouth were smeared crimson with blood. She steadily regarded first Ryan and then Hope in turn with sharp, brown eyes. Ryan instinctively understood that she was the leader among the women.

"Where would we go?" Mel asked Hope cautiously.

"To Addie Sampson at the Marlborough Club. She runs one of the few brothels in the Levee District that isn't controlled by Jack. A word from me and she'll protect you. You can either work for her or go where you choose. I'll provide something for the finances for those that choose to leave. You have my word on it," Hope added quickly when she saw Mel's doubtful expression.

"Decide now, Mel," Ryan said harshly as he retrieved the pistol from the unconscious doorman. He glanced pointedly at Marlo. "The giant's awakening. He's not going to be in a good mood when he does."

Mel looked down and saw Marlo's huge bald head moving from side to side. He mumbled gutturally in a foreign language. She nodded decisively.

"We're going. There ain't time to get nothing from your rooms, so don't let me hear a word about that. Amy, give Molly your robe." When the woman, who was apparently Amy, opened her mouth as if to protest, Mel pointed a finger at her. "If you're gonna whine, then stay behind, Amy. You got a corset on under your robe and Molly's naked. Now, let's go."

"Wait," Ryan said to Mel. "Is Jack unconscious?"

She glanced back into the room and nodded quickly.

"Get my gun from him. And the rest of you—*move*."

He approached Hope as the women began clambering off a sluggishly moving Marlo.

"Stupendous job of following my instructions, Hope," he murmured in exasperation.

"I'm sorry, Ryan, but I couldn't leave you out in the hallway alone. And the women—Jack'll kill them if they stay."

Ryan opened his mouth and closed it. The fierceness of her spirit left him speechless. And of course, she was 100 percent right about the prostitutes who had participated in the attack. Diamond Jack wasn't the type to lightly accept a rebellion against his authority. Ryan met Hope's dark-eyed gaze and nodded once.

She sighed with relief.

"Here. Do you know how to use this?" he asked as he handed her the pistol.

"No," she said, eyeing the gun like he'd just put a snake in her hand.

"The safety is on, Hope, just—"

He paused when Mel stepped over Big Marlo's body, carrying his SIG. Ryan took it from her and gave her the doorman's pistol in return, pausing to give both Hope and Mel terse instructions on how to use the weapons. In fact, he'd been a little surprised at how modern seeming the pistols were despite the narrow barrels. He would have guessed they'd be revolvers, but they were, in fact, early versions of automatics.

"If you should have to fire, shoot to kill. Chances are you'll hit *something* if you do," Ryan instructed.

The women were all assembled now. He told them to wait a moment while he checked out what the situation was in the entryway. A few seconds later he came to the top of the stairs, raised his finger to his mouth to indicate they needed to be as quiet as possible and beckoned for Hope and the women to follow.

Ryan reached the bottom of the stairs first, pausing at the sound of approaching voices. He signaled for Hope to go behind him and lead the women out the front door while he waited for whoever approached. Most of the women had scuttled out the door by the time a middle-aged, balding man who was leaning down as he flirted drunkenly with the woman on his arm looked up to see Ryan holding his weapon on him. Ryan noticed that he had a short-brimmed ivory felt hat clutched in his hand.

"What the—"

"Shut up or I'll hurt you."

"What do you want?" the young woman asked. Ryan recognized her as being the prostitute that had been in the lap of the man Jack had clobbered earlier. Up close, she looked like she was about sixteen years old.

"That hat, for starters. It's mine," Ryan informed the man, who had somehow procured his Coach Stagg hat that he'd left at the bar.

The man handed it to him, speechless. Ryan slammed it on his head, his entire ensemble now consisting of his pants, socks, boots and the hat.

He looked at the girl.

"Mel and a bunch of the women are escaping from the Sweet Lash if you'd care to join them," he told her quietly. When her mouth dropped open as though she were about to barrage him with questions he shook his head. "No time. I'm leaving now. If you want to come—"

But Mel saved him further explanations by hissing from the opened doorway. "Sally, get your ass out here. We're leaving the Sweet Lash for good."

Sally looked up at the bald man, who wore a stunned expression.

A huge grin spread on her pretty face. She didn't seem too upset when Ryan brought down the butt of his gun on the man's temple.

"Bye-bye, Charlie," Sally whispered happily after Ryan had stuffed the unconscious man's body in the entryway closet.

∽ SIXTEEN ∽

An hour later, Ryan wandered around the drawing room of 1807 Prairie Avenue. Hope had hastily lit a gas lantern and several candles upon their arrival. Since their mission was secret, she didn't dare illuminate any of the newly installed electric fixtures. Mel sat in a yellow print chair and watched him as he prowled around the amazing room.

Hope had left just thirty seconds ago, saying she needed to retrieve something from her bedroom. At first Ryan had insisted upon going with her, still worried about something happening to her.

"Nothing dangerous is going to happen to me in my own house, Ryan," Hope had exclaimed in muted exasperation.

Ryan wasn't so sure about that, however. He still didn't know if he was helping to change Hope's fate or nudging events to make her demise more inevitable. The thought brought him close to panic. It was starting to feel like every choice he made—move right or move left?—was somehow inevitably predetermined. The one thing he knew for certain was that the year 1906 was *not* a healthy year for Hope Stillwater.

He needed to get her out of it as soon as possible. For some strange reason, however, Hope had been adamant that he could *not* accompany her to her bedroom before she'd turned away, blushing, and hurried out of the room.

Ryan's nervousness for Hope's safety had slowly been replaced by awe as he took in the interior of the drawing room.

Every nerve in his body seemed to vibrate with mixed shock and amazement as he studied the details of the luxurious room. The only items of décor that remained in the year 2008 were the priceless mahogany panels covering every square inch of the walls and the elaborately carved fireplace. To see all the rich paintings, oriental carpets, crystal decanters and highly polished silver brought it home with more force than anything he'd experienced yet.

He truly *was* walking around in a different century.

One rarely saw this degree of luxury in modern times or if they did, never was it so naturally and elegantly displayed. This was a room that was clearly lived in and enjoyed, not a stiff, stuffy place where Hope and her father occasionally ushered in august visitors with an aim to impress.

Although the furnishings were well made, with fine woods and luxurious fabrics, the couch and several of the chairs by the fire were slightly worn, indicating how much Hope, her father and their visitors sat and *lived* in here. Ryan picked up a delicate blue-and-white porcelain bowl. Granted, he was no expert on the subject, but it appeared to be a genuine piece of Ming porcelain. Alistair had a few Ming vases that Ryan had studied with interest on several occasions.

He looked inside the bowl and saw that Jacob Stillwater used the priceless object as an ashtray for his cigars.

He shook his head in amazement and replaced the bowl on the

table. Hope's father must have inherited his wealth. Surely social reformist ministers didn't make enough financially to afford a Prairie Avenue mansion. He tried to recall if he'd read anything about Jacob Stillwater's roots in the report he'd gotten from Gail, but came up short.

Ryan squinted in the dim light as he studied the portrait of a dark-eyed, dark-haired woman above the fireplace. She wore a lavish sapphire-and-diamond necklace along with matching earrings. The woman's physical similarity to Hope was so striking that it immediately caused a person to seek out the few subtle differences—lips that were thinner in comparison to Hope's lush rosebud mouth, breasts slightly smaller than Hope's, a more aquiline nose—

"Why did you stop that man from beatin' Betsey and me?"

Ryan spun around. He'd been so engrossed in studying the portrait of what must surely be Hope's mother that Mel's question had taken him by surprise. She sat stiffly in a chair near the entryway while they waited for Hope to return, as if she were prepared to bolt at any moment and wanted a convenient location to make her escape. It struck Ryan for the first time that Mel was uncomfortable to the point of prickliness sitting in a room that was almost negligently elegant and grand. Like him, she clearly was not accustomed to being in such a place.

"I have experience with guys like that at my job. You can usually spot them from a mile off." Ryan shrugged. "Sorry I didn't get there before he started hitting you."

Mel gave a bark of laughter. She looked at him as though he were some kind of bizarre alien artifact that had just fallen from the sky and still smoked and sizzled at her feet. It took him a moment to realize she'd been shocked by his apology.

"And then you helped us escape. Why?"

"You mostly have Hope to thank for that. On my part"—he shrugged—"seemed like the right thing to do at the time."

Mel stood slowly and came toward him, her head cocked as she examined him, her squinted eyelids deepening the lines at the corners of her brown eyes. She was still dressed in the robe and riding boots she'd worn to perform in the Slip and Whip. They'd left the rest of the women at the Marlborough Club with a concerned-looking Addie Sampson. The last glimpse Ryan'd caught of Hope's colorful friend she'd been bustling about her private boudoir, barking out orders to maids for towels and hot water and personally seeing to the women's cuts and bruises.

Ryan had asked Hope on their hurried flight to Prairie Avenue to keep their presence secret from the household, including her father, for the time being. She'd agreed, although he thought she was so overwhelmed by the circumstances to question his motives. Hope had snuck them into the house by a side door that Ryan hadn't even discovered existed yet in the early twenty-first century. She'd led them quietly down the back stairs of the darkened mansion, pausing at one point and lifting a finger to her lips as they crossed the foyer. The chandelier in the enormous formal entry hall had been lit, as though to entice the missing mistress of the household back home.

Ryan had seen a light shining beneath a swinging door, which he knew from his own time period led to the kitchen, pantries and back stairs—the servants' portion of the house.

But no one, including the awake, concerned servants, had observed them as Hope led them to the drawing room and whispered for them to wait until she returned.

"Why'd you *really* do all that stuff back there at the Sweet Lash?" Mel asked presently, a small smile playing around her mouth.

"Why'd you stop Diamond Jack from shooting me?" Ryan asked. Mel had given Hope and him a breathless description of what had occurred in the viewing room at the Sweet Lash as the three of them hurried through the dark night, leaving the seedy Levee District behind.

Mel's grin deepened. Ryan realized he'd never seen her smile before—at least in any genuine sense. The single dimple in her right cheek made her look about fifteen years younger. Ryan squinted at her in disbelief.

"Ramiro?"

Mel gave him a "what's your problem, asshole?" look that only confirmed his sudden suspicion that Jim Donahue wasn't the only person he knew who had an existence in Hope's time period.

Son of a bitch, this was amazing.

"What did you call me?" Mel asked suspiciously.

"Sorry. You just sort of reminded me of someone for a second."

She shook her head. "You're a strange man. Nice, but strange. And to answer your question, I stopped Jack because it seemed like the right thing to do at the time."

"Guess we're even, then."

"Guess so," Mel replied, suddenly looking more relaxed than Ryan had ever seen her. They both glanced over when the drawing room door shut softly and Hope hurried into the room.

Ryan's eyes widened in amazement. It struck him for the first time that he'd never really seen her fully clothed. Seeing Hope in the garb of an early-twentieth-century gentlewoman sent another shock wave through him.

"What?" Hope whispered when she saw his face.

Ryan blinked, realizing he'd been gaping. She wore a long, checked tan-and-black skirt with a white ruffled sort of blouse that buttoned all the way up to her neck. Instead of spilling down her back her hair had been affixed to her head. With the black belt highlighting her tiny waist, the few loose curls around her cheeks and the snug, form-fitting white blouse, she looked fresh, feminine and thoroughly alluring.

"Nothing," Ryan replied, clearing his throat.

She drew a long, midnight blue velvet box from a deep pocket in her skirt. She opened the box and took out something that flashed with muted fires in the dim room.

"This is for you," Hope whispered, reaching out to Mel. "I have already told Addie you will bring it to her. Addie has helped me dispose of such things before when I needed funds for various projects. A jeweler she knows will give you a fair price, and you and the others will have some spending money to start anew."

Mel accepted what Hope offered. For several seconds she just stared at her hand. Her brown eyes flickered up to the portrait over the mantel. Abruptly she reached out, using one hand to grab Hope's wrist and the other to return the object into her palm.

"What?" Hope asked in rising confusion. She gently pushed her hand back toward Mel but the older woman was unwilling to take what she offered.

"I may have been raised in an Indiana cornfield and been stupid enough to believe the lies Jack's man told me when I was sixteen years old, but I'm not a fool, Miss Stillwater."

Hope's gaze flickered over to Ryan uneasily as though asking for assistance in understanding. "I'm sorry. I'm not sure what you mean. I told you I would give you something to help you and the others financially—"

"So you're giving me *that*? Are you *mad*, girl?"

When Ryan saw Hope's slain expression he grabbed her hand and pried back her fingers. An exquisite platinum, sapphire and diamond necklace lay across her palm like a supple, jeweled serpent— the same necklace that Hope's mother wore in the portrait.

"Hope . . . *no*, honey."

Hope looked at Ryan, then at Mel and back to Ryan again. A look of grim determination suddenly overcame her face. She took the necklace from Ryan and shoved it at Mel's belly until she grunted and raised her hands reluctantly.

"Stones. *Rocks*. That's what they are. Do you think they mean more to me than human lives? Don't *tell* me they mean more to you," Hope challenged fiercely when Mel opened her mouth to protest.

"No. Of course not," Mel said after a stunned moment.

When Hope noticed the tough older woman's chastened expression she seemed to regret her aggressiveness. Her cheeks colored in embarrassment. "Don't worry. I still have my mother's sapphire earrings . . . and many other mementos of hers as well. Besides," Hope said, raising her chin proudly. "My mother would have approved wholeheartedly."

"With a daughter like you, miss, I'm sure she would have."

Ryan couldn't have said which woman looked more surprised or embarrassed by Mel's tender words.

"I'd best be getting back to the Marlborough Club, then," Mel muttered gruffly.

"I'll escort you to the coach house. It'll only take a moment for the groom to prepare the carriage—"

Ryan never got his protest off his tongue before Mel spoke resolutely.

"No. It's not a far walk, and I'll keep to the shadows just like we did on our way here. I don't want to make any more bother. *Please* . . ." Mel said when Hope opened her mouth to argue. "You've done far too much for us already."

Hope didn't look happy about the proposal, but Ryan said nothing when she looked to him to intervene. He sensed how difficult it was for Mel to sit in this rich room and accept Hope's lavish act of charity. He wouldn't argue Hope's case in this particular circumstance. Knowing what he knew about Ramiro's character made him even more certain that Mel would feel miserable if she were forced to ride in the grand carriage for the twelve blocks to the Marlborough Club.

"Let me at least get you a coat, then," Hope conceded when she saw that Mel wouldn't waver and Ryan would not plead her cause.

Mel met Ryan's eyes and nodded once in thanks before she followed Hope, off to start a different—hopefully better—life than she'd had under the hands of Diamond Jack Fletcher.

When Hope returned a moment later after showing Mel out, Ryan was waiting for her by the door. He grabbed her hand and spun her into his arms.

"Ryan!" she exclaimed softly, her tone slightly scandalized, before he covered her mouth with his.

"Yes?" he said a moment later when he raised his head. He studied her bemused, shadowed face. "Just because you've donned the clothes of a lady doesn't mean I'm not going to kiss the hell out of you every chance I get, witch. I remember what you look like in that excuse for a nightgown. I know what you look like naked—the knowledge is burned into my brain, in fact. So don't plan on getting all proper and ladylike with me now."

Her dark eyes went wide before a grin curved her lips. Ryan couldn't unglue his eyes from the luscious confection of Hope Stillwater's smile.

"The social proprieties between men and women must be very different in the year 2008 compared to now," she said a tad nervously.

Ryan's brow crinkled in puzzlement when he saw her color deepen. "Hope, are you forgetting the things we've done together?"

Her mouth fell open in disbelief, apparently at the fact that Ryan had just been bold enough to mention that they'd had carnal knowledge of one another in the refined atmosphere of the drawing room.

"Are you referring to . . . to . . ." When Ryan just stared at her, his confusion probably writ large on his face, she found it in herself to continue in a nearly inaudible whisper. "Those things happened in the bedroom, Ryan. This is not the *bedroom*."

He just stared at her in amazement before he grinned. How strange. Hope glanced warily around the room as if she thought morally upright, scandalized denizens were going to crawl out of the woodwork at any moment, preaching and pointing their fingers at her accusingly. God, it was going to be a bitch of a challenge to take her to the year 2008.

But challenge or not, he needed to get her there.

He nipped at the shell of her ear and felt her shiver.

"I was wondering when you were going to start acting like an early-twentieth-century woman. Is this modest streak the reason you wouldn't allow me to go to your bedroom with you?"

"Ryan, in my day and age, it would be very ungentlemanly for a man to speak of my bedroom. Even to *think* of my private sanctuary would be considered . . . unseemly," Hope murmured as she turned her head and nuzzled his cheek while he kissed her ear and neck. Her soft sigh and warm breath caused his skin to roughen in excitement.

"I've made love to you in your bedroom, Hope. I *live* in your bedroom. Your bedroom is *my* bedroom," Ryan whispered next to her ear. "Don't you think we might suspend the typical formalities?"

The return of the mischievous sparkle to her eyes made him unduly happy. "I suppose so, considering the highly unusual state of circumstances."

He lifted his head and plucked at her upturned lips. "So let's go to your bedroom then."

"Ryan, I can't think about *that* now! I have to go to my father. I should go this moment. I saw his lights on when I snuck up to my room and I heard voices coming from his suite. I think he's conversing with the *police*. I'm sure the coachman has long ago informed him that I never met him at the carriage. My father must be frantic with worry."

"Hope, listen to me. This is important." Ryan tightened his hold on her, feeling her skirt press against his thighs along with layers of other material beneath it. He would have thought he wouldn't like the sensation of so much fabric separating him from her. Instead he found himself getting aroused by knowing that her warm, responsive body resided amidst all those swishy, feminine ruffles.

As if she were a succulent edible carefully wrapped in silk and lace.

And so much more tasty for it—

He dragged his mind off his dirty thoughts when he saw how Hope solemnly regarded him with her huge, dark eyes. He loved all of her moods, but when she turned all somber on him, she was downright irresistible.

"Let's go to your bedroom first. I need to look at the mirror."

He saw the convulsive movement at her elegant throat as she swallowed. "You . . . you're going to leave now, aren't you?"

"Yes. I have to." *So do you*, he thought privately.

"Would you not like to meet my father first?" she asked hopefully.

Ryan glanced down bemusedly at his bare chest. Addie Sampson had asked one of the men who worked for her to give him his coat, but it was too small for him and he couldn't button it. "I'm hardly dressed for a social call, Hope. And it'd be awkward explaining my presence here. He's likely to believe I had something to do with your kidnapping."

She scowled. "I'd tell him that you saved me, of course! Do you think he wouldn't believe his own daughter? My father and I are very close. We share one mind on most topics."

Ryan ran his hands along her back and side, soothing her pique. "I just don't think it's the ideal time, beauty."

Hope dropped her chin to her chest so that all he could see of her for a moment was the pale part of her hair and the mass of soft, coiling curls pinned to her head. The scent of gardenias wafted up to his appreciative nose.

"No. I don't suppose it is the ideal time. All right, we'll go to the mirror," she whispered weakly.

They extinguished the lights and moved down the darkened

hallway hand in hand, Ryan in the lead. Before they reached the brightly lit entry hall, however, the sounds of men talking reached Ryan's ears.

He pulled Hope back into the shadows.

"You will contact me immediately when you discover anything, won't you, Mr. O'Rourke? I won't rest until my daughter is returned to me safely."

Ryan's brows crinkled in puzzlement. The man who had just spoken possessed a rich, resonant voice that sounded strangely familiar. He could easily imagine him holding a crowd enthralled with his speeches. The Reverend Stillwater must not only be a fine political orator, but popular among his parishioners for his sermons at his church.

"Indeed, Mr. Stillwater. But as we've told you, missing persons investigations are difficult in the city. Every day people go missing in Chicago and are lost without a trace," a man who must have been Detective Connor J. O'Rourke replied, his voice flavored with only a trace of an Irish brogue.

"But my daughter—such a singularly lovely young woman—surely *someone* must have noticed her when she entered that train station."

"Detective McMannis and I will scout the area first thing in the morning, Mr. Stillwater. You're right—chances are somebody noticed something. I recommend you place an advertisement with a copy of her likeness in the major newspapers. In the meantime, do me a favor and keep thinking about who might profit from your daughter's abduction. I'm sure you've made some significant enemies with your political agendas."

Ryan wondered from O'Rourke's steely tone of voice if the detective already harbored suspicions toward Diamond Jack Fletcher even if Jacob Stillwater hadn't yet pointed his finger in that direction.

"I will think on it. I can't imagine who would want to harm such a warmhearted, generous young woman."

Ryan felt Hope startle, as though she reacted instinctively to a need to soothe her father's obvious distress. He squeezed her hand in reassurance, however, and she stilled.

"I'm thinking it's just as likely that it's *you* they want to harm," O'Rourke said before he and the other detective left the house.

"Shall I turn out the lights?" a quiet voice asked a moment later.

"No, Mrs. Abernathy. We'll leave on the entry hall chandelier until my daughter returns home."

"You need to rest, sir. It'll be dawn in a few hours and you've been ill."

"I couldn't sleep if I tried."

"Dr. Walkerton left a sleeping draught and I've had it prepared for you. You'll not do your daughter a bit of good by becoming ill again," Mrs. Abernathy said resolutely.

The sounds of them ascending the stairs followed.

"I think we had better take the main stairs this time," Hope whispered after a moment. "Mrs. Abernathy will use the back stairs on the way back down, as will the maid getting my father's sleeping draught."

Ryan nodded. They crept up the grand staircase and down the shadowed hallway to Hope's room without incident. When Hope closed the door silently behind them they stood in pitch blackness. He heard Hope fumbling by the mantel and soon a flame hissed and flared. She approached him carrying a single taper, her face looking unusually pale and sober in the flickering light.

"We still keep candles and lanterns about. The electricity is wonderful, but it tends to go out easily, especially in storms. Sometimes it seems like the electricity functions only half the time, but we're quite used to it, so fond are we of the modern conveniences of—"

Ryan reached out and grasped her shoulders, hearing the anguish in her shaking voice as she rambled on about undependable electricity. Her eyes rose to meet his and Ryan saw they glistened with tears.

"What's wrong, honey?"

"I—I don't want you to go, Ryan," she whispered miserably.

∽ SEVENTEEN ∽

Ryan studied her face for a long moment. "I'm not parting from you yet, Hope. There's something I need to explain to you. Something important."

They both started slightly when they heard a thumping noise down the hallway.

"The maid must have dropped something," Hope whispered. "You don't think they'll be able to see the candle, do you?"

Ryan shook his head but used his hand to mute the light, anyway.

"Let's look at the mirror and then I need to talk with you about something.

"It's always this clear?" Ryan asked a moment later as he peered into the gilt mirror.

"Clear?" Hope asked, confused.

"In my time, it's grown foggy. But as we began to see one another, to touch, the fog dissipated. Just before I stepped through into the Sweet Lash, the mirror had gone clear in my time as well," he murmured. He experimentally pushed his hand to the surface. Sure enough, he experienced the unusual but increasingly familiar sensation that he could only describe with words as *tactile possibility*, like touching a myriad of different potential realities.

"That's so strange," Hope mused. "I wonder . . ."

"What?" he asked when her voice faded.

"According to my father, the man who lived here before us was a very unusual gentleman. His name was Mortimer P. Chase. He built this house. He was quite an idiosyncratic gentleman and was involved in the spiritualist movement. Some called him a magician. He disappeared without a trace several decades ago, leaving no heirs for an apparently vast fortune."

"Are you saying this mirror belonged to Mortimer P. Chase?"

Hope looked puzzled. "To be honest with you, I'm not sure. We moved into this house when I was eight years old. This wardrobe and mirror have been in my room since then, but—now that I think on it—I don't *recall* it being in my old bedroom on Washington Street."

"I don't know if we'll ever understand the mechanics of how it works, but at this point I wouldn't argue with the idea that it's a magic mirror. God knows I'd believe in stranger things at this point. But there's something more important for us to talk about at the moment, Hope."

He drew her over to an object in front of the fireplace that slowly resolved into a sofa the closer they got with the candle.

"Sit down," he urged. He tore off the constricting coat he wore before he sat down next to her. It felt as if he would burst out of the garment if he took a deep breath and he wanted to be comfortable for this difficult conversation with Hope.

Once he settled next to her on the couch he met her gaze. "I want you to come with me, Hope . . . to my time. Through the mirror."

For a moment she didn't speak, just staring at him as though frozen.

"Ryan, I want to," she finally replied in a choked voice. "I'd love to be able to see a whole different world, to—to be with you, even if only a bit longer." She paused awkwardly and glanced down. "It would be like something from a dream. But I *can't*. You must understand. My father is here. He's been ill. He'll only become sicker if I don't reassure him of my safety very soon."

Ryan sighed heavily. This wasn't going to be easy, but he had to find a way to convince her. He wasn't thrilled with the prospect of what would challenge them in the year 2008 given their vastly different cultures. In truth, he had no idea what he would do with her, their situation was so unprecedented. But in all fairness to Hope, he needed to try and convince her.

Especially since he planned on taking her with him no matter if he succeeded or not.

"Haven't you wondered why I came through the mirror? Why I've been trying to warn you about being in danger?"

"I didn't fully understand in the beginning, but now I assume it was because you somehow knew I was going to be kidnapped by Diamond Jack."

"It was, in part."

"What do you mean, *in part*?" Hope asked slowly.

Ryan dug his thumb and forefinger into his eyelids, feeling the burn of a physical exhaustion that had been held at bay by adrenaline. Until now, anyway. He wished he had more energy for this, but he plunged ahead, anyway.

He proceeded to tell her about the newspaper articles and police reports concerning her disappearance. He put his arm around her when he explained about her death, glossing over the gruesome details of the decomposed body found in the Chicago River. She listened with a quiet, avid intensity but showed no signs of distress. At first he thought she might be in shock but then he began to suspect that the bizarreness of the circumstances made the whole scenario seem far-fetched and removed from her.

Ryan had to agree in part. Who could imagine that the lovely woman who sat beside him, studying him with solemn midnight eyes, could possibly transform into a lifeless corpse sometime soon? Ryan couldn't fathom it.

In fact, that was the main reason he was here.

"You say that you read documents—newspaper clippings, police reports, things of that nature—that reported the year of my death was 1906?"

Ryan nodded warily. Bizarre or not, it wasn't news even the most strong of heart would ever relish hearing. "That's why I want to bring you back to the year 2008. If you're alive in my time, there's no way you could have died a hundred and two years ago."

Hope's eyelids narrowed thoughtfully. "And did any of these documents you read indicate what happened to my father after my death?"

Ryan resisted an urge to state point-blank that she was *not* going to die for a very, very long time. Instead he focused on the facts. "Yes. They said that he went on to champion anti–white slavery legislation and eventually successfully closed down the Levee District."

Ryan's sense of alarm grew when Hope merely stared fixedly at the cold hearth. "Tell me what you're thinking."

"There's been some sort of mistake, Ryan."

"Honey, I know it must be hard to take in—nobody would want to learn the date of their death—but—"

She shook her head adamantly. "There *has* been a misunderstanding. Perhaps you successfully changed history by intervening tonight at the Sweet Lash?"

Ryan thought of those black-and-white photos he'd found in the twenty-first century—photos of Hope and *him* in the year 1906.

"I'm not so sure I've changed anything," he stated grimly. "It seems that history has bent to accommodate me."

But Hope continued as though he'd never spoken.

"I don't mean to place undue importance upon my person, but it is extremely unlikely my father would have flourished as greatly as those reports indicated if I died anytime in the near future. If it were true that I'd been brutally murdered, I would expect my father to be devastated . . . diminished, not infused with a sense of purpose in the manner that you describe from the historical record."

"But isn't it possible your death would drive him all the harder in his mission in order to change the circumstances that allowed your death—"

Hope shook her head again resolutely. "I see your point, but no. You don't know my father like I do. He was devastated by my mother's death, almost to the point of giving up all hope. His grief was protracted and intense. If it weren't for the fact that he had me to live for, I have no doubt he would have just given up and soon followed my mother. Perhaps—"

But Ryan cut her off with a slashing movement of his hand. He abruptly blew out the candle.

"What—" Hope asked, forgetting to whisper in her surprise over his actions.

"Shhhh," Ryan hissed. He heard it again, the rustle of someone moving in the hallway, the sound soft and furtive, as though they'd been leaning in to listen with their ear pressed to the door. The latch clicked open and the door swung silently inward.

"Don't move. I have a gun pointed at you," Marlo said in a deep, sinister voice. "You didn't really believe Jack would let you get away that easily, did you?"

~ EIGHTEEN ~

He's bluffing, Ryan thought after a panicked second. Marlo's eyesight couldn't have accustomed to the darkness yet. The hallway was dimly lit by a distant wall sconce. He knew they were in here, perhaps, but he didn't know *where*.

He mentally cursed himself for removing the borrowed coat and tossing it on the couch. He grabbed it but the gun was buried deep in the one of the pockets. If he tried to extract it, he would waste precious seconds and possibly risk making a noise that gave away their whereabouts in the room.

Instead he delved his fingers into the silky mass of curls piled on Hope's head. She jumped in surprise but had the wits not to cry and betray their location in the darkness. He extracted one of the combs he knew he'd find and flung it toward the far corner of the room. A second after he heard the sound of the comb rattling on the wood floor as it landed, a shot rang out.

Ryan fell on top of Hope, pushing her down on the couch. He pressed his mouth directly next to her ear.

"Stay low and move toward the wardrobe . . . very quietly."

∽

Hope felt Ryan rise from the couch at the same moment that she did. He pushed down on her back, reminding her to stay low. She held her breath as she moved stealthily in the darkness, deathly afraid the intruder would hear her panting.

Her heart seemed to seize in her chest when she heard the man step into the room.

"Where's the damn light?" he muttered in a guttural, lightly accented voice. Hope imagined him running his hand along the wall. Any second now he would switch on the electric overhead light. Ryan must have realized the same thing because he pushed harder on her back. She scurried silently toward the mirror. "I know you're in here. You can't escape. You made a fool out of me and Jack both and *no one* makes a fool of me and my boss."

He made a grunting noise of satisfaction and Hope knew he'd found the switch. The room flooded with light. Hope had a brief impression of an enormous, brutal-looking giant of a man with a black eye and a snarl twisting his thin lips.

Then Ryan shoved her hard. She heard a shot ring out and she was falling. A pocket of air punched out of her lungs when she landed hard on a wood floor. She scrambled up and waited anxiously for Ryan to step through the mirror. He didn't immediately follow her, however, and then Hope heard a truly horrifying sound.

Although it was distant and muffled, she distinctly heard the pop of a bullet's impact and then the sound of glass shattering.

∽

Ryan shoved Hope through the gateway of the mirror at the same moment that Marlo raised his pistol and aimed. The bullet tore a hole in the wood of the wardrobe when Ryan ducked. Another shot rang out. The sound of shattering glass seemed to pierce straight through his heart.

Everything seemed to switch into slow-motion viewing. The bullet blew the glass to smithereens at the point of impact. A crack splintered down the mirror. One large piece toward the bottom separated from the gilded frame.

Ryan dove headfirst into the mirror fragment even as it fell forward.

"*Ryan*," he heard Hope scream before he crashed onto the unforgiving wood floor. He'd landed on top of the borrowed coat and his ribs had slammed against the hard metal of his gun.

There wasn't a damn place on his body that didn't throb in pain at that moment. His heavy fall on the floor seemed to reactivate every one of Big Marlo's punches in the ring.

Big Marlo.

The last twenty seconds came back to him in graphic detail—Marlo aiming his pistol. The shot. The shattering mirror.

Shit.

He sprung up off the floor, doing his best to ignore his aching muscles and joints. He inspected the intact mirror closely. A thin ring of fog had returned around the outer edges. He pushed his fingers to the surface, but there was no give.

Nothing but smooth, impenetrable glass.

Something caught his attention. He reached up and ran his finger over the rough hole on the closed right door of the mahogany wardrobe—a bullet hole that had certainly never been there before, either in Hope's time or his own.

He turned around slowly to face Hope. She still knelt where he'd fallen on the floor, her skirt spread out around her. Her face looked pale in the bright sunlight that flooded his bedroom in the year 2008.

He blinked in amazement and looked out the windows. It'd been the middle of the night in Hope's world. They seemed to have picked up several hours on their trip forward in time. He'd be damned if he understood the details of how that mirror worked.

And he *never* would now.

"Are you all right?" he asked as he approached Hope and sank down to his knees next to her.

"I'm fine. Are you well?" She reached up and lightly ran her fingertips over his brow, pushing back his hair. He saw her looking worriedly at the cut on his brow and wondered if it had started bleeding again.

"I'm okay. Hope . . . the mirror in your bedroom. Marlo's bullet hit it. It shattered."

She froze in the process of caressing his cheek. "I heard it breaking. But I thought . . . I thought since you made it through . . ."

Her voice trailed off when she took in his expression.

"There was one large piece at the bottom that began to fall out of the frame. I dove through it before it struck the floor. I don't think much of it remains in your time. I'm sorry, Hope."

She looked every bit as shattered as the mirror. "I can't go back?"

He tried to pull her into his arms but she resisted him. She twisted around and stared at the room, her mouth agape with shock. He felt a fine tremor begin to vibrate her flesh and knew the reality of her situation had just been slammed home to her.

"Oh my God," she whispered. "I'm really in your world, aren't I? It's the year 2008?"

"Yes."

Her eyes glistened when she looked up at him.

"They're all dead, including my father. Everyone I ever knew or loved—ashes."

∽

Ryan thought it was best to focus on one thing at a time. He'd never once considered Hope frail, but that's the word that came to him as she sat there on the bedroom floor. Her typical, almost tangible vibrancy seemed to drain out of her before his very eyes. He spread his hand along the side of her face, cradling her jaw.

"Hope, listen to me," he said, garnering her attention. She blinked and focused on him listlessly. "I think it would be very dangerous for either of us to try and travel through the mirror after what happened. Your father wouldn't thank you for gambling your life so foolishly, I'm sure. But I want you to know I'm not going to give up on trying to figure out how and why it enabled us to travel through time. This isn't the end of it. Do you understand?"

"You think there's still a chance?"

"I think there are a lot of things about that mirror I don't understand. I'd be a fool to start claiming I have all the answers at this point in time. That doesn't mean we'll always be ignorant . . . or that things are hopeless." He gave her a pointed stare before he stood.

"We're not going to solve anything at this moment. The only thing on your agenda at the moment is a bath and bed. Come on," he said as he reached for her hands and pulled her to her feet.

"But it looks like it's full morning here," Hope mumbled dazedly as she followed him.

"And you've been up all night, hit over the head, kidnapped, witnessed a murder and been shot at, not to mention been made love to . . . rigorously."

He turned in time to see her lower her eyelids. Her cheeks

turned a delicate shade of pink. He dropped a kiss on her mouth and spoke next to her parted lips.

"We *are* in the bedroom, witch."

He took his first full breath of air in several minutes when he saw Hope's lips curve into a weary smile.

⌒ NINETEEN ⌒

Hope had so many questions to ask Ryan about the house—why it seemed so empty, for instance. Didn't he have any family? Why were the servants so glaringly absent?

Other questions were more mundane, but made her burn with curiosity nonetheless. What were the mechanics of the porcelain bowl in the bathroom that had taken the place of the water closet? What awesome scientific advancements had allowed them to so perfectly distill the scent of strawberries in the cleanser she used to wash her hair or make the toilet paper so cushy and soft she almost felt guilty about using it for its purpose?

She wanted to ask Ryan all these things, but he was taking his turn in the bathroom. Meanwhile, her eyelids uncooperatively grew heavier and heavier with each passing second.

She nodded and jerked into wakefulness when she heard the sound of the bedroom door open. Even though she'd been gifted with the sight of Ryan's bare chest for the better part of the night, her eyes widened in amazement presently as though she were seeing him for the first time all over again.

His damp hair hadn't been combed and stuck up adorably at odd angles. She longed to run her fingers through the damp hair on his chest and feel the warm, dense muscle beneath. She noticed that something beige-colored stuck to his forehead, covering the cut on his brow.

"What is that?"

He crinkled his forehead in confusion when she pointed to his head. He reached up and touched his brow.

"It's a bandage. What are you doing sitting there? Why don't you lie down? You're about to fall over." He turned out the overhead light and walked over to pull the drapes on the windows.

"I have so many questions to ask you about the bathroom," she mumbled almost incoherently. It seemed that her lips had grown as heavy and unresponsive as her eyelids.

"The *bathroom*?"

She nodded. Ryan waggled his finger at the pillows. Hope scooted onto the bed—her very own brass bed—and sighed when her cheek touched the pillowcase. Ryan's scent wafted up to her appreciative nose. It smelled like the soap she'd found in a dish by the bathtub but with other odors mixed in—spices, musk, a hint of peppermint and some other scent that she associated singularly with Ryan. She struggled to keep her eyes open when Ryan came down on the bed next to her.

"What about the bathroom?"

"Can't 'member," Hope slurred. She smiled at the sound of his low chuckle. She wanted to purr when he opened his hand over her waist, lazily stroking her. He suddenly went still when he moved up over her ribs.

"What do you have on under this T-shirt?"

Hope cocked open one eye. T-shirt? Was that what one called

the enormous, buttonless cotton shirt Ryan had given her to put on after her bath along with an equally gigantic pair of cotton pants with a drawstring?

"What do you mean?" she asked.

Ryan scowled before he rolled her onto her back and jerked up the hem of the T-shirt. He glanced up at her a second later, his handsome face full of laughter.

"Why are you wearing your corset?" She squawked in protest when he matter-of-factly lowered the pants before he flipped them back up to her waist. "Honey, if you were going to leave on your pantaloons, there was no need to put on the sweatpants."

"You don't expect me to wear these clothes without any underwear, do you?" she asked, scandalized.

He opened his mouth to say something, then closed it. The crooked grin he wore was unlike any smile she'd yet seen on his face. He shook his head, pulled her into his arms and planted a kiss on the top of her head.

"The only thing I expect at the moment, witch, is for you to get some sleep. Something tells me you're really going to need the rest."

Despite her contentment at being in Ryan's arms and her profound fatigue, Hope found that sleep didn't come as easily as she'd thought it would.

"Ryan, do you think that man—Marlo—might have hurt my father or anyone else in the household?"

"No." He opened his palm over the back of her head, cradling it in a gesture that struck her as cherishing. Or perhaps she just wished that were true? She wondered sluggishly if it was uncomfortable for him to have her damp hair on his bare chest but found she was too content and tired to move.

"Why do you say that with so much confidence?"

"Because Jack kidnapped you in order to blackmail your father. He tried to get him on his payroll, but your father refused and went along with his own agenda. Jack wanted to control your father, not harm him and cast suspicion upon himself. Jack sent Marlo to come to your house tonight to reclaim you—and likely to kill me—for a reason beyond the original plan, though."

"What reason?" Hope whispered. She felt his muscles flex as he shrugged.

"Payback. For having defied Jack's all-encompassing authority. The guy's a megalomaniac."

Something occurred to her and she jerked her head off his chest. "What of Mel? What if Marlo stopped her from getting back to Addie? Do you think Marlo saw her? Harmed her?"

"No. I don't."

He held her stare. She wondered if he was being so certain just to still her jitters over things she couldn't control one way or another. Even with that vague suspicion, however, Hope found herself calming.

"No more questions now. Go to sleep," he urged, pushing lightly on the back of her head. She returned her cheek to his chest and closed her eyes.

It was impossible not to be affected by Ryan's quiet, depthless confidence.

∾ TWENTY ∾

Shadows lay thick in his bedroom by the time Ryan opened his eyes. He rubbed the grit out of his eyelids and glanced down beside him.

He bolted out of the brass bed.

"Hope?" he called out, instantly admonishing himself for shouting. The woman had a right to get up out of bed, didn't she?

His eyes flickered over to the gilded mirror. *She wouldn't.* Surely she saw the stark danger of trying to travel using the mirror when its twin had been destroyed in her time.

He headed for the door, deciding even Hope couldn't be that impulsive and headstrong. It still alarmed him to think of her wandering around in the twenty-first century alone. He'd had some of the guidance of history to prepare him and he'd still been shocked to the core. She'd be as innocent and curious as a toddler playing around a steep staircase with no adult present.

He could just imagine her wandering out in front of a barreling truck or asking a whacked-out drug dealer for directions to the nearest respectable jeweler where she might pawn her priceless jewelry.

"Hope!" He saw that the bathroom was empty and that her neatly folded skirt, blouse, petticoat and hosiery were missing. He barreled down the grand staircase and bellowed her name several more times as he checked room after room on the first floor. The memory of the intimate drawing room came to him and he changed direction.

The drawing room stood silent and empty when he reached it. Now that he knew what it'd looked like in the past, the room struck him as hollow and depressing—like an empty tomb.

"*Hope,*" he shouted with increasing anxiety. Where would she go to find comfort in a barren house that had once been a home filled with people she loved, every item that her gaze fell upon likely associated with the memories of a lifetime? Damn. Why hadn't he thought of this? Why hadn't he done something to make the austere mansion warmer, more cheery? As he ran down the hallway a movement outside of the uncurtained window caught his eyes.

A second later he hurried down the limestone front steps and ran across a quiet Prairie Avenue barefoot.

She stood on the sidewalk, shivering as she stared up at the Romanesque mansion kitty-corner from their house. Her long skirt and high-necked blouse didn't strike him as out of place like he might have expected it would. Enough of the elegance and grandeur of Prairie Avenue remained to make Hope look as natural there as in her own time.

When Ryan saw her face he wondered if her trembling was from the cool late November afternoon chill or shock.

"This is my friend Fanny's house. We went on our European tour together. They've made it into a museum," she said dully when he came beside her and said her name.

He put his hands on her shoulders and turned her around firmly. "Let's go back inside. There was something important I needed to tell you before you saw the changes time has made."

She didn't resist him, but she moved like an automaton as he marched her across the street and back up the limestone steps. She cast a sad glance down the north side of the street, her eyes enormous in her white face. Ryan followed her gaze, trying to see Prairie Avenue through her eyes. None of the grand mansions on the Seventeenth and Sixteenth Street blocks remained. Gone was George Pullman's palatial mansion; gutted were the grand homes of Lydia and William Gold Hibbard's many children in a block that would have been known to Hope as Hibbardville due to the family's pervasive presence.

In their place stood blocks of modern brick condominiums, each and every one of which was precisely the same. A few ugly low-rises built in the 1960s added a grim, institutional presence to the street.

Things were much better when one looked to the right, where at least an attempt had been made in the new buildings to preserve the historical appearance of the once-grand avenue. In fact, the new limestone and brick town houses were each unique and built within the strict guidelines of the Historical Preservation Society. A few of the houses were meticulously renovated structures that would have stood during Hope's time. Several of the grand mansions still remained as well, 1807 Prairie Avenue being one of many. Instead of pointing that out to Hope, however, he hurried her into the house.

He understood that it was what Hope was *not* seeing as much as what was there that distressed her so deeply.

When they entered the front door Ryan noticed that the foyer chandelier was turned on again. He was going to have to get an electrician to come out and repair that short. He aimed Hope for the grand staircase. When they reached the bedroom Ryan turned the electric heater on to high and brought it over to where Hope sat shivering at the end of the bed.

"Sorry it's so chilly," he mumbled. "Someone is coming out early next week to check out the heating system. It's been modernized but it still doesn't seem to work very well."

"It never did. Ryan?" she asked suddenly, seeming to stir out of a trance.

"Yes?"

"Why is the house so empty? It's like it's been stripped bare. I tried finding something to eat but there were only bottles of water, milk and a little fruit in that enormous icebox in the kitchen. Has there been some sort of catastrophe? War or . . . or famine?"

"No, not recently, anyway," he answered with a short laugh. His laughter hardly implied amusement, however, only anxious concern for Hope's disorientation at her familiar world being wiped away in a split second. "Remember I explained that I'd just been given 1807 Prairie Street by a friend—Alistair Franklin? It's a long story, but the bottom line is, I just moved in here at the beginning of the week. It's my understanding that the house has stood empty for fifteen or twenty years. That's the only reason it seems so barren."

He walked over to the bedside table and picked up his cell phone.

"How about some Chinese food?" he asked, paging down the list of nearby restaurants that he'd programmed into his phone.

"What about it?" she asked, rising from her sitting position, her gaze glued on his cell phone.

"Do you want to have it for dinner? You said you were hungry. There's a place that has food that might be more what you're used to—chicken, steak, potatoes. Your only other choices at present are Mexican and pizza."

"What does Chinese food taste like?"

"You like beef? Chicken?"

Hope nodded.

"Vegetables—peas, carrots, stuff like that?"

Again she nodded as she came closer to him.

"I'll get a few things. If you're as hungry as I am, at least one of them is going to taste good to you."

As soon as he'd ordered and flipped his cell phone closed Hope reached for it.

"May I?"

"Sure," he replied, handing her the phone. "It's a cell phone."

"So you use this to contact your servants?" she asked finally after inspecting the phone with obvious fascination.

He grinned. "No. Very few people in this day and age have servants."

"I don't understand. Who were you just giving instructions for our dinner then?"

"Oh, the restaurant. They make meals."

"I know what a restaurant is—they have them in all the finest hotels. But you make it sound as if anyone can go to them. And it sounded as if they're going to deliver food to the house."

"Right." Ryan shrugged.

"Have we acquired a socialist form of government, then?"

"No . . . why would you say that?"

"Because you said there were hardly any servants anymore, and that anyone can have food prepared for them. I thought perhaps the government sponsored the restaurants."

Ryan shook his head. "No, good old-fashioned capitalism keeps the restaurant industry alive. That along with a good dose of American laziness and overwork."

"You mean we're going to pay money for our meals?" she asked, clearly disappointed.

" 'Fraid so, honey."

"Oh." She sighed and sat back down on the bed. "Then things really aren't that different from the past. They've just moved the servants out of the house."

"People who work in restaurants aren't servants. They get paid for their work," Ryan explained as he sat next to her on the bed. He was glad to see that some of the animation and color had returned to her face.

"Servants get paid! My father pays the best wages on Prairie Avenue and we offer the staff paid vacations and medical care from Dr. Walkerton as well. Do these people who work in restaurants make enough for their wages to raise their families? Can they go to the doctor for free and do they have paid vacations?"

"Er . . . no," Ryan admitted.

"Well, they should," Hope informed him with a pointed glance. "You should treat the people who prepare your meals well, Ryan, and they'll repay you a thousandfold with their loyalty and kindness."

Ryan opened his mouth to educate Hope on the reality of the modern-day world and shut it just as quickly. Hope may see things from the cockeyed angle of the early twentieth century and the influence of her idiosyncratic social reformist father, but that didn't mean her point of view held no validity whatsoever. Maybe she had a few things to teach him about his time period as well. So instead of lecturing her he tucked one of her errant curls behind her ear, smiling to himself when he felt her go utterly still beneath his touch.

"You know, you're right. I'll make sure I give an extra good tip."

She gave him a radiant smile.

There was no doubt about it. He was going to go bankrupt heating this monstrous old house and giving fat tips to every delivery boy in the city. But if it meant Hope Stillwater blessed him with that smile, he'd be the richest poor man in the city.

∾

Hope sat cross-legged on the bed, her back against pillows that had been stacked next to the headboard. She gave a muffled cry of triumph when she successfully maneuvered the last piece of Mongolian beef into her mouth using chopsticks.

"This is delicious," she told Ryan, who sat opposite her on the bed, his back leaning against pillows and the foot railing and his legs stretched out in front of him. He'd put on a dark blue shirt earlier that only made his eyes look lighter and more striking in contrast to it. He wore a faded pair of the type of the thick cotton pants, similar to the ones he'd had on when she first saw him in the mirror. It was difficult for her to keep her stare off how well they fit his trim hips and long legs. She'd been impressed at how adroitly he handled his chopsticks, as though he had been born in China. "May we use the cell phone to order more of it for tomorrow's dinner?"

"Yes," Ryan said.

"Could you please pass the orange chicken?"

"You already ate it all."

"Oh." She frowned in disappointment and patted her belly thoughtfully. "Perhaps I'm fuller than I thought. I've never tasted food half so good. So many flavors. So exotic. And the delivery boy said he'd been to Hong Kong twice to visit his grandparents! Do you think he'll remember to bring the photographs of his last trip the next time he visits?"

Ryan's low laughter brought her out of her reverie.

"He'll remember all right. It's not likely he'll forget talking to you for a long, long time."

Hope put her chopsticks in the empty carton and carefully placed it on a paper napkin on the bedside table. She'd been unimpressed when Ryan had explained that the rough white paper was meant to be a substitute for cloth napkins and immediately asked why they didn't make napkins as soft as the paper she'd found in the bathroom. He'd laughed at her then just as he did presently.

"I suppose I must seem very foolish to you," she murmured.

Ryan shook his head and swallowed a bite of sweet-and-sour pork. "You don't seem foolish, honey. You make me see my world in a whole different way. I only meant that boy would never forget having such a beautiful woman listen to every word he uttered like she thought he was the most fascinating male on the planet."

Warmth flooded her at Ryan's compliment. He hadn't kissed her and only briefly touched her since they'd awoken from their nap. The heat in his eyes when he looked at her combined with his special small smile made her feel as if he'd been caressing her intimately the entire time, however.

"I *did* think he was fascinating. How many people do you know who have been to Hong Kong twice by the time they were sixteen? And these *airplanes* that he spoke of . . ." She trailed off, gazing off into the distance and fantasizing what it would be like to get on a vehicle and be on the other side of the globe within a day and a night. "Airplanes sound like something right out of one of Mr. Jules Verne's novels. I can't wait to discover the other miracles of your time. I can't wait to tell my father about it all . . . the airplanes, the cell phones, the Chinese food delivery, the toilet paper . . ."

It struck her suddenly that there was a very good chance she'd never have the opportunity to tell her father anything ever again.

A moment later she glanced up and saw Ryan standing beside her through an annoying veil of tears. He came down on the bed next to her. She found herself enfolded in his arms. She buried her face in his shirt, infinitely thankful for his steadying presence as her world rocked precariously. He said nothing as she cried but he ran his hand soothingly along the back of her head and shoulders, once pausing to pull the combs out of her hair.

"I'm sorry," she said wetly against his chest a while later. At some point her attention had turned from her grief to the sensation of Ryan's fingers running through her unbound hair.

"You don't have to apologize. You've been through a lot in the past twenty-four hours."

Hope sniffled and raised her head to look at him. They were so close she could perfectly see the vivid pinpoints of color in his cerulean eyes. For a moment she found herself drowning in the depths of his gaze as though she'd dove down into a warm, sunlit sea.

"I want you to know something, honey."

"What?"

"When I first came into this house—when I first starting seeing you—I was convinced you weren't dead." He saw her crinkled brow and continued. "Ramiro—he's my partner—tried to tell me you were a ghost. The documents and newspaper articles I read stated that without a doubt you'd died in the year 1906. But I didn't believe it, Hope. And now you're here in my arms proving me right."

His hold tightened around her. Her body slid along his several inches, until their faces were only inches apart.

"I don't understand what you mean," she whispered.

"I'm trying to say that I don't think time works the way you and I had always thought. Somehow—some way—I knew you weren't dead. I sensed that we were only separated by something human beings usually don't have the power to penetrate. But you and I—we're solid proof that it's not an impossibility."

Hope merely watched him soberly, emotion clogging her throat. He opened his big hand along the side of her head, his thumb caressing her damp cheek gently.

"I'm trying to tell you I don't think your father is dead . . . not in the way we used to think of it. We're separated from him at present, that's true. But if a gateway could be formed, you would see him, alive and well."

"But—"

He shook his head. "I *know* there's a paradox involved. I used to feel the discomfort of living with that paradox in regard to you. You were both alive to me and not. I had to force myself to choose which reality I wanted . . . which reality felt more tangible to me . . . more *right*. Which one I wanted the most."

She swallowed with difficulty. "Are you saying that it's necessary to believe that my father is still alive, that this house still exists just as I recall it over a hundred years ago?"

He wiped the tears from her other cheek carefully. Hope could sense him deliberating on how to choose his words. "What I think I'm saying, honey, is that it's a *possibility*. Someday, just like I did, you'll have to decide which possibility is your reality."

She stifled a sob of anguish.

"But that day isn't today, Hope. For now, we're here together."

She stared into his eyes, feeling like she soaked up some of the courage he offered her. "We don't know enough about the mirror that remains. I'm just telling you this because . . ."

"You don't want to see me give up hope. I understand, Ryan. Thank you."

He just watched her silently. Hope became preternaturally aware of every point on her body where they touched; how his chest brushed against the tips of her breasts when he inhaled.

"I'm looking forward to learning more about your world," she whispered.

"Do you want to go out right now? See the city?"

"It's dark out now. Perhaps . . . we could wait until morning?"

"If that's what you'd like."

She studied him from beneath her lowered lashes. "I slept all day. I'm not at all tired yet. What will we do?"

"We could watch television."

"What's *television*?" She looked over to where he nodded. She saw a rectangular electrical device with a pane of opaque glass. It was the first time she'd noticed it because Ryan had draped the coat given to him by one of Addie Sampson's men on top of it.

"It's like a radio with pictures."

"I don't understand."

His eyelids narrowed as he studied her. "It's sort of hard to explain. You might just have to see it. That little box over there could tell you a lot about the early twenty-first century, but it might be misleading as well. Maybe it'd be best if you started out by reading newspapers."

Hope bit her lower lip indecisively. She knew what she wanted to do and it wasn't along the lines of reading newspapers.

"I was thinking perhaps we could get to know one another better."

"If it's something you're feeling up to," Ryan muttered gruffly. Her heartbeat skipped into overtime when his magnificent eyes lowered once again to her lips and his nostrils flared slightly. Beneath her layers of clothing she felt the tension grow in his body and the stiffening of his member along her hip.

He remained unmoving, however, and Hope found herself uncertain as to how to proceed. She stared fixedly at his firm, sensual mouth and realized he looked unblinkingly at the same place on her anatomy.

She leaned down and softly placed her mouth on his, fitting her lower lip into the closed seam. Her eyes fluttered closed. She turned her head just a tad, letting their textures rub together, luxuriating in the pleasurable sensations that coursed through her body. They molded their mouths together, discovering textures. After a spellbound moment Hope realized he didn't breathe as she learned the nuances of his lips with her own.

She shyly slid the tip of her tongue between his lips and his hold on her tightened. Feeling encouraged by his reaction, she tilted her head and explored his mouth . . . tentatively at first, but then with growing eagerness as she registered his familiar taste and he began to participate, rubbing his tongue sensually against her own.

Their kiss continued, exploratory, languid . . . more delicious than she could begin to describe. Liquid heat swelled at her sex, and she pressed against his hard chest to alleviate the throb in her nipples. His hand opened along her ribs inches below her armpit, his palm lightly caressing the sides of her breasts. His other hand came up to twine in her unbound hair. He tugged gently and broke the magical kiss.

She saw that he watched her with hawk-like intensity.

"So this is how you would like to spend the evening, witch?"

She met his gaze solemnly and nodded. "If you would find that agreeable."

His low laughter caused the back of her neck to roughen. She couldn't resist leaning down and touching his curving lips with her own.

"*Agreeable* seems like a pretty lukewarm description to describe how I feel at the prospect of making love to you."

Hope swallowed. "I was hoping that . . ."

"Yes?" he asked when she faded off in rising discomfort.

"I was hoping that you would allow me to make love to *you*, Ryan."

"It's always a mutual endeavor, honey."

"Yes, but last night . . . you . . . you made me feel good again and again, and yet you . . ."

"Only came once? Is that what you mean?"

She stared at his chest and nodded.

"Hope, look at me. It's true that I can come more than once, but in general women have shorter refractory periods between orgasms." Her puzzlement must have been clear because he continued, "A man usually can't come as frequently as a woman in the same amount of time."

"Oh, I see."

His mouth quirked. "I'm not so sure that you do, but you will soon enough given the amount of time I plan on making love to you."

Warmth spread into her cheeks and downward from her belly to her sex when she heard he intended to make love to her often. Didn't that imply he wanted to spend a considerable amount of time with her?

"So may I now?"

"May you what?"

This time instead of a gentle warmth, heat scalded her cheeks. "Make you . . . *come*?" she asked tentatively, trying out the word in this new context for the first time.

He gave her a slow smile that made her clamp her thighs together to still the dull throb between them.

"Be my guest, witch."

⌒ TWENTY-ONE ⌒

Hope's heart began to throb in her ears as she leaned on her elbow and reached for the hem of Ryan's shirt. She slowly drew it up over his torso. When the shirt reached his chest he obligingly shrugged out of it with a fascinating flex of ridged muscle and tossed it on the floor. She looked down at the breathtaking male landscape just inches away from her face.

She ran her hand over the delineated muscles of his abdomen and up over his ribs. They shivered in tandem.

"I've never seduced a man before."

"You're wrong."

She glanced up at him in surprise even as her hand continued to discover the fascinating sensation of dense muscle gloved in smooth skin. Ryan watched her hand fixedly as she slid it down his arm and palmed a bulging bicep.

"You've been successfully seducing me ever since I first saw you in that mirror."

"But I wasn't really *doing* anything, then," Hope whispered distractedly. Most of her attention was focused on the manner in which Ryan's small brown nipples pulled into erection the more she touched him. She experimentally flicked her fingernail over the stiffened flesh.

She glanced up into his face to gauge his reaction when he made a hissing sound. The rigid set of his features made her lightly scrape his nipple again.

"So you want to do more? Is that it, witch?" he asked gruffly.

Hope nodded eagerly.

"You might consider taking off your clothes for a start then."

"Oh. Of course." She rolled on top of him, making him grunt in surprise, and clambered off the bed. "I suppose you want me to take off my clothing here . . . not in the bathroom?"

"That's right." Her eyes widened when he put his hands behind his head and stretched on the bed, as though he were getting comfortable for some sort of spectacle. She saw the long ridge of his erection pressing against the cotton material of his pants and realized her undressing before him *was* the spectacle. The knowledge made her hands tremble a little in nervous excitement as she unbuttoned her shirtwaist and then reached around to do the same to her skirt. Once she'd removed both garments and placed them neatly over the bottom railing of the bed she drew down her petticoat.

She found it increasingly difficult to meet Ryan's stare as more and more garments were added to the pile of clothing.

"Hope."

She glanced over at him through lowered lashes, all too aware of how hot her cheeks were. He leaned up on one elbow, his expression tense as he stared at her breasts encased in an ivory, lace-trimmed, strapless corset. His hot stare lowered over her, making her skin

feel prickly wherever it touched. She'd just removed her pantaloons. She had to resist a strong urge to cover herself when his gaze
fixed between her naked thighs.

"That will do. Leave the rest on."

"But . . . I'm still wearing a corset and my garter," she mumbled
as she came toward him awkwardly.

"A lot of guys fantasize about having a woman undress for
them and seeing that she's wearing stuff like a garter belt and hose,
Hope."

"Are you one of them?" Hope asked in dawning amazement.
What else would a woman wear beneath her clothing?

He dragged his eyes up to her face. "I like it all right. But something about the fact that it's not a getup in your case—not contrived to be sexy, but just the way you dress all the time . . . I don't
know. It's more of a turn-on than I'd ever thought it'd be. Come
here."

He reached for her and she came onto the bed. He settled her in
his lap and drew up his knees. Hope straddled him in a sitting position, her back comfortably supported by his hard thighs.

"Ryan," Hope whispered when he ran both hands over her
corset-encased breasts. She moaned softly when his fingers trailed
down her lace garters and down over her pale hose. A shudder of
excitement went through her body.

"These are silk," he said, amazement flavoring his tone.

"Yes. What else would they be?"

"Nylon. It's a synthetic fabric. That's usually what hose are
made of in this day and age." He opened his big hand and caressed
the length of her leg. She clearly felt the column of his penis surge
beneath her bottom.

"So soft," he murmured. He looked up at her face. "You're unbelievably beautiful."

Her lower lip dropped at the stark compliment.

"You're unbelievably beautiful as well. And . . . and I'm the one who is supposed to be seducing you, Ryan," she reminded him with difficulty. Most of her attention was on his long finger as it moved over the top of her breasts where they swelled over her corset. His light touch made her nipples prickle and pinch against the tight material.

He blinked and took a deep breath before he dropped his hand to the bed. "The seduction was complete long ago, but if you want to touch me, go ahead, honey."

She smiled happily and once again began her exploration of his magnificent body. He didn't speak but just watched her as she delved her fingers through his crisp chest hair and ran her hands along the tantalizing slant that ran from his narrow waist up to his wide chest. She felt his skin roughen when she lightly scratched him with her fingernails just inches below his armpit. That physical reaction along with the feeling of his erection throbbing against her bare bottom informed her that he liked having his skin lightly scraped.

She once again focused her attention on his nipples, using both her fingertips and fingernails to stimulate him. She grew so excited by how stiff they became that she leaned down to feel how the hard little button felt pressed against her tongue.

"*Hope.*"

Her eyelids flashed open in alarm. She glanced up at Ryan with the tip of her tongue still savoring his nipple. Why had his voice sounded so hard?

What she saw in his rigid features emboldened her. She flicked her tongue rapidly over the stiff disc, letting him watch.

"Unbutton my jeans and touch my cock," he ordered.

But she recalled all too well the way he'd set the pace for her when she'd begged him while he suckled her breasts last night. This tense, coiled excitement that built and built was the *true* meaning of seduction, Hope decided.

So instead of doing what Ryan demanded she smiled and pulled her long hair over to one side, out of her way. She placed her mouth over his nipple. He groaned when she applied suction and scraped her front teeth over the sensitive flesh, just as he'd done to her last night. She thought he might chastise her for not doing what he ordered, but he remained silent and tense as she used her lips and tongue to explore his chest and abdomen. As she nibbled her way down his body he slowly lowered his legs so she could move downward more easily, so Hope expected he liked her explorations even though she wasn't doing precisely what he asked.

Yet, anyway.

She cradled his ribs in her hands and spread kisses over his stomach. When she moved up slightly, the tips of her breasts slid across his belly just above the pants that he'd called *jeans*. He groaned and she glanced up into his face. She saw where he stared so fixedly and looked down to see the flesh of her breasts spilling abundantly over the edge of her tight corset.

Her smile up at him was a tad devilish before she planted a kiss on his belly button and dragged her tongue down the strip of dark brown hair just beneath it.

"You're buying yourself a one-way ticket right over my knee, witch."

She glanced up at him in trepidation but then snorted softly with laughter when she saw the grin curving his handsome mouth. Still—when she saw how hot his stare was, she wondered for a moment if he hadn't been at least partially serious in his threat.

"You make it sound like I'd never come back," she told him archly before she lightly licked the skin just above his jeans. He started at the caress.

"You'll come back all right—with one very sore butt."

"All right. I'll do what you asked."

He gave an exasperated grunt. "I'll believe that when I see it."

She sat up and narrowed her eyelids at him before she scooted her bottom down his thighs, pressing against his clearly defined erection in the process. He gritted his teeth and drew his breath in sharply. Hope pulled on the fly of his pants, practically ripping the metal buttons through the holes.

"Hold *on* a second," Ryan muttered when she started yanking on his jeans frantically. He leaned up from his reclining position to try to help her. His tone had sounded surprised. Well, what did he expect? Did he think he was the only one here who was eager for her to touch him?

He lifted his hips and between the two of them they wrestled his jeans and starkly white underwear down to his thighs. When Hope saw his cock lying erect along his belly, however, she gave up trying to help him and lowered down to inspect him more closely. Her long hair fell forward and slithered across his stomach, partially obscuring his penis. Hope pushed it back impatiently.

Ryan went still as she studied him just inches away from his erect member. Several blue veins distended along the length of the staff. The head was shaped like the cap of a paddy straw mushroom, smooth and succulent in appearance. She inhaled and caught his musky, male scent.

Liquid heat surged between her thighs.

"I can't believe you put that inside me," she whispered. Her wide-eyed fascination only mounted when his cock slid an inch on his belly as though drawn to her warm breath.

"Well, believe it. I'm going to *put it inside of you* more times than you'll ever be able to count."

She shifted up on him slightly. He gasped and fell back on the bed.

"*Christ*, Hope."

"What?" she asked, alarmed that something was wrong.

"Your hair," he grated out. Hope noticed perspiration dampening his brow. "It's like . . . coiled silk."

She glanced down and saw a swatch of her dark hair had spilled again over his belly and cock. She instinctively moved her head, swooshing it back and forth.

"You really do want a spanking, don't you?"

She grinned. "It feels good, doesn't it?"

He swallowed thickly and nodded. Hope gathered some of the hair in her hand and wrapped her fingers around the girth of his penis, lifting the weight off his belly. When she moved her hand up and down, sliding his cock amongst a dense thicket of curls, he clenched his eyes shut tightly.

"Oh *yeah*."

Hope's smile widened. It did something to her to see Ryan so transported by pleasure. It really did. She could easily become addicted to the experience. Her hand squeezed tighter and her pumping motions grew more rapid. She watched in fascination as his breathing came faster and a slight coat of perspiration began to gleam on his muscular, flat abdomen.

"That's right, honey. Don't stop. It feels so good."

She glanced down and saw the head of his penis poke out amidst the long strands of her dark hair. For a moment or two she merely watched the fat crown while she stroked him with her hair-lined fist and he moaned in pleasure. A globule of clear liquid gathered around the slit and began to stream down the head. She leaned down even further to watch its progress and saw it was about to flow into her hair.

Without thinking she swiped her tongue over the head of Ryan's cock, capturing the liquid.

He started. She stared up at him in alarm only to see his eyes pinned to her opened lips and partially exposed tongue. His essence melted on the tip of it and she caught his flavor. She closed her mouth and swallowed.

"*Hope*."

"Yes, Ryan?" she asked shakily.

But he didn't speak even though it looked like he knew precisely what he wanted to say.

"Remember . . . remember last night when you put your mouth on me?" she asked.

He merely nodded, his eyes glowing like embers between narrowed eyelids.

"Would you like me to do—"

"*Yes.*"

She smiled before she slid the crown of his cock between her lips. His girth stretched her lips wide when they encircled the entire head. She tightened her mouth around him and began to slide the stalk of his penis between her fisted curls.

He moaned.

"That's it. Now move your mouth up and down a little bit, honey. Follow the rhythm of your hand."

Hope looked up and saw that Ryan had come up on his elbows and watched her with profound focus. She loved the weight of his penis on her tongue. She bobbed her head up and down on the first several inches of his cock. When she experimented with suction his expression turned rigid . . . even a little feral. He met her stare while she moved over him even faster both with her mouth and hand.

"Witch."

Her smile stretched around his cock. She felt him throb in her hand, sensed his mounting excitement. He clenched his eyes shut. Hope lost herself in the sensation of giving him pleasure.

"I'm going to come," he said eventually.

Hope's eyes went wide at his harsh proclamation. What did he want her to do?

His big body shuddered and he opened his eyelids into narrow slits. "Come off me unless you want to swallow, Hope."

Swallow? His seed? She wasn't sure if she wanted to do that or not, but she couldn't bring herself to move away from him. It was thrilling to be so intimately touching him as he reached his moment of crisis. His cock jerked in her hand. She kept the head fixed tightly in her mouth and continued to pump him with her fist.

His sharp shout of release segued into a deep, guttural groan. Hope whimpered in wonder as his warm semen began to shoot into her mouth. She struggled to swallow at first, but then his taste penetrated her awareness—musky and rich, the very essence of Ryan Daire. She took him deeper into her mouth then, suckling him while he continued to grunt in pleasure and erupt in orgasm.

Finally his convulsions lessened and the former jets of semen waned to irregular spills on her tongue. It struck her as being a little sad—poignant—for some reason when she'd licked off the last seeping drop and he fell back against the pillows, breathing heavily.

She slid his sticky member out of her mouth. Although he was noticeably less hard, his cock still looked ruddy and full, she noticed.

"Come here."

She felt her cheeks warming at the sound of his low, gruff voice. The intimacy of what had just occurred seemed to crash in on her when she looked into Ryan's face and heard his tone.

"Would . . . would you like me to remove your . . . jeans first?" she asked uncertainly.

He scowled. "What I'd like is for you to come here, Hope."

She leaned down over his chest and he pulled her into his arms. She snorted and then giggled when he put his face next to her neck and rubbed her lightly with his whiskers.

"Oh, stop!" she shouted, squirming on top of him to get away from the torture. "I'm extremely ticklish."

"I can see that." He swatted her fanny once as she wiggled around, trying to get away from him. Hope jumped like the smack of flesh against flesh had been a gunshot. Before she had the opportunity to squawk, however, Ryan was already at the business of soothing her with firm, warm lips that curved into a grin. He scraped his front teeth lightly along her nape.

She writhed again on top of his long, hard body, but her restlessness had nothing to do with panic this time.

Ryan groaned and spread both of his hands over her hips and bottom, holding her into immobility.

"I've never known a woman who squirms as much as you do."

Hope gasped when he nipped at the shell of her ear and then placed a kiss on the opening.

He lightly licked at her earlobe and then kissed the entire opening once again. This time the slight suction he applied made warm juice flood from her sex. Hope pressed down on her hips and wiggled, desperate for pressure where she most needed it. "Oh, you *make* me squirm, Ryan. Don't be mad at me when you're the one who makes it happen."

He chuckled and leaned back onto the pillow, inspecting her. His long fingers began to knead her bottom. "Why would I be mad at the fact that you have such a sensitive little body?" He smoothed both palms over her bottom and parted her thighs. Hope moaned when he penetrated her slit with a long finger. His penis lurched against her hip. "Or that you get so wet from a few kisses and making me come?"

Hope's mouth fell open and she stared blankly as he stimulated her with his finger. A sound of protest left her throat when he withdrew. He brought his finger to his mouth and sucked it, his cerulean eyes never leaving her face.

"So sweet," he murmured after he'd taken his finger from his mouth.

Hope groaned and ground her pelvis against him again, her body moving more sinuously this time compared to her former desperate writhing. If she interpreted Ryan's knowing grin correctly, he knew precisely what she was experiencing. His hands went to the back of her corset.

"How do I get this thing off?"

"There are hooks—" Even as she spoke, however, he popped open several of the fasteners.

"It's like getting off a bra times fifteen."

"What's a bra?" Hope asked, but she wasn't really paying any attention because Ryan had rolled her onto her back. He paused to kick off the remainder of his clothing before he came down on his side next to her with an eager look on his face.

"I'll have my mother explain to you the dynamics of a bra, I think. Suffice it to say it's an abbreviated version of this thing and I'm guessing a hell of a lot more comfortable," he muttered as he removed her stiff corset and tossed it to the side of the bed carelessly.

Hope scowled as he tossed away the garment but she was much more interested in Ryan's casual reference to his mother.

"I meant to ask you about your family. When will I get to meet your mother?"

"Hmmm?" Ryan asked after a moment. She realized he stared fixedly at her bared breasts, a small smile curving his mouth that reminded her of a tiger about to feast—and feast *well*.

"Ryan. We were speaking of your mother."

"*You* might have been. *I* was talking about your breasts. Or thinking about them, anyway."

Hope swallowed as she stared up at him. The secret flesh between her thighs twanged sharply with arousal. Why did the hungry look in his beautiful eyes make her feel as though she was about to be ravished and cherished at once?

Then he lowered his head and caught a nipple between his lips and teeth and Hope thought she began to understand what it meant to be both nourishment and a source of worship to a lover at once.

A *lover*, she thought as she arched her back, feeding him her flesh even as he added fuel to her flaming desire with his firm suck and lashing tongue. She ran her fingers through his thick, soft hair and thought: *I have a lover.*

And *what* an exquisite, awe-inspiring experience it was to desire and be desired full measure in return. Never. Never when she'd read Shakespeare or Whitman or imagined the tawdry romps in the Levee District had she imagined the fullness of this experience, the intense, blazing carnality of it.

She glanced down and saw Ryan's cheeks hollowed out as he suckled her, the taut, firm squeeze of his lips, the surprisingly touching sight of his closed, smooth eyelids—as though she witnessed him at a moment of sublime, peaceful bliss.

Her womb seemed to clench inside of her, the pain so great she cried out.

"Ryan!"

He opened his eyelids slowly.

"I . . . don't think you should continue doing that. It . . . it hurts."

His dark brows and the sticking bandage went up on his forehead, but his lips remained sealed around her nipple.

"Well, not *hurts*, precisely," she admitted rapidly when the divine suction of his mouth lessened noticeably. His firm suck resumed and Hope's fingers clawed desperately in his hair, making him grunt in discomfort. Despite what she'd just said she cried out "no!" when Ryan released her nipple.

"Do you want me to tie you down again?"

"Surely that's not necessary, is it?" she whispered weakly. Ryan gave her a wry look as he came face-to-face with her, pressing her down to the bed. It felt delicious to take even part of the weight of such a big, solid . . . hard man.

"It will be if you keep clawing me and writhing around while I take my time making love to your mouth and breasts and anything else I damn well please for a good part of the night. I want complete access to you, Hope."

Her mouth fell open to reply and Ryan silenced her by sliding his tongue between her lips.

She moaned as pleasure inundated her. Surely Ryan wasn't concerned. Couldn't he tell he had complete access to everything from her pinkie finger to her very soul?

∽ TWENTY-TWO ∾

Ryan's consciousness rose sluggishly into the waking world the next morning. He existed in a warm cocoon of sunlight and body-warmed blankets. He kept his eyes closed, hesitant to break the spell of profound relaxation and contentment. The most amazing, erotic memories clung around his awareness like a dream lover's embrace.

His body tensed immediately, however, when he heard the wooden floor next to the bed squeak, the sound somehow cautious, as though whoever neared him did so furtively.

"You're such a hog with the covers. Let me in there with you. I'm freezing out here."

Ryan's eyelids popped open. He felt afraid to move for a second as the strongest sense of déjà vu he'd ever experienced in his life swept through his awareness. He turned around slowly and gawked at a naked, glorious, sun-gilded Hope Stillwater as though he were witnessing a miracle of the highest caliber.

She literally dazzled him. After a second he noticed that the stunning vision before him had tilted her head and that her dark brows furrowed in puzzlement.

He whipped back the covers and grabbed her before she could fade away like a dream. He brought her onto the bed and yanked the blanket over them, hardly aware of her surprised laughter. Most of his attention luxuriated in the sensation of Hope's body pressing against his. Her skin felt like smooth, cool silk flowing beneath his hand as he drew it along the side of her torso.

He looked into her face and saw laughter in her midnight eyes.

"Just who do you think you are, sneaking around naked at this hour of the morning?" he asked before he brushed aside a swath of dark hair and buried his face in her fragrant neck. His fingers tightened in the silky strands when he recalled climaxing while his cock was buried both in Hope's coiling curls and hot little mouth at once.

She wasn't a dream. And she really *was* right here beneath him, naked and beautiful. Maybe she wasn't a dream, but she was a miracle. The degree of distilled lust he experienced at the sensation of her soft, firm body beneath him, her erect nipples pressing into his ribs was like a blade lancing into his flesh.

He groaned when he felt her hands in his hair and then running hungrily over his shoulders.

"You've accused me of being a witch often enough. Is that the answer you want?" she teased him in that low, smoky voice he'd come to love. His cock lurched against her satiny smooth belly. Despite a night full of mind-bogglingly great sex he realized he had to have her again.

Now.

He needed to prove to himself that she was real; that Hope truly was there with him.

"It's the only answer I'm going to get for now," he growled. "By now you know the only conversing I like doing while I'm fucking is dirty talk."

He saw her black, velvety eyes surrounded by a lush thicket of lashes widen. She pressed two fingers to her smiling lips as though to seal them.

"*Witch*," Ryan muttered before he fell on the luscious pink bow of her swollen, well-kissed lips. He'd explored her mouth all night long, ravaged it . . . made love to it again and again. Still, he wanted more. When he registered her taste he sought out her pussy with his hand. He grunted in sublime male satisfaction as his fingers glided over creamy, plump labia and a slick, erect clit.

He penetrated her snug slit with his forefinger.

"You're so wet. I'm sorry, I can't wait," he mumbled after he broke their kiss roughly. He dove for the bedside table where a box of condoms lay opened, his supply largely diminished after his and Hope's night of intense, abandoned lovemaking. He noticed her eager expression as he rolled on the prophylactic, glad to see she'd gotten over her initial disgust of him using a condom.

"But it's so *cold*," she'd complained when he'd pressed his rubber-covered, lubricated cock to her slit for the first time last night. "I like the way you feel much better—so warm and smooth."

Ryan had thrust into her when he heard her sweet compliment.

"Don't worry, witch," he'd grunted in pleasure at the sensation of penetrating her tight clasp. "You'll warm it up in no time."

Presently he put his upper body weight on one elbow and fisted his cock, positioning the tip at the gate of Hope's wet pussy. He flexed his hips.

She gasped as he came down over her. His gaze zoomed up to her face.

"Are you too sore from last night?"

Her cheeks flushed with blood. "No, it feels so good."

He bent to take a tender bite from her fragrant neck and pushed his cock into her to mid-staff. She'd said *so good*, but the sensation felt so fantastic to him that it nearly ripped at the limits of his consciousness. Heat emanated from the muscular walls of her pussy, taunting him. She squirmed beneath him, trying to seat him further in her tight channel. Ryan felt an overwhelming desire to pound his cock into her until he came in what promised to be an explosive climax. Instead he grasped her hip with one hand.

"Keep still," he grated out as he fought for control amid a cyclone of desire that pummeled him from all directions. He grabbed her wrists and pinned them down above her head with one hand while his other continued to immobilize her hip. She arched her back up off the bed, straining to brush her erect nipples against his chest.

"Quit teasing me, Hope, or I'll turn you over my knee when I'm done with you."

He already knew somehow that she'd give him a look of pure seduction at his threat but knowing didn't diminish the result of her witch's smile in the slightest. His cock jerked in her tight pussy. He bent down and nipped at her bee-stung lower lip with his teeth. "After I fuck you I'm gonna—"

"Daire!" a man called somewhere far outside the confines of the battering, relentless storm that held Hope and him as its hostages. She squirmed beneath him and he instinctively accepted her challenge. A harsh groan tore at his throat as he thrust and pressed his aching balls to her damp cunt.

His shout of triumph blended with her cry of excitement and Ramiro's call. Christ, why did that part of his former dreamlike experience of making love to Hope have to be the same?

"Shhhh, don't move. It's my partner, Ramiro. I'll get rid of him," Ryan soothed when he looked into Hope's big eyes and knew from her shocked expression that Ramiro's voice had finally penetrated her arousal. His belly expanded and contracted against hers wildly as he restrained himself mightily from not fucking her sweet little pussy like there was no tomorrow.

He waited expectantly, knowing what would likely happen, but Hope started beneath him when Ramiro banged loudly on the door.

"Don't you *dare* open that damn door, Ramiro," Ryan roared over his shoulder. "I'm not alone in here."

"What the *hell* are you doing, Daire?" Ramiro shouted from behind the closed door. "Why didn't you show up for the briefing about Donahue yesterday? I thought you said you'd be back in time for it! I had to make up a story about a family emergency and told Crenshaw I'd brief you today myself."

"*What?*" Ryan bellowed.

"Donahue. You remember him, right? We're going to arrest him tonight. What are you doing fucking . . . *fucking*?"

Ryan stared in shock at the clock on the bedside table. He'd been sure it was Friday morning. He had his alarm set to make sure he was up in time for the ten o'clock briefing.

"It's *Saturday* morning?"

"Hell yes, it's Saturday morning. What, are you caught in some kind of time warp, you idiot?"

Ramiro had unintentionally got it right. Apparently he hadn't only lost a few hours traveling back and forth from Hope's time, he'd also lost an extra twenty-four hours. Thank God he hadn't lost more. He held Hope's stare and shouted over his shoulder.

"Just wait downstairs. I'll be down in a minute."

"I'll wait out in the car. This house gives me the creeps."

"He's the one who thinks you're a ghost," Ryan told Hope softly, a trace of apology in his tone. He stared at her beautiful face and a profound sense of satisfaction went through him. Unlike his dream experience, she was still here. And he was still buried fast in her sweetness.

"A ghost? But—"

"Shhhh, I'll try and explain later. But right now—"

"*Ryan*—" Hope protested weakly when he began to thrust his cock in and out of her.

"There's no buts about it, honey. Nothing . . . *nothing* is going to stop me from having you this time around."

The headboard began to clack against the wall loudly as he became more enthusiastic about celebrating her existence.

∽

"Feeling a little less tense, I hope," Ramiro said sarcastically through his opened car window twenty minutes later.

Ryan grinned. "As a matter of fact, I feel fantastic, thanks. Come inside. I want you to meet someone."

A few seconds later Ryan shut the mansion's front door behind them and turned to examine his friend. Ramiro didn't look any more comfortable in the twenty-first century than he had 102 years ago when Hope had dragged Mel inside this same magnificent house.

How was he supposed to go about introducing Hope to Ramiro, anyway? He'd already thought of just making up a cover story to explain her presence in the house with him, but there were a few people—Ramiro, his mother and Alistair—who he wouldn't feel comfortable lying to about the entire ordeal.

Besides, he had to tell Ramiro about Diamond Jack Fletcher's connection to Jim Donahue.

His partner stuck his hands in his coat pocket, hunching slightly as he glanced around the entry hall warily. The whites of Ramiro's eyes showed when they both heard the sound of heels tapping in the upper hallway.

Hope came down the grand staircase slowly, her long skirt and petticoat swishing behind her on the mahogany stairs. The fact that she hadn't pinned her long mane of curling hair back up on her head but wore it spilling around her shoulders and back didn't take away from her regal appearance in the slightest. When she reached the bottom of the stairs she paused and gave Ramiro a shy, warm smile.

Ramiro returned it with a slack-jawed gawk.

"I told you she wasn't a ghost," Ryan said quietly.

"What the hell? You mean *that's* the chick in the mirror?"

Ryan nodded when Ramiro stared at him incredulously.

"Ramiro Menendez, meet Hope Stillwater."

"It's a pleasure to make your acquaintance, Mr. Menendez." She put out her hand when she approached. Ramiro returned her formal gesture after giving Ryan a "you've got to be kidding me" look.

"She feels like the real thing," Ramiro admitted after enveloping her small, elegant hand in his big paw. Ryan bristled when his partner's limpid, bedroom eyes rested on Hope's corset-encased breasts as he spoke. "But if you're not a ghost, how come you're dressed like that, beautiful lady? Don't tell me—Ryan is taking you to the gala tonight at the Field Museum and that's your getup. Some kind of costume or something?"

Ryan and Hope spoke at once.

"Donahue's arrest is official police business. Not something you ask a date to, Ramiro."

"The Field Museum still exists? That's one of my favorite places in the city. It reminds me of all the magic of the Chicago World's Fair. May I go with you, Ryan? I'll promise to stay out of the way of *official police business*."

Ryan threw Ramiro a dirty look, letting him know this was his big mouth's fault. "I'm afraid that's not possible, honey."

"Special Agent Crenshaw's bringing his wife. He asked if we were bringing dates—or at least someone who checked out and didn't get in the way of official business. He thought it might look strange to have fifteen men standing around like a gang of dateless losers crashing the high school prom. I mean, what guy in his right mind would take the time and effort to put on a tux if he wasn't trying to impress a lady, am I right?" Ramiro asked Hope confidentially. "Jim Donahue'd notice that quick as a huge, pussing boil on the nose. I'm bringing Gail. Couldn't keep her away once she heard she'd get to see me in a tux."

"*Tux?* Do you mean tuxedo, Mr. Menendez?"

"Yeah, I do . . . uh . . ." He looked at Ryan as if for advice. Ryan just glared at him forbiddingly. "Er . . . *Miss Stillwater*."

"Oh, so the official police business is taking place at some sort of ball?" Hope enthused.

Her animated expression suddenly collapsed.

"What's wrong?" Ramiro asked.

"I just realized that I don't have anything to wear. I didn't bring any gowns on the . . . journey."

"You don't need a gown for the gala tonight, honey, because you're not going," Ryan stated firmly. He was ignored by both of them.

"Ryan could take you over to his mother's. I'm sure Eve'd set you up. Sweet lady and *so* tempting even though Daire gives me dirty looks like that one"—Ramiro hitched his thumb at Ryan's face—"every time I mention it. All the women at the Field Museum will want to scratch your eyes out if you show up in one of Eve Daire's dresses."

"Oh . . . well, I couldn't impose," Hope said, her eyes downcast.

"Honey, I'm not going to take you into a potentially dangerous situation just so you can see the Field Museum. I'll take you there another time. I don't even think it's in the same place that you're used to—"

"You know as well as I do that the chances are slim to none that anything dangerous will actually occur in the midst of a room

of crowded partygoers," Ramiro interrupted. "We'll arrest Donahue quietly as he leaves. Chirnovsky will get him to talk about his
slimy white slaving plans and Donahue goes to prison."

"You know as well as I do that things are rarely ever that cut-
and-dry."

"Ryan, you're trying to stop a white slavery operation?" Hope
interrupted.

"We've been working on putting away the kingpin—Jim
Donahue—for over a year now. Daire and I were the ones who
brought the whole operation to the FBI's attention. Donahue's a
powerful son of a bitch, though. We have to nail him just right or
risk losing the whole case. Tonight's our moment of victory," Ramiro
said smugly.

Ryan started to reply when he noticed the way Hope regarded
him.

"I'm very sorry to hear that white slavery continues to occur,
but I'm so proud of you for fighting it, Ryan."

The sound of Ramiro clearing his throat tore him out of the
trance induced by Hope's glistening, midnight eyes.

"Do you really think it would be safe at the Field Museum, Mr.
Menendez?" Hope asked.

"Crenshaw would never sanction us taking down Donahue in
the midst of a crowded event, Miss Stillwater." Ramiro's temporary
awkwardness at using Hope's surname immediately diminished
when she bedazzled him with a warm smile. "You'll be as safe there
as you would be on a regular museum attendance day. More so,
with all the cops and federal agents that will be there."

Hope glanced up at Ryan hopefully through a thicket of dark
lashes. "I would love to go with you."

Ryan opened his mouth to explain why she couldn't, but then
he saw the trace of anxiety in her eyes. He was forced to acknowl-
edge that it might be difficult for her to be on her own, even if it

were for only one night, when she was still so emotionally raw from her leap forward in time and the loss of everything dear to her. Not to mention the fact that this house was like an empty tomb. He didn't treasure the idea of leaving her there alone, either.

"You can come on one condition."

Hope nodded eagerly.

"You have to get in a cab and go to my mother's condominium when I tell you to. There's a good chance Donahue won't give us the goods until Chirnovsky and him go to the Sweet Lash after they meet at the Field Museum, anyway."

Hope and Ramiro spoke at once.

"Why the hell would you say that?" Ramiro asked sharply.

"*The Sweet Lash*?" Hope exclaimed. "Do you mean the same establishment that Diamond Jack Fletcher owned?"

Ryan nodded. "The very same. Only in the year 2008 it's a nightclub, not a brothel like it was in 1906. From what I learned while I was in your time and some references from Detective O'Rourke's notes, Jack used to do all his high-level business at the Sweet Lash. I'm betting he might do the same in the present day."

Ramiro stared at Ryan like a second head had just sprouted out of his neck. "Nineteen hundred and six? *Her* time. What do you mean, *her* time?" His dark brown eyes rolled over Hope's apparel, this time with a trace of panic.

"Look, there are a lot of things I've got to explain to both of you and I guess now is as good a time as any. Why don't we go up to the bedroom? There's no place to sit down—"

Ryan paused abruptly midsentence when he noticed Hope shaking her head desperately, her eyes beseeching him not to continue. He sighed. Well, in all fairness to Hope, it really was too much to ask of her to allow a man she didn't even know into her bedroom. Given her culture and upbringing, he should still be counting his blessings over the fact that she tolerated *his* presence there.

He dropped down on a step. "On second thought, the staircase seems like a great place for us to talk. Maybe we should start with the mirror and then move on to the fact that Diamond Jack Fletcher and Jim Donahue just happen to be the same man."

⌒ TWENTY-THREE ⌒

Eve Daire showed Hope the bathroom in the storeroom of her boutique and told her to meet her back up front when she'd finished. She lifted her eyebrows pointedly at her son when she rejoined him behind the checkout counter.

"You might as well have driven a Mack truck through the front of my store."

He sighed regretfully. "I'm sorry, Mom. I didn't know how else to tell you except for to just, well . . . *tell* you."

Eve shook her head, speechless.

"Do you believe me?" Ryan asked when he realized that the glazed expression of amazement hadn't faded from his mother's pretty face in the slightest even though Ryan and Hope had been explaining the circumstances of their time traveling almost non-stop for the past hour—minus the more intimate details, of course.

"Of course I believe you. Can't a grown woman walk around in stunned amazement when the circumstances totally warrant it? I believe you because for one, *you* told me. You're obviously not insane even though the story is absolutely crazy. And also because of that young woman." Eve shook her head again incredulously. "She's *clearly* not from this time. Even if it weren't for you telling me or the incredible clothing she's wearing, I would have figured that out eventually."

Ryan couldn't help but smile. "I couldn't talk her into leaving the front door wearing my sweatpants that were about to fall off her. Hope is . . . unique. I don't think it's just the time period differences, either. She must have raised quite a few eyebrows in the early 1900s."

"You're in love with her."

Ryan started slightly. His mother hadn't asked a question, she'd made a bald statement. He opened his mouth to say something along the lines that it was too soon to tell, that he hadn't known Hope long enough to know if he was in love with her or experiencing an intense infatuation.

Actually, Ryan didn't like to dwell too much on that aspect of their strange circumstances. After seeing Hope firsthand in her time period, he was all too aware of what would be expected of him if he were a man with even a semi-stiff backbone who lived in the year 1906. Decent men didn't go around seducing gentlewomen like Hope Stillwater, let alone do what he'd done to her in that bordello bedroom, and then just walk away.

Problem was, Ryan wasn't an early-twentieth-century man. He existed in a very different time, one where people didn't proclaim their love after a few days of knowing each other, let alone get married like Hope's father—and possibly even Hope—would expect of him.

The situation was so confusing it was just easier for him not to think about it for the time being.

Eve didn't seem to mind his muteness over her disturbing

proclamation about him being in love with Hope. She stepped toward Ryan, her eyes shining with amazement.

"Do you know that young girl back there—*Hope Stillwater*—is the kind of woman we read about in our history books? An activist for women's and children's rights?" Eve asked, her voice laced with barely restrained excitement.

"Yeah. She said the name Miss Addams a few times last night. I finally realized she was talking about *Jane* Addams. Hope regularly gives lectures and attends meetings at Hull House. Apparently *Miss Addams* was a sort of mentor of hers," Ryan admitted, referring to the founder of the field of social work in the United States.

Eve shook her head in continued amazement. "Wow. She knew Jane Addams. *The* Jane Addams. Can you imagine the chutzpah a girl like Hope must have *had* to possess to be so nontraditional during that time period?"

Ryan rolled his eyes. "There's no need to remind me of Hope's chutzpah."

Eve gave a chest-deep chuckle. "I'm glad for you, Ryan. I always hoped you'd find someone special someday—someone who means to you what your father did to me. And Hope certainly is special."

There it was again, that casual, anxiety-provoking reference to Hope and him being a couple. Once again, Ryan ignored it.

"I suppose you could call the fact that she was born a hundred and twenty seven years ago and wears pantaloons underneath sweatpants 'special.' "

"Ryan, you know what I meant," Eve scolded even though her eyes sparkled with amusement. "She's so . . . *alive*. I've never known anyone like her. You know that saying, 'light up a room'?"

"She does, doesn't she?" he admitted gruffly after a pause.

"She certainly does."

"She has other characteristics that aren't quite so stellar, though. She's as impulsive as a three-year-old sometimes. Once Hope gets an idea in her head there's no stopping her."

"And you love her for it." Eve chuckled before she took a sip of diet soda. "She's exactly what you need, a big, strong, dominant man like you. She'll put you in your place quicker than you can say 'mercy.'"

"I'm scared she's going to try and go back through the mirror."

Eve paused with the soda can tilted to her lips. Her blue eyes widened at his sudden intensity.

"She *wants* to go back," he added.

Eve swallowed thickly and lowered the can of soda. "Honey, that's only natural. She loves her father. She's left a whole way of life behind."

"I know," Ryan said. Why'd he say that, anyway, when he'd just been thinking about the impossible complications of Hope and him having a relationship? It was because he was worried about her safety, of course. "But there's no telling what would happen to her if she tried to use the remaining mirror. I wish I understood the mechanics of it."

"It's stranger than fiction. I can't help but feel some kind of mechanical explanation would be woefully lacking. Maybe you should ask Alistair about it?"

"Do you really think he knows something about the mirror?"

Eve shrugged. "I don't know for sure. But you yourself have said the circumstances of him giving you the Prairie Avenue mansion were strange. Now we discover there's a mirror in the household that serves as a portal between time periods and you bring this amazing woman back with you—a woman who's clearly as much in love with you as you are her."

Ryan's heart bounded in his chest. Did his mother really think so? He got his answer when she gave him a knowing smirk.

"You're right. About Alistair I mean. I'm going to talk to him about it tomorrow. The strange thing about it is that Hope and I saw each other, communicated and spoke even, by means other than the mirror . . ." he trailed off thoughtfully.

"What else is bothering you, Ryan?"

He grimaced. The photographs of Hope and him making love in the Sweet Lash had come to mind. He'd re-hidden them in the secret compartment in the mantel the day they returned.

"There's something I haven't told Hope yet—something about some photographs I found of her at the mansion—"

"Ryan, you never told me you found photographs of me."

He looked around in surprise to see Hope pushing through the swinging door that led to the storeroom.

"I, uh . . . there were some photographs of you in the information Gail gathered for me from the Chicago police archives," he mumbled uneasily. Hope didn't appear to notice anything suspicious in his behavior, thank God.

"I keep forgetting to ask you how those toilets work. It seems quite the miracle the way they flush without a tank above my head," Hope stated matter-of-factly as she joined them.

"And what did you think of the toilet paper?" Ryan asked, his lips twitching with humor.

Hope colored and glanced at Eve apologetically. "Ryan thinks I'm silly for thinking the paper in the bathroom is a miracle of softness."

"I always wondered what people used before toilet paper—" Eve began, but Ryan cut her off.

"Hate to interrupt what I'm sure'll be a fascinating conversation, but I told Ramiro I'd meet him to go over some things I missed at the meeting yesterday."

"You go on, Ryan," Eve said as she grabbed Hope's hand and drew her into the boutique's showroom. "Hope and I will be busy getting her ready for the gala tonight."

"I can't thank you enough for letting me borrow one of your

gowns, Mrs. Daire. They're so beautiful, like something an elven princess would wear. I'm a little concerned about the . . . er . . . lack of material involved, but if you tell me they're sufficiently modest for this time period, I'll take your word on it."

"We'll get you all set up, darling. You're going to be the belle of the ball," Eve said as she began drawing down dress after dress from the rack.

"Oh, and Ryan said I was to ask you about the specifics of 'bras' as well."

Hope turned when Ryan touched her shoulder. He dropped a kiss on her parted lips.

"I'll be back in an hour or two to get you. We should have time to look around the city a little more before we have to show up at the Field Museum," he whispered near her mouth a moment later. Hope slowly lifted her eyelids and stared at him bemusedly. It made him feel like a god that his kiss put that silly, dazed expression on her face. "And don't start wearing bras just because I brought it up."

"You would prefer I wore my corset?"

"I'd prefer you wore neither."

Hope glanced nervously at Eve. "I'm sure this is not an appropriate conversation for us to be having in front of your mother," she whispered.

"No worries, Hope," Eve muttered distractedly as she glanced at a green gown and then Hope with a furrowed brow before she rehung the dress. "Believe it or not it doesn't come as much of a shock to me that a healthy thirty-three-year-old male would prefer that a pretty woman not wear a bra." She grinned in a satisfied manner when she drew down a rose-colored gown and held it up to Hope. "Bingo. Looks like Ryan will get his wish."

"What do you mean?" Hope asked a tad nervously as she studied the floaty, silk-chiffon dress.

"I mean that I might have designed this dress specifically for your figure and coloring it's so perfect. And no bra *or* corset is going to ruin that perfection."

Ryan turned and headed for the front door, chuckling to himself at Hope's panicked expression at the thought of going into public with her beautiful breasts unbound.

❧ TWENTY-FOUR ❧

Ryan dug his fingers into the collar of his white dress shirt, attempting to loosen it just a tad. He tied his bow tie and glanced at his face briefly in the gilded mirror, scowling when he noticed the cut on his brow that hadn't yet fully healed. His jacket hung on a rail of the brass bed so his holster and gun were in full view. He looked exactly like what he was—a cop dressed up in a monkey suit.

He grabbed his jacket, shrugging into it as he walked down the hallway. Hope'd been locked up in the bathroom for well over an hour now and he was starting to wonder what the hell she was doing in there. They still had to pick up Ramiro and Gail and he wanted to leave early so he could take a different route to the Field Museum than the one he'd driven this afternoon driving to his mother's. It had been a strangely gratifying experience to show Hope the city and see her wide-eyed expressions of wonder as she exclaimed over the towering high-rises, the speed at which cars flew down Lake Shore Drive and the scandalous fact that women showed their *legs* in public.

He'd also had his smugness punctured a few times in regard to the modern advancements of his world in comparison to hers. As they'd pass Navy Pier on Lake Shore Drive he'd pointed at the Ferris wheel.

"That's a copy of Ferris's original wheel from the Chicago World's Fair in 1893." He noticed that Hope'd looked at the wheel and glanced over to him as though she wanted to say something but was too polite to do so.

"What?" he asked.

"That's not a replica of Mr. George Ferris's wheel, Ryan."

"Are you sure? I could have sworn I read it was."

"Of course I'm sure. That," said Hope as she pointed at the wheel, "is nothing compared to Mr. Ferris's wheel. The original Ferris wheel was as tall as many of these high-rises, as you call them. There were thirty-six cars and each of them held sixty people. It was an engineering wonder. He built it to rival France's engineering feat for their World's Fair, the Eiffel Tower, you know. He surpassed it as far as I'm concerned."

No, he hadn't known. "Over two thousand people could ride it at once?"

Hope had nodded as she gawked at the thick orchard of towering buildings to the left of her. "My mother and father were intimate friends with Mr. and Mrs. Ferris. I rode the wheel on several occasions. Once while my mother and I were on the Ferris wheel a man had a terrible attack of nerves because of the great height. He began shouting and racing about the car, knocking people over. He was inconsolable and of course there was nowhere for him to go. It was quite frightening, as you can imagine, especially for us children to be locked in that small space with a madman. But my mother just matter-of-factly removed her skirt and threw it over the poor man's head. She began to soothe him with her voice and he went quite still under her skirt until we made a full turn of the wheel."

"She took off her *skirt*?" Ryan had asked incredulously, especially now that he'd learned firsthand about a woman from Hope's time period's modesty in regard to matters of dress.

Hope had chuckled when she saw his expression and nodded. "Yes. Not only was the panicking man shocked into silence. Everyone was speechless, but the men on board were flabbergasted at the sight of my mother in her petticoat. I wish you could have known her. She was a very beautiful woman in addition to being quite unique."

"I guess it's clear where you got it from," Ryan had said under his breath.

Later he'd taken her to the top of the Sears Tower so that she could see a panoramic view of the city. He'd been a little unsure about taking her up to the 110th floor, and initially the paleness of her face as she slowly approached one of the windows on the skydeck hardly reassured him. His mother had provided her with a skirt, boots and a sweater to wear. Was he going to have to remove the skirt and fling it over her head to stop her from panicking?

His partially amused, partially concerned thoughts ceased when Hope had turned around and he saw her exultant expression.

After that he'd had trouble keeping up with her as she rushed around from one side of the skydeck to another, identifying known landmarks and exclaiming over the massive growth of the city.

"He lives on our block, you know," Hope had murmured happily as they descended. The elevator was crowded with tourists and Hope was sandwiched between the corner and Ryan's body.

"Who?" he asked, only mildly interested. He pressed his body closer to her and dropped a kiss on top of her head. Her scent filled his nose. She felt so small against him, so soft . . . very, very nice. She tilted her head back and regarded him with eyes that never ceased to capture him completely in their velvety soft snare.

Nice place to be trapped. He found himself wondering idly if there was enough time to take her back to Prairie Avenue, strip her bare and bury his nose in every inch of her smooth, fragrant skin. Maybe if he broke a few land speed records on the way home and wrangled a promise out of Hope that she'd get ready for the gala in twenty minutes flat he'd have time to—

"Mr. Joseph Sears. He lives just two houses down from us. I look forward to telling him of his family's towering contribution to the city someday."

His eyebrows had gone up at her casual melding of their time periods. She'd noticed his amusement and smiled.

"I thought you said I should try and think of my father as still being alive—accessible to me. If it were true of him, wouldn't it be true for everyone?"

Ryan had shrugged. "You love your father, Hope. You can picture him with the clarity that only intense emotion can bring. I'm assuming you don't feel the same way about Joseph Sears, but I may be wrong."

She'd lowered her eyes and blushed so intensely it'd surprised him. Did she really believe he thought she had a thing for Joseph Sears? She cleared her throat.

"Are you saying that was how you did it, Ryan?" she whispered. She looked up at him cautiously through thick lashes. "Is that how you traveled through time?"

Ryan's mouth gaped open stupidly. He grasped for something logical to say, but the elevator door opened and everyone inside crushed to get out.

It wasn't that he was trying to avoid answering her, he assured himself presently. It just seemed like one thing had led to another since they'd returned to the car and then Prairie Avenue.

And now Hope had disappeared into the bathroom for over an hour.

He knocked on the door.

"Hope? We need to get going. We're going to be late."

"Maybe you should go without me, Ryan."

"What are you talking about?" he shouted through the closed door. "You *begged* me to go." He tried to open the door but it was locked. "Open up, honey."

His brows furrowed in concern when nothing happened for several silent seconds.

"Hope? Are you all right?"

He heard the snick of the lock being released. The door opened slowly.

Ryan stared.

"Is it . . . bad?" she whispered.

"Bad?" Ryan muttered, poleaxed by the sight of her in the sleeveless, rose-colored gown. The fabric over her breasts was pleated but fit very snugly. Silver beading just below her breasts further highlighted the most succulent décolletage Ryan had ever imagined. Below the beading the fabric fell to her toes in a graceful, wispy cloud. Her long, curly hair fell around her shoulders in a sexy spill. She wore no necklace, but the flawless expanse of skin on her chest, neck and shoulders required no adornment. His mother must have loaned her the long, delicate silver filigreed earrings that glittered next to her midnight hair.

She looked ethereal . . . otherworldly.

"You're beautiful," he said as he met her anxious gaze. He wished his words hadn't sounded so lame, so inadequate. Ryan was used to seeing professional models wear his mother's designs. As a matter of fact, he thought he'd seen a blonde with legs that went up to her armpits model this very design at one of his mother's shows last year. But nothing could have prepared him for seeing Hope standing there in the same gown, looking so uncertain when she deserved tributes of poetry and song to her unsurpassable beauty.

She gave him a tremulous smile. "I feel naked."

"You look like something from a dream. And nobody at the gala is going to think anything other than that. But if that doesn't help any, think of your mother taking off her skirt to calm that panicked guy on the Ferris wheel." His eyebrows rose when her black eyes sparkled. "Surely you have as much courage as her."

That did it. She went to the sink and picked up the tiny silver beaded purse that matched her ensemble. She took a long, deep breath, mastering her anxiety.

"Well, it certainly is easier to do *that* without a corset," she admitted with a witch's smile.

∽

Ryan noticed Hope's broad grin as they climbed up the white marble steps of the Field Museum.

"Guess you're not disappointed, even though it's not the Field Museum you remember from Jackson Park?"

"Oh, it's exactly what I'd hoped it would be when I heard Mrs. Potter Palmer coaxing Mr. Burnham into building it several months ago at a dinner party given by the Glessners. He recaptured a bit of the magic of the White City and the Chicago World's Fair. I don't think you present-day Chicagoans have any idea what you owe Daniel Burnham for his elegant city plan," Hope said, referring to the renowned Chicago architect.

She stared up at the fantastic, white marble, neoclassical structure. Glowing lanterns had been set at the edge of every step. Hope felt as though she were attending a party at an enormous Grecian temple. Ryan didn't comment on her proclamation but merely gave a shake of his head, a restrained expression of amazement on his face.

Ryan opened the massive front door for Ramiro, Gail and herself. Hope drew near him and paused for a moment in the doorway.

"I didn't get a chance to tell you how nice you look in your tuxedo," she said when Ramiro and Gail passed out of hearing distance. Her gaze lowered over his bow tie and wide chest. She swallowed with difficulty, but the great lump in her throat didn't prevent her from speaking the truth. "You're the handsomest man I've ever seen."

"It's not fair to tease me while I'm working."

"I'm not teasing you!"

Ryan's crooked grin and laser-like stare caused a tingling sensation of excitement in her breasts and belly.

"You've got a lot to learn, honey. You think seduction is all about taking your clothes off in a bedroom, but you get me hard with just a glance. Never mind what you do to me with your kindness."

He leaned down and seized her lips in a quick, fierce kiss. Hope craned up for him, forgetting where they were or who might be watching them immediately when she registered the firm press of his molding lips and inhaled the clean, spicy scent of his cologne.

He kept his dark head lowered over her upturned face when he finally broke their kiss.

"I wasn't being kind, Ryan. It was the solemn truth."

He brushed a curl off her cheek. "I've asked Gail to look out for you at the party, and Ramiro will be there whenever he can be."

"Don't worry about me. I like Gail very much. Imagine—a career woman. I could talk to her about her work at the police station all night. I'll wager that's why police officers are so hardworking and dedicated in your time versus mine—because *women* are allowed to work alongside them. At any rate, you have important work to do. You know I have as much interest in you arresting Jim Donahue as anyone," she said, giving him a significant look. She'd been amazed to the point of muteness (a rare occurrence) when

Ryan had told Ramiro and her this morning that Diamond Jack Fletcher lived in this time period—and was as corrupt and evil as ever.

"I do," he said quietly, his eyes wandering over her face intently. "But it would help me a great deal to know you weren't getting into any trouble. Stay away from Jim Donahue or anyone who looks like they're associated with him. Do you understand?"

"Of course! I'm more than happy to let you and Ramiro capture that woman-hating, white slaving, rotten-to-the-core, vicious, kidnapping scoundrel who—"

"Hope?"

"Yes?" she asked, a little flustered at being interrupted in the midst of her tirade.

"I don't want you wandering around this museum alone gawking at the exhibits or anything. I'll bring you here another time. Stay with Gail and Ramiro."

"I will. Ryan, please don't worry about me. I promise to stay away from Diamond Jack Fletcher. Or any of his future or past incarnations. Lord knows I wouldn't actually *choose* to be around that lout or any of his henchmen," she added under her breath.

"Nice to hear. I probably won't be able to speak with you again until after all this is over. Ramiro will have to leave at some point as well, but you and Gail are going to catch a cab to my mother's place."

Hope nodded. "Be careful, Ryan."

He put out his arm for her. "I always am."

∽

"Nice of you to show up, Daire," Crenshaw said pointedly when he met Ryan and Hope in the high-ceiling entryway.

Ryan thought it was best just to ignore Crenshaw's disgruntlement at his absence at the briefing yesterday and go ahead and introduce Hope.

"It's a pleasure to make your acquaintance, Mr. Crenshaw," Hope told him with her perfect elocution and a smile tailor-made to immediately melt even a hardened federal agent's tough hide.

"Where you'd find that girl? Fairyland?" Crenshaw asked after Gail suggested to Hope that they check their wraps at the coat station. They'd arrived early at the Field Museum in order to check out the lay of the land and to get wired up with their own invisible surveillance devices so that the task force could communicate amongst themselves. Ramiro would remain on the first floor of the museum where the gala was taking place along with eight other members of the squad while Ryan would be stationed someplace covert where Donahue wouldn't notice his presence.

"You'd never believe me if I told you."

Crenshaw's wiry, graying blond eyebrows went up on his head. "You know, I just might believe you. You don't find women that look like that on every corner." He inhaled and got back to business in a split second. "Agent Pearson will take you back to the room we're using for tactical communications. A couple agents are fitting up Chirnovsky with the recording equipment as we speak. We have a van set up for mobile surveillance as well, just in case Donahue should leave the party with Chirnovsky before he says anything of importance. I'm not expecting that to happen, though. According to Chirnovsky, Donahue specifically asked him to meet here tonight along with Manny Gutierrez in order to discuss their plans. Gutierrez is making a rare visit to Chicago. He usually works exclusively in Mexico procuring men for cheap labor and women for the slavery ring."

"Yeah. I'm familiar with Gutierrez's work," Ryan said dryly. "I'd make extra certain that the mobile unit is ready to roll."

"What's that supposed to mean?"

Ryan shrugged. "I just have a hunch Donahue won't say anything substantial until he's at his nightclub—the Sweet Lash."

Ryan returned Crenshaw's steely-eyed stare.

"A hunch, huh? Well, your hunches have usually been bet-worthy in the past. I'll tell Agent Alvarez to be extra sure their unit is alert and ready to go, then. The last thing we need is for Dona-hue to slip through our fingers after all this planning. Our warrant for wiretapping expires at midnight, and I really don't want to have to go in front of a judge for another extension. Speaking of plans going awry, you make sure you keep out of Donahue's sights, you hear?"

Ryan nodded before he went to find Agent Pearson. He couldn't tell Crenshaw about the information he'd gleaned from traveling to a time period where another version of Jim Donahue lived. Be-sides, it was his intuition more than anything else that told him there was a good chance Donahue wouldn't say anything of sig-nificance in regard to his running of the white slavery operation until he was at the Sweet Lash. Old habits died hard—even if they were habits formulated over a century ago.

Agent Pearson showed him the location of the room they were using for tactical communications. Ryan was outfitted by one of the technicians with a Sonic neckloop that went under his shirt. The covert system contained both a microphone for talking and a trans-mitter. A tiny, nearly invisible wireless earpiece kept him connected on a common frequency with the entire squad while they were all in this general location. A remote control monitor that he slid into his pocket allowed him to push a button and be heard by the rest of the squad even if he spoke in a low voice.

An hour after they'd arrived Ryan stood on the second-floor balcony that completely surrounded the enormous central hall of the Field Museum and watched the luxurious charity event unfold-ing below him. Crenshaw had just informed him that Jim Donahue was five minutes away on Lake Shore Drive and Gutierrez wasn't far behind. Crenshaw was taking the opportunity of peace before the storm to dance with his wife.

A hundred or so small candlelit cocktail tables had been set amongst exhibits and the towering menace of a pouncing Sue, the most complete *Tyrannosaurus rex* skeleton known to exist. A sixteen-piece orchestra played a Frank Sinatra classic while dozens of couples danced to the music, the women's colorful long dresses making a kaleidoscope of swaying color beneath him. People were lined up at the three bars that had been set up even though white-jacketed waiters were constantly working the room, offering champagne and hors d'oeuvres.

He felt a little guilty when Ramiro escorted Gail out onto the dance floor and Hope remained at the table alone. One of the waiters approached her. She asked a question and took one of the hors d'oeuvres and a glass of champagne. She gifted the waiter with one of her luminous smiles and nodded her head in approval when she took a bite of the morsel.

After the waiter left—a little too hesitantly for Ryan's liking—Hope sipped her champagne and stared fixedly at Ramiro and Gail as they danced. He could almost sense her energetic mind working as she tried to memorize the dance movements. He scowled when a blond, tanned guy in his late thirties approached her but gave a sigh of relief when Hope smiled and shook her head.

He felt bad about her not being able to dance, but not so bad that he wanted some dude that looked like he spent all his free time on a tanning bed touching her silky skin.

He began to circle the long stretch of the balcony, checking out the faces in the crowd carefully. A few minutes later Crenshaw finished his dance and walked away from the crowd. He asked all the members of the squad to check in.

"All right. Look sharp," Crenshaw said a few seconds later. "Our guest of honor is pulling up to the entrance as we speak."

A minute later he spied Jim Donahue's unmistakable tall, bulky form entering the open forum of the museum with a platinum blonde on his arm.

His spine tingled when his gaze flickered to Hope and then

targeted Jim Donahue again. Ramiro and Gail hadn't reached her yet and she still sat alone at the table.

Alone and vulnerable, Ryan realized with rising discomfort. Donahue and his date were being shown to a special reserved table by a gray-haired man. Apparently being a *woman-hating, white slaving, rotten-to-the-core, vicious, kidnapping scoundrel* got you some special treatment at an affair like this, Ryan thought with grim amusement, picturing Hope as she animatedly enumerated Donahue's faults.

What had he been thinking allowing Hope to be in the near vicinity of Donahue?

Ramiro and Gail reached Hope and he breathed a sigh of relief. Unfortunately, the tingle of warning in his backbone remained.

∽ TWENTY-FIVE ∽

Hope beamed at Ramiro and Gail when they returned from their dance and joined her at the table. "You two dance beautifully together."

Ramiro double pumped his eyebrows at Gail, who both rolled her eyes and blushed at once.

"Sorry I can't treat you to my smooth moves at the moment, Hope. Duty calls."

"That's all right," she assured Ramiro. "I'm sure I wouldn't be very good at it."

"You don't like to dance?" Gail asked conversationally as she sat down. Ramiro, Ryan and her had agreed it would be best to tell as few people as possible about Hope's anachronistic existence in the twenty-first century, so Gail wasn't in on the secret.

"The type of dancing I was taught is a bit more—formal."

Ramiro flashed his white teeth in a happy grin and tapped the table twice. "Time to James Bond it, beautiful ladies."

"He's very funny," Hope said even though she had no idea what Ramiro meant. They both watched him walk away with a bounce in his step.

"That's one way to describe him."

Hope met Gail's eyes and they both laughed. She listened in rapt fascination for the next half hour as Gail expounded on the thrills and doubts of courting Ramiro Menendez. It shocked her to hear how openly her new acquaintance talked about sex.

"But he's so damned cheesy sometimes, you know? If it weren't for the fact that he's phenomenal in bed, I wouldn't put up with his Don Juan act. Don't you dare tell him I told you that, though. He's got a gargantuan head as it is. But then again, he is cute, isn't he?" Gail mused with a small smile as she took a sip of something called a martini. She didn't seem to notice Hope's dazed expression of wonder. "Speaking of which, how did you do it, girl?"

"Uh . . . do what?"

"Every woman at the station would kill to have Ryan Daire stare at her like he does you. He looks like he's going to *eat you alive*." Hope's brows crinkled in confusion when Gail patted her hand over her heart frantically and then waved her face as though she'd overexerted herself. "Just seeing that look got me all hot and bothered and it wasn't even *aimed* at me. You lucky, lucky girl. So . . . what's the verdict?"

"Verdict?" Hope asked, completely at a loss.

"What's Daire like in bed? Jenny Martin from the organized crime unit said he was *amazing*. She told me she was addicted to the sex with him, you know? But Daire is never forthcoming on a long-term supply. So is it true he tends to be *controlling*?" Gail asked with a knowing grin.

Hope stared, mouth agape. Her cheeks flooded with heat. It was one thing to be joyful that women had progressed so much in claiming their sexuality but quite another to suddenly be chatting casually with a virtual stranger about a topic that Hope's culture considered not only extremely intimate, but taboo under these circumstances.

And as far as the rest, Miss *Jenny Martin* better be prepared to expire from her addiction, because she was never, *ever* going to touch Ryan Vincent Daire again if Hope had her way about it!

Fortunately Ramiro saved her from having to respond to Gail when he approached the table.

"Daire's leaving. He wanted me to let you know," Ramiro said softly when he perched at the end of his chair.

"What happened?" Gail asked in an undertone, allowing the swelling music of the orchestra and the crooning singer to muffle their voices for anyone but themselves. Hope had come to understand that although Gail wasn't officially "on the Donahue case," as she'd put it, her work in the research lab made her aware of the generalities of what was occurring tonight.

Ramiro shook his head slightly, his dark brown eyes making a casual-seeming surveillance of the room.

"Something's going down. If it screws up this operation, I'm gonna be 'roid-rage-caliber pissed off, too. Before Chirnovsky had the chance to get Donahue to talk, Gutierrez got a call. He said something was arriving and Donahue ordered Chirnovsky to go to the Sweet Lash."

"The Sweet Lash," Hope murmured. Ramiro met her eyes and she knew he was thinking what she was—that Ryan had predicted Diamond Jack Fletcher's old brothel might be involved somehow tonight.

"Yeah. Crenshaw ordered Ryan to the Sweet Lash in the mobile unit since Ryan was the one who warned him this might happen."

Gail swung her long blonde hair over her shoulder and glanced to the right of her at the same time. "But Donahue is still here."

"Yeah. So are a couple of his boys. All we can hope for is that Donahue relocates to his nightclub and Chirnovsky can get him to talk before the warrant for covert recording expires at midnight. If not, all this tonight will have been for nada."

"Well, shit," Gail muttered in sympathy. She picked up her evening bag from the table. "I need to go to the little girls' room. Care to join me, Hope?"

Hope shook her head. Ramiro asked if she'd mind if he made a circuit of the room and she assured him she was fine. Once she sat alone, however, she became hyperaware of the area just behind her—the place where Gail had just covertly looked over her shoulder and said *but Donahue is still here*.

She couldn't seem to stop herself. It was just like when she was little and her friend Fanny shrieked "*don't look*" at some childhood horror like a huge, smashed spider.

Hope had to look.

Her breath caught in her lungs when she twisted around and her gaze landed dead center on Jim Donahue. For one thing, he looked very similar to his former self—same dark hair and large, bold features going to fat. He sat at a larger round table than the rest at the edge of the gathering with two men and a blonde woman. Beady, cold eyes ran over her body speculatively just like they had several nights ago when Hope lay naked beneath a thin sheet—or 102 years ago, however you wanted to look at it.

And just like then, Hope shivered.

Gail returned and drank another martini. Hope was distracted from the unpleasant feeling of Jim Donahue's stare on her back by a steady stream of men asking Gail and her to dance. The feeling was only caused by her overactive imagination, anyway. Why would Donahue be singling *her* out of the crowd?

Ramiro gave one of their potential dance partners a fulminating look when he returned to the table. The man beat a hasty retreat, undoubtedly aware of Ramiro's gaze burning a figurative hole through his back.

He gave Gail a quick kiss. "Gotta go."

"Yeah, I saw him leaving," Gail whispered. Hope didn't have to ask who they were talking about. She'd seen Jim Donahue's date putting on her fur wrap earlier and Jim accompanying her through the crowd to the exit.

Gail sighed dispiritedly a few minutes after Ramiro left.

"Are you ready to leave, Hope? You don't look like you're having much fun, and both Ramiro and Ryan are gone now. It's not like I want to dance with any of these yahoos."

Despite her cavalier attitude Hope suspected Gail liked Ramiro very much. She agreed, also feeling the flatness of the affair now that Ryan was no longer here.

"If you could point me to the ladies' lounge first, we can be on our way," she told Gail.

Hope had to restrain herself from pausing at every exhibit she encountered as she made her way through the main floor of the museum. She briefly wondered if she'd misunderstood Gail's directions when she saw how dark the staircase was that led into the basement. But she saw bright light at the other end so she ventured on, relieved to see the sign for the ladies' lounge to the right when she reached the bottom. She passed machines that looked like they held children's toys and an exhibit called McDonald's that had an iron barricade blocking it while the museum was officially closed. The corridor where she walked appeared to stretch the entire length of the enormous facility.

The silence was broken by two young women talking animatedly as they exited the ladies' lounge. Hope heard their laughter echo in the high-ceiling, marble-tiled corridor as she entered the largest lounge she'd ever seen in her life. Instead of individual water closets there were perhaps fifty or more narrow stalls. Hope pushed on one of the doors and peered in curiously.

She finally shrugged and entered. Obviously the Field Museum needed to be prepared for gigantic crowds, although apparently she was the lounge's sole occupant at present.

Once she'd used the toilet and determined that the Field Museum toilet paper was noticeably less soft than either Ryan's or Eve's, Hope made her way to the sinks and mirrors in the lounge.

After washing her hands she glanced into the mirror. She inhaled sharply when she saw a man with a dark complexion and black hair next to her own visage. He gave a grin that hardly connoted amusement to Hope's bewildered awareness.

"Good evening. My name's Manuel Gutierrez."

Hope's anxiety escalated a hundredfold when he raised his hand next to her head and something metallic slithered between his fingertips. She stared in amazement at her silver locket. She'd last seen it in the year 1906 . . . in the hand of Diamond Jack Fletcher.

"Jim Donahue asked me to show you this for some reason, miss. Do you know him?" the man asked in a hoarse, accented voice.

"No," Hope replied as she began to edge away from the sink and the man. But he reached up and grabbed both of her shoulders in a strong grip. Hope lunged but he pulled her back in front of him with a hard jerk. Despite her growing fear, his cold eyes held her gaze in the mirror.

"Well, he seems to know you. And he specifically asked me to bring you to him so the two of you could discuss your acquaintance."

Hope twisted wildly in order to escape, but Gutierrez cocked his fist and struck her temple.

Her knees sagged. The room dipped and swayed. She started to scream but Gutierrez covered her mouth.

"Let's be on our way, sweetheart. I know a back entrance, which is a good thing, because I think you've had a little too much to drink," Hope heard him say sarcastically.

She stumbled precariously alongside him as he held her against his side and forced her out of the lounge. He pulled and dragged her down the empty hall, cursing in Spanish when Hope used her legs to resist him and then staggered frantically to regain her balance when he jerked her hard.

Abruptly Gutierrez shoved her down a darkened side corridor. She slipped on the marble tiles as she attempted to twist away from him. Damn these high heels Ryan's mother had given her to wear.

Ryan. He was going to be so irritated with her.

But she had no more opportunity to worry about Ryan at the moment because Gutierrez pushed her front side into the wall. Hope opened her mouth to scream but then felt the unmistakable hard barrel of a gun push against her spine.

"Keep your mouth shut or I'll shoot you. I don't care if Donahue wants to nail your ass or marry you. There's *nothing* I hate more than a screaming, whining woman, do you understand?" He sounded so hard and hateful that she had no problem comprehending him whatsoever. She nodded, wincing when he ground the pistol further into flesh. "I'm glad we got all that settled. Now . . . you're going to walk on your own two feet out that door at the end of this hallway."

When he released her Hope slowly stepped back from the wall, her legs trembling like they were made of rubber. A hand at the back of her neck gave her a hard nudge toward the door in the distance.

∽ TWENTY-SIX ∼

Ryan heard a tapping noise and flipped back the lock on the van door. Ramiro clambered in wearing his dark blue Chicago Police Department tactical coat in place of his tuxedo jacket. The two agents wearing headsets and sitting amongst all the surveillance equipment looked up.

"Menendez, Alvarez and Myerson," Ryan said perfunctorily.

Alvarez and Myerson nodded once before they went back to focusing on their work. They were parked in the driveway of a darkened house that had access both to the alley behind the Sweet Lash and the street on the next block.

"What's happening?" Ramiro hissed softly as he slid the van door shut.

Ryan took off his headset. No covert surveillance devices needed here. "You can only make out every tenth word they're saying the damn music is so loud. I think Chirnovsky is holding up his end of the bargain, but I don't think it'll do us any good with the shit the Sweet Lash is blaring out of the speakers."

"*Fuck*."

Ramiro's assessment was concise, for once, and Ryan whole-heartedly agreed with it.

"Where are the others?" Ryan asked.

"There are units farther down the alley and stationed at all entrances to the Sweet Lash. Crenshaw's listening in to this," he waved at the two technicians who were trying doggedly to single out the men's voices from the booming music, "but he says we have to sit tight until Chirnovsky delivers."

"We're running out of time," Ryan said tensely. Frustration rose in his chest, feeling like burning acid. *Damn*. They'd worked so hard for this. Ramiro signaled for him to give him his headset.

"Did Hope and Gail leave the museum?"

"They were still there when I left," Ramiro said as he started to put on Ryan's headset. He grimaced when his cell phone rang. He scowled at the number and turned away to answer it. "It's *not* really a good time."

At first Ryan hardly paid attention to Ramiro's annoyance at the inconvenient phone call but then he saw his dark brows furrow.

"Did you go and look for her?" A pause ensued. Ryan's muscles tensed. A thousand buzzing little alarms started to go off in his brain. He leaned forward in the passenger seat of the van when he made out the distant voice of Gail talking rapidly.

"What's wrong?" Ryan demanded.

"How long ago did she leave?"

Ryan swatted Ramiro's arm to get his attention but Ramiro just held up his hand and nodded as Gail talked.

"Try to get a museum official to search around the museum with you. Maybe she *did* get lost. Before you do that, though, call the station and have dispatch put you in touch with Marty Simon . . .

Yeah, I spoke to him earlier and he's on duty tonight. Tell him I asked him to come by and help you look for her."

Ryan tried to grab at Ramiro's cell phone at that point but Ramiro leaned back, avoiding him. Marty Simon was one of their many cop friends who worked patrol. Jesus, they were talking about Hope being missing, weren't they?

"Yeah, okay. Let me know as soon as you do." Ramiro held up his hands in a "mea culpa" gesture when he disconnected the phone and Ryan glared at him. "I've got all the information. You weren't going to get any more out of Gail. Let her start looking for Hope again."

"What happened?"

"Hope went to the ladies' room forty minutes ago. They were supposed to leave as soon as she returned, but Hope never came back. Gail's been looking for her for the past fifteen or twenty minutes but came up short. Hope probably got lost or caught up in looking at the exhibits. You know how excited she was to see that museum."

What Ramiro said made sense logically. So why was his stomach churning with panic?

"Look . . . there's nothing you can do about it right now. Marty'll get there before we could, even if we weren't busy working."

"She promised me she wouldn't wander off by herself," Ryan muttered, fury, fear and frustration flavoring his tone in equal measure.

"She'll be fine. Don't—"

"*Hey.*"

Alvarez signaled to the headset when they glanced over at him. Ramiro shoved the headset down over his ears. Ryan gave the agent a querying look.

"The target has just moved locations. He's headed toward the back of the facility. Communications are clear. Crenshaw wants you to move in," the agent explained tersely.

Something caught Ryan's eye. He moved to the front of the van and peered out the window.

"We've got incoming traffic in the alley . . . from both directions."

Ramiro covered the mouthpiece. "Happy fucking day. Let's go," he said with barely restrained excitement.

"What?" Ryan asked as he flipped open his holster and extracted his gun. He took the headset Myerson handed him and put it on hastily.

"We've *got* that red-handed fuck and not just on tape, either. He's headed with Chirnovsky to the rear of the Sweet Lash at this very moment to receive a delivery of women from Mexico," Ramiro explained, grinning like a man who saw his enemy's remaining minutes waning.

They exited the van and waited, crouched behind a hedge and some garbage cans. The night was cool but pleasant for November. The throb of the bass from the Sweet Lash emanated into the still night. People who lived around here must possess a vast collection of earplugs.

"That's not something to be transporting eight women in from Mexico," Ramiro whispered in confusion when a Lexus passed in the alley, gravel popping out from under its wheels.

"There's a vehicle coming from the other direction," Ryan explained, knowing Ramiro hadn't heard him earlier because he'd been listening to instructions from Crenshaw.

They heard a car door slam in the distance. Crenshaw gave the order for several units, Ryan and Ramiro among them, to tighten the perimeter around the Sweet Lash's rear parking area.

Ramiro and he crossed the alley. They took position behind a warehouse just west of the Sweet Lash. Back pressed to the side of the building, Ryan peered cautiously around the corner. He could hear the muted sound of men's voices.

The large van was parked in the center of the lot while the

Lexus had pulled up closer to Ryan and Ramiro. He could see
three men standing in the lot: Chirnovsky, Donahue and one other
man—presumably the driver of the van. Because of his particular
vantage point he could also see movement in the passenger seat of
the van and also in the driver's seat of the Lexus. He flipped the
switch on the headset and softly described the situation to Crenshaw in case he didn't have clear sight due to the hulking van.

The driver of the Lexus got out of his car and Ryan recognized
him. Gutierrez called out something jovially and Donahue came
toward him. The two men drew close and spoke too quietly for
Ryan to make out what they said.

Ryan heard Crenshaw curse through the headset. "Have you
got Donahue, Daire? The van is blocking us."

"We've got Donahue and Gutierrez," Ryan said just above a
whisper. He mouthed *Gutierrez* to Ramiro and signaled for him to
move around the other end of the Dumpsters where he'd have a
straighter rush at his prey.

Gutierrez handed Donahue something. Donahue gave a low,
sinister chuckle and walked around the front of the Lexus. Ryan
could see his puffy face perfectly. Something about his narrowed
eyelids and smug, sharklike smile sent an alarm bell to clanging in
his brain.

"Pearson and DiMarco will cover you from the south, Daire.
All units stand ready."

Several tense seconds passed. Ryan's heart hammered in his
ears even though the beat was slow and even. The adrenaline of
a takedown always focused his attention to a knife's edge. He
watched as Donahue opened the passenger door of the Lexus. The
order to move in came at the same moment.

"No. *Wait*," Ryan muttered into the headset when he saw what
Donahue part lifted and part guided out of the passenger seat—a
woman.

Shit.

He hadn't been able to see the female because the seat had been lowered. Despite his surprise he was already in motion, rushing his target as silently as possible.

Shouts and a few subsequent curses filled the still air.

"Freeze and put your hands above your head. Do it," Ryan added forcefully when Donahue's body sagged slightly at the shock of his voice, the woman's body falling back to the seat. Donahue's wide back blocked the car entrance.

"Put her down and get your hands in the air. *Move away from the car*," Ryan barked furiously when Donahue merely looked over his shoulder.

"*Daire*," he hissed. He twisted his broad torso and lifted the woman in one fluid movement. He sat in the car seat, draping her body over his for protection from one of Ryan's bullets.

Ryan saw the gleaming, dark hair and the spill of the frothy rose-colored gown. It felt like a jolt of electricity had suddenly slammed into his heart and lungs. He aimed his gun carefully, setting aside his fear the moment he recognized it. He saw the silver duct tape covering Hope's mouth and binding her wrists. She began to struggle in Donahue's hold.

"Let her go or I'll shoot you."

But Donahue must have sensed his doom because he behaved like an irrational, trapped animal energized by fear and adrenaline. He clambered wildly over the console, jerking up on Hope's waist brutally and pulling her along with him. Ryan experienced Hope's muffled cry of pain like a blade to the flesh.

There was a possibility Gutierrez had left the keys in the car, he realized. Besides, all Donahue needed was a few seconds to retrieve his gun and hold Hope hostage in earnest.

For a microsecond Hope looked up between disarrayed, glossy curls and met his gaze. The same weird thing occurred that had happened when Marlo had been shooting at him and shattered the mirror.

Time stretched. A second became an agonized eternity. He stared into Hope Stillwater's frightened eyes and wondered if destiny was an even stronger force of nature than time. What if he'd brought her to the year 2008 only to experience her murder here? *Now?* What if he hadn't saved her from anything . . . just delayed the inevitable?

Recognition flashed in her midnight eyes. As if the sight of him had galvanized her, she started to struggle wildly. Ryan gritted his teeth and aimed his SIG. *Damn*, that woman was a squirmer. He held on to her panicked gaze like it was her hand and she was falling over a cliff and ground out two words.

"Stay *still*."

She froze in a position that left a portion of Donahue's right shoulder and arm unprotected. It might as well have been a mile-wide target, as close as Ryan stood. He fired. Donahue grunted.

Ryan lunged forward and grabbed Hope's shaking, bound hands as Donahue's grip faltered. He yanked her up and shoved her behind him while he continued to keep Donahue in his sights. Two agents rushed to the scene, guns drawn.

The whole encounter had lasted less than ten seconds, Ryan realized with dawning amazement. He saw Donahue grabbing his shoulder where Ryan had shot him. Three guns were aimed point-blank at Donahue's head, a fact that Ryan was only too pleased to tell him.

Donahue held up his hands in surrender, grimacing in pain. He lifted his dark head. Beady, brown eyes filled with hatred focused on Ryan.

"When I realized it was the cops I had a funny feeling it was going to be you behind me, Daire," Donahue rasped. He panted and was starting to sweat profusely.

"It was all just a matter of time," Ryan told him.

"Where'd you hit him?" Pearson asked as he inched toward Donahue.

"Winged his right shoulder." Ryan blinked at his own words. It was the exact same place he'd shot Diamond Jack Fletcher earlier in the week.

Weird.

Donahue let out a howl of rage and pain when Agent Pearson shoved his hand beneath his tuxedo jacket in search of his weapon. He withdrew an automatic a second later and handed it to Agent DiMarco. Donahue's curses and complaints escalated when DiMarco helped her partner yank Donahue into the passenger seat of the car. Pearson held him while DiMarco secured his wrists behind his back.

"I've been shot, you bitch! What're you doing cuffing me? I need to go to the hospital before I bleed to death."

But Agent DiMarco just kept on reading him his rights with no inflection whatsoever in her voice as she secured Jim Donahue.

Donahue groaned like they were torturing him.

"Now *that's* a sweet sound," Ramiro said as he approached. He smiled broadly at Donahue's glare before he looked at Ryan. "We've got 'em. Crenshaw has set up roadblocks to keep out all but official personal. No one is getting in or out of the Sweet Lash until they check out. There are nine very scared young women in the back of that van."

Ryan felt Hope start behind him. He lowered his hand down over the curve of her hip, pressing her tightly against him, needing to feel her flesh. He partially turned and looked down at her.

"This is going to hurt a little," he said softly before he removed the duct tape from her mouth. She didn't even wince but just continued to stare up at him with enormous eyes.

"Hope?" Ramiro said incredulously.

"Are you all right?" Ryan asked at the same moment.

She nodded. "I'm fine."

Ryan gritted his teeth in helpless fury. Despite her assurance at being "fine," her face was about as pale as the snowy white dress shirt he wore. He glanced over at Donahue, who sat cuffed in the passenger seat of the car, the stain of blood slowly growing on his shirt.

Too bad the only viable target on the asshole hadn't been directly over his shrunken little heart.

"What did you want with her?" Ryan asked, his voice quiet since Pearson was communicating their situation on his headset.

Donahue's mouth twisted angrily. For a second Ryan thought he'd give him a smart-ass answer or refuse to respond, but instead Donahue nodded at the gravel a few feet from his shining black leather shoes. Ryan saw something glittering on the white stones. He regretfully stepped away for a moment from Hope's trembling body.

"Ramiro, get that tape off Hope's wrists. DiMarco?" he asked, making sure the agent who currently had her weapon trained on Donahue understood that he was going to be bending down within kicking distance of Donahue's feet. She nodded and Ryan crouched. He lifted the delicate chain from the rocks. He immediately recognized the silver filigreed locket.

"Where did you get this?"

His response was an insolent stare.

"Tell me," Ryan grated out.

"I found it between one of the floorboards of the Sweet Lash years ago. I carry it with me for a good-luck token. I suppose you're going to tell me that's a federal crime as well?"

Ryan stared down into Donahue's eyes, dragging his soul for lies. Surely he didn't retain memories from his previous lifetime, did he?

"The photos on the inside of the locket are of a beautiful woman who lived a long, long time ago. You can imagine my surprise when I walked into that party tonight and saw her sitting there at a table—very much alive. I had my coworker ask her to come here to talk about the coincidence, that's all." He paused and for a second Ryan sensed Donahue examining *him* deeply, as though he searched for answers for the strange circumstances as well.

Ryan exhaled and relaxed a little. Donahue didn't have any solid memories. He might have glimpses of understanding—flashes of emotion and perceptions from another lifetime. Maybe that was why he seemed to take an instant dislike to Ryan when Ryan's father had introduced the two of them years ago. Certainly that must have been why he was so drawn to his criminal lifestyle and the Sweet Lash . . . and Hope's locket. More than likely Donahue'd been as captured by Hope's image as Ryan had been.

The wail of sirens approaching distracted him from the unsettling thought of having anything remotely in common with Jim Donahue. A moment later an emergency medical technician rushed over to the Lexus. DiMarco and the EMT helped a grimacing Donahue to stand.

His longtime foe glared at him as they led him toward the ambulance, but Ryan turned away, all too glad to put Jim Donahue and his alternate identity in the past—where he belonged.

Hope paused in speaking to Ramiro when Ryan approached. She looked up with that solemn, big-eyed stare that always got to him. He grabbed her hand and dropped the silver locket into her palm.

"I guess Donahue's luck just ran out," he said quietly. He ran his gaze over her, looking for cuts and bruises. He saw nothing, but recalling some of the strange parallels between the past and the present, Ryan asked, "Were you hit in the head?"

She lightly touched her temple. "Oh. Yes, that man—Gutierrez punched me in the ladies' lounge. How did you know?"

Ryan shook his head distractedly as he turned her head with his hand on her chin. "I don't see any mark. Do you need the EMTs to check you out?"

"No, I'm fine."

"Then come on. I'll take you over to the van. You can wait there until all this is settled. It might take a while."

"Ryan, Ramiro was telling me that those poor women that were in the van are very upset. He's going over to try and calm them. I think I should go, too. Ramiro said it would be helpful to have a woman with him."

He just stared down at her as some strange, potent mix of emotions brewed in his gut. Some of the color had returned to her face, but she was still alarmingly pale. She'd just been hit over the head and abducted for the second time in days and she wanted to run off and play trauma worker to other people. Even though he was usually so controlled, Ryan abruptly felt like he was going to erupt.

He flashed an annoyed look at Ramiro.

"They speak Spanish, Hope," Ramiro said, obviously trying to minimize the damage he'd done.

"I'm fluent in French, but I do speak some Spanish. You'll be able to help me, won't you, Ramiro?"

"*No*," Ryan said.

The sound of a woman crying behind him pierced his awareness. Hope peered around his chest, her lovely face the very image of compassion and concern. He hesitantly looked over his shoulder and saw a group of females huddled together. An EMT checked the cut and bleeding face of a girl who looked no older than sixteen or seventeen. Even Ryan had to admit the medical technician's manner was brisk and businesslike . . . hardly reassuring to the weeping girl.

"Please, Ryan?"

He shut his eyes briefly in mounting frustration. When he opened them he pinned Ramiro with his stare. "Don't let her out of your sight." He switched his gaze to Hope. "If Crenshaw or anyone on the squad tells you to get out of the way, do it. I'm serious, Hope."

She nodded soberly. She smoothed her hair out of her face and straightened her gown as though girding herself for battle. Ryan sighed and shrugged out of his CPD coat.

"Put this on."

She accepted the coat with a radiant smile.

Jesus. His mother had been right. Hope had conquered him with her fierce, vibrant spirit, her courage and her sweetness. Her attack had been so quick and all-consuming that Ryan really never did have the chance to shout for mercy.

⌒ TWENTY-SEVEN ⌒

Hope jumped in nervous tension when Ryan slammed the door shut behind them. The chandelier in the entry hall blazed with light even though it hadn't been turned on when they'd left for the Field Museum hours ago. Ryan said there was an electrical short, but Hope didn't think he really believed that. Like her, he undoubtedly recalled her father's words.

We'll leave on the entry hall chandelier until my daughter returns home.

She turned and faced Ryan hesitantly. He'd hardly said ten words to her since he'd picked her up at his mother's and drove them home.

She'd spoken to the abducted women, doing her best with Ramiro's help to soothe, reassure and provide whatever information was available. After a half hour or so, Ryan had come over and grasped her shoulder. When he'd told her he'd arranged for transportation for her over to his mother's, Hope had gone without protest. She could tell by the tense lines around his mouth that she'd tried his patience enough for one night.

It was now two thirty in the morning, but she was the polar opposite of tired. She felt anxious about Ryan's formidable silence . . . about the tension she felt coiling in him just beneath the surface.

She pulled the lapels of Ryan's huge police jacket more firmly around herself as she studied his cold visage.

"I want you to know that I was very careful while we were at the Field Museum."

Ryan regarded her silently as he leaned against the door. He looked handsome as the devil with the top two buttons of his dress shirt unfastened and his bow tie falling loosely from the collar. He pinned her with his singular, intense stare. Hope shivered in a strange mix of anxiety and excitement.

"You told me you wouldn't wander off by yourself."

"Well . . . I know I did, but Jim Donahue and all of his men had left by that time—"

"Did somebody *tell* you that all of his men had left?" Ryan asked as he straightened. He slowly started to come toward her.

"No, but—"

"Because they clearly hadn't."

"I realize that now," Hope admitted sheepishly. "But—"

"Do you remember what happened the last time I told you not to wander off by yourself because you were in danger?"

She froze with her mouth gaping open. The powerful, carnal memory of him paddling her bottom crashed into awareness as though she were experiencing it right at that very moment. Her cheeks flooded with heat. Ryan's nostrils flared slightly as he stared down at her. For the first time she realized that at least part of his rigid tension was sexual in nature—the savage lust of a warrior following battle.

I think I might have to give you a punishment.

"I see you do recall," he said softly, obviously referring to her flaming cheeks. He grasped her elbow and turned her toward the grand staircase. "Time to face the music, honey."

Hope's heart pounded so loudly in her ears by the time Ryan shut the door to the bedroom that she wondered if she might burst a blood vessel. Her excitement was like nothing she'd ever experienced. The scandalously tiny underpants Eve had given her to wear felt damp at the crotch. She heard him crossing the large, dark room. The dim bedside lamp switched on and he turned to face her.

"Take off the jacket and your dress."

Hope stood unmoving.

"I told you I'd never harm you. You *are* going to get it harder than you did at the Sweet Lash, though," he said grimly. He jerked the bow tie off his neck and unfastened several more buttons on his shirt. Hope considered protesting, but he looked so hard at that moment she knew arguing would be pointless. He paused in unbuttoning his shirt.

"Well?" he asked darkly.

She shrugged out of Ryan's jacket and draped it over a box. Her trembling fingers found the zipper just below her armpit and she drew it down. "I want you to know I protest at the unfairness of your treatment," she told him a tad haughtily when she'd removed the dress and placed it carefully alongside Ryan's jacket. It was really shocking how quickly a modern-day woman could strip to nudity.

Or at least near nudity, Hope conceded breathlessly as Ryan's hot eyes dropped over her body. She still wore the scrap of silk panties that Eve had given her, along with her shoes and the ingenuous stockings that required no garter because they merely clung to her thighs with an elastic band. She held her breath when Ryan slowly walked around the footboard of the bed.

"Don't all impulsive, headstrong individuals say something similar when they've been caught?" he asked as he sat down on the edge of the bed.

"I can't believe you want to . . . do whatever it is you want to do right now because some criminal kidnapped me!"

He surprised her by merely shaking his head silently at her outburst. "I'm not going to spank you right now for Jim Donahue's or Manny Gutierrez's crimes. I'm going to because you deserve it for being so damned reckless with your safety. And I'm going to spank you because I want to, Hope. Got it?"

She swallowed in the face of his potent intensity and nodded.

"Good. Come over here."

Hope approached him warily, but then he did something that banished all her doubts. He spread his big hand across her waist and hip and pulled her toward him. He lowered his dark head and pressed his face to her belly. Her hands tangled in his thick hair because there for a split second—ever so briefly before he'd buried his face in her flesh—she'd seen naked anguish on his handsome face.

A moment later he raised his head and looked up at her.

"Lie down across my lap," he ordered gruffly.

The wild beating of her heart when she came into the room was nothing in comparison to what she experienced as Ryan guided her down over his thighs. The sensitive undersides of her breasts pressed against the wool material of his pants, abrading her slightly . . . exciting her greatly. She made a small squeaking noise when he spread his hand over her bottom as though he tested the dynamics of the arrangement. He shifted her slightly in his lap, making her all that much more aware of the long, stiffened column of his penis lying along his left thigh.

When he drew down her panties, exposing her bottom to the cool air, Hope squirmed.

He responded by smacking her bottom with his palm.

"Oooh," she cried out. He soothed her right buttock with his hand, but at the same time he pressed gently on her neck.

"Put your forehead down on the mattress. That's a girl, keep it there."

She'd been resting on her elbows. Ryan's gentle, firm insistence that she fully submit to her punishment by lowering her head and blinding her eyes from the proceedings caused a forbidden vein of hot desire to flood her genitals. She tensed when he raised his hand, knowing what was to come.

Crack. Crack. Crack.

Hope tried not to squirm beneath Ryan's stinging palm but she couldn't stop herself. It felt exciting . . . almost unbearably so. Heat emanated from his thighs and groin. She became hyperaware of his hard cock pressing against her. He cracked her bottom again and she felt it lurch in his pants. She pushed down and rubbed against him.

"Why, you little—"

Hope yelped when he spanked her hard enough to make her hop in his lap. He used his left hand to fix her more firmly in place and paused, his palm rotating over the flesh of her stinging bottom. She shivered in excitement when he leaned down and spoke near her ear.

"Had enough?"

"Yes," Hope assured him as she nodded into the mattress.

He palmed one of her stinging buttocks, molding the flesh in his hand in a gesture of bold possession. "That's too bad. Because I'm not so sure I have yet."

He sat up and Hope waited, so tense with anticipation she could hardly breathe. But instead of spanking her more he merely continued to shape her buttocks in his palm, squeezing her in a lewd manner that shouldn't have excited her . . . but did. He finally released her. Hope tensed.

She cried out in broken excitement when he suddenly sent a long forefinger between her thighs. He rubbed the ridge against her wet, swollen sex and grunted in primitive male gratification. He was gone too quickly, however, and Hope once again struggled not to twist in excitement as he cracked her bottom with his palm. Her flesh grew hot and tingly beneath his spanking hand. She supposed it hurt a little, but overwhelmingly what she experienced was sexual excitement.

That and the feeling of trembling anticipation as she waited for Ryan's descending palm.

"Enough," Ryan finally grated out. He smoothed his palm over her burning flesh while Hope tried her best to suppress her moans of arousal. "I want you to get up and kneel on the floor now."

Hope's eyes widened at not only the content of what he said but also the hard edge of urgency in his voice. She didn't think she'd ever heard that tone before. Knowing how aroused he was, how close to losing control made her clamber off him quickly. Her panties fell down over her knees and she quickly kicked them off.

Her cheeks burned in intense arousal and embarrassment as she went down on her knees in front of him. Even though she suspected what he planned to do—she had all those lewd references from her drunken neighbor Colin Mason, after all—she still whimpered when he stood up. He towered over her. His cerulean blue eyes glowed like the white-hot center of a flame as he stared down at her.

He rapidly unfastened his pants and shoved them and his white underwear down to his thighs. She found herself staring fixedly at his long, firm erection just inches from her face. He encircled it with his fist and stroked it surely. His other hand rose to the back of her head, garnering her attention.

"You're being punished so I want you to put your hands behind your back." Hope complied, although she was a little surprised by his request. "Now keep them there until I say otherwise. Understood?"

Hope looked up at him soberly. "Yes, Ryan."

For some reason his upper lip curled slightly in a snarl. His eyes felt like they could burn holes straight down to her very soul.

"I swear, you *are* a witch," he muttered as he took a step closer and lifted his heavy penis to her mouth. Her lips parted hungrily when she felt the smooth, warm surface of the head brush against them. Her mouth stretched to accommodate his girth. He gave a guttural groan as he slid along her tongue.

Hope closed her eyes and focused exclusively on the sensation of his turgid flesh filling her straining mouth. He pushed further back. Her eyes opened in panic when she felt him near her throat, but he gripped her hair in his hand and backed out of her clamping lips.

She sighed in relief, eagerly rubbing his cock with her tongue when he slid his weight off it. When she batted at it briskly, his fingers clenched in her hair and he thrust back into her again. Hope accepted him hungrily, her cheeks hollowing out as she tightened around him. His growl was her reward.

"That's right. Suck it good and hard, witch."

Hope did what he asked, focusing all of her being on Ryan's pleasure. How many times had he done the same for her so unselfishly? He took a small step closer to her, one foot next to her knee and began to buck his hips, plunging the first half of his cock in and out of her mouth rapidly. It was a bit of a challenge to keep up with his rate while her mouth strained to contain his thick flesh, but she loved his grunts of excitement as he thrust with increasing excitement. His hands curled into fists in her hair. He lowered one hand and fisted the root of his cock, moving it up and down on the shaft at the same rhythm he pumped into her mouth.

He groaned like a tortured animal and pressed back further than he'd done so far. Hope's eyes widened as she felt his penis swell in her mouth. His fist pumped ruthlessly and his hand tightened on her head.

He growled, deep and guttural, and his seed began to erupt into her mouth. Hope instinctively ducked back at the sensation of all that coiled power being released. Even in the midst of obviously intense pleasure he gave a little in his hold, letting her move him back to a position on her tongue where she could comfortably tighten around his spasming member and swallow his abundant emissions.

Her eyelids closed as she focused on the exquisite sensation . . . on his familiar taste. A stretched, sublime moment passed while she suckled Ryan's most sensitive flesh and his big body convulsed in pleasure.

"Hope."

She opened her eyelids heavily after an undetermined period of time and tilted her head back as best she could with her mouth so full of thick male flesh. Ryan stared down at her with fiery eyes. His penis slipped slightly in her clamping lips as she looked up.

She sucked to bring him back into place.

His lips thinned and his penis jerked in her mouth. Despite her murmur of protest he spread his hand along her jaw gently, holding her in place while he withdrew from her mouth. He leaned down and grabbed her elbows, drawing her up. She felt his powerful muscles flex. Instead of just pulling her onto her feet, he lifted her off them. Hope moaned in sheer ecstasy when he covered her mouth and gave her a blistering hot kiss.

One of her shoes slipped off her foot and fell some ten inches to the floor but Hope hardly noticed, so caught up was she in the heaven of being held against the hard planes of Ryan's body and being consumed by his kiss.

They both came up for air a while later. Hope panted against his lips like she'd just run up and down the grand staircase a dozen times.

"What am I going to do with you, Hope?"

Her lungs burned in her chest when she saw the way he stared at her lips as he spoke. A little cry of wonder vibrated in her throat when she realized that although he'd just experienced a powerful sexual release, he was still nearly as tense and hungry as he had been when they'd stood in the entry hall earlier.

"You could just love me, Ryan."

She bit her lip, already regretting her impulsive statement when his gaze leapt to meet hers. He slowly slid her down the length of her body. She couldn't read his expression as he cupped her jaw and lightly skimmed the pad of his thumb over her cheek. It surprised her when she saw his firm lips curl slightly into a smile. His palm curled around her bottom and molded her still tingling flesh.

"Actually, I was referring to things in a more practical manner. I'm trying to think of a way to get rid of this itch that won't go away. I'm going to have you again; I was just trying to think of how . . ."

Hope's eyes widened when he seemed to come to a decision and released her in order to kick his pants and underwear off his feet.

"Come here," he said, reaching for her hand. She tried not to stare but she couldn't seem to unglue her eyes from the bottom curve of his taut, muscular buttocks beneath his shirt as he pulled her over to the bottom of the bed. That was why he could thrust into her with so much strength—because of those big, powerful muscles in his thighs and buttocks. When he turned it was equally mesmerizing to see the long, still stiff spear of flesh that jutted out from the bottom of his dress shirt.

He must have noticed where she was staring because a smile ghosted his lips.

"Bend over and put your hands on the top rail," he told her steadily. "I'm going to restrain you. God knows I need the evidence that I'll be able to control you in at least *one* area of our lives."

⌐ TWENTY-EIGHT ⌐

Ryan waited tensely, wondering how Hope would respond to his statement. It pleased him when she slowly leaned over the brass bedstead, but her quick, scolding look gratified him almost as much. He turned and unbuttoned the rest of his shirt while he scanned the large bedroom for the box he wanted.

"My father and I don't believe that men should try and control women," Hope told him as he ripped open the tape sealing the cardboard box.

"Hmmm," Ryan responded distractedly as he riffled through the various sex toys he'd acquired over the years. He found what he was looking for and whipped his shirt over his shoulders before he retrieved the items.

She still was bent over the bedstead, but she'd twisted her face around on her shoulder to watch him as he approached, her gleaming, dark curls falling in her face. He saw her eyes widen when she saw the spreader bar.

"Is . . . is that all you're going to say?" she demanded, her voice a little higher than usual. He set the bar and the ankle restraints on the bed and picked up a pair of padded wrist cuffs. He quickly buckled it around Hope's wrist and then used a hook to fasten the cuff around one of the vertical brass posts.

"About the fact that you and your father don't believe that men should try and control women?" he asked as he went around her and did the same to her other hand. She continued to rest her hands on the top rail of the bed, but she was restrained to it now.

"Yes."

Ryan grabbed the ankle restraints and spreader bar and knelt at her feet. He pulled on her slender ankle, placing it where he wanted it. He smoothed his palm down her calf, wondering again at the softness of her skin before he buckled the ankle cuff.

"I seem to recall a very wise, brave woman once telling me that ladies should feel free to please their lovers in whatever way they feel comfortable." He looked up at her when he'd buckled the other cuff around her ankle. "Are you trying to tell me that you aren't comfortable giving me control over your pleasure in the bedroom?"

Her already flushed, dewy-looking cheeks colored deeply. "I . . . I trust you, Ryan."

"Good," he murmured as he knelt behind her. He stared up at the jaw-dropping sight of Hope's plump ass. It was noticeably pink in comparison to her shapely, white thighs due to her spanking. Her dark pink, swollen sex lips glistened with moisture.

His cock tugged impatiently as he encircled her leg just above her right ankle restraint and slid her stocking-covered foot along the wood floor, holding her steady so she didn't fall. He instantly felt the tension in her muscles as he spread her very wide.

"Ryan . . ."

"Shhhh," he soothed. "I know it's hard for you to open yourself for me . . . to have me look my fill . . . lick it." He looked into her sweat-dampened face and sensed her profound arousal, making his cock throb with a dull ache. "But it would give me so much pleasure to have you at my mercy, witch."

She licked her upper lip nervously. "All . . . all right."

He smiled and transferred his gaze to the intoxicating sight of her opened, damp flower, the petals spread wide. He salivated at the veritable feast before him. Deciding that he had her about at the right height for what he intended, he attached one end of the spreader bar to her ankle. He adjusted the length to fit the distance to her other foot by sliding the inner bar out of the outer and then screwing the release at the end to tighten it at the length he wanted. When he'd attached the bar to both of her ankles, it became impossible for her to close her legs.

He stood and lifted one of his heavy boxes of books, sliding it until the bottom corner fit snugly along the outside of her foot. He did the same to her other foot. When he finished he noticed she was staring at him like she thought he'd gone nuts.

"It'll keep you secure," he explained as he reached out to caress her round bottom. "The bar will prevent you from closing your legs but the boxes will stop you from slipping on your hose and pulling a muscle."

"Oh," she whispered. His cock batted up at her wide-eyed expression of mixed arousal and trepidation. Her mouth looked puffy and red. The thought of plunging his cock between those luscious lips caused his cock to lurch up again in mounting excitement. She wasn't used to giving head and he'd tried to go gently on her, but his excitement had been unprecedented—as her swollen lips testified.

"Are you ready for me to eat your pussy now?"

She bit her lower bee-stung lip and nodded.

He needed to do this—to control her, to somehow manage the

almost unbearable emotion that frothed inside him ever since he'd realized it was her that Jim Donahue used to shield his body.

He needed to control himself.

Something primal pulled at him . . . a feeling that made him feel prickly and restless and combustible, like he was going to burst out of his own skin. He'd soothed the beast for all of about ten seconds after he exploded in Hope's sweet, suckling mouth.

But now it reared its head again, more demanding and fierce than ever.

He grasped her shoulders and explained that he wanted her to slide the hooks on her wrist restraints down the posts of the bed until she could rest her hands on the mattress comfortably. He guided her down until her hands were braced on the mattress. Her spanked ass and swollen pussy stuck up further than any part of her body now.

The stab of lust that shot through his cock caused him to squeeze just below the head briefly, trying to alleviate the pressure. He went to his knees behind her and sat back on his haunches. She whimpered when he placed his hands on her soft, firm bottom and separated the cheeks even further.

He could understand why.

He didn't think he'd ever had a woman spread this wide for his unrestrained consumption.

She was *his*, he thought as he leaned forward and inhaled the scent of her arousal. He detailed the delicate, pretty, slick folds of her pussy and the tiny rosette of her rectum.

Hope was all his.

He swiped his tongue once over her labia, pressing just enough to part the folds slightly and flick across her clit. She hopped and made a muffled choking sound. He knew she'd squirm, restraints or no. It was in her nature. So he tightened his hold on her ass, tilted his head and opened his mouth. When he closed over her and agitated with his tongue, her juices flooded his mouth. He grunted in pleasure.

Yeah. Hope tied up, spread wide and at his mercy, her firm flesh squirming in his hands and her honey flowing down his throat.

This would go a long way to soothe the beast.

∽

Hope blinked the sweat out of her eyes and stared blindly at the head of the brass bed. Ryan continued to eat her pussy with a strength and determination that was unabated, despite the fact that he'd made her come three times now. The convulsions that had shuddered through her body during her most recent climax had quieted to tiny spasms that zinged through her flesh whether he playfully slicked his tongue over her clit or rubbed it good and hard. The electrical pulsations had been going on now for several minutes. It felt like she was having a continuous, low-grade orgasm. Her muscles bunched and trembled. Her nerves quaked at every caress.

But that didn't stop Ryan. No, he just continued to torture her super-sensitized flesh. Lord help her. She tightly fisted the bedspread once again. Didn't he know how hard this was for her? How untenably forbidden it felt to be spread so decadently wide for him while he built her desire only to consume it so hungrily again and again? He stretched her so tightly on a rack of sensual pleasure she thought she'd snap from the tension.

She moaned loudly when he sent his tongue deep into her slit and vibrated her. It felt so good, but she burned like she was at the center of a fiery star. She *burned* when what she needed was to *explode* into a million pieces again.

Oh *God*, did she need that.

She pressed back against his tongue, desperate.

"Please, Ryan . . . Please, *please*."

She hadn't realized she'd been begging him out loud until he raised his head, depriving her. She wailed in protest at this new form of torture.

"What do you want, honey?" he asked, his voice deep and raspy.

"I want to come . . . like before."

He stroked her bottom and hip soothingly. "Does it feel like you can't come big because you're so sensitive that you keep coming small?"

Hope looked over her shoulder incredulously, although she really couldn't make him out because of the angle and her wildly mussed hair. "How did you know that? Wait—don't tell me," she muttered, suddenly thinking of Gail talking about Jenny Martin being addicted to having Ryan make love to her.

She'd scratch Jenny Martin's eyes out if she as much as batted her eyelids at Ryan, but Hope had to admit, the woman told the bald truth.

She suddenly realized that Ryan was unbuckling the ankle restraints.

"What . . . what are you doing?" she asked breathlessly, none too keen on the idea of his God-gifted tongue moving farther and farther away from her throbbing pussy.

"I've released your feet. You can move them in now some, if you want."

She did what he suggested, grimacing slightly at how sore her muscles had become fixed in place for so long with her thighs stretched wide. She peered around, trying to see Ryan.

"I'm going to fuck you," he explained. "Besides the fact that I'll spontaneously combust if I keep eating your sweet little cunt, you need a cock in your pussy to send you over the edge."

Hope blinked at his coarse language, although in truth it didn't offend her. She was becoming increasingly used to Ryan's bluntness during sex . . . increasingly aroused by it. It never struck her as crude, actually, but honest and always perfectly matched to their level of excitement.

She gasped in surprise when he stood and leaned down over her, spreading his hands just above her breasts.

"I'm going to lift you. I want you to put your hands back up on the top rail. That's right," he said when she grasped the top of the brass bedstead. He moved behind her again. Her breath froze in her lungs when she felt him dip his knees, his hair-sprinkled thighs brushing against her own. He reached between them and she knew he grasped his heavy erection.

They both grunted in excitement when he pressed the steely, smooth head to her slit.

"Aren't you going to—?"

"I won't come in you. I promise. I want to feel you completely right now"

Hope nodded her head and gasped when she felt him push the knob of his penis into her. His knees pressed into her spread legs and she realized how much he had to bend down to match their disproportionate height. He made it work, though. His cock slid into her hypersensitive slit, setting off little detonations of pleasure deep inside her body. She closed her eyes and moaned in pleasure when he pushed into her to the hilt.

He paused and pressed tight, as though he strained to kiss the edge of her womb.

Hope's rough groan might have suggested to some that she'd never been raised as a lady.

"Brace your arms," Ryan ordered tensely. He wrapped his forearm beneath her belly and slowly lifted her feet off the floor for the second time that night. Her mouth gaped open at the sensation of him pulling her up his body. He stopped and she gasped raggedly. It'd felt fantastic to have him in her before, but it was as if he'd just locked her in place for the perfect fit.

He leaned down over her. One hand came down and braced

next to her own on the bedstead. The other held her tightly against him.

He flexed his hips.

She keened at the shock of the pleasure when he rocketed into her body. Her feet dangled in the air. Her hands were bound. She held on to the brass railing for dear life as Ryan pumped in and out of her with increasing force. His forearm held her in the air below her belly, but he didn't use it to push her body into him. Instead she just draped there, held immobile and helpless while he nailed their flesh together again and again.

Hope's hands slipped on the bedstead but she was so close to combusting, so mindless with need as he barreled into her that she barely noticed.

But Ryan did. He paused, making her groan in agony.

"Hold on tight, honey, and I'll bring us home," he muttered, his voice barely above a strained whisper.

She strengthened her grip on the rail and stiffened her arms. Ryan seemed all too ready to resume once she'd secured herself. Once again he crashed their bodies together. The entire brass bed began to rattle as a result of Ryan's forcefulness. Her lips stretched into a snarl. She cried out every time Ryan thrust deep and his pelvis whapped loudly against her ass.

"Yes, yes, yes," she chanted mindlessly each time he smacked into her.

The tension she'd been harboring finally reached the breaking point. She clenched her eyes shut and exploded as the spark from the friction ignited into a roaring flame.

Distantly, through pulsing waves of pounding pleasure, she became aware of Ryan's roar as he jumped into the conflagration with her. The knowledge only added to her firestorm of raging desire.

They still panted heavily by the time Ryan unbound her wrists. He retrieved several tissues from the bedside table and carefully wiped his semen from her back and bottom. Afterward he pulled her over to the bed and they collapsed like two survivors from a great storm in each other's arms. He kissed and nuzzled her breasts as their bodies slowed.

Hope knew Ryan slept when she felt the warm mist of his even breath falling on her breast. She thought of being bent over, spread wide and restrained while she stared up at the headboard of the bed—a bed that she'd slept in since her eighteenth year.

Never in a million years would she have thought she'd experience such grandeur, such depths of the human experience as she had while staring at such a mundane object as the brass bed in her bedroom at 1807 Prairie Avenue.

Ryan turned his chin in his sleep, brushing his lips across her nipple. Her fingers tightened in his thick hair as a powerful wave of emotion crashed into her. Tears burned her eyelids.

She loved him. She loved him so much. Illogically, perhaps, for there really hadn't been enough time to truly understand one another's true selves.

But what was a *self* compared to a soul?

A sob shuddered through her.

She carefully lifted Ryan's head from her breast and slid a pillow beneath his cheek. He scowled slightly in his sleep, as though he hadn't cared for the replacement. Still, he didn't waken.

Hope stood and went over to the mantel, pausing at the side of the hearth. She placed her hand upon the ledge and bent over, thinking. It was actually a familiar pose of pensiveness. The fire that was usually in the hearth was warm, and she was naturally drawn to it, but her father always worried about her long skirts catching fire if she drew to close.

So she reserved her thoughts—and her tears—for the periphery of the mantel.

For the first time she allowed the image of what Ryan had looked like when she'd asked him earlier today if he'd been able to travel through the great barrier of time to reach her because of his love for her.

For a split second, he'd looked cornered—trapped at the idea of having to answer.

Profound love, even if it did exist mutually, didn't mean they could necessarily bridge the cultural differences of a century. What it meant to Ryan to care for her . . . even love her, didn't have the same consequences in the year 1906 as it did in the year 2008. As much as Hope had yet to learn about Ryan's world, that much had been made abundantly clear to her.

Hope lifted her head and stared at Ryan as he lay sleeping and peaceful upon the brass bed. Such a big, supple . . . beautiful male animal. Again, tears smarted behind her eyelids.

Is this what true love entailed? That she be willing to sacrifice everything in order to gain an even fuller, richer existence?

And what if she made the wrong choice?

She swung around abruptly and stifled a frustrated sob, pounding her fist against her thigh. The tension inside of her spirit felt nearly as untenable as the sexual friction Ryan had built in her flesh. How to soothe herself without breaking into wretched tears and disturbing Ryan while he slept so peacefully?

She decisively reached toward the carved mantel, pressing on the well-worn center of a twining branch of leaves. The secret drawer popped forward.

Who knew? Perhaps her copy of Mr. Walt Whitman's *Leaves of Grass* was still secreted inside after all these years? Hope had always read to soothe her stormy moods, and she doubted anything—even her beloved Shakespeare—would offer a better match to her volatility than Mr. Whitman's carnal prose that spoke so honestly of the joys and sufferings of the human spirit.

Hope's brow crinkled in confusion when she drew out a number of large photographs instead of *Leaves of Grass*.

For several stretched moments as she looked at each one, nothing moved. Nothing in the universe. Certainly her heart didn't stir, did it?

A memory that she hadn't considered significant at the time suddenly sprang into her consciousness. She recalled the expression on Ryan's face when she'd exited Eve Daire's storeroom just this afternoon and interrupted him as he talked.

There's something I haven't told Hope yet—something about some photographs I found of her at the mansion—

Now that Hope reflected on it, his lame explanation about the police archival photos of her didn't really adequately explain that statement.

He'd been referring to *these* photos—the ones she held in her hands at this very moment, Hope suddenly knew with certainty.

Ten seconds or thirty minutes later—she couldn't be sure because so much went through her mind in those electrical moments—she glanced over at Ryan and inhaled raggedly. She looked at him, the photographs that shook in her hands and back to Ryan's still form.

Her path had been made clear to her.

She now knew what she had to do.

∽ TWENTY-NINE ∾

Ryan awoke with a start. For a few seconds he remained very still, wondering what had awakened him so abruptly. Rain spattered on the windows, but the sound was pleasant and muted. It hadn't been that which jerked him out of a deep slumber.

He was cold.

He sat up from where he'd been sprawled on the brass bed and stared around the large bedroom. The lamp was still on, allowing him to see that he was alone. Hope must have gotten up to use the bathroom.

His brows furrowed when he noticed that the bedroom door was shut.

And the door on the wardrobe where the gilt mirror hung was open.

He scuttled up off the bed, shivering in the cool dawn. He

opened the bedroom door and walked down the dark hallway. The bathroom door was partially opened, the muted light of morning casting it in gray shadow. It was empty. He turned around in the silent hall, a sense of panic rising in his gut.

"*Hope?*" Ryan shouted. His voice echoed through the corridor. He called her name again, but the truth already rattled hollowly in his bones.

He was alone in this tomb of a house. He raced back to the bedroom and opened the second wardrobe door. Hope's long skirt, high-necked blouse and lace-up shoes were gone.

"*No,* honey," he mumbled miserably. His gaze fell on the mirror. She'd tried to go back in it. He just knew she had. But what had been the result? Was it even possible without the corresponding mirror? What if she existed in some formless state of nonexistence and couldn't return to either world?

The thought of her leaving caused a dull throb of grief in his chest, but the thought of her disappearing from *any* time—her vibrant essence being wiped from history altogether—was a far worse consideration.

Something occurred to him. He hastily pulled on a pair of jeans and raced out of the room. He peered into the thick shadows as he descended the grand staircase, his footsteps echoing hollowly off the bare walls.

He'd hardly ever seen the entry hall darkened. The chandelier continually blazed to life of its own accord, no matter whether the switch was in the on or off position. Ryan flipped the switch to turn it on.

But the crystal chandelier hung cold and lifeless.

We'll leave on the entry hall chandelier until my daughter returns home.

Jacob Stillwater's voice reverberated in his head. Ryan fell heavily to a sitting position on the stairs, the wood creaking beneath him in protest. A strange, potent mixture of relief and grief struck him like a tidal wave.

Chances were Hope'd returned safely to the year 1906. The chandelier had finally gone out. She was in her world, where she belonged. He was here in his, where he belonged.

He glanced around the gray, barren hall. The life had gone out of the house. He felt every bit as empty and hollow.

Why had she done it? He thought of the previous night, of his volatile mood, of the manner he'd insisted upon making love to her when they returned home. Had he pushed her too far? Asked too much of her?

Regret settled on him like a weight. Of course he'd asked too much of her. He'd demanded that she give every last ounce of herself, insisting that she trust him wholly even though she was still shockingly innocent when it came to matters of sex.

Wasn't it best that she was back in the home she loved with her father and friends? What could he really offer her here? A woman like Hope deserved a husband and a family. If he'd lived in the year 1906 and had been as intimate with Hope as they had been, he would be expected to marry her. He would likely even expect it of himself if he'd been raised in a culture that dictated marriage as the honorable action given what he'd done with her.

But he didn't live in Hope's time . . . *hadn't* been raised in her culture. The idea of them marrying after he'd known her for less than a week was ludicrous.

Maybe that's why she'd gone. After she'd lived in his world for a while, she must have learned what he'd already known—their respective worlds were incommensurate. Their time periods and cultures couldn't meld even if Hope and he could. Time had stepped in and had the final say, cleaving their unnatural bond.

He rose slowly from the steps, his body feeling strangely achy and old. He reentered the bedroom and stared around dully. Something struck his eye and he walked over to the fireplace.

His heart seemed to forget to beat for several seconds when he saw the photos on the mantel. Hope must have found them in the secret drawer after they'd made love last night.

Jesus, what had she thought when she saw them? She must have been shocked . . . Furious?

Ryan tossed down the black-and-white photographs hastily. She'd drawn all the wrong conclusions, that much was certain. She hadn't left him because she'd realized their values were too different. She'd left him because she found those pictures. God only knew how she'd rationalized their existence.

He spun around, suddenly galvanized into action. If Hope had chosen to leave because she saw the impossibility of their being together, that was one thing. But it was another thing altogether for her to have fled last night because she'd been disillusioned by those photographs.

Disillusioned by him.

He had to go back, Ryan thought frantically as he opened the wardrobe, looking for viable clothing to wear for the time period. If Hope had done it, surely he could. The thought of her existing back in her world and believing that he'd tricked her into having sex so they could be photographed was just too god-awful. He searched for something to wear, his impatience and frustration mounting.

The stark white of the dress shirt he'd worn last night with his tux caught his eye. He lunged for it but before he could get it on a buzzing noise reached his ears. He paused, at first not recognizing the sound as the doorbell since he'd heard it only a few times when food was being delivered in the evenings.

Who could be ringing it at six a.m. on a rainy, cold Sunday morning?

It didn't matter. He needed to get going, he thought irritably as he tossed on the white shirt. He needed to go back so he could explain to Hope—

The buzzing continued in an insistent manner. Whoever was out there wasn't going to be ignored, he realized.

He swung open the front door a few seconds later. His irritation quickly segued to incredulity.

"Warren?" he greeted Alistair Franklin's driver. Warren stood on the wet front steps as raindrops fell across his round features.

"Morning, Ryan. I brought Alistair over. He was insistent upon seeing you this morning. Wouldn't let me talk him into waiting until a decent hour no matter what I said," the stocky driver explained with a rueful grin. He hitched his thumb out to Prairie Avenue. A black Mercedes sedan was parked at the curb. " 'Fraid you'll have to go out to the car to see him. Since his stroke he has to use a wheelchair and it might be kind of hard to get him up these stairs—"

"No, that's fine. I'll go out," Ryan interrupted distractedly, his eyes still on the black sedan. Something about his elderly friend's strange visit on the cold, rainy dawn felt eerily familiar—*right* somehow, like Alistair and he had scheduled the appointment long ago and Ryan had forgotten.

"Just let me grab a jacket and I'll be right out to see him, Warren."

∽

Jacob Stillwater entered the brilliantly lit ballroom, his eyes immediately finding his daughter where she stood by the enormous fireplace. He looked very distinguished and handsome in his formal attire as he came toward her, smiling. Hope's return smile never faltered despite the fact that it broke her heart to see the slight drag in his left leg. Her father maneuvered extremely well using the cane Dr. Walkerton had left for him, however. Hope consoled herself that very soon her father's limp would be hardly noticeable to those unfamiliar with his recent illness.

The fact that he'd experienced a stroke while she'd been gone from his side would likely haunt her until her dying day. Still, she found strength in knowing for a fact that her father would live and prosper for many years to come.

"Happy birthday, Father." She gave him a kiss on the cheek when he reached her. "I'm so sorry we couldn't celebrate it with the party I'd planned. But with only you, Mary and Mrs. Abernathy knowing I'm here—"

"Oh, posh. I'd rather just have a nice dinner here with you. I'm too old for a birthday ball, anyway. Certainly can't dance around on this old clunker," he said matter-of-factly, tapping his left thigh. He offered her his arm and they slowly made their way over to the table Mrs. Abernathy had meticulously laid for their supper.

Hope had requested that her father's dinner be served in the ballroom for several reasons. First of all, the huge room usually stood empty and unused, making it unlikely that servants would disturb them. This was important since only Mary, Mrs. Abernathy and Jacob knew of her return to 1807 Prairie Avenue. That had been something she and her father had decided on the first evening she came back to her own time.

The second reason was because the grand piano was in the ballroom. She'd been working for several months now on a special composition for her father and she looked forward to playing it for him on a night that was poignantly special to both of them for more reasons than it merely being her father's birthday.

Before they could take their seats, Jacob spoke.

"Show me again, dear, how they dance in the year 2008," Jacob said with a glimmer of amusement in his black eyes.

Hope laughed, the sound echoing off the walls. She obligingly walked several feet into the enormous ballroom while her father sat down at the table. She closed her eyes, perfectly imagining Gail and Ramiro moving in tandem to the unusual, exciting music. She positioned her hands, picturing herself touching Ryan's broad shoulder while his big hand spread at the back of her waist. She began to softly hum a tune while she swayed to the music, occasionally inserting remembered lyrics.

Fly me to the moon and let me play among the stars, da da da ta da, ta da on Jupiter and Mars . . .

The train of her blue satin gown and her petticoats swished behind her as she circled the ballroom floor in her solitary dance. She opened her eyes after several moments and looked over at her father, laughter curving her lips. He shook his gray head in amazed satisfaction as she came over to the table.

"Very unique and lovely. You were always as graceful as your mother on the dance floor." Jacob stood as she approached. "You know, I was thinking a good part of the night about something you told me about the future, dear. How is it that, do you suppose, these airplanes don't crash into those towering skyscrapers?"

"I'm not sure how they contrive it," Hope admitted after she'd puzzled on it a moment. Her father moved to seat her and Hope put up her hand. "Wait. I have a special gift for you. Sit back down, Father."

She started over toward the piano, pausing when the light level in the ballroom seemed to magnify for a second and then return to normal. She experienced a prickling feeling on her neck and twisted around.

Her eyes widened in amazement. For a second she thought she'd been imagining the dance she'd never gotten with Ryan at the Field Museum so perfectly that she'd magically conjured him. He even wore his tuxedo. His greenish-blue eyes were trained on her but he didn't move or speak. Suddenly his dark brows rose as if in silent query.

"Ryan," she gasped.

"Hello." He glanced over at her father and nodded. Her father looked every bit as stunned as Hope felt. "I'm sorry for interrupting."

Jacob used his cane to stand slowly, his eyes never leaving Ryan's face. "Why . . . you're Ryan Daire, aren't you?"

Ryan glanced over at Hope. She didn't understand the trace of unease in his expression. "Yes, sir. I am."

Hope's shock faded enough for her temporary paralysis to fade.

"What are you doing here?" she blurted out.

Ryan inhaled slowly. "I came to see you, of course." He glanced out the La Farge windows and his brow furrowed. "It's nighttime here. How long have you been back, Hope?"

"I've been back two days. This is my second evening," she answered as she came toward him. "How long ago did I—"

"Leave without a word?" Ryan finished the sentence for her. She couldn't interpret his expression, however. As she knew by this time, he could be impenetrable when he chose to be.

Even so, the sight of him literally stole her breath. It felt like an eternity since she'd looked into his singular eyes. He gave a small smile suddenly and she found herself relaxing.

"Since I'm not sure at what point you left, I can't say for certain. But it couldn't have been much more than three hours ago, by my time, anyway."

"Amazing!" Jacob declared. "Hope told me about this slight discrepancy between dates when one travels through time, Mr. Daire. Have you formulated a theory on why this occurs?"

Ryan shook his head. "I have no idea, Mr. Stillwater. I'm woefully ignorant on the mechanics of the whole thing. I am starting to realize it's not as much of a cut-and-dry situation as I thought." He met Hope's eyes. "Our being able to meet isn't just about the mirror. It's about this house . . . or something."

Her father snorted. "My daughter had already figured that out,

Mr. Daire. She realized the two of you had communicated in ways other than the mirror, and that while the mirror was a handy object on which the imagination could grasp, it wasn't the *source* of the magic. The true magic relates to the two of you."

Hope's cheeks flamed. She loved her father like mad, but his outspokenness could mortify upon occasion. She sensed Ryan's steady gaze on her and met it with difficulty.

"You didn't use the mirror to get here?"

He shook his head.

"How did you do it, then?"

He opened his mouth as if to speak and then glanced uneasily over at her father. "I just pictured you in my mind . . . Imagined you here, moving about a house that was filled with all the things I'd seen before, held your face in my mind, heard your laughter, thought of the way you walk . . ."

His voice faded but he continued to hold her stare. She remembered what he'd said while they'd been in the elevator of the Sears Tower about her father. *You can picture him with the clarity that only intense emotion can bring.* That's how she'd known how to return.

"Love."

Both Ryan and she started out of their mutual stare and glanced over at her father when he uttered the single word.

"That's the driving force behind the phenomenon. Oh, maybe that strange man, Mortimer P. Chase, built some of his magic into this house," Jacob said with a wave of his hand, "but clearly it takes something very special to mix with that magic in order to create the miracle of time travel."

"Father," Hope said excitedly as she neared him. "Perhaps this means you will be able to visit me in the year 2008?"

"Excuse me?" Ryan asked sharply.

Hope turned toward him. He didn't look impassive at all at the moment. He looked like he'd just been unexpectedly punched.

"Oh, I didn't get a chance to tell you, Ryan. There's so much that I have to explain."

But Ryan didn't seem concerned with all the other details. "You were planning on coming back to me in my time? Even after—" He drew up short and glanced uncomfortably at her father.

Hope stirred restlessly on her feet. She hadn't meant for Ryan to find out this way. She'd rather have prepared him first by explaining about the plans she'd made—the plans that hopefully would help him not to feel trapped by her presence in the year 2008.

"You know," Jacob began, clearly following his own line of thought versus the exchange between Ryan and his daughter, "I don't think it's best that I breach the barrier of time, dear. You know I'll always be with you in spirit. But some things just weren't meant to be. I'm afraid my existence in the year 2008 just doesn't seem . . . right."

"And it does seem right to you, Hope?" Ryan asked her intently.

She nodded her head solemnly. "That's what I was going to tell you when I returned later on tonight. My father and I have made plans, Ryan. You won't have to look out for me. I won't be a burden to you—"

"You weren't going to be a *burden* to me," Ryan interrupted, scowling. "I was worried that you might feel uncomfortable with the way we do things in my time." Once again he glanced at her father, clearly uncomfortable. "I didn't want to take advantage of you, Hope."

Hope's heart stopped and then resumed beating again in an ecstatic dance. "That was very kind of you to be concerned about me, Ryan. But I'd already decided to go back. I mean forward. Besides, I don't belong here anymore. They found my dead body yesterday, you know."

∞

Ryan had experienced shock so many times in the past week that he would have thought the experience would lose some of its power. That was definitely not the case, however.

"What do you mean they found your dead body?" he demanded, feeling rattled.

"Well, it wasn't really her dead body, obviously," Jacob said.

"It was Sadie Holcrum's body they found in the river, Ryan. Remember the woman Jack killed in the Sweet Lash? The woman who helped kidnap me?"

Ryan came nearer to her and put his hand on her back, needing to touch her. The news that she'd been planning on returning to the year 2008 . . . to *him*, had left him stunned. He'd already known what he was going to do when he came back to find her, but the fact that she wasn't furious at him after finding those incendiary photographs, the fact that she'd decided to return to his time moved him deeply.

His fingers skimmed over the satiny smooth skin of her exposed back. She looked absolutely gorgeous wearing a formal blue satin gown with an ebony ermine border around the hem and over the shoulders. Once again he had to admit he'd been wrong about so many of his ideas concerning the culture of the 1900s, because the neckline of the dress was downright racy, displaying the creamy curves of Hope's beautiful breasts to jaw-dropping effect. The silver locket glittered on the flawless skin of her chest.

He blinked in shock, recognizing for the first time that she was dressed precisely in the manner he'd seen her on that first day he entered the mansion with Ramiro here in this very room . . .

"Ryan?" Hope interrupted his thoughts.

Ryan cleared his throat, forcing himself back to the present. "How do you know it was Sadie Holcrum they found?"

"Her face and body were damaged by being in the river for days," Hope explained sadly, "And she appeared to have been badly beaten, which is just awful, because . . ."

"It must have been done after she was dead," Ryan finished grimly. He suddenly recalled what Jack had said on their first meeting in the Sweet Lash when Ryan had asked him where Marlo was.

He's taking care of some business for me. He'll be along.

Undoubtedly the *business* to which Jack had been referring was to beat Sadie's body until it was unrecognizable so that no one could trace her back to the Sweet Lash and Jack himself.

"When I arrived home the other day, I was surprised to find myself in my father's suite. I suppose since I was concentrating on him so greatly it makes sense that was where I would appear. When I arrived, my father was having a meeting with the detective—Connor O'Rourke."

"You can imagine my shock, Mr. Daire," Jacob spoke up, a wry smile tilting his lips, "when I glanced up while in the midst of Mr. O'Rourke telling me they'd found a woman's dead body that generally matched Hope's physical description . . . only to look up and see my daughter standing on the far side of the room. I thought I was seeing a ghost."

"I can imagine," Ryan said. "What happened then?"

"I'd already determined before I returned that it would be best for those in my time period to believe that I'd died in the way you described to me from the records," Hope said. "How else to explain the fact that I'd returned only to disappear again a few days later once my father and I had made our plans?"

"Much easier for history to believe as it did," Jacob agreed. "I myself would know that she was alive . . . that she was happy and where she'd chosen to be. Once I'd understood what that man—Jack Fletcher—had done to her, I vowed then and there that nothing would stop me in my aims to stop him and those like him from hurting other young women like my Hope."

Ryan's gaze flickered over to meet Hope's but he couldn't quite interpret her steady stare. One thing was for certain, he was enormously relieved to hear that there had *never* been any time or any reality where Hope's body was found beaten and decomposing in the Chicago River.

"Didn't O'Rourke want you to identify the body?"

"Indeed, that was the purpose of his errand," Jacob said. "He was in the midst of explaining to me that although the body and face were sadly unrecognizable, there *was* one identifying feature to the corpse that might help us determine if it was my daughter or not."

"A gold tooth. Right here," Hope said pointing to her right incisor. "That's how I knew the body they found was Sadie. I remembered she had a gold tooth in that precise location."

"At the moment Mr. O'Rourke asked me if Hope had possessed a gold tooth, I was hardly listening to him. I was staring at what I thought was the ghost of my daughter standing fifteen feet behind Mr. O'Rourke. He hadn't noticed her ghostly presence. However, it quickly became very clear to me that I was seeing no specter, for Hope was acting very un-ghostly-like, frantically nodding her head and mouthing, *Yes, father. Say yes*, and pointing wildly at Mr. O'Rourke and then her tooth." Jacob chuckled at the memory.

Hope snorted with laughter. Ryan looked down at her and smiled. Hope's laughter was like hearing sunshine.

"Mr. O'Rourke turned around because you had such a queer look on your face, Father. I barely had time to hide myself behind the sofa."

"That's when I knew for sure I was seeing no ghost. Spirits don't dive behind furniture in order not to be seen. So I was only too happy to mislead Mr. O'Rourke and tell him my daughter did, indeed, possess such a tooth. I think he thought grief had driven me mad when he saw that I couldn't repress a grin of delight upon being told of my daughter's heinous end."

All three of them joined in laughter.

"But come, Mr. Daire. Pull up a chair," Jacob invited once his mirth had quieted. "There are many things that I need to ask you in order to provide for Hope in the future. It's very fortunate that you're here, because there are so many details about the way things work in the year 2008 that we didn't know. Financial functioning, for instance—"

"You seem to have figured things out admirably, Mr. Stillwater," Ryan said as he crossed the room and grabbed a chair.

"What do you mean, young man?"

Ryan set down his chair at the table and held out his hand to Hope. He seated her before he took his own place at the table.

"As strange as this whole situation is, I don't suppose it should come as too much of a shock to you that there's yet another surprise," Ryan said, looking first at Hope and then Jacob. He took a deep breath in preparation to explain what he'd learned this morning from his friend Alistair Franklin. "You see, it seems that I was given the Prairie Avenue mansion under your specific direction, Mr. Stillwater."

For a moment, Jacob just stared at him blankly. Then a smile began to curve his lips. "I had planned to provide for Hope through a trust that would pass into the guardianship of my descendants with each successive generation. Since I have no other children besides Hope, I designated the guardians for the trust to be the descendants of my sister, Mrs. Margaret Tanser. Mr. Daire, do you by chance know a relative of mine who lives in your time period?"

Ryan looked over at Hope, who was watching him with open-mouthed incredulity.

"You never told me you knew my relative, Ryan," she exclaimed.

"Well, I didn't know he was your relative until this morning when he told me he was. The man who gifted me with the Prairie Avenue mansion is named Alistair Franklin. And yes, he is a direct descendant of your sister's family, Mr. Stillwater. You can imagine how amazed I was when he visited me this morning and showed me the document of your highly unusual last will and testament. You handled it all admirably. Hope is currently a very wealthy woman. A fortune is awaiting her in the First National Bank of Chicago. In addition to the wonders of compounded interest, it would seem your guardians have invested your inheritance very wisely, Hope."

"Excellent! Excellent, I'm so glad to hear of it," said Jacob with glee as he struck the table briskly.

"And of course this," Ryan glanced around the elegant ballroom, "is yours, Hope. Your father just directed for it to be given to me by the guardian living in my time period."

"I did? How brilliant on my part!"

Hope just stared at him fixedly, her dark pink lips parted in wonder.

"But it's *your* house, Ryan," she whispered.

He smiled and reached for her hand. Jacob Stillwater had arranged things so perfectly that the deep divide between Hope's and his culture had just narrowed to something Ryan would dare to leap in a second.

Because of Jacob's plans, Hope now was independent and could do what she pleased. He didn't have to feel guilty about the fact that he was forcing her to live with him. Hope believed herself to be a progressive thinker, and she was for her time period—no doubt about it. But no amount of education and insight could have prepared her enough to leap into living permanently with a man outside of marriage. Ryan would have offered to move back to his loft and give her use of the house, but he knew Hope well enough to know she wouldn't have abided him supporting her.

Sure, she could find work, but what were the chances that she'd make enough to continue to maintain the house? Ryan would have gifted it to her in a second, just as Alistair had gifted it to him. He doubted, however, that he'd be able to keep the truth from her about the enormous amount of money Ryan would have to take from the trust from his father in order to pay the taxes on the mansion.

Now Hope could maintain the dignity that she deserved, given her background and culture, while he could behave in the manner of any other guy from the twenty-first century that had fallen flat on his ass in love.

Maybe the difference between the two situations didn't look huge on paper. Hell, he doubted he'd be able to spend too many nights without her in his arms. But Ryan knew how important it was that neither of them be forced into behaving in a manner that clashed *too* drastically with their culture and backgrounds. Jacob Stillwater's arrangements had allowed that to happen. He already knew that Hope was the woman for him and that nothing was going to change that.

Still . . . it would be nice to have things evolve in their own time.

He leaned forward and spoke to Hope quietly. "I only belong in the mansion if and when you want me there, honey. I have my own condo, you know."

A small smile tugged at her lush lips even though she still looked flabbergasted. "Ryan," she chastised with a smile. "Of course I want you there."

He suspected from the gleam in her midnight eyes and the brilliance of her smile that the advantages of the situation weren't lost on her, though.

"It's amazing, isn't it? All of it . . . it's just amazing," she murmured.

Ryan squeezed her hand tightly. It was amazing all right. In fact, there was one other awe-inspiring fact that he hadn't yet told her. He glanced over to an ebullient-looking Jacob Stillwater and back to Hope. But she'd find out the truth for herself when she was back in the year 2008. With him.

Where she belonged.

～ THIRTY ～

Ryan stalked back and forth nervously in the entry hall clutching his cell phone in his hand. He'd told Hope to call him from the car on her way home from Alistair's. Warren, Alistair's driver, had assured them she could use his phone on the drive back from Alistair's Morgan Park estate.

She hadn't quite mastered the cell phone yet, however. She either disconnected after shouting in his ear, "Ryan, are you there? Ryan, can you *hear* me?" or else remained connected for extended periods while she bemoaned the fact to Warren that the cell phone didn't seem to work for her, and Warren—jovial and infinitely patient as he was—saying at one point, "No, no, stop pushing down on that button," and Hope replying, "Well, you said to *press* it, Warren!"

So other than knowing that Hope was on her way home and

that cell phone tutorials were high on his to-do list, he had no idea how things went between Hope and Alistair.

They'd returned to Ryan's time following a special evening spent with Jacob Stillwater. Hope had played the piano and to Ryan's untrained ear, she'd done so with the skill of a concert pianist. Who knew how many talents and skills she possessed that he'd never considered?

Nice, though, to think of discovering each new treasure of Hope's personality and history one by one.

As it'd grown late Hope became more and more subdued, letting Jacob and Ryan hash out many of the details of his will and the transference of Hope's estate through history.

When Jacob finally said it was time for them to go, Ryan had told Hope he would wait for her in the hallway and left father and daughter to say their good-byes. A short while later Jacob had come out of the ballroom and softly closed the door. His eyes found Ryan's shadow in the dim hallway and he'd approached.

"You will take good care of my daughter," Jacob had declared instead of asked.

"I will."

Ryan needed no interpretation for Jacob Stillwater's searching, anxious stare.

Jacob nodded. "I sense the truth of this but it's still difficult for an old man to accept."

"What you said, sir . . . about what caused the connection between Hope's time and my own: You were right. It was love. I don't know how. I don't know why. But it was," Ryan assured quietly.

A warm smile had spread over Jacob's face, even as his tall, thin body seemed to wilt slightly with his outgoing breath. "Hard to let her go. Very hard. But it must be so for all parents when their child leaves the roost."

"She'll be right here. She'll never be far from you."

Jacob had nodded. "Yes. I sense that's true. And I also sense she'll be happy there in your time. She always wanted a grand adventure. I'm envious of her, actually. It's quite a daring feat for her, but my daughter has never been short on courage or determination. Can be a bit headstrong at times, however."

Ryan had smiled. "I've noticed that about her."

After Jacob had departed, Ryan had found Hope standing alone in the ballroom, trying bravely to appear as though she hadn't been crying. They'd been able to return to the twenty-first century without incident merely by closing their eyes and imagining being there in the house together. It had been five o'clock in the morning when they'd returned. Ryan was careful this time to check his cell phone date, and indeed, they'd lost not only several hours but also a day and night on top of it. He'd grimaced when he realized he had to get up for work in the morning.

One look at Hope's pale face and he'd insisted she get ready for bed. It'd been so hard on her to leave her father.

Hopefully this final piece of the puzzle would help her to feel more comfortable here in the year 2008, Ryan thought presently as he glanced out a window and saw a car pulling up to the curb.

He felt wired even though he'd only slept two or three hours before he'd gotten up and gone into work. While at the station, Ryan had learned from an irritated Ramiro that Jim Donahue was still at Cook County Hospital. Apparently the gunshot wound itself was fairly superficial but had triggered other complications.

"Apparently he's got unmanaged diabetes," Ramiro had explained with a scowl. "Makes it hard for him to heal. With our luck, the jerk'll finagle his way into staying forever in the hospital and never see the interior of a jail cell."

"You know," Ryan had said slowly, "you might be a hundred percent right about that."

"What do you mean?"

Ryan had just shaken his head, but he'd been thinking about Diamond Jack Fletcher. He'd also weakened after a gunshot wound that *shouldn't* have been mortal, but inevitably had been. It was possible Jim Donahue would suffer a parallel fate.

Ryan couldn't say he was sorry.

He waved at Warren from the open doorway. The driver returned the wave before he opened the sedan and Hope's dark brown boots appeared from the backseat. One of the many fascinating paradoxes about Hope was that she had no compunction about displaying her gorgeous breasts in low-cut gowns, but the idea of showing her bare legs in public absolutely scandalized her. Eve's gift of a pair of boots and several calf-length skirts quieted Hope's concerns, but Ryan still thought she might have felt more comfortable in the sexy rose-colored gown than she did wearing a "short" skirt.

He couldn't read her expression from a distance but as she neared the limestone front steps Ryan saw the exultant, blazing look in her dark eyes. She flew up the stairs and into his arms. He lifted her instinctively, laughing when she dropped several enthusiastic kisses along his neck, jaw and cheeks.

"What did I do to deserve this?" he asked.

"You're just you." Her eyes radiated joy when he set her back down on the ground. "I'm so happy, Ryan. He's so wonderful. Why didn't you tell me? Why didn't you tell me that my father's spirit exists here in this time in the body of Alistair Franklin?"

"I wanted you to be the one to decide if that were the case or not, honey. I suspected it was true, but only someone who loves him as much as you do could ever be really sure."

Her expression sobered. "He doesn't realize, you know. He knew from the secret documents that had been passed down to him from the former guardian that I was from the past. He doesn't understand about who he was, though. But it's strange . . . sometimes, the way he looked at me . . . I wondered if he really *did* know."

Ryan nodded. "It was the same with Jim Donahue. Maybe they

don't have the specific memories, but part of them knows the truth."

"Yes. I think that's true. And it's so strange . . . the patterns, the synchronicity. Alistair told me that he had a wife and daughter, and that he lost both of them in a car wreck when the girl was only ten years old. He showed me a picture of her, Ryan. She had dark hair and dark eyes. I think . . . I think when he looked at me he thought of her . . ." She trailed off pensively, looking a little sad. But then she rallied with her characteristic ebullience.

"When did you begin to suspect the connection between Alistair and my father?"

A brisk lake breeze blew a gleaming dark brown curl into her face. Ryan pulled her inside the house, closing the door behind them.

"When I heard him talking on the staircase that night when we were here with Mel. I remember thinking his voice sounded familiar. I pictured him holding a crowd of people enthralled with that powerful voice and thought of your father's church and the speeches he gave for political purposes. But I didn't realize until I spoke to Alistair the other day it was *his* voice and charismatic speaking that I was recalling. He was incredibly popular among the students when he taught at the University of Chicago."

He grinned.

"What?" Hope asked.

"He made history come alive."

Hope's smile widened. It did something to him to see her literally brimming over with happiness. He grabbed her hand and pulled her into a loose embrace.

"Alistair said you were his best pupil."

Ryan rolled his eyes. "His best pupil would have gone on to become a scholar. Not a cop."

"That's not true," Hope defended hotly. "Alistair and I have discussed it and agree completely."

"Have you?" Ryan asked wryly, amused by Hope's automatic tendency to ally herself with Alistair in stating her opinions just as she used to do with Jacob Stillwater.

"Yes. Alistair says that you could have become a fine historian and an excellent lawyer, but that you have a very practical nature. He says that you possess a first-rate intellect, but that you wouldn't be happy theorizing about problems or hashing them out in a courtroom. You want to go out and deal with them firsthand, as they're occurring. I understand that perfectly, because that's how I felt about the white slavery problem in my time. My father could deal with things on the political front, but me—I just wanted to help those young women one by one. Alistair says I'd make a very good social worker and when I told him I already was, he just laughed and said I was right. What?" Hope asked, apparently noticing the intensity of his expression.

Ryan just shook his head. He saw Hope's eyes go wide in surprise just before he kissed her hard.

"Where are we going?" Hope muttered several seconds later as he carried her up the grand staircase, taking two steps at a time.

"To bed."

"Oh," was all she managed to get out.

∽

A while later Hope fell gasping onto Ryan's chest. Her body rose up and down as Ryan also struggled to get his breath.

"You certainly are a passionate man, Ryan Daire," Hope panted next to his nipple.

He buried his fingers in her hair. "You make me a little crazy, honey. I've never had to work so hard to find my control than when I'm with you."

She lifted her head and regarded him soberly. "I like it when you lose control," she whispered. "But I want to thank you for being so patient with me that night, Ryan . . . at the Sweet Lash."

"I knew how much you wanted to console those women, honey. It's part of who you are."

"No. Not on that night." He paused in stroking her hair. Her throat convulsed as she swallowed. "The night in the past—when you made love to me. The night Jack Fletcher was having us photographed."

Ryan supposed the silence that followed was only a few seconds, but it felt much longer.

"I didn't want to do it, Hope."

She put her fingers over his lips and made a hushing sound. "I know. I know. When I first saw the photographs I was shocked. But then I recalled the details of that night and of our escape: your insistence that I be very quiet when I spoke familiarly to you, but didn't reprimand me when I was loud during our lovemaking; the tense, pained expression I saw on your face at times; that room where Diamond Jack stood . . . the fact that he had your gun."

"Jack forced me to do it. He had us at gunpoint the entire time."

"I guessed that might be the case when I stood there in shock staring at those photographs. What a vile creature he was. But even so, Ryan, Jack couldn't mar the experience. You made love to me that night—made something that could have been a nightmare into something rare and beautiful." Her velvety eyes gleamed with tears as she regarded him soulfully. "Thank you for that."

"I'm just glad you didn't jump to the conclusion that I would have taken part in something like that willingly."

She shook her head. "I know you wouldn't. Seeing those photographs made me go over again in my mind everything that happened that night. Suddenly everything fell into place and I realized what I had to do."

"What?" Ryan asked, puzzled.

"I had to go back and retrieve those photographs, for one thing! Do you think I wanted my father to *see* those? Do you think I wanted Jack to blackmail him?"

Ryan sat up slightly as he stared at her in dawning amazement.

Hope's lips curved into a witch's smile before she got up from the bed and padded over to the fireplace, her long curls swishing sensually around her curving hips. A second later she reached into the hidden compartment and pulled out the black-and-white photographs that had started his strange, awesome story with Hope Stillwater.

He hadn't replaced them in the compartment before he returned to her time, Ryan recalled in rising confusion.

"Just where I left them," Hope said with a satisfied grin.

"You left them on the mantel."

She shook her head and came back to bed, setting the photos on the bedside table. "No. I put them back in the compartment several nights ago—in my time. That was after I'd learned the possible identity of the photographer from my friend Addie Sampson—you remember her? The madam at the Marlborough Club? She's in the know about so many things that take place in the Levee District. I went to the flat of a Mr. Michael Divorak. He was indeed the man Jack had hired to photograph me being supposedly ravaged and debased. Mr. Divorak was more than willing to trade the photographs and the film, which I destroyed, in exchange for my grandmother's diamond brooch, especially since Jack had become very ill after you shot him and never paid Mr. Divorak for his labor."

"Why didn't you just destroy the photos as well?"

Hope gave him a puzzled look as she crawled back into his arms. Their perspiration-slick skin slid together in an erotic glide as he pulled her close. "Destroy them? I couldn't do *that*."

"Why not?" he asked with a bark of laughter.

She gave him a look like she thought he'd temporarily reverted to being a three-year-old child. "Well, it's only logical, Ryan. I had to make sure that you found the photographs someday, didn't I? How else was *this* ever going to happen?"

She glanced down significantly to their naked bodies pressed heart-to-heart.

Ryan began to laugh. Hope seemed surprised by his reaction at first, but then she joined in his mirth.

"It's hardly logical, witch." He leaned up and brushed his smile next to hers. "But it doesn't have to make sense to be right."

To be perfect, he thought to himself before he seized Hope's mouth in a kiss.